CHASING THE WINTER'S WIND

A NOVEL BY

DAVID TRAWINSKI

outskirts press

Chasing The Winter's Wind

v4.0

This is a work of fiction. The events and characters described herein are imaginary and are not intended to refer to specific places or living persons. The opinions expressed in this manuscript are solely the opinions of the author and do not represent the opinions or thoughts of the publisher. The author has represented and warranted full ownership and/or legal right to publish all the materials in this book.

Outskirts Press, Inc.
http://www.outskirtspress.com

Paperback ISBN: 978-1-4787-9130-0
Hardback ISBN: 978-1-4787-9149-2

Cover concept by Matthew Wisniewski
Görlitz Coverphoto © 2017 Elizabeth Marie Trawinski. All rights reserved - used with permission.
Katyń Monument image cover overlay used by permission of the National Katyń Memorial Foundation in Baltimore
All Interior Photos © 2017 Elizabeth Marie Trawinski (except where accredited elsewhere herein). All rights reserved - used with permission.
Edited by Deborah Chapman.

Outskirts Press and the "OP" logo are trademarks belonging to Outskirts Press, Inc.

PRINTED IN THE UNITED STATES OF AMERICA

Chasing The Winter's Wind
David Trawinski
KATYN 1940

Dedicated to the Memory

of

Albert

Michael

Wisniewski

A Little Polish Language Found Throughout This Story…

English	Polish	Rough Pronunciation
Yes	*Tak*	*Tock*
No	*Nie*	*Nyeh*
Good	*Dobrze*	*Dub zah*
Good Day	*Dzień dobry*	*Jane Doh bree*
So Long/Goodbye	*Do Widzenia*	*Doh Vee zen ya*
Please	*Proszę*	*Prah shem*
Thank you	*Dziękuję*	*Jen Koo yen*
Mr./Sir	*Pan*	*Pahn*
Mrs./Madame	*Pani*	*Pahnee*
Derriere (One's backside)	*Dupa*	*Doo pah*
Truth	*Prawda*	*Pravda*
No way! (Disbelief)	*Nie Prawda*	*Nyeh Pravda*
How are you?	*Jak się masz*	*Yak shem mash*

W's are pronounced as V's (Prawda is pronounced Pravda)

J's are pronounced as Y's (the name Jaruzelski is pronounced Yar OU Zel Skee)

Cz is pronounced as Ch (as in pronunciation of Czech)

Ch is pronounced like "k" in Lech, pronounced "Lek"

The ł sounds like "w"; the ę sounds like a "en", Therefore "Lech Wałęsa" is pronounced "Lek Va WEN sa"

A family name is gender sensitive, therefore:

Pan Kazimierz Danuski. (ski is the male ending)

Pani Agnieszka Danuska. (ska is the female ending)

Many thanks to the National Katyń Memorial Foundation for their assistance, and for all they do to keep the memory of this tragedy from being lost to the tides of time…

Chasing the Winter's Wind

Frozen Blue in The Hammer's Stroke,
Fire and Force Juxtaposed,
Captives Freed, Their Prison Broke,
Sins of The Father Forge the Son's Mortal Yoke.
The Fire Flickers, Yet Fails to Warm,
Days Elapsed, I am Duly Warned,
"Allow the Years to Pass, The Days to Thin,
Seek Nothing Else than to Chase the Winter's Wind."
Now Memories Crawl Like Wounded Dogs,
A Heart Once Chaste, Now Beating Raw,
As Lilies Lay White on a Pure Snow's Thaw,
The Call of the Winter's Wind Still Unresolved.
When All is Taken – Life, Love and Need,
By Souls Embittered of Corrosive Greed,
Forced to Act, Stained Scarlet in Sin,
Burn your Remnant Breaths
Chasing the Winter's Wind.

Chapter One
A Chilling Friday in November

Death is thought to be cold, immobile, permanent. Yet, it is the fear of death which drives men to uncontrolled and unexpected actions. Death is anything but final, as the remembrances of those long dead are the driving forces of generations. Love survives death. Often, in a perversion driven by the fear of death, the greatest sins of man are justified in the name of love.

Mid – November Friday Afternoon,
CIA Headquarters, Langley, Virginia

"WHO THE ***F**K*** sends me a *MANDATORY* on my first Friday off this year?"

The words hung with accusation in this sixth-floor office in the CIA headquarters in Langley, Virginia. The accuser was flush with anger, his eyes carried the November gray skies indoor with his temperament. Jack Trellis was visibly angry, crashing the Italian leather briefcase used to carry his files, laptop and documents onto the office desk of his professional adjutant, Ellison Redmond. Trellis had come directly to Redmond's office, avoiding his own on the floor above, located just down the hall from the DCI's own office. Trellis often treated Redmond as nothing more than a personal vent for his tirades of anger, which were not well accepted elsewhere within this institution. Today was no exception.

"Sir, you have a meeting with the DCI in a little over two hours," said Redmond, crisply. Redmond knew his boss inside and out, and knew when Trellis flew off the handle in his emotional outbursts, it was his job to cut him off and get him back on point. Redmond described this function as "sheep dogging" Jack Trellis.

"What the *f**k* is so damn important? This is the first Friday in forever I got my boat out of Spa Creek." Ellison noted Trellis' use of the Colonial-British "*Spar*" pronunciation, just another manifestation of his elitist, *nouveau riche* persona that had been draped over his "coarsest graduate in the history of Yale" reputation. His wealth was thanks to the inheritance of his wife's father's estate - gigantic house on the Annapolis waterfront, 62-foot sailboat, Breitling watches, the whole deal, all fully vetted and cleared by the CIA's money watchers.

Trellis didn't miss a beat. "Then I get the *MANDATORY* and had to take in the sails I had just hoisted to motor it back to the dock at the house. Now I drive down from Annapolis like a bat out of hell. Good damn thing I was going against the traffic on route fifty all the way. OK, *El-li-son*, what is so *f**king* important it's crawling up the DCI's ass?"

Ellison Redmond, like his boss Jack Trellis, was a longtime operative of the CIA. He was smart enough to notice Trellis only dragged his first name into three over-pronounced syllables, contorting the "El-lie" in "El-lie-son" into an effeminate, derisive form when he was exceptionally furious. Ellison decided for the sake of time to cut to the chase.

"We received an *IMMEDIATE* cable from Warsaw station, sir. There's been an assassination in the Old Town. About three hours ago. Data still coming in, but..."

He was interrupted, as he expected to be, by Trellis' fury, which was yet to hit its zenith, given what "Ellie" was about to pass on.

"That's not even *my* territory any more," thundered Trellis, cutting off Redmond. "Hasn't been my territory for nearly two decades. Who the *f**k* would even notice an attempt over there anyway..."

"Not an attempt, sir, a confirmed kill," Redmond returned the interruption. "And I hate to remind you, sir, but as Deputy Director for Operations, it is all yours, now."

Jack Trellis sucked in his breath, to come down from the explosive orbit he was in. He had previously been head of Eastern European Operations. He had successfully ridden the wave of credit for destabilizing the Soviet Union in the nineteen-eighties, leading to its ultimate death throws and destruction by Gorbachev's policies of *Glasnost* and *Perestroika* in 1991. Trellis was rewarded a few years later to become ostensibly the second most powerful member of the CIA, behind only the DCI, or Director of Central Intelligence himself.

Trellis calmed somewhat. "Okay, who got taken out – Polish President or Prime Minister? Let me guess, the Russians are overstepping their bounds again? Have they grown restless with the Poles already, since nearly the entire Polish government got wiped out in that plane crash in Smolensk in 2010?"

"No sir – doesn't appear to be related to the Russians at all - victim was an American business executive from Global Defense Analytics. One Langston Powell."

"*F**k!*" Trellis re-exploded. "*That Mother F**ker!* He was just named as successor to their CEO yester-*f**king*-day. What the hell?"

Trellis leaned over, placing one hand on the desk. He was trying to stabilize himself from the shock of one of his closest affiliates in the defense industry being murdered…and just at the time when he was about to become most useful to Trellis.

"Who do we think is behind this?" muttered Trellis, uncharacteristically looking down at the floor while he gripped the reality of the moment. "Is it one of the terrorist factions out of Yemen? That would be the perfect payback for Powell's Daedalus Destroyer Drones and the damage they are doing for us over there."

Trellis' eyes were now glazed over and searching the distance in disbelief.

"No sir," Redmond struggled to continue his brief. "It appears from all internal data we have, at this point, that it was a member of his traveling party."

"Makes perfect sense," Trellis jumped in. "Powell had the most inflated *f**king* ego, and sooner or later someone was going to deflate it, one way or the other."

"Sir – It was one of us, sir, a company man, working on his staff," said Redmond sheepishly.

"One of who?" boomed Trellis.

"Well, ex-company, sir. Retired CIA," Redmond said definitively.

"No. Tell me it wasn't that bastard Stanley…" Trellis said, anticipating.

"It was Stanley Wisniewski, sir," Redmond spoke over his boss hoping to cut off the explosion sure to follow.

"This just keeps getting *f**king* better..." Trellis' voice exploded.

"Stanley shot him at the Warsaw Monument for the '44 Polish Resistance," Redmond wedged in.

"Had to be there, had to be right *f**king* there, didn't it? What the hell were they doing there together? What the hell is Stanley doing coming out of his nice quiet retirement, anyway? I thought we had taken care of him."

Trellis looked visibly disturbed, something Redmond had rarely seen. He had seen the explosion of profanity, had seen the tantrums, but these were always part of the process in taking on new, emerging issues. For the first time that Redmond had been assigned to him, Trellis looked anxious, frustrated and disbelieving. Had Redmond not known him so well, he would have thought Trellis was scared.

"Sir – our preliminary data suggests Stanley was working as an interpreter for Powell in Posen two days before..." said Redmond, before being cut off by Trellis.

"Poznan. It's a part of Poland now. Has been since '45. Poznan, not Posen; Gdańsk, not Danzig. Can we at least get the *f**king* names right, Ellie!"

Trellis was now in full annihilator attack mode on Redmond, official bearer of bad – no, the worst – news. Trellis paused, drawing a deep breath before asking aloud, "Are we sure Powell is dead? Or is he in some shit-hole Warsaw hospital clinging to life? Do we know if he is coherent? Is he talking? Can he tell us anything?"

Ellison looked directly at Trellis as he answered, but his boss was staring off into the far corner of the room. "No sir, two shots, from a Luger – of all weapons. One to the heart – likely killed him instantaneously at point blank. Second shot to the forehead, expect we'll find it to be posthumous. Anyway, I already have a visual confirmation from Warsaw station."

Trellis' fury re-detonated, "Shit! Shit! I can't *f**king* believe this! Tell me Stanley's in custody..."

"No, Sir. He just walked off into the dusk. Back towards the Old Town section. Just dropped the Luger next to the body and walked away."

"He'll blend in like a *f**king* pierogi in Poland," Trellis' voice trailed off, as his eyes moved from the blank corner of the room to the TV monitors continuously running in Redmond's office. "Has this hit the news cycle yet?"

"Not yet, sir. We've worked with Warsaw to keep this as quiet as we can, but the seams are already ripping..."

Trellis raised his voice, but not to the level Redmond expected, "No *f**king* kidding. 'Global Defense Analytics' CEO in waiting, father of the killer drone, gunned down execution style by CIA Operative' – and they won't say ex -CIA, or retired. It will be 'CIA operative'. *F**k*."

"Sir – something else. Global Defense Analytics is saying that Stanley had access to very sensitive information. They read him into ARTEMIS."

"Project ARTEMIS? Why?" Trellis asked.

"Seems they were using him to vet Powell for the CEO successor position. Their leadership was concerned Powell might have had some complicity in the death of another of their executives, Ted Barber. He was found drowned in Amsterdam."

"I thought we assessed that was a drug induced accident?" Trellis was running through his memory, but thought this was what he had been briefed...

"That was our preliminary assessment. Our man inside Global Defense, Marlow, said Stanley was brought in to assess Powell's potential for possible involvement in Barber's demise. Stanley cleared him. Sent the report in to Marlow just before he boarded Powell's Exec Jet to Europe."

"Yeah, so he could follow him to Poland and gun him down. In the very spot where his parents had been held by the *f**king* Nazi's." Trellis looked away from Redmond, his gaze now was not focused on anything but his thoughts definitely were.

Trellis became unusually quiet, pensively closing his eyes, as if trying to solve a great riddle.

"What the *f**k* are you up to, Stanley?" Trellis asked aloud.

Trellis addressed his next question to Ellison Redmond, "Have you tossed Stanley's house yet?"

Redmond expected the query and began to reply. "No sir. We don't have the Court Order..."

"What the *f**k* are you waiting for, Ellie, an accomplice to get a signal to go in there and clean the place up. Now get your damn away-team's asses up to *f**king* East Baltimore and toss every *f**king* inch of that bastard's house."

Redmond had never seen his boss so willing to move on a domestic residence in advance of the appropriate court orders, and the look of hesitancy, doped with disbelief, was showing on Ellison's face.

Trellis recognized Redmond's reticence and decided to forcibly swing his clout. "My God, Ellie, I can't believe this isn't already *f**king* done. What are we becoming down here, a *f**king* country club? Now move your little bisexual ass!"

Ellison was waiting for the sexual orientation threats, wielded ever so blatantly by Trellis as a threat in times of pushing Redmond beyond the norms of acceptable CIA behavior. While these verbal threats were once reason for having Redmond drummed out of the agency, in today's world they were reason enough to have Trellis himself dismissed. Ellison did not know why he continued to put up with these offensive references, other than fear that Trellis would viciously retaliate against him if he were to report him. However, Redmond did know, and very clearly, that breaking into an American citizen's home, even one accused of murder, was strictly off-limits to the CIA. Even under these conditions.

"Yes, sir. We'll move out immediately based upon National Security implications given Stanley's background." Ellison walked out of his office to give the direction. He would later note in his daily log the direction came verbally from Trellis himself. Just to cover his bisexual ass.

Trellis turned and looked at the model of the Daedalus Destroyer Drone on the ledge behind Redmond's desk. He thought "Langston, I always told you to tone down that damned know-it-all, superior prick persona, didn't I? *F**k it. F**k it all.*"

As Jack Trellis awaited his briefing with the Director of Central Intelligence, Stanley Wisniewski roamed the Polish night, an ocean and continent to the east. His seventy years hung on him like a weight, now that the adrenaline was ebbing back to his normal levels. His emotions, so overwhelming when he had pulled the trigger taking Langston Powell's life, had receded like the tide, exposing only the bare rock of his professional tradecraft as he effected his escape.

To Trellis, Stanley had always represented a silent threat that had crept into the clandestine darkness in which the deputy director had structured his life. Those who choose to live in darkness soon learn to fear the depravity of other men's hearts, should they be as corrupt and conspiring as their own. However, Trellis' fear of Stanley was not due to the darkness in Stanley's heart, but rather the naïveté, idealism and unpredictability of the aged spy. Trellis thought his concerns were addressed years earlier when he had forced Stanley into the silence of retirement.

Now, Stanley had shattered the silence. To Trellis, Stanley declared with the murder of Langston Powell, "I will not be swept silently away. You have taken away my innocence, you have taken away all that I loved in life. Now, I will crawl out from the darkness if only to drag your sins into the light of day. You have made the creature of me that you must now fear."

Treading carefully through the Polish night, Stanley knew that Trellis would indeed fear him now. Enough to silence Stanley forever, to keep the truth of Trellis' crimes unknown to mankind.

After shooting Langston Powell, Stanley had carefully laid the luger next to the lifeless body. The Aerospace Executive had been the partner in Trellis' greatest corruption. Stanley's fingerprints on the luger were his declaration of war against Trellis. He would no longer be silent; Stanley would expose Trellis' greed.

Stanley had walked away from behind the three-dimensional bronze and granite monument dedicated to the Polish Home Army's resistance to the Nazi occupation. This was near the site where his mother and father had been chained like dogs by their Nazi SS captor. Stanley would no longer be captive to Trellis' manipulations.

Stanley walked briskly away from the monument just before the crowd began to grow in response to the two gunshots. He walked with conviction along a carefully planned route that rapidly took him into the Friday night mayhem of activity that was Warsaw's Old Town - the *Stare Miasto*. He walked its alleywidth streets blending in with the festive crowds, who were collectively unaware of the murder that had just been committed a few blocks away.

Stanley used his tradecraft, doubling back upon his route to assure he was not being followed. He watched the reflections in the shop windows for signs of the professionals he knew would soon be relentlessly hunting him. He did this out of training, but Stanley had calculated that he was safe inside a cocoon of anonymity amidst the Warsaw night, which was soon enough to become aflame with the shock and commotion of a brutal execution. Stanley knew his anonymity would last only for a few brief hours. The Police of the capital city were only now responding to the crime scene, but soon the entire city would be consumed with the hunt for the killer.

Stanley had returned to the *Rynek* - that is, the old town square - where his accomplice Jean Paul awaited the signal that the act had been committed. As they had agreed, Stanley stood in the center of the square near the statue of *Syrenka*, the mythical sword and shield bearing mermaid who was the protector of Warsaw. Stanley now found Jean Paul across the square, still amongst the displaying artists, where earlier in the evening he had passed the luger to Stanley, hidden in the core of a rolled canvas painting.

Stanley assured Jean Paul's eyes saw him across the large crowded square. Stanley executed the signal, slowly sweeping back his long grey locks with his left hand, its palm outstretched to the watching world. He knew Jean Paul would recognize this "tell", just as he knew the cameras in the square would record it. But he instantly wondered if Jean Paul, or those watchers who would assuredly be reviewing the video in a few hours, could detect what Stanley himself was surprised to discover. His hand trembled as he executed the tell. For the first-time Stanley could ever remember, both his hands shook, gently, but uncontrollably.

Jean Paul recognized the tell, and responded in the pre-arranged manner by removing his scarf and retying it around his neck. Immediately, Stanley and Jean Paul exited the square in different directions. Jean Paul negotiated the labyrinth of the Old Town's pedestrian streets to reach the adjoining city avenues. Here he had parked his vehicle, an older model green Audi sedan, which he had recently purchased on Stanley's direction. Stanley then began his much longer sojourn. Stanley understood his steps would, in a few hours, be recreated by the watchers at the agency by meticulous review of unrelated video streams across Warsaw. In fact, the trail that Stanley now set upon was selected to assure the watchers had no difficulty in following his steps.

Stanley slipped effortlessly through the crowds and the maze of streets in the Old Town until it opened onto the *Krakówskie Przedmieście*, the promenade that connected the Old Town to the Presidential Residence, the Royal Palaces, and several ministries and academies. This expansive open area was crowded every weekend night, full of the street performers and the crowds they drew. Just past the Column of King Zygismund III, the pedestrian area yielded to the modernity of the city. Here, Stanley climbed into the taxi that would take him through Warsaw to its very center. Once there, across the street from the international hotel where Stanley and Langston Powell several hours earlier had begun their long Friday tour of Warsaw, Stanley emerged from the cab alone and descended into Warsaw's submerged central train station. It was here he knew he was most vulnerable, as he waited the thirteen minutes to board the east bound train that would carry him to the small town of Siedlce. He wondered if the watchers would have trouble pronouncing its name - perhaps butchering it to a close English equivalent of "Shedleetza".

The minutes dragged on as Stanley awaited the train. He knew by now the Warsaw Police would be combing the Old Town looking for him. He had gambled that he could make this train before they would eventually close the station. Just then, the train arrived, and Stanley climbed aboard and soon was heading east to Siedlce.

The train ride was approximately one hour. Stanley sat with the few other patron riders - a few individuals, and a family of three returning home from Warsaw. The parents of the family were older, perhaps in their early forties. Their young girl could be no more than five or six, but she was bubbling with the excitement of her first trip to the capital. She had seen so many wondrous things - palaces and churches and glorious parks. She was totally unaware that when her parents were her age, they were not even allowed to move freely throughout their own country as she was doing now.

Stanley watched his companion riders' faces. All were totally ignoring him, caught up in their own existences. He continued to feel the shaking of his hands, which he had unconsciously buried in the pockets of his topcoat. He scanned the faces, which he knew would be recorded along with his upon exiting in Siedlce. He knew they would all ultimately be traced by the agency and interrogated about the old man who rode for an hour in the darkness of the night with them. That was only if the agency, the police, or others in the shadows were not waiting for Stanley when he emerged from the train.

Stanley knew he was taking a gamble by this train ride east, but to him it was a strategic investment in his overall escape. Yes, he was essentially trapped in this train car for about an hour. However, Stanley was betting the Warsaw Police were not possibly able to establish so quickly that he was the companion of Langston Powell, that he had shot Powell, and that he had fled through the Old Town only as a rouse to cover his real objective of reaching the train station. Nor did he believe that they could track his movements in real time, nor obtain his photograph and distribute it throughout Poland in the roughly two hours since Stanley had pulled the trigger twice on the old luger.

The investment would pay dividends in the next few chaotic hours. Stanley was taking advantage of the frenetic confusion to feign towards the east, towards Belarus, or possibly the Ukraine, and mother Russia that lay beyond. He knew that even the agency would take a few hours to organize its search for him. This false move east was meant to cast their initial efforts in the wrong direction.

The task of tracking Stanley would initially fall to whatever inexperienced analysts happened to be on duty. They would track him through a string of unrelated video feeds through the Old Town and to the Warsaw train station. They would watch him board the train to Siedlce, but by the time they accessed these videos from half a world away, Stanley was sure he would have long emerged from the Siedlce train station. The analysts would assume he was moving East, possibly for the protection of the Russians, as the defecting NSA analyst Edward Snowden currently enjoyed. Stanley now felt that he was somewhat of a kindred soul to Snowden, acting beyond the perceived bounds of socially acceptable behavior to point out to the populace of America what acts were committed by the country's security apparatus just beyond their view.

Stanley would not travel onward to Russia, but would want the agency and INTERPOL to think this was his intention. They would move resources in this direction, cutting off the border with not only Belarus and the Ukraine, but Slovakia to the south and Lithuania to the north. There was even the Kaliningrad Oblast enclave further to the north, which was a floating piece of Russia that bordered Poland at the Baltic Sea, but was not contiguous to the main of Russia itself. Watching these borders would consume precious resources, Stanley hoped, thanks to what he thought of as his "False Demetrius" misdirection.

The False Demetrius was an episode from Russia's Time of Troubles following the reign of Ivan the Terrible. Ivan IV was the first of Russia's rulers to declare himself Tsar. As a child, he was known to have tortured animals. As Tsar, it is said that after viewing the majesty of his newly built St. Basil's Cathedral - the onion domed spires of today's Red Square - that Ivan had his architect's eyes put out so they could never construct anything more beautiful. The moniker "Ivan the Terrible" was indeed well earned.

Ivan's family life was nothing short of disastrous. Ivan's first son had been drowned as an infant in a boating accident. Decades later, Ivan killed his adult second son in a fit of rage by hitting him in the head with his Royal staff. Ivan's feeble third son, Feodor, survived to inherit his title as Tsar. There was, however, a fourth son of Ivan named Dmitry. After Ivan died, and Feodor had become Tsar, the Tsar's then ten-year-old brother, Dmitry, was found dead of stab wounds to his throat. The tragedy was astonishingly explained away as "accidental" as the young heir was playing with a knife.

Years later, a man named Demetrius arose in Poland claiming to be the not-so-deceased Dmitry, youngest son of Ivan the Terrible. As such, he claimed to be the rightful Tsarevich, or heir to the Tsar. He had said years ago his mother had hidden him in a monastery, fearing he would soon be assassinated by his brother, then Tsar Feodor. The child found stabbed in the throat was a substitute, Demetrius claimed. Demetrius was the right age, well educated, and with the support of the Polish nobility. Demetrius soon raised an army to march against Moscow.

Demetrius and his army reached Moscow. The ruling Tsar had just died. Demetrius was accepted by the Russian populace. In 1605, he was installed as Tsar Dmitry the first. However, his rule was short and contentious. He quickly normalized relations with the Poles who had backed his claim, despite their longstanding rivalry with the previous Tsars. Soon Dmitry was also viewed as having favored the Poles' historical religion, Catholicism, over the well-established Russian Orthodox church. The Russian ruling class soon declared him a false Prince, an agent of the Poles and the Pope. Ten months after being installed as Tsar Dmitry, the Kremlin was stormed by an angry mob. Demetrius escaped by slipping out of his robe, even after its arm had been seized. He then leapt from a window, but broke his leg in doing so. He was soon captured, found to be an impostor, murdered, and his remains burned. His ashes were then loaded into a cannon, and ceremoniously fired in the direction of Poland.

As Stanley's train pulled into Siedlce station, the spy turned executioner knew he could not hope for any better treatment from the Russians than what they long ago had served to Demetrius. Stanley had spent his entire professional career working to free Poland from Communism and to bring down the Soviet Union. He then had continued to spy upon the Russia that emerged from the Soviet collapse. Stanley knew he would not be welcome there. What he knew more, in his heart, is that what little remained of his future awaited him in the West, not the East.

Stanley marched out onto the platform of this eastern town of about 80,000 Poles. No one stood waiting for him, no Polish security officers, no shadowy figures of the agency, only the deepening chill of the Slavic night.

Stanley walked for the next half hour through the darkened town, along a route he'd planned in detail, to bring him to the edge of the countryside. He was well past the town's structures and their video surveillance. Alongside the road in front of him, abreast a shadowed farmer's field, sat the automobile that Stanley was so eager to protect from any surveillance. Stanley walked slowly towards it until he was sure to be seen by the silhouetted image of Jean Paul behind the driver's wheel.

Stanley again executed the tell, pushing his long grey hair off his forehead with his left hand, palm outstretched. This distinctive motion was answered from within the car. Jean Paul lit a small lighter, extinguished it, and lit it again. The warm glow of its light assured Stanley it was indeed Jean Paul. They had agreed to this signal, with the second flame to indicate that Jean Paul had not been compromised.

Stanley approached and climbed into the car, reaching to pat his driver on the shoulder as he did so. In Polish, he said, "The most difficult is now behind us. Drive to the villa of the woman we both love."

"As you say," responded Jean Paul. The stocky, dark haired Frenchman, who had once been Stanley's thin blonde Polish agent code named *Syrenka*, eased off into the chill of the November night, and they headed west.

Trellis sat in Redmond's office awaiting his briefing to the Director of Central Intelligence. He knew if he went up to his own office, he was fodder for too many interruptions, including perhaps a drop in from the DCI himself.

Here in the relative anonymity of Redmond's office, his gaze was hypnotically affixed on the bank of televisions, that were turned to Fox News, CNN and BBC Sky News. Trellis hoped all would remain quiet at least until after his briefing to the DCI. Trellis was working out in his mind just how this would be laid out to the DCI. Which details to divulge, and which had to remain hidden until Stanley could be caught and silenced.

All the cable news programs were spewing soft pieces as it was up to that point a very slow news cycle on this Friday before Thanksgiving. Pieces on the preparations for the upcoming Thanksgiving Day Parade in New York, and workers stacking shelves in advance of shoppers who would be lined up for hours in the bitter cold to cash in on Black Friday sales a week from today.

Meanwhile the BBC was featuring a piece on the intricacies of the Euro-zone banking crisis.

Then nearly simultaneously, with the BBC leading by what appeared to be more than thirty seconds, the explosion snapped and all three networks frenetically regurgitated the limited facts known to them. The rapid succession of "Breaking News" flying logos competed for attention as they hovered across the side-by-side digital television screens.

The British cable channels led the assault:

"And this just being received from our European Syndicate - An American Defense Executive was gunned down today in Warsaw, Poland by an unknown assailant. A terrorist operation is rather suspected, but not confirmed at this time. The executive, Langston Powell, was only yesterday appointed Chief Operating Officer, and effectively Chief Executive Officer in waiting, for Global Defense Analytics, the pre-eminent international defense firm. Powell was the self-professed creator of the Daedalus Destroyer Drone system used with great efficiency in Afghanistan, Yemen, Iraq and Syria by the American Intelligence Community."

The American channels were quick to add speculation to the facts:

"It is thought that his assassination could be the work of terror cells that may have tracked his movements to Poland. The current CEO of Global Defense Analytics, Everett Roberts, could not be reached for comment."

Making matters worse, these narrations were over video of a lifeless corpse in a body bag being removed from Warsaw's massive outdoor monument commemorating the Polish Home Army insurgents taking on the Nazi's in August 1944.

The last channel to the party was the first to have a digital representation of the Daedalus Destroyer Drone that Powell was inherently connected with. It rotated in a three-dimensional ray-traced rendering before the screen cut away to the aftermath video of the damage this system produced in Syria, Afghanistan, and Yemen.

"The devastation from this drone was significant, and it was had not escaped the terrorists' notice. It is telling in itself that Langston Powell was gunned down the day after being announced COO, and effectively as successor-to-be for CEO Everett Roberts." The report suggested, without stating directly, that terrorists had used the timing to make their point.

Trellis watched silently, bracing himself for the storm that he knew was coming in his direction. Just wait until the news bureaus discovered the killer was not an Islamic terrorist, but rather an ex-CIA operative. Why the *f**k* couldn't Stanley have just laid low for a couple more years enjoying his damn retirement until Trellis himself got out of the game and had the time to enjoy all the trappings he had labored so hard and long for? This was bound to get messy, and had to be dealt with great tact and agility, out of view of the now watching world, and with the bluntest force and most permanent finality.

Trellis thought next about Langston Powell. They had been associates ever since Powell had pitched the Daedalus Destroyer Drone to the agency after its operational failure with the US Air Force. Trellis saw the promise of the device, but even more so, the greed of its creator.

Greed is a powerful motivator, and in Trellis' world one of the main tools in compromising men, bending them to your own will. Powell was, of course, greedy in relation to fortune, but he had already amassed a large enough financial empire to secure his family's future.

It was the power and recognition Powell lusted after most. His drive was to be Chief Executive Officer of Global Defense Analytics, and now, just on the brink of that becoming reality he is taken out by none other than Stanley Wisniewski.

Stanley, who was ever the idealist, never satisfied with the world's developments. Stanley, who had so significant a role in promoting the *Solidarity* trade union in Gdańsk, Poland through his agent, the secretive *Syrenka.*

Stanley, who was not satisfied when the strikes and demonstrations in Poland led to the fall of the Communist regime there.

Stanley, who was not satisfied when the events in Poland spread throughout Eastern Europe culminating in the fall of the Berlin Wall a short while later.

Stanley, who was not satisfied when the Soviet Union collapsed under its own massive, corruptive weight after the cracks in it were introduced by *Solidarity*, Stanley and his agent *Syrenka.*

Trellis' thoughts drifted to his own early career, when he first introduced the novice Stanley to international covert operations. Stanley came to their agency somewhat later than most recruits, but his language skills were remarkable, and with CIA training Stanley would soon become readily inserted into Eastern Europe, specifically the country of his love, the then Communist Poland. Stanley detested Poland's Communist rule, and this was the greatest motivator of all for this idealist American-born Pole.

"Stanley, we would like to post you into Warsaw," Trellis recalled. The scene in his memory, dustily restored like an old film clip, was showing its age, but playing true none the less.

Not long after graduating his initial training at the CIA's "farm", a training site in the Virginia countryside, Stanley had been flown to Oslo, Norway. After a night in the city to rest, enough for Stanley to absorb the excitement of its international energy, they drove the newly recruited agent into the rugged mountains for several days of training in a country safe house operated by the agency. Later that week, Trellis walked alongside the young Stanley outside in the chilled Norwegian air. This was a respite to the dank, restricting safe house that Stanley had been confined to for the past four days and nights. It had been set up for them amid an alpine clearing covered on three sides by the primal solitude of a Nordic mountain forest.

Trellis could sense the excitement Stanley felt, of his being measured up for his first operational posting overseas. It was late summer, 1973.

"What do you know of Polish history?" the young Jack Trellis asked the young Stanley Wisniewski.

They were both in their late twenties, with Trellis being actually a couple years younger than Stanley. This was a fact that any casual observer would immediately miss, as Trellis, through his experience to that point in his career, already carried a weight, a *gravitas*, that foretold his dramatic rise to come within the agency. He would quickly rise to run covert operations throughout all Eastern Europe. Trellis himself had turned the highly valued double agent code-named *Erasmus,* from within the East German Secret Police, *the Stasi.* After the fall of the Soviet Union, his star ascended to its zenith, as he was soon named Deputy Director of Operations. Trellis' and Stanley's careers became intertwined. It was this trip to Norway where the recruit first came to the attention of Trellis.

They walked through the bucolic alpine meadow, following a

footpath among its tall spurting growth of early August. The feathered stalks surrounding them were a hip-high palette of ochre and pale crimson earth-tones that danced on the already cooling breeze as it swept up the mountainside. Narrow as the footpath was, it was necessary for Trellis to walk in front of Stanley. It truly was a case of the blind leading the blind – the leader blinded by his own all-consuming ambition, the follower blinded by his Utopian idealism. Neither had yet been tempered by the scars of time.

The path that had led them through the alpine clearing, now brought them to a majestic overlook. The drop at their feet was several hundred feet, but the mountain sloped away from their precipice, offering a natural panorama of a beauty unlike anything Stanley had experienced in his young life to that point. Below them lie a Norwegian fjord, shimmering a vibrant blue among the muted green of the mountain forests that rimmed it like a monarch's cape.

Trellis allowed the incredible scene to have its effect on young Stanley. Then, he played his opening card, "Go on, Stanley, tell me what you know of Polish history."

Trellis laughed as he recalled the naïveté of Stanley's response. Stanley started with King Bolesław the Brave unifying Poland in the year 1025. He then skipped forward to 1410 when Poland, aligned with Lithuania, defeated the Teutonic Knights at the Battle of Grunwald. Then, Stanley jumped to King Jan Sobieski defeating the Turks at the siege of Vienna in 1683.

Trellis, put his arm around Stanley in a fatherly way, even though he was actually a few years younger than Stanley. Trellis whispered into his ear, "Stanley, just shut the *f**k* up!"

Stanley was stunned. Trellis removed his arm. Looking out over the fjord, he gently kicked a stone at his feet, as if to demonstrate to Stanley the very danger of the heights at which they stood.

Trellis watched Stanley's eyes follow the accelerating pebble until it was lost, buffeting in the winds blowing up the mountainside.

"Stanley, why do you think we recruited you? For your academic knowledge of Poland? *F**k*, no. We have experts to go to who understand that subject in a much deeper level than you ever will. But I can't insert an academician into a communist regime, can I? The answer is no. *F**k*, no." Trellis paused. "Sorry, does my language upset you? Well, I don't give a *f**king shit*."

Trellis could see the confusion in Stanley's eyes. For days, he was indoctrinated in the discipline and rigor of tradecraft, and now on the last day Trellis appears undisciplined and unprofessional in his use of profanity and his apparent lack of interest in the cultural details of the very country he wishes to infiltrate.

Trellis pushed on, "The reason I wanted you so badly is the linguistics guys tell me your Polish is spot perfect, if not a little too corrupted by the émigrés slang, but we can fix that. Also, the Psych Ops teams tell me you have a real aptitude for working in isolated environments, and you won't get any more isolated than this."

"Than what?" asked Stanley, not looking directly at Trellis. Trellis ignored Stanley's question, out of the sheer belief that Stanley had no right to be asking Trellis anything at this point.

Trellis continued, "And finally, Stanley, the cultural assessments show a really deep rooted hatred of both Germans and Russians alike. So that is like hitting the trifecta for me. Now, what I am offering to you is very big, very important."

Stanley now listened with eager interest. Again, his naïveté was displayed. "Penetrating the Communist eastern bloc? US versus Soviet Union? Good vs. Evil?"

"*F**k* that, this is beyond good and evil," snapped the angry young Trellis.

"You don't realize it, but you just quoted Nietzsche," replied Stanley.

"Screw Nietzsche, that *f**king* kraut bastard." Trellis' eyes seemed to screw back into their orbital sockets, scaring the young recruit.

Trellis noted the scent of fear and pressed on. "This is exactly what I am worried about, you just are not ready for this assignment. This is not a casual game, Stanley. You must realize this could be life and death. Your life and your death, Stanley. It doesn't get any more personal than that."

Trellis watched the young recruit's face, not wishing to push him past the point of interest, just to increase the intoxication of the assignment to him. He went on, "The Russians don't particularly like us meddling in their front yard. Especially Poland. It's a powder-keg for them. Hungary in '56, Czecho in '68. They sense Poland is next."

Stanley objected, "I am very ready. So, what is the correct version of the agency's history of Poland that I should know?"

Trellis grinned. "There you go, now. That's what I like - a high potential recruit willing to listen and learn."

His slate gray eyes beamed in the afternoon Norwegian sun. They both stood, now a mere half mile from the unassuming country house, looking out over the glacially formed, majestically placid, pristine Scandinavian fjord.

What would have been a pregnant silence was filled by a rolling thunder of the nearby mountain stream, greedily falling over itself down the mountain, in its rush to come to rest in the fjord below. The green alpine mountains dived vertically on either side, creating a natural funnel into which the icy waters sacrificed themselves noisily. To Trellis, it figuratively represented the chasm that Stanley would or would not cross in the moments ahead.

Trellis watched as Stanley took in the magnificence of the surroundings, to which the recruit had been in such proximity to for four days and never realized. Trellis guessed Stanley's very thought, "Don't waste a single day more of this life, as there is so much beauty in this world to discover".

Trellis knew, but would not offer the corollary that evaded Stanley, "And there is so much terror in this world to be subjected to as well."

Stanley's thoughts of not wasting the beauty of life, a close variant of which he had indeed been feeling, were exactly what the majesty of this Nordic vista, after days inside a darkened cabin, had been intended to convey.

Trellis laughed inwardly. This was the hook, and it damned always worked. First, have the recruits spend four days in a remote safe house cramming the potential operative with political and cultural briefings, instructions in tradecraft, and even a little self-defense and martial arts training. Even the small arms handling refresher instruction was done inside, out of sight of passers-by, including the potential Soviet satellites overhead. The timing of these assets was known to the agency, and there were no satellites overhead now.

Stanley now stood at this gloriously inspirational vantage point after four stinking days, running long hours off only adrenaline and perspiration. Of course, this formula was played out over the world with agency recruits. There were six trainers to only one trainee, this devised to wear the recruit down to a fatigued state of being. Finally, Trellis himself would take the nearly exhausted recruit out to some picturesque location a short walk or drive away, almost saying "What we talk about now is so important even the rest of the staff can't be let in on it."

The recruits always struck at the bait with their near-adolescent cocktail of energy and idealism coursing through their veins.

Trellis began with setting the hook. "Your beloved Poles have been wedged in between competing European powers for the last thousand years," he said emphatically over the raging Norwegian stream. Its waters were not quite visible, being a short distance below their feet, but were audibly and proudly professing their existence.

Trellis faced out over the fjord, projecting aloud as if to tell Stanley this is a soliloquy, so don't *f**king* interrupt me with your ratty facts, dates and eloquent pronunciations. And for God's sake, don't correct me if I get any of them wrong – it really doesn't matter.

Trellis knew how terribly important all these truly were, but this was part of the act. Take confidence in my cocksure bravado, my young recruit, and I will take you places. Besides, Trellis knew the instructors had drilled into Stanley the importance of the details. Trellis began his monologue.

"The Russians to the east, the Germanic tribes to the west, Scandinavians coming from across the Baltic on their northern border with the sea. Austrians and Turks to boot in the south and west, and throw in a Mongol Golden Horde just to spice things up. This turned out to be an Eastern European chemistry class, with all these reactants thrown in, stand back and let's see what happens. Your beloved Poles did well, absorbing the Lithuanians and defeating the Teutonic Knights in the end of the Middle Ages. But after that, it was basically 500 years of being fought over until eventually the Germans, Austrians and Russians carved up the country in 1795. After this, there officially was no country of Poland in existence, at all. For over 120 years, until just after World War I, the country literally did not exist. Again, in September 1939, the re-established Poland was then partitioned between the Nazis and Soviets, and once again is literally wiped off the map. So, in 1945 the Soviets win big at the Potsdam conference, consolidate and consume their eastern European spoils, and here today we have a communist version of Poland, not so very far from where we stand and talk."

Trellis sensed Stanley's euphoria, from moments before, plummet like the stone he kicked over the cliff, and Stanley's pride of Polish culture was now buffeted in the winds of reality. The rich heritage of the proud Polish people was often reduced to a throwaway discourse of being Europe's doormats. The problem was, this was the view of the world. Not recognition of the proud and peaceful culture Stanley had been raised to cherish.

Trellis sensed this was where his mind wandered. "So, Stanley, do you want to know what the agency thinks about the Poles?"

Trellis allowed the question to age for a few seconds before continuing. "We love the Polish people. We adore the Polish Culture."

Stanley looked confused.

Trellis now set the hook. "They are fighters, Stanley. They will do whatever has to be done to save their culture from extinction. To have a culture survive for well over a century, with no formal country in existence, with the Germans, all the while, attempting to *Germanize* them, the Russians attempting to *Russify* them, and the Austrians, who were most lenient so long as they walked away with most of Poland's natural resources from Galicia and its part of Silesia."

Trellis waited for Stanley to comment on his knowledge of historical geography, which did not come. So, he continued.

"Insurrection after insurrection by the Poles were crushed, but the Poles kept organizing, kept resisting, kept planning for the return of their country - and not the Soviet puppet version of it. The Poles do not *f**king* give up. No matter which world power they are up against. The agency needs to find a way to tap into that defiantly resistant spirit, and help them break free from the Soviets."

This was the most lucid Stanley had ever seen Trellis. He was actually making sense.

Trellis turned his view from out over the fjord to scour the muscles below Stanley's face. He saw no telltale twitching of indecision he was trained to look for. His recruit stared back at him, but even in doing so, Stanley's stare evaded Trellis' eyes directly. Stanley knew he was being measured, the cloth of the suit still unknown to him.

Trellis looked back over the fjord and continued, "After Stalin died in the fifties, the Politburo realized the Soviet Union could not continue to kill off its most productive leadership in psychotic purges as Stalin had done. In comes Nikita Khrushchev, and with him his attack on Stalin's 'cult of personality'. Almost imperceptibly, there was a softening of the paranoia that ruled in Stalin's lifetime - and this led to the de-Stalinization of the Soviet Union. So, in 1956 in the city of Poznan, the Poles react to intolerable working conditions by rallying 100,000 strong in the streets. Just like in Hungary that same year, the Russians send in the tanks, put down the protest, dead bodies are strewn in the streets, thank you very much. So, what do the Poles do? They resist and organize. They begin setting up secret networks inside one of the most oppressive regimes outside of Russia itself. This is their intuitive response to living under the threat of torture, murder and oppression. They did not cower, for what they cherished most was at stake – the Polish culture. The very Polish culture that their ancestors had kept alive under tyrannies from many sources wishing to grind its flower into an unrecognizable dust."

Stanley's face actively showed his interest. Turning out over the fjord once again, Trellis now went further.

"Even more recently, in 1970, the Polish Communists raised food prices radically, and the Poles took to the streets in the Polish Baltic cities of Gdańsk, Gdynia, Elblag, and Szczecin in the thousands. The Communists again send in the tanks, over five hundred of them, killing and wounding over a thousand Poles. However, we now see something very interesting. After the revolt is put down, Leonid Brezhnev, Khrushchev's successor in the Soviet Union, replaces the Polish Communist in-country leadership, lowers the food prices back to pre-protest levels, and even raises wages slightly. The Soviets fear total civil unrest, and lessen their stranglehold. Just a little bit."

Trellis now stopped talking out over the waters below, and turned once again to face Stanley, boring hard directly into his eyes.

"Stanley, we want to insert you into Poland to help us tap into the resistance that we know is already building there. We have information that the Baltic shipyards are already beginning to organize secretly. We need to support them, as they are up against a brutally totalitarian state. We already have developed a cover story for you, arranged through a small Canadian classical music record label. You are their talent scout looking for the next Arthur Rubinstein or Vladimir Horowitz."

"Horowitz is Russian," Stanley corrected him. He searched Trellis' eyes expecting an outburst, but found calm reasoning instead.

"Good, Stanley, because you will need to know that. Once we insert you, you will have to be able to stand on your own two feet. We do not have a large infrastructure behind the Iron Curtain. You will mostly be on your own. And make no mistake, alone means at risk, and the risk is your very life."

Stanley's young heart was pumping wildly. He opened his mouth to ask of the details of the assignment, and as his brain struggled to formulate its thoughts, "I'll do it!" came forcibly and uncontrollably out of his mouth.

Trellis looked out over the fjord, impassively. He thought to himself, "It always works. They cannot resist. They know the risks, yet always strike at the glittering lure."

Jack Trellis took the elevator to the DCI's office on Langley's seventh floor. Trellis knew his job was to clean up this mess, before it crossed the Potomac into the political confines proper of Washington, DC.

The meeting with the DCI was small and in the conference room connected to his office. The Director of Central Intelligence is a presidential appointment, and one that was increasingly reserved for those who had come from outside the ranks of the Intelligence Community. Technically, it was no longer the DCI, but more accurately D/CIA since 2005 when the Director of National Intelligence (DNI) office was formed. Today, the D/CIA reports to the DNI. But internally, the Director of the CIA was still colloquially called the DCI.

This particular DCI was a throwback to the days of old, an operative who cut his teeth in South America and was closing his career at the professional pinnacle. This was the position for which he had aspired, over the last forty years. He had no further ambitions. This was no political stepping stone for him.

He said simply, "Let's get started."

At this hastily called session, there sat the DCI, his Executive Assistant, and his legal counsel. In addition to these three, attending were Jack Trellis - the Deputy Director of Operations (formerly Covert Actions), Carter Norris the Deputy Director of Analysis (formerly Intelligence), and Jonathan Williams, the Liaison to the NSA.

Trellis began the brief. The briefing papers, hastily prepared and classified by Redmond's team, were passed across the table. Trellis's outbursts were now long behind him. He was fully vented, and had slipped behind the facade of the career operations professional.

"Sir, at approximately seven PM local time, Warsaw, an executive from Global Defense Analytics, Langston Powell, was murdered in apparent cold blood. Powell had been announced as the next COO of that firm only yesterday, and was expected to succeed Everett Roberts as CEO when Mr. Roberts retires as expected next year. Our head of station Warsaw has visually confirmed the corpse. We are treating this as an assassination, sir. The assailant is not in custody."

The DCI's face was expressionless. Years of handling explosive issues had trained him not to react at the initial unfolding of emerging issues. They could in a few hours or even days seem much more straightforward than they do at first hearing. Or conversely, quite often, the magnitude of the explosion yet to come could be tremendously magnified once the full impact was understood. The DCI was right to suppress his reactions, for this would turn out to be the latter case.

"Why Warsaw?" he asked. He was intentionally non-specific as to draw the full breadth of the briefing from Trellis.

"If you intended, sir, 'Why was Powell in Warsaw?', then the answer is very straightforward. His business had taken him to London earlier this week, and Powell travelled from there to conduct a business negotiation with the Poles in Poznan on Wednesday. He had been in Warsaw Thursday evening as he joined the conference call where he was announced to financial analysts as Global Defense Analytics' new COO and successor to the CEO."

Trellis looked to the DCI, whose face was a blank slate that seemed to speak in response – "Yes, I understand, go on."

"Sir if you intended, 'Why would an assassin pick Warsaw of all places?', we believe there was a very solid reason for why this location was picked."

Trellis paused, and was obvious in the fumbling of his briefing sheets as he prepared to utter the most distasteful briefing points he had ever uttered to any DCI during his long career.

"Sir, he was one of us. An agency man eight years retired."

"*Really*," crept unexpectedly through the DCI's restrained mask. His rigid face slackened slightly.

"Stanley Wisniewski, sir. Deputy Head of Warsaw Station through the 1990's. We recalled him in 1996. He retired with pension in 2007."

The DCI seemed for a moment to search his memory. He quickly found his recollections, captured like prey in an inescapable snare.

"Operation INDIGO, wasn't it? Yes. And that was with Marshall Analytics, wasn't it?" The DCI was holding the 8 x 10 photo of Stanley from the dossier. But the recollections were in advance of the rest of the briefing sheets he had not touched yet. His eyes transitioned from uninterested blanks to reflecting the sparks of recognition of how dirty this was about to become.

The room seemed to pause in a sterile electronic white noise while the DCI leafed through the dossier. He looked up and said simply, to no one in particular, "Continue."

"If I may, sir," chirped in Carter Norris, Deputy Director of Analysis, "Operation INDIGO was the breaking of a burgeoning espionage ring in the mid-eighties within Marshall Analytics, one of the two legacy companies that merged to become Global Defense Analytics in the mid-nineties. The agency was called in on a joint activity with the FBI, domestic stuff being their turf, by Marc Constantine, the firm's CEO at the time. Marshall's leadership had noticed several failures of deployed systems and wanted to assure critical classified systems information was not being fed to the Soviets. Mr. Constantine's hunch was right. Stanley was critical in resolving this case, and the capture of one of their chief technologists, Dr. Bennet Palmer."

Not even a mention was made of Bryce Weldon, rest his soul, thought Trellis.

The DCI had turned his head slowly and purposefully to look at Norris in a disapproving manner. The DCI's eyes glazed with boredom and indifference at Mr. Norris.

There had been a level of tension between these two shortly after the DCI took over and had decided to keep both existing deputies. While Trellis connected instantly with the DCI, for they had both "grown up" in operations, the DCI seemed to be put off by the dismissive and condescending manner in which Norris regularly briefed him. "It was as if Norris acted as if he was the only person in the room possessing any intelligence at all," the DCI was often overheard saying.

"Yes, Carter. I was around back then, you know," he said icily. He paused and turned to Trellis, "Jack, what makes us so sure this wasn't random violence? Beside the fact that Stanley was present. Could the two of them just been assaulted by someone in the streets? I mean, it is possible, isn't it?"

"Well, sir, your having been operational in eastern Europe throughout your long career, you are aware that violent crime is very atypical in that part of the world. Even with the Russian syndicates moving westward, they are very well behaved in Poland and Germany, virtually zero violent crime. Basically, petty theft, some drug infiltration, but even that not high by our standards."

He held the DCI's full attention. Carter Norris fumed quietly, once again left out of the inner circle.

"Besides,"Trellis continued, "Stanley had been seen with Powell all day throughout Warsaw on what appears to have been a walking tour. They ended up in *Stare Miasto* - Old Town Warsaw - before visiting the Polish 1944 Insurgency Monument. You may remember that massive monument sir, its photo is in the dossier – that is where Wisniewski appears to have planned, all along, for Powell to be gunned down."

Throughout the conversation, Stanley's name was mentioned in the Polish pronunciation, "Vish – NEV – Ski".

"How odd," added the DCI looking at the photo of Powell's body lying at the bronze feet of Polish insurgents emerging from the metallic rubble of this World War II Warsaw monument. "How odd that Powell was even out of the country when his appointment was announced. You'd think he would have loved the limelight, taking a victory lap around the corporation, wouldn't you? I mean he must have known the announcement was coming?"

A silence paused heavily over the men seated around the DCI's conference table. The question hung in the air like an unwelcome guest in one's doorway.

"There is another aspect of this that is somewhat unseemly, sir." Trellis addressed the DCI before legal or any others could wedge in with their opinions.

Trellis continued, "Stanley had been hired by Global Defense Analytics to vet Mr. Powell before the Board of Directors confirmed Powell's selection. You recall several weeks ago another GDA Executive, Ted Barber, was found dead in a canal in Amsterdam..."

"I was about to bring that up, sir," interrupted the legal counsel. "We now have two dead Global Defense Analytics executives. Could these be inter-related?"

The legal counsel looked proud of himself, for having contributed something other than a precedent of a legal ruling.

"How very astute of you, Paul." The DCI said without bothering to turn and look at his counsel. "You just interrupted the briefer who was about to explain that interrelationship to all of us. So, for the value of all of our times' sake, can we please allow Jack here to finish his briefing." The silence settled even more heavily across the conference table, pinning them all in their frozen positions.

The DCI waited for effect before breaking the tension, "Jack, please go on."

"Well, sir, Stanley was paid by Global Defense Analytics to vet Powell, specifically to clear him of any wrongdoing in the death of Barber. Powell had dinner with Barber the night Barber later drowned in the canal. By that time, Powell was jetting back to the US in his Gulfstream G650. By the information we currently have, Stanley cleared Powell, just before joining Mr. Powell on the trip to Poland. Powell had asked Stanley to serve as interpreter with the Polish Government in Poznan. Chances are Powell was aware of what Stanley had been hired to do. However, Powell was unsure of the outcome, that is of his being cleared, until the last minute. Must have created a lot of angst for Mr. Powell, not knowing if he would ascend to the zenith of the corporate world until just before the scheduled announcement."

The DCI was putting the pieces together. "Not a bad ploy. If you suspect someone is weighing heavily in the most important decision in your career, most possibly only negatively, best case neutrally, then you get him out of the equation by taking him abroad."

Williams, the liaison to the NSA was waiting for the entry point to interject their preliminary findings. He addressed the DCI.

"Sir, over at Fort Meade, we had a team on this as soon as the news broke a few hours ago. I believe we can contribute some insight on this."

"Go on, please," the DCI said respectfully. He always had tried to show impartiality in these briefings by treating the NSA with respect and dignity. God only knows the horrors they were going through with that Edward Snowden betrayal...

"The most preliminary review we performed turned up multiple intercepts between Wisniewski and an accomplice known only as Jean Paul. All very much in the open internet traffic with only rudimentary encryption. They appeared to have very little attempt to hide communications, save for some rather simplistic code words."

"And where did these COMMs originate from?" asked the DCI.

"All appear to be from Wisniewski's laptop while he was in California, and his accomplice was very readily traced to Paris, Amsterdam and London, mostly using cyber cafes and unprotected hot spots throughout these cities."

"So, you weren't able to identify this accomplice?"

"No sir. It appears he is skilled at avoiding detection. Even his transmissions to Wisniewski were rerouted through several unprotected servers across the US and Europe. They were programmed to wipe themselves clean after transmitting to the next link in the chain. It took us a while, but we were able to rebuild the links."

The DCI asked. "If they were wiped clean, how were you able to recover the trail?"

Williams looked at him. "It's called burning servers, like burning bridges behind a retreating enemy. We deal with that all the time. It is what we do. We traced Jean Paul to Paris, Amsterdam and London. But even then, we couldn't pinpoint him to anything other than a hotel or internet cafe computer."

The DCI gave an impressed look to his rep from the NSA.

Williams continued, "Our conclusion from the intercepts is that the Jean Paul accomplice was retained by Wisniewski to investigate the Barber death, found that Powell was at least complicit of manslaughter, if not murder. Yet even given this information, it appears Wisniewski intentionally cleared him to the Global Defense Analytics Executive team. It would appear your man Stanley had decided at some point to take matters into his own hands, with the further assistance of the Jean Paul accomplice."

Trellis had been coiling, but now unleashed. "That's the third time you called him 'Wiz NEW Ski'. His name is 'Vish NEV ski'. Stanley would have corrected you the first time if he were here. Let's know our subject, please."

Trellis was not being obstinate, he firmly believed one had to know the personality of those that one was hunting.

"Yes, of course," said Williams, passing a look to the DCI that said this is your game, your rules. The DCI looked impatient, waiting for the briefing to resume.

Trellis, wanting to regain the lead on the briefing, jumped in strongly, "Well, it sure would have been convenient if our brothers in Fort Meade had shared that treasure trove with my organization."

Williams held up his hands, outside of his chest, in a very open gesture. "Well, Jack, not like we had a great bit of time since your man, Stanley *Vish NEV ski,* went operational again."

The term "your man, Stanley" incensed Trellis, but being in the presence of the DCI, he calmed himself in response. He found and reapplied the Intelligence Professional facade he had been wearing before reacting to the NSA briefing.

"Yes," Trellis said sheepishly, "None of us saw that coming. Even our man on the inside at Global Defense Analytics thought this was too mundane to report back to us."

Trellis took a deep breath, as if the momentary pause somehow cleansed the incompetence of the last statement from the otherwise pristine atmosphere of the DCI's office.

Trellis continued, "Except in this case, Stanley appears to have had a pre-ordained agenda. Today in Warsaw, as our team is still working this out, this 70-year-old walked Powell all over Warsaw, no stops for meals or rest, ending up at the '44 Insurgency Monument as evening was falling. He intentionally wore down Powell's guard, and then got him just where he wanted him, before pulling the luger on him."

"My God, a luger? Why on earth would he use a luger?" the DCI was reacting unguardedly now.

"He used the luger as a symbolic weapon, sir. Stanley's own parents had been held not very far from that monument by the Germans in War World II. We are running German war records, but we believe the Luger was that from the SS Officer that held them both in '44."

"He blamed Powell for this?" The DCI seemed astounded.

"No sir, but I believe our *PYSCH OPS* team will assess he attached

Powell as a symbol of power. Somehow he viewed Powell as the same unopposed power that held his father and mother." Trellis' gut contracted, and he quickly continued the brief to avoid questions.

"This also explains why he left us two very pristine prints on the barrel of the luger, when he knew we would have had trouble getting a positive ID from the knurled grips. He wanted us to know it was him, sir. Left us the luger at the scene of the crime when all training he ever had would have said to pitch it into the Vistula, who's banks were but a very short walk away."

"Incredible," reacted the DCI. He attempted to regain his self-control. "Does he have a gripe with us? You said he retired in good standing. He worked for you in Operations at the time, right?"

"Sir, I was leading the Eastern Europe Division when we called him back to the states, just after the Ames affair."

Aldrich Ames was the worst mole the CIA had ever had until his arrest in 1994. He was personally responsible for the deaths of many operatives revealed to and later executed by the Soviet KGB and their later Russian equivalent – the FSB.

"After Ames' capture, many of those with direct operational exposure to the Russians, including our Polish teams, were brought back to Langley for debriefing, to assure they were not at risk of having been turned double by the Russians. With regards to Stanley, while we decided to put him back in place as Deputy Chief of Warsaw station, we noted some irregularities. We conducted a thorough audit of the Polish networks operational funds."

Trellis arched his eyes at Legal, sensing they might interrupt his briefing at this point, but they did not. Trellis continued.

"By the time we permanently recalled him in 1996, there was five million dollars missing from an operational account under his control. It was later assessed that the money had been siphoned off, but the forensic accounting team could never tie it back to him. We decided the best course was to bring him back stateside, give him access to nothing, and wait for him to retire."

"Smart move," now chirped in Legal. "Would have cost us a hell of a lot more in bad press if he went public and we had no proof. Surely would have drawn a lawsuit, undoubtedly."

The DCI cut him off again. "Don't worry, Paul. I think he will be getting us plenty of bad press now. In fact, it has already started. Having you seen the news in the last hour? Wait until they start piecing together the facts."

Having dismissed Legal again, the DCI turned back to Trellis. He appeared impatient. This was going to be a first-rate scandal for the agency. "Where is he now, Jack?"

"Still at large in Poland," Jack began, "last sighted at the central train station in Warsaw. Our team is reviewing video, but it takes a little longer over there. We now have teams on board the train routes to Berlin, Moscow and Vienna, among others, and we don't think he will make any moves to the airlines, as by now he knows we have an INTERPOL alert out for him. We initiated a border contain, and got our own agency's best people on the borders immediately, and initiated a full manhunt as well."

"So, we should have him pinned in Poland, you think?" asked the DCI hopefully.

"Perhaps, but I doubt it. Even if he still is in Poland, he will lay low, and blend in perfectly. He is more comfortable there than in the states. He will most likely try to cross the unprotected borders into Germany, or east towards Russia. There is a lot of border to cover there. Also, he could easily slip into the Czech Republic, Lithuania, Belarus, Slovakia or the Ukraine. Even with border alerts, it is not like the days of the cold war, ever since the Schengen Agreement was put in place."

All present knew well that the Schengen Agreement, named after the town in Luxembourg where the convention creating it was held, instituted the means to what is now known as the Schengen Area of Europe, composed of 26 nations and offering several hundred million Europeans free travel across most of Europe's internal borders. Often thought to be tied to the European Union, it actually is more expansive, including non-EU states as well.

Each of the men in the room thought the same thing. The ease of international travel within the Schengen Area would be no more difficult than Americans moving between states. This meant Stanley had relative ease in moving across borders, including Poland's, unless the agency happened to have agents watching. There simply were not enough agents to cover every possible crossing.

"What do you need, Jack?". The DCI asked. His eyes said there would be nothing held back. Ask and you shall have.

"Not what, sir, but who?"

The DCI rephrased the question, "Who do you need, Jack?"

"I need Diane Sterling," Trellis said to the DCI with a sideways glance to Carter Norris, for whom she worked. Trellis could see this caught him unaware, as his face flushed with anger and he began to object.

"Diane, *The Huntress*?" asked the DCI aloud.

"Exactly, sir. I need *The Huntress* to find Stanley so we can bring him in." Trellis' tone was more demanding than requesting, putting Carter Norris on the spot.

"Jack, you're not even briefed on what she is working for me. I simply cannot let her go for even a couple weeks."

Norris caught the eye of the DCI and his disapproving response to Carter's objection. Norris at this point knew he would be donating his best agent to Trellis' Covert Ops to track Stanley.

Trellis still could not believe that Norris was caught unprepared. Diane was the best in the agency at hunting men. Especially agents on the run.

The DCI weighed in. His measured response silently said, "do not waste your efforts to appeal this, Norris, this is final". He added aloud, "Jack, you get Diane until Stanley is caught or his body is found and confirmed deceased. But let's not be mistaken, I want him brought in alive if possible. I want to get to the bottom of this wretched affair. Thank you, Gentlemen, I have what I need to brief the DNI. That is all."

The DNI was the Director of National Intelligence. The DNI was created after 9/11, when inter-agency bickering contributed to missing the terror strike, even though several of the hijackers were under surveillance immediately before. It effectively separated the two functions of the DCI up to that point - running the agency, and coordinating all the National Intelligence Agencies. Only in America, could the answer to an inefficient bureaucracy be to strap on another layer.

Rising from the conference table, Trellis gave a snort of appreciation he had survived the briefing in one piece. To Norris he said, "God knows she won't find him in two weeks. He's too good operationally for that. He knows our playbook in and out. But if I were on the run, she would be the last person I would want to track me down."

"There's not a man alive she can't bring down..." someone said in the clutter of bodies exiting the seventh-floor office. It was exactly what they were all thinking.

Diane Sterling was somewhat of a legend in the CIA. She was smart, tough, resourceful and unrelenting. She had worked closely with Stanley on the Project INDIGO investigation, and her recognition from that ultimately got her assigned to the two fiercest manhunts in the history of the country's Intelligence Community. The first was the hunt for Aldrich Ames, the CIA mole and Soviet/Russian informer. The second manhunt was even more impressive, as it ultimately caught Robert Hanssen, the FBI Soviet counter-intelligence officer that was secretly on the payroll of the Soviets and later Russians themselves.

Both manhunts started as searching for the mole within the CIA that was evidenced by the Russians rolling up our networks at an alarmingly efficient rate. The latter investigation ultimately caught the FBI's Hanssen in its net. Robert Hanssen, working for the FBI perhaps did more damage to this country than any other single traitor in its history, including Aldrich Ames. Diane had been crucial to both investigations, and her financial insights led to both the eventual capture of both Aldrich Ames and Robert Hanssen. It was the money trail that led them to both spies, and Diane followed that trail relentlessly.

Diane's time on the Project Indigo Joint Task Force made her name well known throughout the agency, pulling her into the two manhunt teams, where she contributed impressively. Her time working jointly with the FBI demonstrated her knack for inter-agency abilities. As a result of this highly valued capability, Diane had been stationed for the past dozen years in London, working as one of the primary CIA liaisons to British Intelligence.

Trellis, now having access to Diane, hesitantly called her back for a few days of briefings.

"She'll lose valuable time she could be searching for Wisniewski," Redmond had argued, regarding Trellis' decision to bring her back to Langley for briefings.

"Can't release the bloodhound without giving her a sniff of the prey!" Trellis had said in their quiet conversation in his office. "Besides, the team working it already is in *The Blind* in Berlin and is competent enough to run the drill until Diane spins up. They don't stand a chance of catching Stanley, though."

"Why not?" asked Redmond.

"He is that damn good, especially over there. Fits right in - blends into the background. Best operative we ever had over there. When he gets into his safe location we'll have a hell of a time finding him. So, we need *The Huntress*, and she needs to know everything we have on Stanley, right up to the latest."

"But wouldn't we know all his safe locations from when he was operational?" asked Redmond.

"Ellie, you have never really been stationed in the field, in a hostile country, have you?" asked Trellis.

"No, sir, I can't say I have had that experience," said Ellison, unapologetically.

"Well, my friend, the first thing almost every operative does instinctively, without any training from us, is to burrow out a safe haven – an apartment, a home, a cave in the mountains – that he can retreat to in times of great peril." Trellis explained the ways of the covert world to Ellison Redmond. "At least the operatives that stay around for a while do …"

"But we would know about that, right?" Ellison asked innocently. "Surely they would share that safe haven site with the agency?"

"F**k, no, Ellie. The last thing they would do is share that with us." explained Trellis. "Sure as shit, one thing every covert op out there fears more than the Russian KGB, the East German *Stasi*, or in Stanley's case the Polish ZOMO, is the unknown mole within the agency that feeds their secrets to the enemy. They fear the betrayal by any one individual within the massive bureaucracy that could cost them their life in the middle of the night. So, one thing I know for sure is that Stanley has a safe haven that he kept from us, fearing someone in the chain might sell him out."

One thing Trellis did not know was if Diane would even accept this assignment. Yes, of course, there would be no choice in it for her from the CIA perspective. But, unlike almost every other operative worldwide, Diane was financially independent. Filthy rich, one might say. Family money from a deceased financier father. She could walk away from the CIA at any time. Not unlike Trellis himself.

The question at hand was would she refuse to track down her old mentor and friend, Stanley Wisniewski?

She could simply retire from the agency and set up shop anywhere in the private sector. Or live off her family fortunes. She had no children, no family. She was as independent as one can be. Trellis knew her well enough to know she wouldn't refuse the assignment. Even if it meant hunting her old friend, Stanley. In fact, she might want to find him before some other more reactionary faction of the company found him. Trellis convinced himself that Diane would immediately pick up the hunt, if she was convinced that it was in Stanley's best interest.

Diane was born in Bucks County, Pennsylvania, to an investment banker father who had a flair for the good life. Diane was denied nothing growing up, save for the love of her parents, who divorced when she was only eleven years old.

Her mother, forced into the divorce by her father, was crushed by it and broke down into a physical and emotional wreck. Diane witnessed the drinking and pills followed by the rehab followed by the pathetic attempts to regain her husband, all to no avail. Diane was hardened in the crucible of insensitivity of the father against her darling mother. As so often is the case, witnessing this insensitivity manifested in Diane an insensitivity of her own. She vowed to herself to never fall prey for the emotional dependency of another.

It wasn't that Diane did not love her father, she just could not understand how his love of money, possessions and lifestyle could numb him to the trauma he was inflicting on her mother.

Despite this, Diane still spent time with her father as she matured, with trips to New York, London, Paris, Rotterdam and Zurich. Her father taught her the ins and outs of amassing and maintaining financial wealth. She clung to these trips, as they represented her only real relationship she was ever to have with him. This relationship was financial in nature, and its clinical, even analytical, perfunctory nature had further hardened her. She had become what she hated most about her own father – cold, insensitive and materialistic.

Though she did not see the elements of it in herself today, she saw her father over the years for what he really was – an unemotional man who's only love was for personal fortune and all the excesses of life it could afford its owner.

She saw the weakened shell of a woman that her mother became, and told herself she would never become this dependent on any man. She decided to dictate her own terms to life, and no man was to control her as her father had controlled, and ultimately destroyed, her mother.

By the time Diane entered Princeton, her mom was remarried to a man Diane cared not to know. Her mother was seizing the remnants of security on which to rebuild her shattered life. Diane now became emotionally separated from both her mother and her father, but discovered herself in her collegiate years.

She had immersed herself in her studies. Economics. With a minor in Criminal Justice. An unusual paring, but one that captured her interests. She soon realized other interests as well.

A friend had coaxed her to join the women's Rugby club, if nothing else, for the legendary partying. To Diane's surprise she soon loved every aspect of being a member of this team. She soon found herself starting A-side as a wing forward, thanks to her innate and previously unknown skill in tackling - a skill she never knew she had growing up as an only child. She loved the physical contact, the exhilaration of dominating an opponent, and the camaraderie of being with her teammates. Less for the post-game kegger parties, and the debauchery that was often the allure of so many to collegian club Rugby, but more for a sense of belonging amongst her teammates.

However, it was the game itself, though, she found most intoxicating. The sport itself was unlike most things in her life - fast, unspoiled, and when best played, fluid. And most of all, physical. Incredibly physical.

More than anything, she loved the physical competition of the game. Once taught the fundamentals, she took quickly to it, and craved the exertion and self-sacrifice, knowing it could result in the satisfaction of dominating an opponent. She loved to tackle her opponents.

The truth of the tackle could not be denied. You either brought down your opponent or you did not – it could not be debated. She was so skilled in bringing down the competition, that she soon earned a reputation that she could tackle anyone.

Diane became so praised on the women's team that the scent of her reputation wafted over to the men's team. So much so, that Bill Berrault, the 260 pound loose-head prop from the men's A-side team challenged her outright that she could not possibly tackle him. So, it was set in her third season on the team, on a lovely late fall Saturday, before both their games, on a practice field, the wager was put to the test. Players from the both women's and men's teams showed up to witness the contest, unbeknownst to both coaching staffs.

Berrault took the ball at the 22-meter line, with only Diane between he and the try, or goal, line. The wager was simple. Berrault would have three attempts to score – if she brought him down once before he crossed the goal line, she won.

Berrault was a massive, mauling man, and when he began running he did so in a tight loop backwards to assure he got up a good head of steam. Diane was not small at 5 feet 9 inches, but her 140 pounds or so were doubled in Berrault's mass. As it came toward Diane, she suppressed the fear of the impact that was coming, concentrating only on the fundamentals of the tackle. She concentrated on the physics of where to drive her shoulder, what to grasp with her hands.

She could hear the cheers of the crowd as Berrault closed in on her, but her eyes focused on his hips. The hips do not lie. The legs, the shoulders, the head, the knees would feint one direction or another. Focus on the hips, tackle the hips.

Tackle the hips. Wrap him up. He will come down.

Diane lowered her shoulder, head up, eyes on his hips. Then the impact hit like a freight train. The force drove Diane back, but her hands were now squarely around Berrault's waist. Her shoulder already was screaming in intense pain, but she forced herself to hold on.

Don't let the explosion of the impact throw you.

Berrault drove his massive thighs in high steps to break her grasp. His right knee came up with violent momentum and crushed directly into Diane's nose. She felt it break, as if a water balloon had ruptured on the sidewalk. A pain like she had never felt followed, and immediately she could taste the warm salt of her blood choking in her throat.

Don't let the bastard go. Hang on for all you've got.

She held on. She did not loosen her grip. Her hands remained locked around his waist. He was dragging her towards the goal line, still pumping those massive thighs. She knew she could not survive two more attempts at this. She had but one opportunity to bring him down. She knew she would be in no condition for rounds 2 and 3.

Ignore the pain, focus. Do this now or you won't survive.

She released her right hand, now grabbing the thick, cinched waste band of his rugby shorts. Sensing this he now moved frantically, trying to shake her loose, like a bronco throwing its mount. She did not release her left hand, but Berrault was dragging her more readily now.

The blood ran down her arm freely. She could see it flow in all this physical mayhem, the amount startling.

Ignore the blood. Focus on what must be done.

Diane looked beyond the blood and took measure of Berrault's left ankle. Amidst her pain and concentration, time had slowed. The actions were moving in slow motion. The pain was seemingly more intense, as if it had been concentrated by the slowing of time.

Now, you must do it now.

She timed her reach to his frantic steps and her right hand found the fat massive instep of his cleated left foot. Not releasing the waist with her left hand, she mustered every bit of strength, above the searing pain of her shoulder and nose, and pulled his foot as hard as she could against the cheek of his huge fat ass.

She knew she had him when she felt the physical panic in his frame. He was still standing upright, dragging her, but now only able to hop on his right foot. She slid her hand forward, his ankle now in the crook of her elbow, her right hand now relocked with her left.

She dug her toes in the soft soil under the grass, and this resistance was enough to knock him off balance. Berrault went over as if from a logger's ax – slowly, but undoubtedly, he was going down.

Don't let go. He is coming down. Don't pass out.

Diane held firm to him. If she let go now, there was always the chance he would regain his balance. Even though he was falling, she had to see this through to the end. She knew the impact of their hitting the ground together would tear through her shoulder and head in a wave of pain like she had never felt in her life.

But she held the waist and ankle right to the ground, and the impact ripped through her like a violent fever, attacking every sinew and nerve of her being.

He is down. You have done it. Release.

Diane rolled off Berrault's massive, muddied hulk, only a few feet from the goal line. He was soon raising himself to his feet, frantically, as if it was to distance himself from his shame. Diane rolled onto her back, the blood from her free-flowing nose smeared across her face, and then began to pool below the sockets of her eyes. The pain was overwhelming, now that her focus was released from her task. It was then that she blacked out.

When she came around it was in a matter of seconds that some of her teammates thought infinitely long. Berrault and the crowd now stood over her, blocking out the sun, making the air heavy and tight with sweat. She lay on the field covered in her own blood. Her nose was broken, shattered. Under her jersey, she had a hematoma on her shoulder that prevented her from moving her right arm without searing pain.

Berrault mocked her, standing over her. "You know Diane, for such a pretty piece of meat, you're not looking so good to me right now."

The crowd immediately jeered at Big Bill for rubbing salt into the wound. "Asshole!" and "What a jerk!" were heard distinctly. His smile broadened at the censure of the crowd.

Diane craned her neck and spit blood from her mouth. She looked up at Bill's jersey, shorts and socks, smeared in her own rich, crimson blood.

"Bill, you jackass!" she yelled from flat on her back. "Just make sure when all your buddies ask you how you got so bloody before a game, that you tell them this little bloody piece of meat brought your fat ass to the ground on the first try."

The crowd whooped and hollered, most vocally from the men's team members who bore witness to her feat. She could hear their mocking of Berrault begin, just before she yielded to the pain and passed out on a more permanent basis.

She did not play again that season, in fact never played again after that day, but she won that bet. Thus, began her legacy. *"There was not a man alive she could not bring down."*

Chapter Two
Saturday's Dawn Breaks

THE AUDI CRAWLED slowly westward, quietly through the blackness of the Polish night. Jean Paul drove, his hands and arms in near constant, agitated motion. Stanley sat stoically, looking through his window into the night. The interior's glow betrayed his isolation, as his accomplice Jean Paul stole glances of the reflection in the passenger's window across the Audi's cabin.

The only motion that Jean Paul observed in his glimpses were those he had never seen before in the long gray haired seventy-year-old. Jean Paul noted the continuous tremor in Stanley's hands.

"*Jak się masz?*" he asked Stanley, softly, as if not to step blatantly on the old man's cell of introspection.

"I am fine," Stanley responded in Polish as well. His gaze was still fixed into the depth of the Polish countryside that the night hid from him. He added, as if to cleanse himself of the inaccuracy of his response, "It is done."

"Yes, it is done. Of course." Jean Paul raised his eyes to see only Stanley scanning the darkness. "You know they will come for you now, with everything that they have."

Jean Paul's hands were still evidencing his nervousness, as he reached again for the Audi's console's display panel. The Audi drilled deep into the dark Polish country side, progressively to more remote, lesser traveled roads exactly as Stanley had instructed Jean Paul. The Audi shook violently at times, not for lack of it's quality construction, but more so for the poor quality of roads on the route which they now executed. Stanley felt comfort in the rough ride, knowing the new, smooth autostradas would be the first routes watched by the Polish authorities, especially as these highways were equipped with state of the art camera systems. So instead, the dark green Audi negotiated country roads where the larger threat was breaking an axle, or otherwise becoming stranded.

Stanley continued to look off into the night, whose edges were highlighted in the faintest purplish warning of the dawn's advance. He was waiting for the snare to snap, for a blocking vehicle to skid in front of them before additional cars closed in from a side or rear access. But Stanley knew operationally, this would take a few hours to set up. So, long as the last known trail was hot to the east, Stanley knew they must have still 2-3 hours in front of them to get to their most westward of destinations. Stanley had to get to the safe house. To get to *her* home.

Stanley broke the silence in the Audi, only to calm Jean Paul's angst - whose constant arm movements were now annoying him. They flailed like the dance of flags announcing an oncoming storm.

"Where will you cross the border?" he asked Jean Paul in Polish. "You know they will watch for every new person who has checked-in to a hotel or inn across the country in a matter of hours."

Jean Paul's younger voice caught and cracked on his response. "I will drive south as the sun rises and approach the Czech border. I will take the Polish country roads toward the Czech town of Liberec. There are no border checkpoints anymore, but even if the authorities hastened a roadblock, I am a tourist on my way to Prague, with my EU passport, it should not be an issue. Besides, by then they will be looking for a tall graying man with long locks and a close-cropped beard. Even the most imaginative policeman would not see how an international killer fitting that description converts himself into a short, pudgy middle-aged Frenchman."

Stanley scoffed of the thought of Jean Paul as a Frenchman. True, he had lived in Paris for decades since Stanley rescued him from the closing snare of the Russians, a trap that would surely have been lethal. Stanley knew while Jean Paul's fluent French language skills and identity papers were more than convincing, Jean Paul would always be his Polish agent from Gdańsk.

"Be aware they will be looking for you, of your own accord, soon enough. Be very careful my friend…," Stanley said, still peering into the black night.

The statement hung between them like a shroud. Black and ominous. They both knew it to be accurate. Jean Paul decided to clear the air.

"So, let them look. I knew of this when we met in London. I knew exactly what you were asking me to do. I have committed to you, my friend. You saved my life not so long ago. You saved my mother's soul. This is my chance to return the favor."

Stanley looked at him quizzically. He needed to set the record straight with his final confidante.

"Jean Paul, if you think somehow you can save me, you cannot. I am already dead, my friend. My movements are but the writhing of the snake who has lost his head to the shovel's thrust. Now I only wander until I wander no more. But I have done what was needed. You know all else that needs to be done."

Jean Paul looked at Stanley's right hand. It still trembled. Stanley may have made peace with his actions, but his body's wrestling with his memories were still ahead of him.

Stanley was also aware of the tremors, as he thought of a quote from Nietzsche, *'I did that' says my memory. 'I could not have done that,' says my pride, and remains inexorable. Eventually, the memory yields.*

Stanley knew that he would not live to realize the benefits of time that Nietzsche described. He would be naïve to think that Trellis would allow that. Stanley was no longer the naïve young man he had once been.

After driving slowly across Poland throughout the night, they pulled into the western Polish town of Zgorzelec on the German border. The Audi soon crawled past a small Polish villa near the center of town, overlooking the Neisse river that separated Poland from Germany. Stanley made careful inspection of his refuge as they passed. The first hues of morning were battling the still violet edges of the night, so they needed to unload the contraband that was Stanley before the full glory of morning descended.

The Audi crawled down the road before doubling back. Jean Paul handed Stanley the key. "It is stocked for thirty days. Food, water, vodka, clothes. Even hair dye. Scissors. Razors. There is a loaded Glock 9mm in the desk drawer, should you decide you need it. If you change your mind and stay any longer than that, you are on your own."

"*Dziękuję bardzo*, my friend." Stanley took the key. "But, if I stay any longer than ten days, I will be in the custody of Director Trellis. Or worse, waiting to be judged in the afterlife. Director Trellis fears the secrets of his that I carry. No, I will see you in Vienna on the sixth of December. Remember your tradecraft."

"Of course, I will, of course," answered Jean Paul. He remembered to himself, not to be repeated aloud. To Stanley he quipped, "It is a simple code for our meeting in Vienna. I will follow our tradecraft. It all comes back like an old lover. And, my friend, we Frenchmen never forget our lovers, *c'est impossible*."

The Audi pulled past the villa, one final look for Stanley. It would be only minutes before the town awoke to begin its daily routine. The Audi would be noticed, and so Stanley grabbed the prepared rucksack from the back seat, and moved in a determined motion to the villa. His motion was as brisk as the night air, and Jean Paul became startled.

"How will ***you*** cross, my friend?" Jean Paul asked in a desperate attempt to hold onto Stanley, if only for a second longer.

The question hung unanswered. Stanley re-opened the front passenger's door, and peered at the man who was but a teenage boy when Stanley first came to Poland. The boy was still nervous, but the man he had become was trying to hide it.

"Please do not ask me that, just meet me in Vienna on the sixth of December. And prepare yourself that you will never see me again. Know that I will never give you up my friend. If I do not show, never show, I am gone. Do not come back here. It would only be trouble for you. Go on and enjoy life with the funds you have earned. Should I never make it to Vienna, assure me you will do this. If circumstances require that you must forget me, know that you have done your duty. You have done all I have asked. I can ask nothing more."

Only then did it dawn on Jean Paul that this might be the last he would ever see the man who had saved his very life so many years earlier. His eyes began to flood as his mind grasped with the catastrophe that had yet to happen.

"I would give my life for you, my friend," he said to Stanley. His voice frothed with emotion.

Stanley was now backing away from the Audi, its door still open in his hand. The light of morning was slowing crushing the veil of night.

"You very well may still have to. May the Lord protect you, my friend, and may His grace be with *her* tonight, for the shelter *she* provides me." Stanley's right hand then gently flipped, swinging the door on its arc to closure with the Audi's cabin.

"May His grace be with *her* tonight and always," Jean Paul rapidly wedged in as the door swung, instantly realizing the irony of a freshly minted murderer and his accomplice invoking the blessings of the Lord. The car door slammed with a condemning thud.

Jean Paul drove off into the sparseness of the town. Small as it was, he was soon down the hill, and parked for a moment upon the square that sat on the border. The Neisse river, which flowed into the Oder downstream, bisected this town, separated Poland from Germany across its icy November banks.

On the eastern bank of the Neisse, the smaller and less developed half of the city was known as the Polish town of Zgorzelec. Across the modern, new, beautifully arching footbridge over the river, the other half was the revitalized German town of Görlitz. This was the product of the Potsdam Conference agreements that essentially set the post Second World War borders of Poland.

The Soviets had since 1945 controlled both lands, with Görlitz being in East Germany. With both Poland and East Germany under the communist sphere, one would think there was no need to separate the two. Not the Poles, who held fiercely to their culture like life's last breath. They demanded their own nation, outright, even if it was to be under the shackles of Soviet Communism. President Truman and Winston Churchill demanded free elections in Poland after the war, along with the new borders. Stalin agreed, knowing he would fix the elections to produce a Communist puppet state, and refused the Allies request to have the elections internationally monitored.

The Poles demanded the Polish flag be unfurled proudly once again, and the victorious Allies of the West were with them.

Jean Paul watched the mist of the river slowly shroud the footbridge in nature's own red velvet curtains, as the strongly rising morning scarlet hues of warmth reflected from last cold vapors of the night.

Jean Paul looked at the white over red border markings along the near bank, reminding him of one of the greatest feats of Polish nationalism. It was when Arthur Rubinstein, himself a Polish Jew, but then living in America, was asked to play at the ceremonies commemorating the institution of the new United Nations. Angered that the Soviets refused to allow the Polish flag to be flown as a sovereign state at this point, he finished his entertainment with a powerful crescendo forte of Poland's National Anthem, "*Poland Is Not Yet Lost*", drawing a thunderous ovation.

Jean Paul glanced across the river to the beauty and majesty of the German city of Görlitz. It climbed majestically from the banks of the Neisse, with the twin spires of the Church of Saints Peter and Paul dominating the town's riverbank.

Conscious of not staying too long along the river border, where the ever-watching cameras would likely be mounted, Jean Paul took in the beauty of Görlitz as he slowly allowed his Audi to roll forward. He took comfort in knowing the car had no titular connection to himself, as he bought it on Stanley's direction on the black market for cash. It likely was stolen, but was old enough not to have any GPS or tracking signal generators installed. Again, this was done at Stanley's direction.

Jean Paul took one last look at the modern footbridge spanning the river. There had once been a footbridge, the *Altstadtbrücke* (German for the old town bridge) at this location prior to War World II, but in 1945 the retreating *Wehrmacht* destroyed it in a desperate attempt to slow down the advancing Soviet Red Army. This span was a testament to the new European cooperation. It was rebuilt, reopening in 2004. In 2007, its border crossings would soon come down as the Schengen agreement allowed unrestricted crossings between the two countries.

Jean Paul wondered if Stanley would be so brazen to stroll across the pedestrian crossing itself? Certainly, there would be agents watching this crossing. Jean Paul could not help but wonder how difficult it would be for Stanley to make that short walk in the days to come across the river from Zgorzelec into Görlitz. From Poland into Germany. From the land of Stanley's mother (and the man he considered to be his father), to the land of his monstrously defective natural father. From the land of the beauty and sensitivity of Frederic Chopin, to the land of the insensitivity and atheistic nihilism of Friedrich Nietzsche.

Jean Paul pressed the accelerator, and drove south out of Zgorzelec along the Neisse, as the rising morning sun now fully brightened the stillness of the boundary river.

Above him, on the overlooking hill, Stanley had turned the key in the lock, letting himself into the villa that had once been the private recluse of himself and the only woman he would ever love.

He slipped through the door into the stale warmth of a vacated property which only recently was brought back to life by Jean Paul. The recently restored heat hung moist, permeating the dank emptiness that for so long had been this forgotten villa. It carried airborne the residue of the long-settled dust that had been recently cleaned away. However, as old memories can never be completely purged, the dust dispersed into the thick putrid air reminding Stanley of the emptiness that would always be present in some form within him, for her love had been taken from him.

The word villa was misleading, as it was more of an antique apartment in the Polish sense of the word than the splendor conveyed by the Italian sense. It was a respite from the dangerous tension that both he and his love existed under - never knowing if they were watched and tracked by either the Russians or the Americans alike. Stanley was betting his life that he had been successful in keeping this reclusive site from both. This villa was the most cherished and most temporary of freedoms in his life once, and now Stanley could only hope to escape his most desperate of actions, the killing of Powell, in its stale warmth.

Stanley held his right hand to his face for the first time since sacrificing Langston Powell. He had come to terms with himself by rationalizing Langston's killing as a sacrifice. It was needed to prevent Powell's Orwellian planned expansion of drone deployment over the world, including the West, and the United States itself. Stanley felt nerves of his hand flutter on his cheek like the uncertainty of his days ahead. His Polish step-father, the man he loved, would have said it "swayed like the stalks of grain trembling in the harvest wind awaiting the scythe."

The more he attempted to control the motion of his hand, the more his nervous response rebelled. For Stanley, a man accustomed to severe strain over the decades of his assignments in Poland, this was an unaccustomed reaction. He had always controlled himself in the threat of grave danger. Now, he realized that danger had been replaced by the certainty of his own grave.

A great fatigue came over Stanley as the rising Saturday morning sunlight crept through the villa. Stanley walked through the kitchen, recently replenished with stores of food, water and *Luksusowa* potato vodka. He checked the drawer containing the Glock, and pulled back its upper mechanism to check the chamber, which was empty. Stanley completed the motion that would load the first round into the chamber, deciding that the speed of reaction now outweighed the safety of an empty chamber.

Stanley walked past the small, simple wooden table of the dining room where *they* had first shared the forbidden joy of tender smiles over nervous glances. Down the hall, he walked into the bedroom. This room which he had remembered so repeatedly and vividly throughout his lonely retirement half a world away. Stanley remembered the smells of *her* closeness - sweet, clean and subtly fragrant, enticing his desires. All the more, this now frustrated the romantic in him, knowing he could never see or smell or touch *her* again.

He lay himself, fully clothed, onto the bed, only slipping off his shoes. His entire body now began to tremble. And every inch of his being remembered.

He remembered not the recurring loop that had been running through his mind since it happened - of Langston Powell's terror as Stanley had just pulled the trigger; of Powell's realizing his earlier certainty of Stanley's weakness was wrong. Mortally, terminally wrong.

Stanley did not remember himself standing over Powell's fallen body and squeezing a second round into the instantly lifeless corpse. For the first time in the few hours since these events came to pass, Stanley did not recall them in his agonizing, inescapable loop of memory.

Instead Stanley now lay remembering his body trembling uncontrollably, another time, long before. It was in this very bed, as he lay beside her body, exposed to him for the first time. Stanley remembered his fluttering touch as he traced the curves of her delicate, feminine form. He then had also tried to control his nerves, and then also they had intensified in rebellion.

A rebellion that was not quelled until his lips met hers that evening. Their passions, long suppressed, exploded as they mutually lowered their walls of restraint. A fire had lit the kindling of compassion from their years of working together so intimately, so secretively. It had now raged into an inferno which would consume every desire they had each told themselves could never be dared to be acted upon. The inferno would rage uncontrolled until no fuel was left to feed it .

It was quelled by a night of satisfied passion that was Stanley's first. Ever. A night that revealed to Stanley how wonderful the touch of another human being could be, and how close two individuals could become through it.

It was foreign to him. He was raised in a family full of love, but devoid of intimacy. A family of survivors who felt the guilt, the shame, of existing while those they loved, and so many million more, had perished to the greatest evil of their time.

It was *she* who had saved him from that very gnawing emptiness that was his lack of intimacy. Before *her*, he could only see himself as a hunter. A man, cold and hardened by the hunger in his belly, seeking his prey through the darkness of the thickets and forests. His prey eludes him, and his hunger overtakes him even more. Then one day, on the edge of the clearing, from the forest emerges a delicate fawn. The hunter raises his bow, but in sighting the youthful beauty and innocence of his prey, he is overtaken by its simplicity and dignity. In the sunlight, every detail of its marking shimmers like gems of revelation of the stark void of his own inner self. The hunter sights the fawn, but cannot release the arrow. Despite his deepening hunger, which he knows can ultimately lead to his own destruction, he cannot destroy what he has come instantly to love.

It was in this very bed, years ago, that Stanley's *fawn* offered his first taste of true freedom. *She* shared herself freely with him, first sensing, and then fulfilling, his need to feel the tender touch of another.

For *she, herself,* was another who also knew the horrors that life can force us to witness, to bear. Another who knew that the relief from this world of horrors lies in the most fleeting and tender of caresses of another's warm and gentle human soul. She sensed this was missing from his life, as much as freedom itself was missing from *her own*. For he had given *her* freedom, and now *she* would lead him on his path to intimacy.

She lay naked before him then, as the fawn lies exposed beyond the edge of the forest, into which it blends so protectively. *She* reached out taking his quivering hand, softly pulling it to the precious vale between her full, lovely breasts. He looked into her eyes, open wide like those of a most delicate and sensitive creature. His thought, at that moment, he remembered now clearly - "How I have wasted my life, for only today do my fingers feel the pulse of the heartbeat of another."

Now, on this day when Stanley had returned to Zgorzelec, to the villa, to this bed, there would be no *fawn*, no touch, no freedom. No anticipation. No escape. Only the tremors remained.

Diane looked out the cabin window of the agency's executive jet as it bore its well-worn route to Washington, DC through the North Atlantic skies. The Saturday sun glistened on the seemingly peaceful, greenish-gray ocean below in an unusually clear November morning. The pattern of its waves, mere textured ripples from this altitude, became hypnotic to her view.

She had been awakened in her Westminster flat just hours earlier with news of her priority assignment. She immediately rose and packed a single grip and headed in the desolate London night to the agency's waiting aircraft. A part of her resented giving up her Saturday, scouring the shops of Chelsea and Kensington. These were her pleasurable diversions from her rigorously clinical and methodical existence. There would always be time enough later for these simple pleasures, she thought to herself.

When she boarded the jet, Diane was handed a classified dossier on Stanley Wisniewski. Diane was the only passenger on this jet designed to carry twelve. She strapped herself in behind the conference table that otherwise would itself seat four. As the jet taxied to the runway, she spread the papers that mapped Stanley's life, as it was known to the agency.

She had digested its information on the long flight, with only the most recent facts being new to her. It began with Stanley Wisniewski, being born May 7th, 1945 at Johns Hopkins Hospital in Baltimore to freshly emigrated Polish parents that had just survived the war. Eerily, Diane noted that this was the very day of the German surrender to the Allies ending the war in Europe.

Stanley's upbringing in Polish East Baltimore was spartan, but thanks to his uncle who had emigrated years earlier, Stanley's family had a modest row home on Shakespeare street to themselves. There was also a resettlement grant from the US Government, in return for his father's Nuremberg Trial deposition. The Fell's Point neighborhood was effectively a Polish micro-community. In this waterfront "bubble", Stanley was raised speaking only Polish in his home, and at many locations - Polish grocers, butchers, bakers - throughout the community. He attended Saint Stanislaus elementary school, graduating at the top of his class. This earned him a placement in the city's most prestigious high school, the then all-male Baltimore Polytechnic Institute. With no social distractions, he graduated with honors, completing the academically rigorous A-course. With the assistance of an academic scholarship from a state congressman of his district, Stanley then went on to obtain his Bachelor's and Master's degrees, from Maryland's

Loyola University. His focus had been his own love of language and European history.

In 1972, he sought to scratch out a living using these talents. After taking language proficiency and intelligence tests for what he thought was a position with a firm doing interpreting work in nearby Washington, DC, Stanley was recruited into the Central Intelligence Agency. He underwent orientation in 1972, followed by European field trials in 1973 and 1974. In 1975, he returned to the states to tend to his father, dying from cancer.

Returning to the agency after his father's passing, Stanley was soon thereafter inserted into Poland. The first two years were predominantly assimilation of himself into the culture of Warsaw, but in 1977 his first real activity in developing his network began. By 1978, Stanley had been reporting back to Trellis his product (informational reports) detailing the burgeoning underground resistance movement within the country. Stanley's work product was sourced from his agent *Syrenka*, named after the mythical sword and shield bearing mermaid who protected Warsaw. Stanley adamantly resisted any attempts to identify his agent *Syrenka* by name, even to Trellis, in order to protect his most precious source.

The other critical event in 1978 in Poland, and around the globe, was the election of the Polish Cardinal of Kraków, Karol Józef Wojtyła, as the new Pope John Paul II. This stunned the world, as the new Pope was the first non-Italian pontiff since 1523, over 450 years. The Polish Cardinal and new Pope had been supportive of the underground network, formally known as KOR (short for the Polish *Komitet Obrony Robotników* or Workers' Defense Committee) that had existed in secret since 1976. Cardinal Wojtyła, many would later say, was instrumental in its formation. The new Pope also had been crucial in establishing what were called *Flying Universities*. These were underground classes that Poles could take to educate themselves. The word *Flying* alluded to the fact that they were secretive, constantly changed locations, usually in individuals' homes, to evade the Communist Polish secret police, known by the Polish acronym ZOMO.

In 1979, the Pope John Paul II returned to his homeland with the papal message, ***"Be not afraid"***. This was continuing his tradition, as when he had been Cardinal of Kraków, of speaking direct messages of non-violent resistance to the Polish people, couched in the holy language of Our Lord Jesus Christ. Even the Communist State could not prevent his doing this.

Certainly, the Poles took his message to heart – "Be not afraid" of the communists who constantly seek to control ever more of your life and eradicate your culture.

A few months later in early1980, *Syrenka's* products were validated by a series of events which took place in the massive Lenin shipyards of Gdańsk. Following the firing of a beloved crane operator and worker's right activist known affectionately as *Pani Ania*, only weeks before her scheduled retirement, the shipyard ground to a halt as the workers refused to continue their activities until she had been reinstated. The Workers' Defense Committee, that is the KOR, had supported the Gdańsk Shipyard Strike, and coordinated sympathetic strikes in other industries throughout Poland.

From this situation emerged a leader in the form of the charismatic, mustachioed electrician and workers' rights activist, Lech Wałęsa. Stanley's secretive agent *Syrenka* had identified Wałęsa a year earlier as an activist personality to be watched as a potential organizer and emerging protest leader. With the *Solidarity Trade Union* being legitimized in the resolution of the strike, it formed the first social movement of workers organizing and rising against their so-called

Worker's Party Government. *Syrenka* was now treated within the agency as a grade A source. *Syrenka* was second only to the even more secretive source code named *Erasmus*, the East German *Stasi* Secret Police agent that Trellis himself had turned. Stanley's star had risen high within the agency as these events came to pass. CIA money began pouring into Poland through Stanley to *Syrenka*, and on to *Solidarity*.

The next year, 1981, with the Soviets threatening an invasion to control the Poles, the newly appointed Communist Polish Prime Minister Wojciech Jaruzelski imposed martial law. Thousands of members of *Solidarity* were imprisoned, including Lech Wałęsa. Jaruzelski's actions were an attempt to destroy the *Solidarity* social movement that would eventually grow to 10 million members – one of every three working Poles. The threat to the Communist regime could not be more real. Stanley and *Syrenka* remained the pivotal connections tying the CIA to this movement which was now driven underground.

Syrenka's product continued to flow from Stanley, giving the CIA its most accurate glimpses inside the Polish police state during a social crisis. *Syrenka* predicted the pressure of work slowdowns by the millions of workers loyal to *Solidarity* across Poland, as protest of their imprisoned leaders. These actions crippled the Polish economy, which unlike other Communist states owed huge sums loaned from Western banks. The pressure of the work slowdowns, and their resulting potential state default would force Jaruzelski to end martial law in July 1983. This capitulation only emboldened the Poles, and as a result *Solidarity* thrived throughout the 1980's.

Stanley continued to run *Syrenka* from Warsaw, until the summer of 1985. The Soviets had suddenly and effectively been rounding up networks and executing agents throughout Eastern Europe. Fearing

Stanley himself was endangered, he was recalled back to CIA headquarters in Langley, Virginia. With Stanley back in the US, *Syrenka's* output immediately stopped. *Syrenka's* output began again when Stanley returned to Poland in 1987. In the mid 1990's *Syrenka* went silent, permanently.

Since the agency never knew *Syrenka's* identity, that is outside of Stanley himself, it could not validate if *Syrenka* was even still alive. Was *Syrenka* another casualty of the Soviets actions? Stanley refused to identify *Syrenka* by name upon his return to CIA headquarters, nor would he give any insights into *Syrenka* suddenly having gone so deafeningly silent.

In 1985, Diane, then a new associate with the agency was assigned to Stanley upon his return stateside. They would both be assigned to a new project codenamed INDIGO. It was later, after Project Indigo, when Diane became active on the teams that frantically hunted the source of the Soviets newfound efficiency in rolling up the Western networks throughout Eastern Europe. Moles in the CIA were suspected. First, the agency mole Aldrich Ames had been captured in 1994 and confessed to turning over much of the information that had sent Western operatives to their deaths. Then, however, betrayals continued that could not be traced back to Ames or the information he had access to. It was then that Diane was drafted onto the team that hunted and caught the traitorous FBI counter-espionage agent Robert Hanssen.

Only years later, after seeing the deaths and carnage attributed to the Russians from the information passed on by Ames and Hanssen, did Diane fully come to understand the urgency of Stanley's return. Fearing that Stanley's cover had been blown and his status as an operative of the agency was made known to the Soviets, Stanley was repatriated to the United States.

Project Indigo was to be Diane's first action in the field, assisting in inserting Stanley into a Defense firm to evaluate whether an executive on its staff was culpable in handing technical information over to the Soviets. She loved the excitement and diversion from her earlier staff intelligence postings, where she developed background information on various countries, their organizations and their known indigenous intelligence personnel.

While the Staff Intelligence work was initially very exciting, Diane tired of it quickly. She found the work to be mundane, lacking urgency, and she soon felt isolated from the true *raison d'être* of the agency - operations. She knew she would love her first true operational posting with the now experienced Stanley Wisniewski, even if it were a joint exercise with the FBI on American soil.

Diane, in her first field assignments, would support Stanley in penetrating the defense firm Marshall Analytics. Diane aided Stanley in befriending Bryce Weldon, a young engineer who had been drawn into this scheme unwittingly. Stanley later would use the nubile, young Diane as the very bait to draw Weldon to the snare.

Diane thought back to her initial meeting with Stanley. He was forty years old when they first met. She thought him somewhat reserved at first, but in a quiet, polite way. Not standoffish, nor condescending, just a polite distance, as if by the stain of the culture in which he had been immersed.

Project Indigo, a joint operation with the FBI counter-intelligence unit, was a trial in cooperation that was historically non-existent between the two agencies.

The counter espionage unit of the FBI would typically handle these domestic issues, but the political climate at the time was driving the two agencies to collaborate in these national security issues. The CIA was still recovering from the thrashing it had taken during the 1970's, at the hands of the Senate Investigations into its practices led by Senator Frank Church from Idaho. By the mid 1980's, the agency was ascending again, and covert operations were once again *en vogue*.

Project Indigo was the pet project of the agency leadership, but came with heavy congressional oversight. The CIA spying on US citizens, even those suspected of committing treason against the US, was a very sensitive nerve indeed. Therefore, Indigo was officially a FBI operation with CIA assistance.

Stanley was inserted as a Lean Manufacturing process flow expert onto the Staff of the Executive Vice President of Technical Operations, one Lincoln Meredith. Dr. Meredith was a PhD of Systems Engineering for Marshall Analytics.

Diane's first two weeks with Stanley were briefings to him on the emerging science of Lean Manufacturing and Quality Science – all taking from the writings of those who taught the new science to Japanese manufacturers – Deming, Juran, and company. She provided a detailed understanding of basic concepts, so that after Diane drilled Stanley rigorously on its tenets, he would be able to bullshit his way throughout the industry.

She worked closely with Stanley, and loved the fact that he recognized she was his lifeline. She was the source of the knowledge flow that prevented his cover from being blown.

"I will only be as successful as you are in preparing me," he would tell her over and over. She was young, smart, lovely, and aspiring to advance her career. She respected Stanley's operational experience.

She would come to learn over the years that respecting others could be a costly trait in the CIA.

The view of North Atlantic, outside her cabin window, lay sprawled before her, muddled and seemingly infinite, like her many thoughts of Stanley.

"Why does a retired spy turn vigilante? What drives an old man to sacrifice a comfortable retirement for a meaningless act of murder? Where does one who knows the process of the hunt run to? How does the hunt change when the fox knows the way of the hound?" she thought repeatedly during the long flight.

"And why the hell was Trellis treating this like he just found Russian Nukes in Cuba? One, even two, dead aerospace executives were hardly a national crisis in her book. What was running below the surface here? Something in this story appeared to be untold, as if protected by the calamity that was Stanley's attack and killing of Langston Powell."

In the villa in Zgorzelec, Stanley awoke late Saturday afternoon. Awoke was a misrepresentation, for it suggested the concept of rest.

Stanley lay motionless, clothed in the bed. His exhausted frame was still, his mind was anything but. It wrestled with multiple anxieties. The memories of sacrificing Langston Powell had returned, as had the new concerns for the safety of Jean Paul.

The recollections of *his most delicate fawn* had abandoned him, and during what little sleep he fell so shallowly into, his mind skipped one fear to the other, and finding no solace, skipped again. The result over the past several hours was a mental fatigue that was accompanied by an angst of impending personal demise. This he was sure was his destiny.

However, Stanley was accepting of this destiny. Even if he could not turn off his racing mind, for now, at long last, he was free. Free of fearing the loss of the family who had loved him so. Free of the encumbrance of materialism that seemed to drive society today. Most importantly to him, now he was free of the burden of the last promise made to his dying father.

"Protect the weak from the strong, my Stashew, always protect the weak," he could hear clearly in his mind.

Stanley was free, as the sacrifice of Powell accomplished this. The threat of Powell's greatly expanding the use of the Daedalus Destroyer Drones had been dealt with. The poor of the world were no longer subject to the spreading of the abuses as envisioned by the creator of this destructive, indiscriminate technology. But Stanley knew he had also struck hard at Trellis himself, the one whose very power came from deploying this lethal technology.

Stanley was free, not of the anxiety of the world that searched for him, but even of the need to survive. He knew his future was limited to days, if not hours. In a strange way, this certainty of his own fate calmed him. They no longer had anything to take from him, other than his life itself. Stanley was now ready to yield even that to them, if necessary.

Stanley soon realized that the sacrifice of Powell was the very acid that etched away at the smooth monolith that was the boredom of his retirement. He knew even if it were possible, Stanley could never return to that quiet, empty life on Shakespeare Street. He was not the man he had been even two weeks before.

Stanley stared eyes wide open at the remnants of light reflected on the ceiling, slowly being subjugated by the darkness of evening falling. He had laid there and stared at this spot most of the short November day. He had watched the darkness creep and consolidate, slowly driving out the light. Now the darkness appeared to almost be nearly static, as if waiting to gain confidence before it began its final assault on the remnants of the day.

But the final assault would be rapid, and complete. Stanley knew no matter how complete it may seem at times, that the battle between the light and the dark, between good and evil, would go on. He was confident it would go on, even after his own death.

Stanley had thought of Trellis and the training in Norway in 1973. It went on for several years throughout Northern Europe, always in non-communist settings. Scandinavia, West Germany, Holland, Belgium, and France.

Stanley knew he was not only being trained, but measured. His Polish was tested in long sessions with Polish emigres in Paris.

His tradecraft was measured everywhere. How many of the agency trailers could he spot on the streets of Munich, Brussels, and Copenhagen?

How well could he trail someone undetected in Amsterdam, Oslo and Aarhus?

How well could he remember recognition signals in Sedan, Cologne and Narvik?

How well could he execute emergency escape instructions in the forests of Finland outside Helsinki?

All the while he was aware of having the American stamp slowly washed from him. His clothing, his mannerisms, his very thinking became "of the continent".

Except for the return to be with his dying father in 1975, he remained on the continent of Europe, always in the north.

"I see you are growing strong," his dying father had said to him. "I know why they send you to Europe."

While his father could not know the details, he could read the changes in his maturing son. "Always protect the weak from the strong," Stanley would hear him plead among the last of his breaths.

After years of extensive training, Stanley was finally inserted and operational in Warsaw. 1976 was an austere year in the capital. His cover as a talent scout for a Canadian classical music label had now been established.

Stanley was amazed at the depths undertaken by the agency to create a life's history of background for the Soviets to plow through, as he and all new western businessmen would immediately be suspect to the KGB and their sister agency in the Communist Polish government.

Stanley's Polish heritage was deepened with each day that passed in his existence in the land of his mother. Stanley's salary was sent to his mother for her wellbeing in Baltimore. Stanley lived a meager existence within Poland, but there was not much available to do otherwise.

Stanley had indoctrinated himself within the capital in his first year. During this time, Stanley developed a strategy to make contact and penetrate the shipyards in Gdańsk. He knew from his agency training that this was the center of the underground Polish resistance.

The agency had only a modest presence in Poland. Trellis could not join Stanley inside Poland itself, as it was assumed Trellis would be too well known to the Soviets. So, Stanley entered Warsaw with only his cover identity and a list of emergency contacts and extraction plans. With his Canadian cover, even his visits to the American Embassy would have to be very limited for appearance's sake.

Stanley had long strategized his own approach to contacting *Solidarity*. His research from informal discussions with the people of Warsaw soon allowed Stanley to focus on an individual likely to be sympathetic to his advances. On a cold winter's night in 1977, Stanley's strategy would be put into play operationally.

Stanley had found a potential but somewhat risky contact. He had targeted the Economic Minister's wife, Agnieszka Danuska. Agnieszka was as beautiful as her name was in the native Polish tongue. In English, the name Agnes is hard and craggy off the tongue, let alone the even harsher sounding "Aggie". In Polish, however, the name Agnieszka flowed eloquently: *Awn-YEZ-ska*.

Agnieszka's young son had recently been appointed to a low-level state management position in the Gdańsk shipyards. This appointment was a courtesy to his father, the minister. Stanley's strategy was to play upon Agnieszka's Polish heritage to convince her to allow Stanley to use her son as a conduit from the agency to the KOR.

The trick would be in either using her own desires for a free Polish state to enlist her son, or if necessary, and only if necessary, blackmail her with any incriminating material Stanley could find.

The risks were many. Most notably, she could report any contact with Westerners, and the noose would likely close around Stanley very quickly. Even if she did not report the contact, she would certainly be watched closely as the minister's wife.

Finally, the trick would be in turning her son, who had grown up in the Communist State. This could be the most difficult part of the assignment.

Stanley felt confident in his plan. *Pani Danuska* was a few years older than Stanley. The research that Stanley was slowly able to do over the last few years suggested a background that could be readily exploited.

Agnieszka's father was a Major in the Polish Army, fighting bravely against the Germans and Soviets in the overpowering September invasions of 1939 that started the Second World War.

Her father was captured, held by the Russians until finally in the Spring of 1940, he and as many as 22,000 other Polish officers were transported to the forests outside of Smolensk, Russia. Each and every Polish officer who was assessed as not willing to serve faithfully in the Soviet Red Army was murdered upon Stalin's orders. They had their hands tied behind their backs before a single bullet was shot into the base of their skull. Their bodies were dumped, one after the other, in great open earth trenches dug by bulldozers. Thousands upon thousands of Poland's military leaders were laid to waste in this quiet Soviet forest. This was the demonic horror that was the Soviet massacre in the Katyń Forest.

Surely this was something that had stayed in the mind of Agnieszka, who was a very young girl of four years old when her father was captured. Stanley reasoned that she would remember the torment of the war, the captivity of her father, and the Nazi confiscation of their home in what once had been Western Poland.

She would surely remember the Nazis driving the Soviets deep into Russia in late 1941, and their discovering the mass graves at Katyń. The Nazi's were quick to propagandize this massacre, showing the Poles how much better they were under German control than the brutality of the Soviet Union. It was a false choice to the Poles, who despised Nazi and Communist rules equally.

Agnieszka would likely remember the lists of the dead exhumed by the Nazi's that were made public and would inevitability contain her beloved father's name.

Agnieszka would have seen the personal turmoil wreaked upon her loving mother. Stanley knew that even in Agnieszka's later life as the wife of the economics minister in Communist Poland, these memories would still gnaw at her heart.

Finally, Agnieszka Danuska would remember the Soviets shamefully blaming the Katyń Massacre on the German army during its early occupancy in 1941, never admitting to the horror they, the Soviets, had perpetrated in 1940. As well, she would remember the Soviets ultimately and greedily consuming all of her beloved Poland as a Communist regime after the war. Agnieszka would perhaps most remember her beautiful mother, widowed and out of sheer necessity marrying a Red Army officer. She did this only to feed the precious, young Agnieszka through the post war famine. A marriage of necessity to the very enemy that had taken her own mother's true love in the forests of Katyń.

That same wounded mother's heart would drive her to convince her only child, Agnieszka, to marry Bronislaw Danuski, a Pole in the young Communist Government. *Pan* Danuski would feed her, clothe her, impregnate her, and make her comfortable. He just wouldn't love her. The now maturing Agnieszka could never love him, because she despised his betrayal of what all Poles cherished – a free Poland. The man she was forced to marry represented what sickened her most in post war Poland - Poles seeking to align themselves with the Communist Party to escape the harsh life they now faced. The cost of which was excusing every crime the Soviets had ever inflicted upon the Poles, which included the barbaric killing of her own father, along with so many others, in the forest of Katyń.

Agnieszka could not excuse the Soviets out of necessity as her mother had done. She surely could not excuse the atrocity that was Katyń. It remained the horror that consumed her loving father. It took the innocence of their family. It took her childhood.

Being the wife of the current Minister of Economics brought physical comforts, but with a guilt of privilege. For if anyone saw the inevitability of failure of the Communist structure, it was surely her husband's analytical, financial prodigy of a mind. Stanley could not know at this point how deeply Agnieszka despised the way he chose to ignore the truth of the erosion of the Polish economy at the hands of Moscow and Warsaw's Polish Communist Government.

On a cold winter night in 1977, Stanley waited outside the Warsaw Philharmonic Symphony hall. He watched impassively as the crowds filed into the hall for the Chopin piano concerto recital. He watched the icy plumes of breath drill outwardly from the mouths and nostrils of these citizen comrades as they waltzed deceptively, gracefully across the icy sidewalks and through the snow where necessary. Seeing her husband's car pull up, one of very few vehicles on the street, Stanley knew now was the time to make his way to his seat.

The building itself was relatively new, as the original Symphony Hall had been completely destroyed in the war. The hall was rebuilt in the mid-fifties, but thanks to the Soviets, without the elegance that was so characteristic of its predecessor. The interior of the new building was plain by the concert hall standards of Europe, but none the less was fully functional as a symphonic auditorium.

Stanley followed Agnieszka Danuska, and waited until the elegant woman had seated herself. He watched her carefully from across the concert hall. She sat alone, as usual, as her minister husband was too busy to attend the event. Agnieszka Danuska sat upright in the worn velvet interior of her seat, tugging gently downward at her woolen country jacket. Her blonde hair, short to the nape of her neck, was topped with a matching wool hat, fur lined inside for the winter weather outdoors. Her face was of a pale complexion, but not without a winter's blush of rose coloring her flawless cheeks. She possessed a panache that otherwise was devoid of her surroundings.

She was the classic Polish mature beauty, complete with confidence and composure. These she wore in the place of freedom and independence - the cold, reserved facade of domination masks the desire for the expressive joy of self-determination.

The orchestra went through its cacophonous tuning, the concerto was now only a few minutes from beginning. Stanley moved now in a mocked rush into the vacant seat next to the beautiful Agnieszka, and in his self-affected rush brushing his arm up against the arm of her jacket.

In his best Polish he said to her, "Please forgive me, *Pani* Danuska, my humble apologies".

"*Proszę, Pan*, (Please, sir), are we acquainted?" she said, surprised at his knowing her family name.

The symphony was just now coming to silence just before the conductor was to walk into the concert hall from the wings.

Stanley lowered his voice to a whisper, "*Nie, Pani*, but everyone in Warsaw knows the beautiful Madame Minister's wife. My humble apologies, I do not mean to embarrass you. Please forgive my intrusion."

The conductor came to the rostrum. The hall applauded politely, over which *Pani* Agnieszka Danuska, looking forward, said aloud to Stanley, "I am humbled, of course, please enjoy the concertos".

Stanley clapped and smiled politely. He had broken the ice, which was his single objective for the evening. Anything else, would be welcome, but unexpected.

The featured pianist was introduced, and the first concerto began. The symphony breathed deeply to life with the stirring of the strings and wind instruments. It was music that nearly everyone had committed to memory, as Frederic Chopin had only composed two concertos for piano and symphony, with the vast majority of his work being virtuoso piano expressions. Even now, the pianist sat motionless at the mirror finish of his black lacquered grand piano, awaiting the several minutes of symphonic introduction before he demonstrated his proficiency of the Polish master.

Stanley followed the performance movement by movement, note by note. The pianist, after beginning his work in earnest, was clearly accomplished. He was a Russian prodigy, on tour from Moscow. Playing Chopin in Warsaw was somewhat of a rite of passage for him, as well as other Soviet pianists. Warsaw had been a venue of honor for Edvard Grieg, Igor Stravinsky, Sergei Prokofiev, Arthur Rubinstein and other world class performers over the years. Tonight's pianist played the concerto somewhat stiffly, however, not having accomplished the sensitivity and feel Stanley had learned to love of Chopin's music.

During the intermission, following the last movement of the first concerto, Stanley remained in his seat, next to the minister's wife. She was staid, somewhat uncomfortable at his presence. Stanley watched her gloved hands for signs of restlessness, but they merely remained silent, immovable in the lap of her heavy wool skirt.

"*Pani* Danuska, did you enjoy the first concerto?" Stanley asked turning slightly towards her. He was pressing slightly, and he knew she would be uncomfortable with this second intrusion.

He also knew her culture would not allow her to be rude in this social setting. She turned her face ever so slightly towards his, but not so much as to draw the attention of others in the crowd.

"*Tak*, I enjoyed it very much, but I adore Chopin, all of Chopin."

There was no smile, not the slightest, to cross her beautifully plain but plump lips. In his peripheral vision, Stanley noticed the crease at the tip of her beautifully sculpted nose. It was exactly as he had noted from her photos, a trait that was atypical to most Poles, and as such very identifiable.

"*Proszę, pan,* did you enjoy the performance?" she responded hesitantly, but politely.

Stanley now turned full faced toward her, lowering his voice. "Yes, but of course, what is not to be enjoyed of Chopin?"

She continued to look at him only in shallow, angled glances.

After a brief pause, he added, almost at a whisper, "but I am sorry to say I find the Russian's interpretation somewhat stiff. Oh, I am sure that is fine for playing Rachmaninoff, or Tchaikovsky, but a Russian could never understand the tender, tortured inflictions of Chopin's Polish soul."

Her face turned to the stranger. These were words that could readily be deemed treasonous in this state, so dominated by the Soviet masters.

Her eyes met his directly as she responded, "So my mysterious friend, you know my name, you know my manners, and apparently, you know my Polish soul. But your slight accent betrays you. You are not Polish, are you, but a visitor to our land?"

"*Tak, Pani*, almost all you say is true. My name is Mariusz Krajewski, and I visit your land, my homeland. I was raised listening to Chopin played by the Polish soul of Artur Rubinstein. He feels, even in his old age, the stirrings of Chopin as a calling to the country he still loves. One can hear Rubinstein's longing in his mastery of the nocturnes, the mazurkas, the Polonaises. It is the same longing for his country that Chopin himself felt after leaving just before the insurrection of 1830."

Her eyes were expressive now, not the cold polite discs they had been, frigidly weary of contact with this apparent westerner. They made direct contact with Stanley, but only in brief periods of engagement, as if somewhat fearful of taking too deep a plunge in an unknown pool. In her eyes, Stanley read a whisper of wonderment, not of infatuation, but a far weaker shade of this emotion. It was more of a young girl engaging a puzzle unknown to her. It was a sense of something outside her crushingly routine life, but its unfamiliarity told her to proceed ever so cautiously.

"*Pan* Krajewski, you speak of the master Artur Rubinstein, who lives in America today. This is not a time we that see many Americans in Poland. Are you American, *Pan* Krajewski?" She played her question with a cautious, but not unwelcome look.

"*Nie, Pani* Danuska. I am Canadian, but I am very close to America. I live in Toronto; do you know Toronto?" he asked, engagingly.

"Of course, I know of your country, but I must admit I personally am not sure where your city lies."

"But you know Niagara Falls?" he followed.

"But of course. Very beautiful. I have seen it in the cinemas." She blushed slightly as she responded.

Stanley noticed her face, and could not resist its beauty. He concentrated to formulate his reply. "Toronto is directly across these falls from Buffalo, New York. There live a great many Poles. Some would say the powerful beauty of the waters is all that distances me from my countrymen."

Her eyes engaged him more directly now. "But, *Pan Krajewski*, you speak in such cryptic metaphors. Beauty, Power, Country, distance. And you speak of Americans in New York as Poles."

His mouth creased into a gentle smile. His eyes warmed. Her beauty was disarming. Stanley found this deception to be an enjoyable task. He felt comfortable talking to her, despite her caution. Agnieszka's beauty and dignity were hers naturally, and she wrapped them in a cloak of apprehension. Stanley sensed the way to pierce the cloak was through her love of her country's denied freedom.

Stanley pressed her, "Have you been to Canada or America, *Pani* Danuska? *Nie*? You would be most pleased to know the Polish

Culture flourishes there, in cities like Buffalo, Chicago, Philadelphia, New York and Baltimore. It is understandable to you, as perhaps you are aware, the Polish Culture survived here in this, our homeland, when the country did not exist for over one hundred years because of the greed of our neighboring powers."

She became stiffened and offended. "*Tak, Pan Krajewski*, I am familiar with my country's history. You make your point. It appears the intermission is over. Enjoy the second concerto, *proszę*. I have enjoyed our discussion."

Stanley sensed he had lost his advantage, that he had pressed too far. "I apologize if I have trampled upon the solitude of your evening, *Pani Agnieszka Danuska*. But Chopin felt in his sensitivity, his longing for his native land, the embers of a great flame which once roared. I feel it in his music, even when too played stiffly by a Russian soloist."

She chirped at him, "And yet you speak of our native land. You are a far away from Toronto, *Pan Krajewski*."

"Ah, but my *matka* was from a peasant farm in Katowice. She lost her parents to the invading Nazi's, among much else. My father was held in Auschwitz by the SS for over three years. I was conceived here in Warsaw, *Pani Danuska*. Yes, I was born abroad, but in a very direct way I am a product of the suffering of our country, *Pani*."

Stanley feared he was too forceful in making his last points, laying claim to his share of the culture and suffering of the Polish people. But the veil of her eyes seemed to flash a sensitivity Stanley had felt *Pani* Danuska had kept protected somewhere deep inside her.

Up until this point, she had been speaking in a very formal tense of the Polish language. Now an inkling of what Stanley took as compassion, known only to those who share similar griefs and tragedies, overtook her countenance. Stanley felt badly to draw upon her emotions so strongly. She now changed over to a more informal tense of their shared language.

"My greatest apologies, *Pan* Mariusz. I did not mean to question your Polish heritage. I am coarse, please excuse me." Her eyes pooled with the tears of embarrassment, having felt she had brought this gentleman to confess a painfully private truth. She stood and removed herself, not to return to her seat this evening. Stanley stood in respect, as she walked from the concert hall.

In the days that would follow, she would think over again of this evening. Being a minister's wife, she had been briefed on the way that western spies would attempt to initiate contact with dignitaries' wives. She had not been watched that night by her communist "protectors". When she was, she usually was aware of their complacency and clumsiness. They were not difficult to lose, should she so desire.

Agnieszka wondered if she should report this contact, but in the end, she did not. She wondered if this *Pan* Mariusz Krajewski spoke the truth of his mother and father, of his being conceived in Warsaw. She would come to know, his false name aside, exactly how truthful it all was.

She was, in fact, sure the name he relayed was fictional. Mariusz was her father's name. Her father that had been murdered by the Soviets at Katyń in 1940.

And the surname, Krajewski literally interpreted as from the country.

However, she also knew it could also be roughly interpreted as "countryman". For its root word in Polish "*Krajan*" indeed means "compatriot".

Chapter Three
Langley

DIANE HAD LOOKED out of the jet's cabin as it prepared to land. The view of Washington DC was spectacular. Now the chase would speed up. The next day or so would be the equivalent to gathering the riders and hounds to ready for the scent of the prey.

As she collected the contents of Stanley's file still arrayed before her on the large table, Diane's thoughts returned to that first assignment – Project Indigo.

In early 1985, Marshall Analytics' then CEO, Marc Constantine, had noticed an unusual rash of field failures of their weapon systems. Missiles going off course, rocket systems detonating on launch, radar systems mysteriously refusing to boot, and so on. There seemed to be no common thread, except all the systems were those produced by Marshall Analytics.

Constantine approached the FBI, suspicious that someone in his staff was passing critical systems information to the Soviets. The FBI agreed to review his corporate technical staff, as this team alone had access to the details of all these weapon systems. These systems were produced at multiple Marshall Analytics sites across the nation, and only the corporate technical staff had access to all their detailed engineering. This team came under the leadership of Dr. Lincoln Meredith, Marshall's Chief Technical Officer and VP of Technical Operations.

The FBI and CIA agreed to act jointly, naming this joint operation as Project Indigo. It was agreed that Stanley Wisniewski, having been freshly recalled from his network in Poland, would be inserted into to Dr. Lincoln's staff as Director of Lean Manufacturing. Supporting Stanley would be the relatively new CIA field agent Diane Sterling, assisted by several team members of the FBI counter-espionage office.

Diane did her job well preparing Stanley in the emerging science of lean manufacturing. Stanley was soon quickly accepted by Dr. Lincoln Meredith's staff. Dr. Meredith himself had been thoroughly surveilled, and determined to be clean by the FBI. He was then "read into" Project Indigo. Each member of his staff was definitely still a possible source of the technical information potentially being leaked to the Soviets. How the Soviets could be using the information to sabotage fielded systems was another team's concern. But this team - Stanley's team - had to find the source of the technical data leak, assuming Marc Constantine's theory was correct.

"Find out what drives each of the staff members, and we will find our traitor," Stanley would tell Diane often. So, after Stanley was inserted successfully, Diane's priority was to profile the six members of Meredith's staff. Financial, religious, political and even sexual preferences were researched, examining any potential for blackmail by the Soviets. The field narrowed rapidly on the financial review alone. There was one member of Meredith's staff who was living well beyond the means of his position as an Engineering Director of a major Aerospace Firm.

Dr. Bennett Palmer had been very active over the past several years. He had paid off his modest Virginia suburban home, then he sold it and moved into the very prestigious neighborhood of Potomac, Maryland. He even had joined the very selective Potomac Country Club. The financial forensics team examined every transaction of his, including purchases of a vintage Chevrolet Corvette, an eight-carat diamond necklace for his wife, and quickly assessed these purchases were out of sync with his income and debt levels.

"Follow the financials," Stanley would drill into Diane, "and motive and method are not far behind."

In Palmer's case it did not take long to establish his motive. Dr. Palmer had long been politicking Dr. Meredith for a promotion to Vice President. Diane had interviewed his professional peers and social friends, including those at his new country club. She presented herself as a security clearance investigator, conducting an interview in support of a clearance required for an upcoming promotion opportunity for Dr. Palmer.

Diane knew people are always more willing to talk when a potential promotion for an individual is dangled - friends wanted to pass on praise to help, and the envious wanted to pass on any dirt to derail. Dr. Palmer's motive was soon established, thanks to the envy of his "friends".

The interviews revealed that Dr. Palmer had long griped that Marshall Analytics was getting Vice Presidential performance from him at the discount rate of his current title as Director. This, coupled with his derogatory comments of his boss, Dr. Meredith, made it clear that Bennett Palmer was dismayed at his ability to make VP, and continually complaining to anyone who would listen about this perceived slight.

Motive now being established, discovering Dr. Palmer's methods proved much trickier. Diane's detailed review of Dr. Palmer's accessing of classified files showed no correlations to the information suspected of being leaked to the Soviets. However, the review of these systems all had one thing in common - all had detailed classified schematics checked out over the time frame in question by Dr. Meredith's staff intern - one Bryce Weldon. As the Technical Operations Staff Intern, Weldon was at the disposal of the entire staff, but several members of the staff had complained of Dr. Palmer monopolizing Bryce's time.

It appeared that Weldon pulled the material, somehow got it to Palmer, who in turn would pass it on to an unknown Soviet handler. Now the unknowns in the details needed to be filled in.

Stanley, in his guise of a new member of the staff, struck up a close relationship with the younger, more vivacious Bryce Weldon. Stanley played the role of the neophyte staff member, trying to learn the organization's personalities, their subtle alliances and inter-dependencies. Who had feuded with who? Who was ascending, and who was falling behind? All the secrets a new corporate climber would find necessary enough for his career. It was natural that Stanley would willingly befriend and even subjugate himself to a much younger engineering intern. Stanley played up Bryce's inside knowledge, and was quick to tell Bryce just how valuable it was to him as the newest staffer from outside the corporation.

Bryce's degree was in Aeronautical Engineering. He did not wear the standard introverted persona that most engineers find so comfortable. He was brash, handsome, well-tanned and wore a dark complexion, which contrasted with his marketeer's bright million-dollar smile. A product of his hometown New Orleans and later Louisiana Tech University, Bryce Weldon never was at odds to find a story to entertain you with, or a bar in which to tell it in. Wherever the staff traveled across the country to Marshall Analytics' various facilities, Weldon was adept at pinpointing the local watering hole.

"Darling, what's your name," he would pour out to the inevitably pretty, young barmaid he found as instinctively as a baby turtle finds the sea. He was so practiced at this that his effortlessness was often mistaken for sincerity.

The answer came back in its various forms - Marcia, Brenda, Rachel - it was just a blank to fill in the script. This day in a darkened Georgetown cocktail lounge, the barmaid serving Stanley and Bryce was a beautiful young woman named D'Ette.

"D'Ette," Bryce would say slowly, stretching the name out across a broad, polished grin, his eyes smiling and laser focused on hers. "D'Ette, I like that, yes I do. Fits you perfectly. You are exactly what I'd expect a D'Ette to be."

He would relax his smile but not his lock on her eyes. "Here's what I need, D'Ette. Bring us your two best rock glasses, a bottle of twelve-year-old Macallan, and a bucket of ice. My partner and I have some serious business to discuss. In the meanwhile, I'll be thinking of what I want to know about D'Ette."

Nine times out of ten, he would get a laugh, with a flush inquisitive look that would seem to say "Who is this guy? Is he serious or just another bar crawler?"

Weldon was smooth, and seemed to always get what he wanted, as Stanley was soon to find out.

Turning to Stanley on these occasions, Weldon would loosen him up with a well-worn joke. He seemed to have an inexhaustible supply.

"So Stanley, do you know how to tell an extroverted engineer?"

"Didn't know there was such an animal," Stanley retorted, raising his glass of Scotch in mock salute to exactly such a beast.

"An extroverted engineer is one who looks at your shoes, instead of his own, when he talks to you!" Weldon delivered the line with well-polished sincerity, before exploding his million-dollar smile like glistening white fireworks.

"That's so true," said Stanley finishing his first pull of single malt through a conceding chuckle. His eyes were still adjusting to the darkness of the bar. "Weldon, I have to give it to you, you clearly have no trouble communicating to these young barmaids. If I tried your routine, I would get slapped silly, or at best laughed out of the bar."

"It's all in the delivery," Bryce would say through another overly broad smile. "These girls are handpicked to be bait to us, to capture our imagination. You just have to come in strong, then circle the bait at a distance just outside their grip in order to capture *their* imagination. Then it's just a matter of time. Half the time they drop a phone number on me before I hit the door. Half of those I end up waking up next to."

"OK, now you're just bragging," Stanley played his role.

"It ain't bragging if it's true," Bryce answered with a serious stare, before his face exploded into that handsome boyish imp of a smile that so captured his personality. "Only bad part is some of those bagged are really good bartenders. But, I'm afraid there is no going back to the well once you've plumbed its depth," followed by a smile and a wink.

So these two business suited warriors, their work day behind them, their neckties relaxed and collars unbuttoned, would make a series of assaults on the Macallan bottle. In the middle of this ritual, the prerequisite cigarettes would emerge to complete the illusion of ambiance.

It didn't take long for this recurring routine to establish a close camaraderie between the forty-year-old Stanley and the slicker, more vivacious man a dozen years his junior. As they travelled across the country with the rest of the staff, they would inevitably seek out a bar in which to recap their day.

Stanley increasingly gained the confidence of Weldon, and Bryce more freely opened up on the dirt of the staff. Stanley relayed these stories to Diane, and a trend emerged. When they would turn their discussions to the stodgy Dr. Meredith, Bryce would criticize and almost condemn the man as unimaginative, boring and predictable to a fault. Then as the discussions turned to Dr. Bennet Palmer, Bryce's face would light up, and he would always cap off the discussion with how Palmer should have Meredith's position as Engineering VP and Chief Technologist.

Stanley also noticed every time D'Ette, or one of her professional compatriots was in earshot, Bryce would work in references to his Porsche Carrera, Georgetown apartment, or as the night wore on, his previous sexual conquests.

"There was this beautiful, young woman, not unlike D'Ette here," and he would gesture in her direction with his rock glass, making sure she could both hear him and see the sparkle in his eyes, "who I met in Aspen in a ski bar not too different than this place, except it was holding back two feet of snow outside and a quarter of the patrons were in casts. This girl had a body that demanded the attention of every guy in the place. She got off shift and we did some serious partying. Just about wore me out. Man, we had a good time together."

Weldon flashed the beaming smile for effect. D'Ette was now increasingly flashing hers back.

One other thing Bryce would do, without fail, was to make sure the bartender, D'Ette or otherwise, knew he was picking up the sizable tab. At first, Stanley demanded he get his portion. Bryce would put his hand over the wallet that Stanley had pulled out in protest.

"It's mine," Bryce demanded. He lowered his voice as he came closer to Stanley, "It's an integral part of the routine. Besides, they take care of me pretty damn well."

"I bet they do," Stanley thought to himself, smelling the alcohol on the intern's breath as he neared. "Now, it was just a matter of finding out who *'they'* were."

Later, walking out into the cool night air, Stanley asked Bryce when he would know if his antics with the barmaid would yield benefits.

Bryce just held up the receipt with the lovely hand written "D'Ette" and her phone number scrawled beneath it.

As her plane touched down, Diane smiled to herself. Her heart warmed as she remembered Stanley detailing these stories to her so much younger and more impressionable self. It was an exciting time in her life. Her life was so vibrant then, everything so new, everyone so seemingly more experienced and cultivated than her young self. Now she dreaded having to hunt one of her oldest friends, yet she knew she had to. Stanley had obviously gone off the deep end in his retirement, and she needed to bring him in, if only to protect her mentor from himself.

Stanley was active through the night in the villa in Zgorzelec. He examined the contents of the rucksack he had taken from the rear seat of Jean Paul's Audi. In it he found cash, lots of cash. Roughly ten thousand Euros and a few thousand Polish Zlotys. Stanley knew this would already have been laundered, and was likely from Jean Paul's own "clean" stash he held for emergencies in Paris. Neither Jean Paul nor Stanley could risk using the funds they had recently withdrawn from the European banks in case the serial numbers of the cash had been recorded. So, in the intervening weeks between their meetings, Jean Paul would launder the bank cash and provide some of the clean currency to Stanley at the next meeting.

Stanley also found in the rucksack several forged passports and other identity papers in names he had never operationally used. The forgeries were good enough for street use, but in the rush of time Jean Paul was unable to provide anything that would stand up to official scrutiny by the agency or INTERPOL. However, with Europe's open borders of today, even these documents would not be necessary. Certainly, they would be good enough to pass the inspection of hotel personnel or innkeepers, if needed.

Finally, Stanley found in the bag a few pair of binoculars, two male wigs, and three wool scarfs. Already in the villa, were the two hats that Stanley had left there so many years ago. The first was the traditional Polish *Kapelusz* banded hat, similar to a fedora. This particular hat was bought for him by his Agnieszka, and he kept it here to commemorate his times here with her. It was stylish in its deep olive green felt, and was adorned with a color matched wide satin band. The final touch had been the stylish silver Polish white eagle medallion upon the right side of the band that, while understated, gave a finished look to the headwear.

The second covering was more of a cap than a hat. Stanley had purchased it in Warsaw, and had accidentally left it in the villa on their last visit here. It was a wool *Narciarka* cap. Technically an alpine skier's cap, it was fabricated from light gray wool, with a sportsman's bill and flaps that could be drawn down over the ears. Unlike the *Kapelusz* hat, this cap had heavy wear from Stanley's years in Warsaw.

Along with the wool scarves and sunglasses, these obstructions would shield Stanley from the perils of the facial recognition software that now ran on so many of the cameras that had proliferated modern Europe. The software, which was run on the computers the videos were fed into, had algorithms which made lightning fast measurements of the features and their relational distances of each face, often keying on those of the eyes. These measurements would be compared against known databases. These systems were lightning fast, but suffered in that they were compromised by obstructing the features of the face. In these cold, bright days of winter, this was readily accomplished with hats, scarves and eyewear. What Stanley feared more was the human recognition, as he was sure by now INTERPOL had spread his photos across Europe. Even the follow-up television news pieces on this rare and cold blooded murder in the safe capital of Warsaw would soon include his image, he was sure.

Stanley decided to address his fear of recognition of others by modifying his appearance. In the villa's bathroom, Jean Paul had left electric clippers and manual razors, as well as the hair dye that Stanley opted not to use. Stanley cropped his longish gray locks and his neat trim beard with the clippers. He then shaved his head to a rough bald condition. He did not attempt to achieve the clean sheen bald appearance that was in such style today. Instead, he shaved his head coarsely, intentionally drawing blood in several locations by using a double-edged razor blade to slice the skin of his scalp. Along with the complete removal of his beard and his eyebrows, the resulting face Stanley barely recognized himself. He looked even more anemic than his normal pale complexion; he looked gaunt and drawn, more so than Stanley's normally thin demeanor. In a word, his new appearance was ghastly. The welts just now scabbing over on his close-cropped scalp made him appear sickly. The total removal of his eyebrows gave him an emaciated look.

Stanley had remembered from his training that the most recognizable feature on the human face was not the chin, or mouth or even the eyes. An extremely complex neural cognitive process in the human brain scanned instantaneously for identity, emotion, gender and even danger. It was a process that was readily recognized in infants. Most interesting to Stanley, it was the eyebrows that the human cognitive processes used predominantly to key recognition of other humans. This had been borne out by studies where easily recognizable faces had been digitally reworked removing only one feature. Those with the eyebrows removed, but the eyes, nose, and mouth left intact were most often not recognized by the participants. Stanley did not expect to elude being identified after he was captured, but rather to elude capture by not triggering the instantaneous reaction in those watchers who would be searching for glimpses in a crowded street, or might only have a fleeting glimpse of their prey.

Next, the now shaven Stanley had turned off the lights in the villa and peered through the high-powered binoculars from Jean Paul's rucksack down onto the Neisse river. Both sides were now darkened. There was no traffic at this late hour crossing the Altstadtbrücke footbridge that connected the German Görlitz to the Polish Zgorzelec. Stanley saw no movement of any kind upon the bridge nor it's approaches. It was a few minutes later that he noticed the glint of a reflection on the German landing. He searched the windows of the riverfront edge of the arcade of shops that climbed Görlitz' hilly bank. On the second floor of the shop closest to the footbridge he found what he knew was sure to be there. A figure in the darkness watched the bridge and its approaches.

Perhaps they thought Stanley would make rush across in the deep black of night? Stanley's eye's fixed on the shadowed figure, and as Stanley focused the binoculars, he could make out the long telephoto lenses of a camera. The figure itself even appeared to be wearing night vision goggles. This was surely the agency's watcher.

Stanley had the advantage of height over the watcher. He would not be looking so far up the Polish hillside to spot Stanley in his darkened window nest. Stanley now drew his optics across the footbridge. On the Polish bank, just at the landing of the footbridge, there was a building representing a medieval tower of six or seven stories. It was squarish in shape. It was new since Stanley had last been here, but so was the bridge itself. Stanley assumed it was constructed after the bridge, to take advantage of all the foot traffic coming across the pedestrian arch. At the building's base, Stanley could see signage for a restaurant.

The tower itself would make the perfect vantage point for a sniper covering the bridge. Stanley saw no figures on the roof, but surmised they were on one of the upper floors facing the river. But what Stanley did see upon the roof made him confident of his conviction. Among the flat landing that topped the tower Stanley saw, just lit enough by the evening's moonlight, a ceramic plate with a knife and fork upon it. Someone was assessing the view while they ate. It could have been a restaurant worker taking a meal break, but Stanley thought not as they certainly would not have left the plate on the roof. Stanley could see the sniper having a meal from the restaurant below as he assessed the roof before moving to an upper floor inside. Stanley assumed he arrogantly left the tableware there, as he was done with it. This wasteful act was something a Pole, nor many Europeans, would dare to do.

Having confirmed his suspicions, Stanley rolled away from the window in the darkened room. He now sat on the floor, his back leaned into the wall. He thought of his Agnieszka, and their times together in this room. He could smell her fragrance - not perfume, but the sweet cleanliness of her warm body as it laid next to his. The scent he remembered, in turn, drew memories of his next encounter with her.

It was a mild spring day in Warsaw in 1978. He had been shadowing *Pani* Agnieszka Danuska for several days, until he was able to assure she was alone in the park. She was sketching in pencil a beautiful scene of a pond surrounded by elegant willow trees. *Pani* Danuska was known to him to be an amateur artist.

After an hour of careful observation, Stanley had ascertained that this day she had no handlers. Nonetheless, he was cautious as he approached the bench on which she sat. Stanley was preparing in his mind how he would initiate the conversation when this trouble was taken from his brow.

"And so we meet again, *Pan Mariusz Krajewski* from Toronto," Agnieszka said in Polish, not breaking her gaze from her sketching hand. Stanley perceived skepticism in her voice as she restated his cover.

He suspected she had been awaiting his re-emergence for some time now, and that is why she made herself available to his approach.

"*Pani* Danuska, What a pleasant encounter and sweet coincidence. I thought I should never be graced to make your acquaintance again." Stanley extended his hand, which the ministers wife glanced at, but refused to extend her own.

"*Tak, Pan Krajewski*, a pleasant spring encounter. But, once is a coincidence, twice is a pattern." Her tone was pleasant but cold, and she sensed Stanley detected her detachment.

"I see you are very talented, *Pani Agnieszka,*" he said seating himself on the bench a respectable distance from her, while affording him a view of her sketching hand. Calling her by her first name, even with the title *Pani*, or Madame, was a risk that she might rebuke him. Instead, she returned the familiar greeting.

"*Tak, Pan Mariusz*, you see much." She paused, her attention gathered for seconds only to her sketching. "It has been many months. I was sure you would find me again, but I did not think it would take you this long."

"Forgive me, Madame, I am not aware ..." Stanley started before he was interrupted.

"I thought for many months, who is this man who speaks to me of the Polish culture in America, and who so effortlessly allows me to know his own *matka* was taken by the Nazi's from her childhood farm in Katowice. Who is this man who plays on my emotions, only minutes after he meets me? It becomes clear that was no chance encounter, as much as you might hope I thought it was. " Her eyes remained fixed on the movements of her hands.

"I have offended you, *Pani Agnieszka*." Stanley lowered his voice.

"No, my dear *Pan Mariusz*, you flatter me. You take my father's name, Mariusz, and name yourself Krajewski - countryman. I wonder how much you have knowledge of. You obviously have looked into my life. Please tell me, my countryman *Mariusz*, what do you know of me...?" Her tone now was defiant, accusing.

Stanley weighed how to proceed with caution, but his immediate lack of response triggered her again. She spoke more quickly now, in a halting, agitated manner.

"Tell me now, my friend, or I shall rise and walk away. And once I do, should you never come to me again, I will have you arrested as a western spy. Now tell me that which you are knowing of me." Her hands were tense and still now.

Stanley sensed the women to be thoughtful, perceptive and articulate. She was accelerating the process, as unexpected as it was, but Stanley sensed she did this in a such a manner because she was welcome to what she knew he needed of her. He thought she was only angry for the months it took to re-engage her, and she needed the pace to be accelerated. He sensed *Agnieszka* felt she was running out of time.

"*Pani Agnieszka Danuska*, I know much of you, I have to admit. I know that your family was driven from its home in Zgorzelec by the

Germans before the war. I know you all were relocated eastward to Wadowice."

Stanley looked into her defiant but now moistening eyes. They engaged and looked away from this westerner who spoke her language so fluidly and beautifully, that only the slightest of his inflections betrayed him.

"I know your father, a brave Polish army officer, was captured by the invading Russians, and died, when you were but a few years old, at the tragedy that was the massacre at Katyń. I know that you survived the war only after your mother remarried a Red Army Captain out of necessity. And I know that she arranged your marriage to the Minister Danuski, for your own survival. Finally, I know your son, your precious son, works for the state in the shipyards of Gdańsk. These things I know."

She was failing in trying to hide her soft weeping. Stanley felt she had confirmed her expectation that she had been played at the symphony hall, and that she was embarrassed in her life being exposed aloud. But he watched this remarkable, delicate woman compose herself, before she continued. Even in her vulnerable state of embarrassment, Stanley could not help but to be affected by the beauty she radiated.

"Yes, my son in Gdańsk. Interesting, that this all leads to him," she paused, thinking of the only treasure of her life.

"What would you have with my son in Gdańsk?" She turned from him and began to sketch again.

"I am sorry, *Pani Agnieszka*, I do not know what you are asking," lied Stanley.

He felt her become tense and defiant again. She continued to draw, but the lines she etched were erratic, scratched harshly into the paper.

"You are wasting my time, *Pan Mariusz.* I cannot arrange these opportunities without my government handlers very often, so please do not waste this precious moment."

Stanley noted her anxiety. No matter how cool and aloof she wanted to appear, she was edgy and nervous. She feared being spotted by the secret police, the ZOMO, speaking to this foreign gentleman.

Stanley thought there was no way she was a professional spy, trying to entrap him for the communists. If Agnieszka was, Stanley thought, she was an extremely gifted one, with the skills of an actress overlaid to disarm the westerner.

Stanley decided to go with his first instinct. She is nervous because she wants to engage him, the man she suspects is sent from America.

"We want your son to allow us to assist him in his work with the trade unions." Stanley stated this firmly, crisply. Yes, I am CIA, he might have added, but to do so would confirm what she already knew, at great risk to them both if they were being listened to electronically.

Her eyes flashed in anger, but it was not strong enough to mask the depths of their beauty. The anger in them morphed into a sullen recognition.

"This is exactly as I suspected," she said almost to herself, but so Stanley could hear. "You have no interest in me, only what precious gems I can give to you." said Agnieszka, almost saddened by his lack of interest in her directly.

Stanley pressed forward. "We can provide your son financial support.

Very significant financial support. We just need to know what the unions need in order to organize the workers."

"So it begins," she stated wearily, "I am to risk my son's life so your country's dreams can live with expectation."

"We know your son is already risking his life in his dealing with these unions. They are outlawed by the communists. We only hope to make them as strong as they can become in resisting the Soviets that have overtaken your country."

Stanley now looked at her. She was only a few feet from him. She physically slumped, not so much loosely in defeat, but more tensely as a snake coils before striking.

She unleashed in correcting him. "*Our* country, *Pan Krajewski*. Our country that these Russian bastards have taken from us. They take our dignity, our freedom, yet dare to tell us we are free. We have existence, without hope, without promise, without tomorrow. Only the workers in solidarity with each other gives us hope. Only in organizing in solidarity shall we ever realize these truths."

She repeats the mantra that her son has told her from the resistance that was organizing at the shipyards. She has accepted it. She knows the danger to her son, but accepts it. Why? Perhaps because it gives her the foundation of belief. To truly believe in a future without the Communist overlords. It is as if she was willing to accept the danger to her son's life, and now to her own, so that her country could live with the rarest of luxuries here – hope.

Stanley watched her hand, now rigidly wrapped about the sketching pencil that no longer desired to flow over her half-abandoned sketch pad. Stanley knew that she had allowed her innermost convictions to be exposed to him. Was it a window to her soul, or possibly a facade effected by a communist spy to entrap a foreign operative?

Stanley's instincts told him that they would already have had enough reason to arrest him, and if their discussion was being recorded clandestinely, going no further would in no way save him. But if this beautiful, frail, tortured soul was at all honest to him, as he desperately wanted her to be, then now was the time to forge the bond between them. Stanley knew there are few moments in life where the frailty of honesty has the impact of a blacksmith's hammer.

"*Pani Agnieszka*," he whispered delicately, "I know how you suffer. What the Soviet barbarians have taken from you, for the Nazi barbarians took the same also from me. They raped my *matka*. My father was tortured for three years in Auschwitz. The Germans on the west, the Russians on the east, are but the same. Two claws of the same beast ripping apart the heart of Poland. Time does not matter, as the scars are forever, but if this cauldron of our culture is ever to fill with freedom and pride again, then we must act. Let me help you, help your son, to save our culture."

Her head was bowed now, not in shame, but so this man could not see the tears wandering uncertainly down her cheeks. She said in a soft, choking voice, without raising her head, "They have taken my family's home, taken my father's life, taken my very childhood, and now they imprison my country. And you are so bold as to ask me to risk my son."

"Not to risk your son," Stanley said softly, "but aide him in that which he is already doing. He is making a difference. We can help him with resources. We can work together toward the day Poland is free of the Soviets again. Free from the Russian scourge."

Stanley looked at her. Her face raised to look upon him. Her features, still damp with tears, was lit warmly by the Spring sunlight of the afternoon. She looked hard into his eyes, probing to see what type of man he really was.

"How can I commit my son's life to a man who tells me lies? His name is a lie; his life is a lie. What sort of man would ask of me these things, and lies to me?" The muscles of her face rippled beneath her smooth skin in response to the conflict that battled within her. "Can I trust this man? Can I entrust my son's life to him?"

The weight of the moment hung heavy between them. Stanley sensed her reaching out to him, as if she extended her hand. If Stanley did not take it in return, he knew all risked getting to this point was for naught.

He braced himself. The moment had come to put his Polish heritage above his American patriotism. What he spoke next, he did so in a brisk forceful way, as one who reveals his innermost secrets surely would.

"My name is Stanley Wisniewski. My father was from Poznan, my mother from Katowice. I am American, but my soul is Polish."

He had violated every training he had ever had to secure this connection, to cement this bond between them. With this information, the Soviets could hunt him down and eliminate him. Trellis would be furious if he knew the words he had just spoken, and likely would pull him out of Poland immediately.

Stanley stared at her. "Yes, I ask that your son risk his life for us. But by giving you my name, I have now given you my very life."

Her face now warmed into a heart shaped smile. Her cheeks were high and perfect, as if they were those chiseled by the sculptor.

Her nose straight, fine, highlighted by the beautiful dimple in its tip.

Her voice was soft and tender, "Yes, I know. I know you tell the truth - *Prawda*. Now we hold each other's beating hearts in our hands. I do not know why, but I know you now have told me the truth."

Stanley looked to the ground. As he stretched to rise from the bench, he said these words to her, but not without looking at her. "I shall call your son only '*Syrenka*'. No one other than I myself will ever know his identity."

She looked at her sketching, and said so he could hear, "And what of me? Who will you tell them I am?"

Stanley paused for a second. He had previously thought through this.

"You, they will not know of you at all. They will only know I deal with my agent *Syrenka*. That being said, your name to me, and to me alone, will be '*Sarenka*' - my delicate fawn."

She smiled to herself, but then thought aloud, "These names, they sound so alike."

"All the better to fool whoever might be listening," Stanley answered, having given this much thought in advance. "Should I slip and say *Sarenka* aloud, they will always think I am speaking of the agent *Syrenka*. They will never know of you, my *Sarenka*."

Having said this, Stanley simply walked away into the park.

A few hours later Diane sat with two men in a secure conference room deep inside CIA headquarters in Langley, Virginia. She had arrived weary from the flight, but took a short nap in the back of the car during the drive in from the airport. It had the effect of reviving her, sharpening her edge, that she knew she would need in dealing with Deputy Director Trellis. She knew Jack, but had never worked as closely with him as Stanley had. She did not need to impress Trellis with her sharpness. In fact, if what she had heard rumored of him was true, she needed more to protect herself from him with it.

Across the large modern, non-descript conference table sat Trellis. Jack eyed her, but not in a hungry way. He was clearly anxious to get Diane prepared and on her way to the field to track down the fugitive Stanley.

"You have briefed yourself with the files we provided on your travel over?" he asked, but only for the formality of a response.

"Of course," Diane responded, but not much there I didn't already know, she thought without saying. Then she thought, there was one thing she needed clarification on.

"Stanley ran the agent *Syrenka* in Gdańsk during his assignments in Poland?" she stated more than asked. "What do we know of this agent?"

"Not much," Trellis replied. "Stanley allowed us only the code name, *Syrenka*. We never were able to put an identity to him". Trellis began to say something to the third party in the room, before Diane interrupted the Deputy Director.

"But, Director Trellis (it was customary to drop the 'Deputy' in conversation), you were actually in charge of Eastern Europe Ops at that time. As best I can tell, we infused a lot of cash into Stanley's operation to pass onto *Syrenka*, didn't we? Wasn't there later the accusation that five million dollars were unaccounted for when Stanley was eventually recalled?"

"Yes, Diane, I was head of Eastern European Operations then," he said, chewing on his words, upset that she had made the association sound impure. "Stanley had been running *Syrenka*, in Gdańsk, from Warsaw. His travel was limited, so he likely wasn't meeting *Syrenka* in Gdańsk. He was bringing back tons of very valuable INTEL on *Solidarity*. Back then *Solidarity* was the *f**king* major thorn in the Communist government's paw. *Syrenka* kept shoveling the INTEL to Stanley, and Stanley to us, and we, in turn, shoveled lots of cash back into *him*."

"How do you know '*he*' wasn't a '*she*'? Could have been a wife, a mistress of someone inside?" Diane was under Trellis' skin, and thought she might as well keep probing.

"Could be. Kind of far-fetched for that time in Communist Poland, but still possible. Fact of the matter is, it is possible." Trellis seemed to be reining in his emotions, as he glanced over to the other gentleman listening to this conversation.

While he had been talking, Diane had been lost in thought, looking at the pudgy, balding, goateed gentleman in the wool sports coat that sat with them. His hands lay across the protruding belly tenting out of his jacket, his interlocked fingers looking strong and thick as harbor ropes. His eyes bore heavy bags underneath, coupled with high arching eyebrows and a balding hairline with squared peaks. This gave him an almost owl like appearance. A dark, greasy Mediterranean owl.

The second man stared back at Diane in a measured way. His mouth curled into a half smile. Was he analyzing her? Or just acknowledging that she was analyzing him? So, Diane thought, this is the newest head of PSYCH OPS. This was Dr. Darien Shaw.

Trellis noticed the visual interlude between Dr. Shaw and Diane. He decided to force their conversation.

"Dr. Shaw has some background information to share with us that may be of use to determining Stanley's state of mind when he executed Langston Powell in cold blood. Let's hold the *Syrenka* conversation until later, so we can have Dr. Shaw brief us."

"I would just like to finish up a bit before we move on," Diane said, expecting her rebuke to his recommendation to anger Trellis. His snap temper was legendary, although he hid it as best he could from his superiors. But this is the CIA, and there was no safe haven for secrets. He succeeded despite his irritability. He succeeded because of the victory that was Gdańsk, because of *Solidarity*, because of *Syrenka*, because of Stanley. He succeeded because of *Solidarity* chipping the initial cracks into the long Soviet domination of Eastern Europe, which might as well have been chipped directly into the Berlin Wall itself. For those cracks ran fast and fearlessly through the Communist infrastructure, until the Soviet Union collapsed of its own corrupted weight a few years later. Trellis ascended upon his success, promoted to Deputy Director of Covert Operations. Soon after that, Trellis recalled Stanley from Poland and sticks a five-million-dollar embezzlement charge on him. Not being able to make it stick, Trellis puts Stanley out to pasture and drives him into a shamed retirement.

Odd thing, Diane thought, was Trellis could have written five million dollars off without a question, so long as it was used for bringing the Soviet Union to its knees. Why does Trellis go out of his way to hang the operative who paved Trellis' own path to glory for him? Something was not consistent within this set of facts. Diane sensed the tension that had long strung between Stanley and Trellis.

"So why would the CIA not demand to know the identity of someone they were funneling this much money through?" Diane dredged ever deeper into Trellis' waters. "Why didn't you try to learn his or her identity without Stanley learning?"

Her pointed words now neared accusation.

Diane continued, "It would seem to me you would have been concerned that the cash you were feeding *Syrenka* could have been funding Soviet Ops against us, if it turned out *Syrenka* was a double agent".

Diane could see Trellis tightening like a drum as she proceeded. "Diane, you of all *f**king* people should know the answer to this. The Soviets did have double agents, but they were embedded inside our stateside teams. You were pivotal in bringing two of them down – Aldrich Ames and Robert Hanssen. If you remember this time in our history, we didn't *f**king* know if there was another traitor out there. Fact was we hadn't caught Ames or Hanssen yet. All we knew was that our agents around the world were being rounded up or disappearing, never to be heard from again. We now know they were almost all executed. By the time *Syrenka* came along, we really didn't want to know his/her identity. If we didn't know it, then whoever their mole was in our system wouldn't know, and in turn the Soviets wouldn't know either. Come on, Diane, you should have been able to piece this all together on your own. Can we get to Dr. Shaw, now?"

She nodded, as if to say, yes, we can move on to Dr. Darien Shaw. Still, though, she was not satisfied that all the details of *Syrenka* were being presented.

Dr. Shaw began slowly, but Diane knew his reputation, he would pick up steam as he rolled through his diatribe. Dr. Shaw could talk. He would talk in his accented, broken English. Darien would go on to claim he intentionally held onto his accent as an honor to his past, to his culture. Diane found this to be a sacrilege, especially as she prepared to hunt Stanley, the man who honored his own past, his culture, by ultimately shooting a presumed innocent man in cold blood at the very site where his parents were held by the Nazi's in the second world war.

"Why isn't this making any damn sense at all? I am exhausted, my brain is numb," she thought, as Darien droned on.

Darien claimed to think in four languages, and at speeds much faster than this mouth could ever keep up with. He was known to brag that he was successful because he could program his remarkable brain to think like any man under any given set of circumstances.

"That was your first fault," Diane thought, "you think like a man."

"Stanley Wisniewski, our Stanley," Darien paused for effect, "this man is a very tormented man". The good doctor hissed through his heavy Eastern Mediterranean accent. Turkey, Crete, possibly Malta? – Diane was uncertain. Definitely not Israeli – Diane had dealt with them previously. They listened, deeply, and when they spoke, they were quick to the point. Darien was anything but.

Darien haunched over in his chair, apparently ready to spring in the direction of Diane.

She looked tiredly into his now glaring, beaming black eyes. Diane thought the effect was that of a man massaging his own ego. She knew she didn't have time to waste on Dr. Shaw's self-serving assessment of the man she was to hunt, whom Darien had never met, and knew virtually nothing of. This was crazy. But Trellis had insisted. Jack was the man who had brought Shaw into the agency.

Dr. Darien restarted, "Stanley was long ago a wounded man. From his childhood through to his loss of rational thought last night in Warsaw. It all is tied together, do not misunderstand, for I will show you. In the end, you will see his striking down Langston Powell is no more a surprise than the dog that bites the mailman he barks at each day." Darien chuckled at this own reference.

Shaw was known for legendarily bad analogies, Diane remembered. She just met the man, but disliked him for no other reason than he liked himself enough for the both of them.

The good doctor unfolded his fat sausage fingers so he could speak freely. His hands began to spread and gesticulate while he articulated his theories. Amazingly, the expression on his face was monotone, as if his hands accented and highlighted his words so his face did not bother to.

"Stanley's fiercely proud of being Polish. His parents drilled this into him. Chopin, Copernicus, Dr. Madame Curie. All the smartest people in his history of the world were Polish. Stanley even felt it was necessary to acknowledge on his CIA application that though he was born in the US, he was actually conceived in Poland."

He looked pleased with himself. Diane disliked him.

He continued, "Can you imagine that, a young adult that clung to the concept of being Polish to the point of it mattering that he was conceived there?"

Darien chuckled again, expecting a return amusement from Trellis or Diane. None came. Darien, noted the silence, and continued.

Diane interrupted him, "Doctor, I know Stanley very well. He never thought that all the smartest people were Polish. He was merely proud of those of his ancestry who had made their mark on history. Sure, he loved Chopin, but who can't acknowledge that Chopin's music is beautiful and unlike most other composer's? As for his application, Stanley was, no, is, a stickler for full disclosure. So, when you ask him where he was born, Baltimore was not enough. He wanted to include his parents were immigrants who escaped war torn Poland. Therefore, I find your comments don't fully reflect the essence of the man."

Trellis started to rebuke Diane for addressing Dr. Shaw in this way, but before he could the good doctor held his massive palms out in front of him like they were pressed on a plane of glass.

"Jack, please, allow me," he said, his face smirking as if to say he could handle this himself. "Diane, we have for you a great respect and admiration of your skills. The *Huntress* (Shaw made a face as if to indicate a mock fright of the name) – isn't that what they call you? You have a very strong reputation. But I have a very strong reputation also, I am sure you will acknowledge. I am trying to paint you a portrait, not of Stanley's face, but what is behind his face, inside his head. Not just thoughts, but the nerves, the synapses, the gut response of the man."

Diane thought to herself, so now his gut is behind his face? This is classic Darien Shaw, the reputed mangler of metaphors. He played true to form to the laughable veneer of his reputation.

Diane desperately needed to get on with her background investigation, including a trip to Stanley's home ninety minutes away in Baltimore. What little energy she had was being sucked out of her by this bloviating, Mediterranean egotist.

"I need you to allow me to paint this portrait for us. Please hold your questions and comments until later. The interruption is very disruptive for me. Just think of me as a great master. You may not agree with me, or even like my art. I merely ask that you allow me to finish so I can complete the work before you begin nibbling at its edges." At this, Shaw made the face of a mouse nibbling, which Diane found embarrassing for him.

Darien watched her face closely. Diane restrained her reaction, which was to laugh out loud.

Darien waited for the air to clear, before saying, "Sometimes we need to see things in total, and absorb the depth and intricacies before making a snap decision. Agreed?"

His hands were now spread out before him as if to receive a gift, arms outstretched, palms to the sky.

"Go on, Doctor," she said tersely. She could see that he was unhappy she had not totally acquiesced. She hesitatingly, belatedly, said the word "Agreed".

Dr. Shaw's face lit with a triumphant smile, and Diane instantly regretted allowing herself to agree with him.

"Thank you. I will continue. Stanley's parents both suffered at the hands of the Germans during their invasion of Poland during the second World War. This we know. Stanley's father is held for years at Auschwitz, only saved by his language skills that the Nazis found useful enough to keep him alive. His mother was repeatedly raped by the same Nazi who held his father for years, we know this from testimony prepared by them for use at the trials at Nuremberg. They escaped Poland, and through the assistance of the Allies, resettled to the US, relocating in Baltimore's Polish neighborhood in the east end of the city."

"I know all this," thought Diane.

Darien shifted into second gear. "But Stanley is raised unlike the other boys he is schooled with. His family lived off the kindness of others. Yes, they had relatives who helped them, and they had the modest row house provided in-part by the US Government through the Polish American Society, but not much else. Surely, Stanley was teased by the more Americanized boys for all he did not have. Perhaps not so much at his grade school – Saint Stanislaus – where nearly everyone was Polish, and many were poor. But in his high school and college, he was now in the company of very accomplished students, many of whom were from prominent parents of significant means. Surely Stanley began to feel ostracized in this environment."

Dr. Shaw used his hands to show Stanley's isolation - his left hand, fist enclosed in a tight bubble while his right hand swept a huge arc of volume.

"So, we have a fiercely proud, Polish student who goes on to master languages, like his father. He begins his studies at Loyola University. He feels different from his peers. He is more serious, more somber. Stanley feels like he needs to make a mark of redemption for what the world had done to his parents. He joins the CIA straight out of school for just that reason. To give his parents a protective shield, the same shield they tried but could not provide for him."

"OK, you psycho babbling bag of mixed metaphors. First, I know from actually spending time with Stanley," Diane thought, "that he really did not know of his mother's and father's abuse at the hands of the Nazis until he had been in the agency for almost ten years. Besides, Stanley was the best adjusted person she may have ever met. He was never ashamed of growing up poor, rather he was quite proud of it. Look at me, I come from the all-American success: the rich and broken family. My father was a glutton for whore women and easy money. Even if it meant driving his wife, my mother, to the brink of destitution. My mother was so weak and afraid of losing the man she accepted him for all his failings. So, here I sit a classic, caustic non-believer in anything. Darien knows it's always easier to pick things apart, than build relationships and retain pride. Look what that easy path did for me."

She could see Darien trying to gauge what was going on behind her forced smile. "*You are not getting in here, she thought, no matter what. You are not getting in my damn head.*"

Shaw continued, "Stanley gets trained and dispatched to Poland and could not be happier. He enjoys the old world, but hates the communist regime that suppresses his Poland's culture. The Russians had failed throughout the nineteenth and early twentieth century to 'Russify' the Poles, so after World War II, they are happy just letting them exist as a Soviet puppet state. The Poles hate it, but they at least have their language, some of their culture, retained more or less intact. Stanley nonetheless sees this oppression as an extension of the tyranny that his parents were subject to. He wants desperately to strike against it."

The good doctor has an inch-deep understanding of the world's culture, Diane rapidly concluded, despite his own portrayal of himself as a multi-cultured man. In Communist Poland, Poles were not free to worship, own property, or travel outside of their home areas without government approval. Stanley saw these as oppressions because they were, in fact, oppressions of the first order. When the Soviets were kind enough to allow the Poles to display the White Eagle, the icon that the country had historically tied to sovereignty, they would not allow this emblem of national pride to be displayed bearing its historical crown atop the eagles' head – reminding the Poles they had no true sovereignty.

Nor were the crosses of this historically Catholic nation allowed to be shown in public. Religion was contested at every turn. Priests were detained, tortured, and in several cases murdered.

Diane noticed that Doctor Shaw was picking up steam now. His language becoming increasingly more fluid in its tempo, his hands now periodically caressed his face as he talked, his fingers outlining his goatee as if that lent importance to what he had to say.

Diane was having more and more difficulty in not interrupting his limited analysis with a deluge of corrections and insights.

Darien continued. "Yes, Stanley was successful in developing an agent inside *Solidarity*, and for this he earned great praise. It was this praise in itself that became a drug to him, altering his consciousness such that he honored the adulation resulting from the work, and not the honor of the work itself. He saw the Berlin Wall fall, partly from his work, and soon Poland was a free and sovereign nation again. East and West Germany soon reunited, the Soviet Union was now gone. The Russians were a shell of their former power. But all Stanley could feel after this was a hollow emptiness, ever wanting another great coup, another *purpose*. He was empty, without meaning. Then he got caught in his siphoning of funds, for what? We still don't know."

Diane was fuming. Darien was insane indeed. How far would this go?

"So along comes an opportunity in his lonesome retirement to vet a CEO-to-be in Langston Powell for the untimely death of another executive from Global Defense Analytics. He clears Powell, but not in earnest."

Darien wags his finger, shaming Stanley in absentia, as Shaw looks around the room. His analysis is met with blank stares instead of the rapt attention he expected.

He continues "His accomplice, known to us only as Jean Paul, has detailed information, enough to grant Stanley concern over Powell perhaps having played a role in the death of Ted Barber. Does our poor Stanley raise that concern in his report to Global Defense Analytics? No. He vets him clean. Why? So, he can have his last great moment of fame. He sees Powell as an oppressive force upon his native Poland, extracting excessive funds from a small country trying to arm itself, defensively. Instead, our Stanley allows Powell to be declared CEO-in-waiting by Global Defense Analytics, waiting until only hours afterwards to strike him down. All for the greater glory of Stanley Wisniewski."

"Vish NEV ski," Diane interrupted for a second time.

"What?" the good Doctor was shocked she would again interfere.

"You were finished, right. Good God, I hope so. You kept calling him WIZ New Ski. If you knew anything about the man you'd know he detests that Americanized pronunciation. You write this all off as Stanley being an ego-maniac due to the torture of his parents at the hands of the Germans 70 years ago? I am not buying it. Stanley is as well-adjusted an individual as I have ever met inside the agency. But that might be the problem, you never met Stanley, did you? You don't know the man at all."

Diane looked into Darien's fuming eyes, ready to explode. He was choking back an eruption of response that Diane could only think was ironic, given Trellis' being in the room.

She went on, "For him to have gone through all the planning that was required to pull this off, he clearly had more motive than just striking out for fame and glory."

Dr. Darien Shaw was not about to allow this intrusion stand.

"Diane, I know you are so famous for your work leading to the arrest of Aldrich Ames and Robert Hanssen, but leave this analysis to those of us trained in it professionally."

His voice was now lilting with contempt. Shaw was beginning to mock her, as she suspected he would, for the sin of not accepting his simplistic interpretation of Stanley's frame of mind.

"Please *advise me* of what I may have missed in my analysis," Shaw pleaded sarcastically.

She knew this was meant to belittle her in Trellis' eyes. A glance over to Trellis was greeted with a nod that seemed to say, "Go ahead, let him have it...he's earned it."

"Okay, *Doctor*," she began. "Let's start with Stanley's father. Stanley cherished him. Hung on his every word. It was his father's dying request when Stanley was some thirty years old to take care of his mother, retain his Polish heritage, and to protect the weak from the strong. Three simple requests that Stanley would go on to live his life by. You missed that. You know why – because it's not in the damned files."

"So, miss *Huntress*, if it is not in the files than how do you know this?" Darien was visibly perturbed now.

"How do I know? Stanley told me. It's amazing what people will share with you once you develop a friendship. It's called trust, and Stanley trusted me with his secrets. Now Director Trellis asks me to use those secrets to hunt him down."

"Well, how could I have known this?" Darien offered in his own defense. He held his palms upright again, but now with his arms not outstretched. Rather his elbows were pulled tightly into his waist, protectively guarding his exposed weaknesses. "I cannot be expected to work without all the facts".

Darien's eyes pleaded to Trellis, perhaps to make her stop.

"Here's how you could know this. Don't assume you are so intuitively wise a man you can derive the essence of another man from sheets of paper in a file. Ask people who knew the man. Seems a logical thing to do – listen to somebody, for a change."

Her voice was elevated. Her eyes drilled into him, forgetting Trellis was even in the room.

"It was an electronic file, there were no sheets of paper, as you say," Shaw added childishly, as if it mattered. He looked intently in Trellis' direction. He was afraid to look back into Diane's stare.

"Two," she blurted out. "You completely missed the fact that Stanley was the instrumental force in bringing in Bryce Weldon and Dr. Ben Palmer during Project Indigo in the mid-eighties. Palmer was caught red handed by Stanley of handing engineering data over to the Soviets for cash. That was in the file - you really ought to read them more closely. I know they are pretty thick, but there is some good stuff in there."

Dr. Shaw looked at Trellis, now requesting his intervention.

"Diane, you are over-tired. You don't know what you are saying," Trellis was now trying to de-escalate the situation.

"Stay out of this, Jack," she said, holding out both index fingers to get his attention. "Three. His mother was raped repeatedly by the Nazi who held her and his father. Stanley's father killed the SS officer that held them both." Factor that into your equation, you mediocre, misogynistic shrink, she thought to herself.

She went on, "His father shot him with what I am sure was the same Luger that Stanley so courteously left at the Powell murder scene with intact prints on the barrel. Stanley wanted us to know it was him that pulled that trigger on Powell. Why? This is the question you should be asking yourself. I am sure it was the same gun that his father used so closely nearby back in '44".

Trellis jumped in again. "It was. We had an analyst run it through SS records overnight. Damn Nazis were notorious for their record keeping. All digitized in a massive database now. Not that we get much chance to query it anymore. In fact, the analyst spent more time writing the query than it took to find the record."

Darien continued to plead to Trellis with hand motions and facial expressions. Stop her. Make her respect me. *I am more important to you than she is.*

Trellis' response said he was not. Diane was the needed talent here, not the good doctor.

Diane finally smiled condescendingly at Darien. "Why is Project Indigo so important? Because things did not end so well for young Mr. Weldon. Stanley to this day blames himself, for getting so close to this individual, only so he could trap him and deliver his treacherous ass to Langley. Only for Weldon's life to be ruined at the hands of the CIA. This affected Stanley more than anyone can ever estimate, for Stanley always felt he had failed on his father's wish to protect the weak from the mighty."

"I see. In your mind, you feel justified that" ...he was trying to analyze her now, cut her off, and regain control of this dialogue.

She cut off Darien for a third time.

"I don't justify anything. I am merely telling you what drives Stanley, and it is not in any way to obtain personal fame. Stanley felt he had failed with Bryce Weldon. Personally, I couldn't give a rat's ass about an egotistical hot shot engineer who treated women as sexual milestones. Doesn't bother me if he gets what he deserves. That man, young or not, was a traitor to our country. I also am damn sure that Doctor Palmer deserved more than the life sentence he got."

Diane kept up the high tempo assault, "So my thoughts don't really matter. But Stanley felt Weldon had been sucked in by Palmer for the money, for the excitement of the game, and deserved a lesser sentence than Palmer. Stanley felt he, himself, was personally to blame for what unfortunately happened to Weldon. Stanley felt that he had conceded too much of Weldon's oversight to his superiors."

Darien Shaw arched his eye at the mention of the word "superiors".

"Well, Ms. Sterling, sounds to me you may have some issues with authority, yourself." Darien was clearly trying to assert an offensive foothold against the woman's challenge to his own expertise.

"I've got no issues with men, if that is what you're getting at?" Diane said, accusing Darien of oversimplifying her. "As it were, Dr. Shaw, almost half of the world's population, and most all of my professional peers, tend to be men, so I usually smile a lot and laugh to myself. Except for when they are condescending pricks like yourself, chewing up the precious time I need to be working, then, I blow up at them."

Shaw physically rocked back in his chair. He could not believe the audacity of this woman, and wondered how she had been so successful in her career challenging her superiors in such an outright manner. He did not realize that this rare attribute was exactly the genesis of her success.

"Jack, now, if you don't mind, I need to drive up to Baltimore and visit Stanley's house where I may actually learn something that will help me track him down. If we are done here." Diane was now standing, leaning over the conference table with Trellis and Darien still seated.

Trellis looked back at her in silence. As much as he enjoyed Diane taking apart Dr. Shaw piece-by-piece, he felt a need to defend the agency's head of PSYCH OPS.

"Diane, if I didn't need you so critically to hunt down Stanley, I would be thinking about a written reprimand for your behavior," Trellis said looking tautly into her eyes that were locked on to his own.

"But, Director Trellis, as it turns out, I am still the one you are assigning to hunt Stanley down and bring him in, right? You obviously know not only that I know him better than anyone else in the agency, but that I can bring him in where you fear no one else can…," Diane said, testing her limits with Trellis.

Trellis gave up on rescuing Darien's honor. Without breaking lock with Diane, he said "That's right, Diane, and don't let me down or there will be hell to pay. I'll get you a driver for the trip up to Baltimore. I suggest you sleep on the way up, you certainly are in need of it."

Diane left the conference room. As the door shut behind her, Shaw looked over to Trellis, arching his eyebrows and pursing his lips, as if to say, "this one is crazy for sure …"

Stanley had been very busy throughout the night watching the watchers. From his villa window overlooking the *Altstadtbrücke* footbridge over the river Neisse, he noticed a pattern.

The watcher in the second story apartment on the German bank of the river would periodically leave his post and exit the Görlitz apartment to walk near the landing of the footbridge. Stanley had noticed that he appeared much more bulky outside than he did in the window behind the photographic lens. Stanley could not see him within the apartment after he left his window position, but noticed the spotter had donned a heavy oversized white cable knit sweater for his pacing back and forth along the German footbridge landing. The sweater screamed of New England, and immediately stamped him as American, or perhaps, at best, a British commercial fisherman. Certainly, not continental European, and definitely not German. Stanley had immediately marked him as a CIA watcher, and assumed he was working in conjunction with an as yet unseen sniper in the tower building along the opposite Polish bank of the footbridge.

Stanley began to piece together the ritual - every three hours or so, the rifleman he was sure was in the tower was given relief to stretch his legs, relieve himself, or possible get a bite of prepositioned food. Leaving nothing to chance, the spotter departed his warm German apartment window to cover the footbridge at ground level. If Stanley was correct, they really were leaving nothing to chance, as Stanley assumed the added bulk under that oversized sweater was due to the spotter having donned ceramic body armor.

Stanley was sure the spotter was armed, although he saw no evidence of a weapon. If the spotter came upon his fugitive while the sniper was temporarily out of position, Stanley was sure the spotter himself was also authorized to use deadly force.

Certainly, Stanley had expected they might be donning Kevlar vests, which today were very effective in stopping all but the largest caliber handgun rounds. The fabric vest alone would not account for the bulk Stanley noticed. These vests, Stanley remembered from his training, had pocketed compartments into which specialized ceramic plates could be inserted. This level of protection would be effective against most rifle rounds as well as handguns. The Kevlar would effectively provide a netting to arrest the bullet slug, but for the larger rounds, the energy of the projectile would be absorbed in the shattering of the ceramic plate. The energy would be dissipated as the ceramic cracked and fragmented. Most plates now were covered with a spall liner, a polymeric coating that prevented the ceramic fragments or even the slug itself from ricocheting into the face, arms or other body parts not protected by the armor. The ceramic plates would explain the spotter's additional bulk Stanley had observed under the sweater.

If Stanley was correct and the spotter was donning this level of protection, it meant that the agency was anticipating all contingencies in containing their prey within Poland. Did they think that Stanley would actually try to shoot his way across the border? Stanley searched the rooftop of the tower, hoping to catch the sniper taking a break of fresh air, or to smoke a cigarette. Nothing. Stanley knew he was in that tower, but still had not seen any visual evidence of him, other than the abandoned plate, knife and fork. If the sniper was there, he was a disciplined pro. Stanley was sure he was there. He could feel him.

It was the routine of the spotter that gave him away. Why else would the spotter be braving the cold every few hours, going through the process of armoring himself each time. Routine and protocol - Stanley had always feared he would be spotted during his years of service handling Agnieszka in Warsaw. He had feared becoming too much a creature of habit, such that the habit's repetition betrayed itself and he became apparent to the communists.

Stanley watched the footbridge as he thought of his lovely Agnieszka. They had remained undetected for so long, for so many years. They evaded not only their communist foes, but eventually their own feelings for each other.

After going operational, Stanley and Agnieszka had soon developed a safeguard in their meeting protocol. Agnieszka's lifelong and trusted friend, Zbigniew Księgarski, had years ago been approved to operate a socialist bookstore on the street front parlor below his apartment. The store was forbidden from selling or in any way promoting books from the West, but non-political Polish literature, and of course Russian literature was still allowed. These were the few gems buried in Zbigniew's store, amongst mountains of Socialist propaganda and communist economic publications.

Of course, the store had been approved with the full backing of the Economic Minister, Agnieszka's husband. In addition to advocating her friend's request with the man she was forced to share her captive life, Agnieszka had thought this shop would be a welcome diversion for her terribly lonely days and weeks. Long before she ever met Stanley, Agnieszka loved to spend hours at a time there, reading the classic Polish literature that was approved by the state. She also adored the few forbidden so-called western classics that Zbigniew was able to smuggle into the country. She loved the works of the French authors Alexandre Dumas and Victor Hugo, as often their themes were of overcoming the oppression of the ruling state or political system. She read the classic "*Notre Dame de Paris*" - known to most Americans as "*The Hunchback of Notre Dame*" - and openly wept at its themes of love denied. She had wondered, having been forced to marry to a communist minister to whom she could not bear to open her heart, if she would ever experience the deep love portrayed within its pages. She never for a second realized that even in the freest of all societies, true love is the scarcest of treasures.

Agnieszka's greatest affinity was for those works of the Pole turned world sailor later turned English language author - Joseph Conrad. His Polish birth name was Józef Teodor Konrad Korzeniowski. His stories of the open sea had long ago taken Agnieszka's captive soul to an unobtainable world of freedom.

Born a Pole, Conrad's family was exiled to an isolated Russian wintery outpost after his father was accused of crimes against the

Russian state. By the time he was eighteen, Conrad was able to escape the crushing Russian rule of Poland.

He travelled to the French port of Marseille. He immediately signed up for work aboard the first ship that would take him. From there, he would sail the world's seas that he had fallen in love with through reading and re-reading his father's books during their Russian exile.

Agnieszka always idolized the fact that Conrad, who like herself spoke and read fluent Polish and French, had earned his freedom from the Russian overlords. Conrad had learned the English language only in his twenties, yet somehow managed to become the master of this language's prose later in his life. She thought his writing some of the most beautiful she had every read in any language.

Little did Agnieszka realize just how convenient her friend Zbigniew's modest apartment just above the bookshop would later become as a safe place where Stanley and his *Sarenka* could meet. On each day of their scheduled meetings, Agnieszka would arrive first, and after browsing for something to read, would discreetly retire to the parlor of his upstairs apartment. Stanley would arrive some ten to fifteen minutes later.

The safe word Stanley would pass onto the proprietor was always a specific character's name from one of the classics penned by the polish author, Henryk Sienkiewicz. His zenith as a writer was in 1905, being awarded the Nobel Prize for Literature, for his epic tales of Polish history. Ironically, many of these tales were written of battles the Poles had against their many suppressors. They were written for a people without a nation, as Poland did not re-emerge as a free republic until two years after Sienkiewicz died in 1916.

Stanley entered the bookstore, under his alias – Mariusz Krajewski, (pronounced in Polish as "Kry YEV ski").

"*Dzień dobry, Pan Krajewski,*" called out the proprietor on this day.

"*Dzień dobry, Pan Księgarski,*" replied Stanley, always assuring they were alone within the shop. This was frequently the case, as books were scarce, and not high on the shopping list of families who could rarely obtain meat, fish, or vegetables beyond potatoes and beets.

"I am enjoying the story of the Teutonic Knights by Sienkiewicz that you recommended," Stanley began.

The bookkeeper added, "Ah, yes, of course, Sienkiewicz's medieval masterpiece, *Krzyżacy*. And who is your favorite character?"

"Why, the young knight Zbyszko, of course," replied Stanley enthusiastically.

"Yes, very impetuous young fellow," added the shopkeeper. "I like him also, but still feel myself drawn to the older, more cautious knight, Macko."

With each man having given the expected characters' names, they had communicated to each other, "It is safe to join *Pani Agnieszka Danuska* in the apartment above". Only then would Stanley slip into the back staircase that lead him to his *Sarenka*.

Stanley entered the apartment, and glanced nervously at her. As he always did, Stanley went to the phonograph, and placed the needle onto the revolving vinyl disc of Chopin nocturnes. Stanley increased the volume to mask their conversations to any potentially unknown eavesdropping electronics, much as a white lace veil masks the darkest fears of the unsure bride.

They began in the late 1970's and for several years met undetected in the apartment above the bookstore. Stanley would provide Agnieszka the unwritten list of questions for her son to provide responses that he would pass verbally through his mother.

Agnieszka would also pass on requests for materials and printing equipment, that her son knew was needed by the Worker's Defense Committee (KOR) to sustain the production of underground leaflets and communications. Cash was never requested as such, but Stanley was soon supplementing their requests with increasing amounts of CIA supplied Polish zloty notes. Stanley would commit her answers and requests to memory, never committing them to writing until well after their meeting. All the memorization was challenging, but it protected both Stanley and Agnieszka should either of them be picked up by the ZOMO before or after their meeting.

Stanley would later encode the information and pass it clandestinely to the agents in the secure and legally protected American Embassy. However, given Stanley's cover, he could not enter the Embassy itself. Handoffs were done over dinner, or at outdoor cafes in Warsaw's old town, under the guise of two westerners fraternizing within the communist state.

This day in August 1980, Stanley and Agnieszka sat in the apartment above the bookstore, face to face across a narrow, scratched and worn wooden low table. It separated a worn sofa from a dilapidated over-stuffed chair, well past its prime, but still functional. Stanley looked into his *Sarenka's* doe-like eyes.Open wide, beneath their innocence and magnetic beauty, Stanley could sense the usual meeting day tension of her fear. This particular day, however, overlaying the fear was the electric spark of hope.

"I have spoken to '*Syrenka*' just this morning. Much has occurred over the past two days." Her breath was cut short by her immediate desire to rapidly relay so much news to her Stanley.

"Tell me, please" said Stanley stoically, although he was anxious to get the details of what he already knew were history-making events in the Lenin Shipyards where her son worked.

"It all started a week ago with the dismissal of Anna Walentynowicz (pronounced *Val-EN-tin-o-vitch*)" she started.

"*Pani Ania*? The old electrician woman?" said Stanley, surprised. Agnieszka had often passed on news of this widowed worker and emboldened labor reformist at the shipyards. She was increasingly becoming a nuisance to the Polish Communist state.

"Yes, and she operated the large cranes as well." Agnieszka's eyes showed her raw emotions of hope, joy and caution, as she began to relay the story.

"Last week, the bosses at the shipyards fired *Pani Ania*. It was only a few months before she could be eligible for her pension. They ruined her because she was organizing the workers secretly for their own protection. But they made a massive mistake, for everyone at the shipyards loved *Pani Ania*. This little widower was always the first to push back against the party and shipyard bosses when they were heavy handed with the workers. Because this short old woman could make the bosses cower, the workers at the shipyards always loved her."

Stanley looked deeply into her moistening eyes. "Yes, I remember from *Syrenka's* reports. She was the heart of the worker's movement within the shipyard. So, the bosses finally fired her ..."

""Starting two days ago, *Syrenka* says that the shipyard operations ground to a halt. Everyone refused to work until she was brought back, but the bosses refused. They thought they would fight through the demands of the yard workers, because without *Pani Ania* there, the workers had no real leadership." Agnieszka was now nearly breathless.

Stanley looked at his protege across the table, hoping to calm her. "This is when the other electrician, Wałęsa, came back to the shipyards?"

It only excited her more. "Yes, you remember that *Syrenka* had predicted this. His name is Lech Wałęsa. He was fired from the shipyards in 1976, also for organizing the workers. When the news leaked out all over the town of Gdańsk, Wałęsa went to the shipyard, but by then the gates had been chained shut."

Stanley remembered. He had reported back to Langley, based on *Syrenka's* early reports, that the thick mustachioed electrician had been identified by his agent as a potential leader for the emerging social movement. He pressed her gently, "The gates were chained shut by whom? The workers? The Management? The Party? The Police?"

"It is not clear at this point," she said, lowering her head, as if in shame. Then her shame instantly departed, her head snapped proudly up, and she added. "*Pan* Wałęsa did not let the chained gates stop him, for he found a wall to climb over to get into the shipyard. He then took over as leader of the striking workers." Her smile triumphed across her radiant face. Stanley had never seen her this excited, this hopeful.

"The workers welcomed him back?" he asked.

"Oh, very much so. They always liked him. He is very, how do you say, charismatic?" Agnieszka explained.

"Yes, charismatic," said Stanley, who thought to himself, "we will see how far his charisma takes him."

He looked again at his *Sarenka*. "So, go on. Tell me everything."

Agnieszka exploded, as if his words were the squeeze of a finger on her trigger.

"The first thing *Pan* Wałęsa did was to demand the return of *Pani Ania*. The bosses resisted, but they could see that Wałęsa had given the workers what they direly needed - a voice. The voice that soon said that nothing would be done by the workers until Walentynowicz was brought back. Chants of 'bring back *Pani Ania*' filled the air of the shipyard. Banners demanding her return were raised throughout the shipyard. He had them *whipped in frenzy*, you say?"

"Yes, whipped up in a frenzy." Stanley gently corrected her. "What else did *Syrenka* have to say?"

"Then the rest of the country began to support the striking ship workers. Other workers throughout Poland began to strike in sympathy with them, the whole country was shutting down, did you not sense this?" Her emotion now dripped from her voice.

"Yes, it was apparent, but I eagerly awaited this meeting with you to learn why it was happening." Stanley was telling half-truths. He had eagerly awaited his meetings with Agnieszka, it was true. These had become the events he lived for. To be alone with her for fifteen minutes or so. To absorb her perfumed allure and reserved warmth. But today, her reservation was thrown aside. Her beauty was dynamically enhanced by her pride and joy in telling her American handler the most intimate and potentially treacherous details from her son. Her fragrance was tinged with a faint scent of sweat, a whiff of the danger of her treason she was committing to the Polish Communist State that employed her husband.

She continued in her animated manner. "The Director of the shipyards finally conceded, and sent his own government limousine to *Pani Ania's* home to bring her back to the shipyard. Can you imagine, after firing her a week ago, they send their car to bring her back? Wałęsa insisted that she join him on the negotiating committee. That is where they stand as we speak; the shipyard remains shut down. Oh yes, I nearly forgot, the most thrilling part. *Pan Wałęsa* and *Pani Ania* have added a demand to the workers strike resolution. They demand that the communist government allow for the legal establishment of trade unions within the Polish Communist State. It is so exciting!"

Stanley remembered thinking, "Deadly might be a more appropriate adjective." Here he broke off the meeting with his *Sarenka*, so he could immediately pass on the information to Langley. His agent *Syrenka* had not only predicted the leader Wałęsa rising to rally the workers, but also that the underground movement would soon demand to be a recognized force within Poland. Stanley knew what the leadership at Langley would fear - a Soviet invasion to quell the uprising.

"*Dziękuję*, my friend," he said, rising to his feet. She rose with him, coming around the worn table that had separated them. He placed his arms on her shoulders. "Please take great care, and may our Lord be with you."

Agnieszka then placed her hands, inside of his arms, onto his chest. She rose upon her toes and leaned into him, and for the first time placed her lips directly upon his. Stanley felt a shudder he could not control lurch through him. She pulled back slightly, and smiled broadly only inches from his face. She had felt his body react to her kiss.

"I should say *dziękuję* to you, *my dear*," she said in a whisper. It was the first time she had used this appellation to him. "You have given me this wondrous joy".

He looked confused, his hands still on her shoulders, her body inches away from his. With the greatest of circumspect, he said to her, "I gave you nothing that the Polish people would not have done on their own."

"You give me the joy of one with whom I can share my hopes." Saying this she kissed him again, but now pressing her lips firmly into Stanley's own. He could feel upon his cheek the tenderness of her tears as they rolled from her face onto his.

Stanley recalled the years that followed the Gdańsk shipyard strike of 1980. *Solidarity*, the trade union legally emerged from the strike's settlement. Lech Wałęsa was elected as its first leader. *Solidarity* flourished as more than a labor movement within the still communist Poland. It had become a social movement of unprecedented momentum. Within months, it had ten million members in a country of less than forty million. One of every three workers were represented by *Solidarity*, in fields of labor far beyond shipbuilding. It did not take long for the Polish Communists, as well as their Soviet overlords, to notice that *Solidarity* held the power to completely shut down the Polish economy.

In October 1981, the *Solidarity* trade union was outlawed by the Polish Communist government. In mid-December 1981, with the Soviets threatening a massive invasion to bring Polish populace under control, the new communist prime minister Wojciech Jaruzelski declared a state of martial law.

"My husband is panicking!" Agnieszka relayed to Stanley in their first caucus above the bookshop in the many months that followed the imposition of martial law. Her voice was taunt and edged with fear. There had been no invasion as had been threatened. The restrictive controls of martial law were resulting in a slowing economy, crippling the Polish Communist State. The trade union *Solidarity*, legitimized only some 15 months earlier had been outlawed. Its leadership was now imprisoned.

Agnieszka went on. "Lech Wałęsa and Ania Walentynowicz are in jail along with thousands of others. Thank God, my own son is not. He tells me that the workers are passively resisting, slowing their labor in every facet of life. The economy is stagnant. My husband is taking great blame as minister of the economy. The debt owed to the Western banks is crushing the state. He fears the Soviets will roll in with their tanks and annex Poland as part of the Soviet Union itself."

"Has your husband talked to Jaruzelski about lifting the martial law?" Stanley asked, watching for the expression on her face to yield the answer.

"My husband is a coward," she said, arching her eyebrows, "but much to my surprise he has broached the subject with the Prime Minister. Bronislaw has known Jaruzelski for many years, since he was Defense Minister in the 1960's. The Prime Minister considers my husband a friend, so he answers his queries, but only in private, never in the recorded sessions of the government. He tells me that the Prime Minister is concerned over the Soviets. They have had plans for invasion just before he imposed martial law, but have not yet acted on these plans."

Stanley knew from the agency that this was correct. Trellis' agent *Erasmus* had passed back information from East Germany that indeed an invasion had been planned. Troops were to roll in from the east from the Soviet Union, from the west from East Germany, and from the south from Czechoslovakia. The Soviet Politburo was prepared to act, but had held off at the imposition of martial law in Poland. But the threat of invasion remained.

"What is the Prime Minister to do? Allow the economy to ground to a halt until there is unrest in the streets, as there was in 1970?" asked Stanley.

"I do not know. But my husband knew that Jaruzelski, as Defense Minister, had seen firsthand the carnage of the Soviet invasion of Czechoslovakia in 1968. Bronislaw knew that if the Polish people remembered that brutality, as well as the force used against the Polish workers in 1970, then this invasion would be tremendously more oppressive and might again result in the loss of an independent Polish State."

She paused, with a strained look upon her face, as if she had just ingested something bitter.

"Independent, how could he say this?" scoffed Agnieszka, as if to beat Stanley to the point..

"This is a dangerous time for you and your family," Stanley remembered telling her. "Be cautious. Better days are ahead, but one knows not how far ahead…"

It was true. Stanley and his *Sarenka* continued to meet secretly, and with the greatest of caution. True to Trellis' East German source, the spy codenamed *Erasmus*, the invasion never came. The martial law was lifted in July 1983, but *Solidarity* remained outlawed. Lech Wałęsa was soon freed, but was hounded by the secret police. Wałęsa went on to run *Solidarity* as an underground movement throughout the 1980's. He was awarded the Nobel Peace Prize in 1983. The government would not allow him to travel to Oslo to accept the prize, so his wife Danuta accepted on his behalf.

Stanley found this to be somehow very ironic. Henryk Sienkiewicz was the author who had won the Nobel prize for Literature in 1905 for his historical tales. Stanley had used the characters in his novel *Krzyzacy*, or the *Knights of the Cross,* detailing Poland's struggle against the Teutonic Knights, as codewords for their meetings. Stanley had often used the name of the story's the tragic heroine, Danuta. Danuta was held against her will by the knights. Stanley favored this name because it echoed of Agnieszka's tragedy of being held captive in her loveless Danuska marriage. Finally, Lech Wałęsa called his wife by her middle name Danuta, even though her given name was Mirosława.

Chapter Four

Harbored Secrets

THE COLD NOVEMBER night air in Baltimore was brisk, biting with the humidity of the harbor nearby. Diane, bundled in her full-length Burberry overcoat and scarf, looked up at the massive sculpture towering over the main traffic circle of the newest trendy area known as Harbor East. The area was wedged between Baltimore's highly renown Inner Harbor and Stanley's home neighborhood of Fells Point. It was mixed use, with high rise office buildings in glass and steel bearing the names of the nation's predominant investment firms side by side with five star hotels, upscale restaurants, a cinema, a Civil War museum, and high end retail. Plenty of high end retail.

The centerpiece in this most bejeweled of Baltimore's renaissance zones was a monument to something the casual tourist might find quite unusual. Above the dissipating mist of Diane's breath in the frigid night, rose a majestic golden sculpture of flames some forty-four feet into the air, centered in the roundabout that defined this harborside redevelopment zone.

But this sculpture of bronzed flames erratically dancing skyward was detailed with the recognizable features of foreign soldiers, painfully dispersed throughout the fiery bursts of the monument. The soldiers appeared to be suspended in terror on the precipice of the furnace. And in the center, the cut away area forming the void among the flames, one could visualize the absent form of the Polish White Eagle rising like a Phoenix amongst the carnage. The White Eagle that was complete with the regal crown that was strictly forbidden during the 44 years of Poland's Communist rule.

The words "Katyń, 1940" were etched across its cold, dark gray marble base. This was the National Katyń Memorial dedicated in this emerging section of Baltimore's harbor in the year 2000.

But the monument also celebrated 1000 years of Polish heritage. Amongst the flames were the unmistakable figures of Bolesław the Brave, the first king to unify the fragments of Poland about the year 1000; King Jan Sobieski, whose winged hussar army lifted the Turkish siege of Vienna in 1683, and even Count Casimir Pulaski who died assisting the young American revolutionists.

Diane needed to come here. Despite Darien Shaw's psycho-babble analysis, the trip to Stanley's home yielded little other than proof of a very simplistic existence in retirement. While very little decorated the walls of his home, there was a hand painted canvas of this East Baltimore monument. Why?

The last she had seen of Stanley was at his farewell luncheon the week that he had retired, some eight years ago. It was in a Georgetown restaurant, and after the last remaining observers from the luncheon were washed away by duty, returning to Langley, she stayed after. She and Stanley walked the bright afternoon streets of Georgetown with Stanley reminiscing. They walked among the brick town homes, not unlike his own, and spoke indirectly of project INDIGO and of Bryce Weldon. Stanley always thought of Bryce, his loss haunted Stanley.

Bryce was consumed by the machine that was the CIA, but to Stanley, this was the now retired spy's failure alone, and it gnawed at him. Despite all he had achieved in his career, he allowed this loss to define him.

Stanley retired in his early sixties. At that time, Diane thought the next she would hear of him would be of his passing from this life. Instead, Stanley apparently had gone off the deep end in taking Powell's life. She knew him well. Stanley was not doing this for one last grasp at center stage, bathing himself in glory as the imbecilic Dr. Shaw had assumed.

The darkened narrows of Shakespeare street were eerily reminiscent of Georgetown itself. The row homes huddled together in their quiet preserve, just yards from the ever-ebullient nightlife of Fells Point. While most of the inhabitants were upscale professionals who more recently bought into this more renewed and esteemed neighborhood, Diane knew that Stanley had lived in this modest row house ever since he was born. He lived here not for its capital gain value or its trendy urban appeal. He continued to live here because it was the hearth upon which hung the memories of the most meaningful moments of his life. He lived here out of respect for the parents he loved so deeply.

She did not know while once it was all he ever needed, it was now more than his lonely, tortured soul could endure.

She had walked throughout his modest house. It was a throwback to an earlier age. The downstairs walls had been stripped of its plaster and framing, to reveal the precision of earthy red brick and white mortar. A television, a telephone, an old sofa, a reclining chair and a singular end table were all that graced the living room besides a few wall hangings. The small kitchen was open to the living room. In its center stood a rectangular oak table with elegantly carved, massive legs. The table had a metallic surface hand painted with a beautiful East European design of swans swimming on a genteel lake before a cottage shrouded in edge of a darkened forest.

The upstairs only revealed two small bedrooms, and a single bathroom, with a shower so narrow it was barely wide enough for a man to shimmy his frame into. The upstairs had none of the vanity of the first floor's grit blasted brick. The smaller of the two bedrooms was paneled in an old faux birch, likely from the seventies. From the alarm clock, and the clothes in the dresser, it was clear this was where Stanley was sleeping.

The only slightly larger of the two bedrooms was dim and shrouded in a very old, dried out wallpaper. The musty smell of plaster permeated the room. It was dark, and heavy with the weight of not being used. The dust settled thick on what must have been his parents' original furniture from when they first arrived in this country.

Why would Stanley live like this? He clearly could afford to redo the upstairs. She stared at the bed, it's sheets and covers made long ago in a militarily tight precision, had leaked backed into a tired slouch. Above the bed was only a painted religious image in an intricately carved oak frame. Our Lady of Częstochowa – the Black Madonna – was a highly cherished religious icon to the Polish culture. Diane imagined it was hand carried back by Stanley as a gift for his aging mother. Or possibly as a spiritual salve for his dying father?

Adorning the dresser table, was a singular black and white photograph of a joyful, yet reserved couple (in their thirties, perhaps?) together on a blanket in the grass in a park. Behind them rose a majestic hill, on which rose a beautiful Japanese pagoda. Around the structure's base was layered the delicate decoration of cherry blossom trees in bloom.

The team that tossed the house the day before had identified Stanley's parents, now both long deceased, as the couple. The finely mowed lawns were those of nearby Patterson Park. The picture had no time markings, as it was cut to fit the simple silver frame that held it, but was decided to be from the early 1950's based upon some visual renovation to the pagoda known to have been ongoing in that time period. They speculated the photo was taken by the young Stanley himself, who would have then been between eight to ten years old. This framed photo was the only decoration in the rooms upstairs, other than the Black Madonna. Diane could not help but to notice that the readily tarnished silver of the frame had very recently been polished. Perhaps Stanley's last act of loving respect to his deceased parents before leaving on his journey that would unexpectedly take him back to Warsaw?

Downstairs, was nearly equally scarce of decorations. An enlarged photograph taken by someone of Stanley in Kraków's medieval town square hung proudly on the wall. Diane had been there several times, and the Cloth Hall in the center of the square was unmistakable.

Several pieces of hand-made Bolesławiec pottery decorated the hutch that clung tightly to the wall, separating the living room space from the kitchen. The last decoration, hung proudly over the television, was a stylized oil painting of the East Baltimore Katyń monument.

The painting was almost impressionistic, and it was painted against a dark background, but in such a way as to highlight the Polish Eagle cut from the center of the flames.

Why does a man who has virtually no decorations in his home have a painting of this relatively new monument just a short walk from his own doorstep?

Why was Katyń important to Stanley? And more importantly, why on the back did it bear a brushed signature "***Your Sarenka, 2008***"?

After searching Stanley's home, Diane was compelled to walk the half mile or so in the cold night air to this towering, iconic Harbor East sculpture. She now stood before it's spotlighted grandeur.

She looked up at the monument before her. Autumn leaves, colored brown and red, danced across the circle, attempting to distract her gaze from the enormous flames and their enveloped martyrs. But the dried remnants of summer were unsuccessful, and as such ignored, only left to the wind to inevitably carry them the last few feet into the vast Baltimore harbor. The circular fountain at the monument's base solemnly cried a perpetual cascade of tears for the over twenty thousand innocent Polish lives so callously consumed by the Soviets in this Russian forest in the Spring of 1940.

"Why this monument?" she wondered. "Why Katyń?" What special relevance did it have to Stanley, enough for a painting of it to adorn a wall in a home where every space was seemingly kept vacant as if not to compete with his own memories of his parents and his childhood. What was missing from her knowledge of Stanley's life?

What was motivating him? Katyń was five years before Stanley's own birth. His parents had not perished in Katyń, but had someone else close to him?

Her instincts were telling her that the roots of his ties to Katyń lay in his Polish culture, undoubtedly sewed during his time on station in Warsaw.

She knew Katyń was the massacre of the surrendered POW Polish Army Officers by the Red Army. It was an atrocity that the Soviets committed in this remote Soviet forest in 1940, under direct orders of Beria and Stalin. It had been discovered by the advancing Germans when they double crossed their Non-Aggression Pact Soviet Allies and invaded Russia in 1941. They were keen to spread the propaganda of the brutality of the Soviets. When the Russians drove the Nazi's back into Germany in late 1944 into early 1945, they merely re-attributed the now discovered atrocity to the retreating Nazis, conveniently dating the massacre to 1941.

But 22,000 lives refused to allow this Soviet charade to be accepted, thanks to the efforts of the slain officers' families that survived the war. Thousands of surrendered and unarmed Polish officers and infantry murdered in cold blood, cried from the grave for their oppressors to be brought to justice. The Soviet lie died with the USSR, and the 1990's temporary dance with Gorbachev's *Glasnost* and *Perestroika* lasted long enough for the classified files of the NKVD, the predecessor to the KGB, to be wedged open via international legal proceedings.

By the time this monument was erected in the year 2000, it was a known and established fact that for every foot of height of this memorial, some 500 innocent Polish lives had been ever so efficiently destroyed. Every foot of this monument also represented one of the 44 years of oppression at the hands of the Soviets, from 1945 until the fall of the Berlin Wall itself in 1989.

Deep in the forests of Katyń, near Smolensk, in what was then the USSR, 22,000 Polish families were mortally scarred. Scars that would drive many to never allow the truth to die.

Of course, Diane knew this symbolized Stanley's yearning for all things Polish. She knew his parents had been repatriated from Warsaw in the last year of World War II, via London.

Of course, she knew that his mother was pregnant with Stanley at the time. Just in time for Stanley to be born at Johns Hopkins Hospital in 1945.

Diane also realized that Stanley, in his position as deputy station chief in Warsaw spent most of his professional energies bringing about the downfall of the Soviets themselves.

President Reagan called the Soviets the "Evil Empire", and Stanley knew it true long before those famous words were ever uttered. But thank God, they were uttered, Stanley would say, as the world needed to hear them. The world needed to bring them to justice.

Diane would now have to bring Stanley, the cold-hearted killer she could no longer possibly know, to justice. It would be difficult, but she knew she would.

She had taken a singular item with her from Stanley's home. It was a first edition of *Morfill's Poland*, a history of the country that did not technically exist for nearly a hundred years when the book was printed in 1893. It was bound in beautiful leather bearing the embossed seal of Wellington College upon its cover.

In it was a business card from Peter Harrington's, the Chelsea bookshop from which Diane assumed it was purchased. She knew Peter Harrington's well, as she had browsed its Fulham Road storefront, which was only doors down from one of her favorite interior decorating shops. She had procured a few leather-bound volumes in Harrington's to accentuate her flat at her St. James condominium in Westminster. Books that looked elegantly impressive on her shelf, but remained unread.

The business card seemed to mark a particular reference. As Diane split open the marbled pages of this beautiful manuscript, the card sliced her attention to an excerpt by the Polish poet Julian Niemcewicz that read,

> ***"O ye exiles, who so long wander over the world,***
> ***When will ye find a resting place for your weary steps?***
> ***The wild dove has its nest, the worm a clod of earth,***
> ***Each man a country, but the Pole a grave."***

Diane thought of Stanley, now being chased across Europe, never knowing if he had been spotted and marked, waiting for the CIA to move in decisively and forcibly take its prey.

The cold was now biting fiercely at her face. She gazed upward for a final view of the Katyń Memorial. Why this? Who is *Sarenka*? Is this the agent *Syrenka*? How do these pieces tie together?

There was a winter's wind blowing. It was a cleansing wind, brutal in its origins. From the emptiness that was the open harbor, came the wind that would relentlessly chase its prey, without respite or mercy. It was a wind in which would flicker the flames of Katyń, with their sacrifice of Polish officers, and the wind would demand a sacrifice of its own.

Agnieszka was always notified of their meeting dates by Zbigniew, after Stanley had relayed the request to the shop owner. Usually this was done in person, when Agnieszka next stopped by the bookstore. This request, however, had an unusual urgency, prompting Zbigniew to call her at her home to tell her he had received a new book for which she had been waiting. This telephone call was highly unusual, but demanded by Stanley due to the urgency of the subject. They all knew the telephone lines were listened to, and could only hope this message would draw no overt suspicion.

They sat across the low table, she in a worn but lovely upholstered chair, with Stanley opposite her on a tattered sofa that did not match. Today, Stanley could see a tension in her eyes instead of what had on previous meetings been an increasingly reflective nature. It was full of the sense of gratitude she had for the risks he took in his efforts to secure freedom for her birth country.

Over the years since he first contacted her, Stanley had noticed her often studying him as if gauging him. The looks had, at first, been shallow glances, readily averted whenever Stanley's eyes met hers. Now, Stanley knew he could be briefing Agnieszka for the last time. She seemed to sense this, even before he began to speak. The tension beneath Agnieszka's beautiful blue eyes now pulled at Stanley's heart. A heart, which for the first time in life, ached with the pain of knowing he may never see her again.

"My dear *Sarenka*, I have been recalled to the West. I must leave immediately," Stanley blurted at her, with more offensive force than he intended to impart. Her hand raised to cover her mouth. It was March of 1985.

"*Nie, Nie*. I feared this was coming from the risks you took in meeting with me today with so little caution. Having Zbigniew call me on the telephone! You only come to use me for my son, and now you will leave me here, alone, useless like a flower drained of its nectar." Her anger instantaneously turned into a desperate plea.

"Please do not leave me," she begged. "I have come to love you, my

Stanley, and I need you, though I could never dare express it to you before today. I do not believe that I can exist without looking forward to the joy of seeing you next."

Stanley, caught off guard by her admission of affection, squirmed across from her, as if trying to hide in the many crevices of the thread-born sofa. He sensed Agnieszka probing him, sensing her naked nervousness of having exposed her secret emotions, and now fearing a rejection they both knew she could not bear to stand. As he prepared to speak, Stanley looked deeply into the pools of her eyes, as he had always done. Over the years, he had increasingly been stealing strength and comfort there, ever hoping she would not notice his growing admiration for her. Today was different. He felt her eyes not just meeting his, but enveloping them. She was emotionally clinging to him, and her pools of static tears now began to run in tiny rivulets across her pale lightly powdered cheeks.

"My Agnieszka, I must talk to you. Time is urgently against us..." Stanley began as tenderly as he could, leaning forward, taking her hands in his. Stanley was in mid-sentence when she rose, and slowly negotiating the table. She came to sit next to him on the tired sofa. Stanley had stopped talking, intead he focused on her. Agnieszka then leaned into him, so their faces were inches apart.

Closing her eyes, she delicately, and with the sensitivity of a butterfly's landing on a green summer leaf, kissed Stanley once again.

"I love what you are doing for all of us," she whispered in his ear, as the revolving vinyl disc rendered forth its sweetest and most sensitive passage of a beautifully fragile nocturne. He could feel her tears against his cheek, onto which they flowed before draining into his trim beard.

She breathed into his ear, with a quiver in her voice, "It will not be long now before we will have our country returned to us. I know this. Please stay with me, when we both can enjoy the tastes of freedom for *our* Poland."

Stanley not only heard this statement, but felt her breath warm and moist upon his eardrum. It instantly penetrated him, running through him all directions at once. Stanley thought he had been able to conceal the secret desires of his own from Agnieszka. Now, for the first time, Stanley was confronted with her desires that had been building within her for years, pulsing beneath her fine porcelain skin. It had grown in her, like a living thing, and now consumed her, as it had in him. Over the years, Stanley had been preoccupied with the CIA money and operational details that he was passing on to her, for her to further pass on to her son. He was consumed by the information received from *Syrenka* that she passed onto him. He had failed to sense that he, the watcher, had himself been watched by her. More than merely watched, but that she grew to desire him.

She looked deeply into his eyes, probing for a response. After what seemed many seconds, but surely was only a fraction of one, Stanley flushed and continued.

"*Sarenka*," Stanley said lovingly, pulling back from her, "We have little time."

She continued to probe him. She watched him, and more specifically the features of his face, which he could feel was tight and tortured. Stanley could feel his pulse racing, his face flushed. For the first time, Stanley did not know exactly what to do.

That is when Agnieszka, in sensing his hesitation, raised elegantly to stand over him. Stanley, frozen by a strange sensation of uncertainty, remained sitting. Agnieszka moved forward until she, in her white wool dress, hovered high over him. She straddled him, her knees now outside his own on the sofa. Her warm body slid down over his sitting form, as slow and sweet as the rarest honey, its taste forbidden lest it draw the fearsome anger of the hive.

She sensed him pulling back in awkward politeness, yet she pressed her curved frame more directly into him, draping herself onto him in a movement that was neither awkward nor rehearsed. It felt so foreign, so intrusive to Stanley as she slid her mature but curvaceous form onto his rigid, unexpected body. Within the singular movement her arms framed slowly around his neck, her delicate forearms arched around him meeting behind his head, her breasts now tightening in a frame just below his bearded chin.

"I thank you for risking your life for us, for me," she whispered as she dropped lower onto him, her full lips now only inches from his own. "You must not abandon me."

She pressed her lips hard onto Stanley's. An electric spark jumped through his body, igniting a flame of passion within him. Her mouth wandered, sliding moistly over his own, probing for the response that took every ounce of Stanley's will to deny her.

Stanley, arching his body back onto the sofa, could feel the animal heat radiating from her form onto his. Her full weight bore down upon him, and seemingly spread across his groin in a hot, yet perfumed lightness that he knew instinctively carried a heavy danger. Her breath was warm and thick upon his face, as if it carried more meaning than just the words she spoke to him.

"Do not deny your *Sarenka*," she whispered to him, stretching the syllables of *Sar-ren-ka* in a breathy, earthy tease. She slid across him slowly, draping herself ever more tightly onto him. Her body still warmly weighed upon him. Stanley, feeling emotions he had never before encountered, thought of a dozen actions he could take, but was somehow powerless to move.

She grasped his hand and placed it firmly on her breast, while with her other hand braced his neck such that she could prevent him pulling his head away as her mouth again searched his out. Agnieszka felt his hand tremble upon her aching tender skin. She felt the hesitancy in the nerves of his face as she pressed her full red lips onto his. But she also felt his breathing become labored and restrained, as that of a man struggling to rein in a runaway mare.

"Do not deny me this, please," she whispered again in his ear. "And I will deny you nothing."

Then came the sudden explosion. Stanley, fighting the urges that had been conjured from deep within himself, uncontrollably pushed her away to the farthest edge of the sofa. This was only enough that he could stand to free himself from the situation. His face was crimson, and he seemed angry, but Agnieszka sensed not with her, but himself.

"I am sorry, Agnieszka, I know no other way to tell you this. My life is in danger. The Russians have come to suspect me. My country believes they will act against me. For this reason, I must go back."

Her face seemed to crumple into the recognition that he would leave her this very day. "*Tak*, my dearest. Leave me to grow old alone with a man I not only do not love, but I despise as a traitor to a free Poland. Yes, my Stanley, you go back home…"

As she nearly spat this last word at him, her face drained of the emotion which with it had seconds before overflowed. That was when Stanley cupped her forehead with his hands and tenderly kissed her at its highest point, just below her hairline. They had been speaking in Polish all along, but now in the perfumed French language she so loved to speak, he said to her, "My darling, I promise to you, that you alone are my home. While I must go away now, I promise that I will return to you, my *Sarenka*. I cannot stand to see you in this pain. Just know I will come back for you."

With this Stanley again kissed her forehead, before he rose and descended the stairs that would take him to the street below. It was March of 1985, and the next morning Stanley made his return to the west.

Chapter Five
Diane The Huntress

STANLEY AWOKE LATE Sunday morning after his second night in Zgorzelec. He had finally slept and dreamt the night before of his love, *his delicate fawn, Agnieszka*. In his dream, she had sheltered him from a great beast. She protected him from the fierce predators in the night. He had at once felt safe in her arms, immersed in the depths of her full round eyes.

He had once fanned the embers of her interest for the intention of his professional use, only to later realize instead that it was she had who had kindled its flames into a blazing desire within him. It was she who had stolen his heart.

He felt all this in a swirling watercolor of emotion that permeated the recollection of his dream. It was a pleasant sleep, until he awoke realizing that while he was lying in her bed, she was not beside him. She could not be, of course, and the melancholy of this realization sobered the joys of the young romantic into the pain of the old nostalgic he had become.

Then, as if a vapor, into his awakening crept the image he resisted so strongly, but futilely so. He was haunted again by the shocked face of Langston Powell. Stanley felt the trembling twitch of his right hand, which was not only uncommanded, but actively resisting Stanley's every plea for it to cease.

Stanley felt no remorse in his mind for his action, knowing it had to be done, as Powell's expansive plans for the Daedalus Destroyer would ultimately risk freedom throughout the world. And knowing that Powell's plan would have been fueled by Trellis' own excessive greed.

Stanley showered in the little flat that was his villa. His hunger had not come to him this morning, but the cold Polish chill of November had. The warm water cascaded over his tall aged, but still angular frame. Despite its warmth and plenty, the waters did not chase away his hollow core of cold emptiness. The warmth of the shower shrouded his frame but did not penetrate him.

Stanley knew he had to move. The die was cast, he had to meet Jean Paul in Vienna as planned. Yes, Stanley could stay protected in the anonymity of this villa, unknown as it was to the agency. It was tempting to stay in the rooms where his fawn touched and penetrated his heart, opening his soul to what it was to love. However, Stanley knew with great confidence, that waiting statically in any hiding place would merely benefit the predators that now pursued him. They would eventually sniff him out and close in.

Stanley had decided before sharing his plan with Jean Paul that he must move and evade the pursuit, but Stanley could not evade the realization that he would be caught.

Inevitably, Trellis would take his life, he knew this.

Stanley had decided that evading Trellis would become his life's last great adventure. Stanley would use it to test the retention of his skills that he had allowed to dull over the sedentary years of his retirement. Better to jab sharp daggers at the eyes of the predators, even knowing they would anger to the threat, then to allow the static ticking of the clock to overtake the beat of one's own heart.

Stanley would harness his skills not only to evade the hunters, but to live long enough to accomplish the simple, but unrealized, lifelong wish of his delicate *fawn*, of his beautiful Agnieszka.

She had always longed to perform a simple act - to place a bouquet of white lilies on the cold granite stones of the master's grave. She longed for their scent to grace and permeate the heartless tomb of Frederic Chopin. She had been taken unjustly from this world before she could make this pilgrimage.

For Stanley, he would complete the act in honor of the memory of Agnieszka. Lost to life, she herself had no tomb for Stanley to visit, to commemorate. Her remains were scattered like the joyous gifts she had once bestowed on him - warmth, touch, intimacy. They were why Stanley had returned to this villa - to be as near on this earth, as he ever could, to the memories of his delicate fawn, Agnieszka. The villa was their sacred monument to what had once been them.

The lilies brushing upon the master's gravestone would drive him as if they were one last brush of her fingers upon Stanley's wrinkled, aging face.

Having returned to London overnight, Diane dropped her keys onto the burled walnut table in the foyer of her St. James Residence flat on Buckingham Gate in the Victoria section of Westminster. The keys slid across the magnificent burnished grain under an elaborate silversmith sculpture of several giraffe feasting on the broad leafy trees of the Serengeti. A beautiful work of art, it was hand detailed to her specifications by her favorite Chelsea gallery. It was one of her favorite possessions. It was elegant and understated, yet captured the essence of majesty of the Africa to which she had never travelled. Perhaps that was the greatest aspect of its allure, its ability to generate in her faith a beauty, a simplicity, a power in something that she had never even seen.

She had purchased the sculpture upon the advice that her father had long ago given her - "invest in beautiful works of art that enrich your life and hold their value."

Not "to make sure you give yourself completely to the love of your mother."

Not "to embrace others in need, even as a general concept."

No, you can ditch and run when you need, your mother be damned, so long as one has assets to liquefy. So much for her caring father's advice.

Diane ran her hand over the delicate walnut grasslands beneath the silvered trees and creatures of the Serengeti, assuring herself she had not scratched its lustered veneer. She hadn't. She was careless in tossing her keys. She ran her fingers apologetically across the burled, nearly mirror-like finish.

She barely had enough time to pack her bags for Berlin, where she and Trellis had mutually agreed the hunt should be directed from. "*The Blind*", as Trellis called it. The man had never hunted so much as a Peking Duck on a Chinatown Menu, but he loved his metaphors.

She was sure he had hunted his share of agents, and counter agents, so she supposed he had a right to his vernacular, after all. Diane unbuttoned her Burberry raincoat, shrugging it off her tall shoulders such that it rode down her back as the touch of a lover. At least as she had remembered - it had been quite a drought, recently. She moved to the other end of the sitting room's white sofa and reached across the oriental Rosewood end table. Beneath the hand painted Chinese lamps she searched for the answering machine. It reminded her of her age, becoming quite the 40 something dinosaur - the kids today had no home phones let alone answering machines - everything was off the mobiles today. She thought of Stanley. His home had no answering machine, only the phone and caller ID. Was she beginning to become the recluse Stanley had morphed into? When did he begin to shelter himself from society? To lose his mind?

She pressed play and listened first to a message from the concierge, Henri, about a delivery he was holding from Fortnum and Mason downstairs. She looked over at the Burberry's raincoat splayed out on the sofa, like a twenty-year old bored of the art of active resistance.

"I wish I could relive those years," she thought, "I sure would have a hell of a lot more fun the second time around."

The next and last message was much more important and put her in a quandary.

"Diane, darling, it's your lovely Mad Mal. We have been concerned about you. Appears you were on a Deep Dive at your end of the pond. I would terribly love to meet you for tea at the St. Ermin's. Just ring and give me a quarter's hour notice and I am yours. Keep me if you like. At least for the week's end. Ciao."

Malcolm Devereaux, her liaison at MI6, was her Mad Mal. The Brits loved their little affectionate *Noms de guerre* - their nicknames with the sadistically deprecating twists. She was surprised they knew she was back from DC so quickly, having taken the agency transportation. Was the "*Deep Dive*" reference to tell her they knew she was on the hunt, if so, how possibly could they so fast? And why were they letting her know?

She decided she had to see Malcolm before she crossed over to Berlin that afternoon. She called and gave him 20 minutes to get to the St. Ermin's Hotel. It was just a five-minute walk for her, just around the corner, behind New Scotland Yard.

She decided to pack the kid leather grip she had purchased last season in Florence. What she couldn't fit or she might have forgotten, she'd buy in Berlin. She sure as hell refused to roll a suitcase down the street like the ubiquitous American tourists. She packed the grip, threw on her Cordings of Piccadilly country jacket, grabbed the Burberry trenchcoat, and was off. She would take a taxi from the hotel after her meeting with Devereaux.

"I love this place too much to always be running away from it," she thought, as she heard the solid click of the oak door locking, as if kissing her goodbye.

They sat in the white rococo tea loft just above the lobby at the St. Ermin's Hotel. Malcolm had arrived minutes before her and the tea service was set. Good Lord, Diane thought, were they trailing me?

Malcolm was dressed impeccably as always in his tailored suit, French cuffed, slim fit shirt, violently expensive tie and always complimenting scarf. He was vainly proud of his appearance, she thought, his trim physique, his perfectly coiffed hair. But then he was always on the prowl, wasn't he? While his wife, Pet, kept the family estate outside Cheltenham in the Cotswolds, Malcolm kept a tiny flat in a Mews just down from the V&A - the Victoria & Albert Museum – just off the Cromwell Road. Conveniently, his flat was also just around from the French day school *Lycée Français Charles de Gaulle*, where Mal was known to poach an unsuspecting young mother, aunt, or *au pair* - whoever would fall prey to his dashing looks and spot-perfect French language skills. He was quite willing to talk about his conquests, and Diane knew he used it as the very curiosity subject to judge just how susceptible his partner in conversation might be to his advances.

"Really, it is quite a simple philosophy, love," he had told her in the past, "nothing is as irrepressibly boring as a good woman. And by the corollary, nothing as exciting as a formerly good woman. The trick, my love, is for me to be the doorman enabling the transition. Any interest?"

"Sorry, Mal. Not gonna happen." She flashed a big smile back in the direction of his dark, gentile looks. "As much as you flirt with me, you just push me away all the further."

"How crushingly old fashioned of you, darling. You'll come full round and square the circle. I can wait." He wore the knowing smile of having never gone hungry for lack of the feast.

Despite her protestations, Diane had come to love Malcolm's persistent volleys so indiscreetly peppered throughout their professional engagements, once she had gotten over the shock of them.

It was flattering, and at some points tempting, though Diane knew she could never act on it. It was a game, a dance they danced when the rigors of business became too intense. Besides, his Oscar Wilde "live for the pleasure of the moment" lifestyle was a little too carefree for her.

"Lovely bag, darling," he started as they sat to an early tea. "Going away so soon? You just came home to me. Not very large though. So, either it's a short return or you've packed only a starter kit? Either way, that jacket is absolutely endearing to your figure. I envy it madly, being draped so conformingly to your perfect breasts."

"Malcolm, I know you surely did not invite me here so urgently to compliment my clothing. I am in quite a hurry, I am sorry to say, as I do so enjoy these *tête-à-tête* engagements with you, dear. Now, please let's get to the points of interest."

Malcolm arched his perfectly shaped chestnut eyebrows. "Yes, right, precisely the tack I was on, I rather thought."

He ignored Diane's disapproving look as he pulled a long sip of the delicate St. Ermin's China tea cup, almost hiding behind it momentarily. "Except I rather do not wish to complement your wardrobe, as I would much prefer to compete with it for the right to drape your nubile form."

"Malcom, please! I am terribly pressed for time," pleaded Diane.

"Fine darling, here it is, all out, with a shredding of advice chucked in, gratis. Rumors about the palace are that you're going continental on us, doing a bit of field work. I am under direct orders from his majesty, George *the fith* (no typo) was George Chartwell, Devereaux's section chief who was the chief watcher of their American counterparts in Europe. Devereaux always thought him "*f**ked in the head*", hence George the "*fith*". "Inside joke, darling," Malcolm once said, "don't tell a soul. That one is for you and me only to muse over."

Diane arched her back, and screwed herself into her seat, revealing her discomfort.

"Malcolm, my dearest, we both are quite knowledgeable of the on-going animosity between Chartwell and Trellis. Now is not the time for subtle shots at our leadership. We are merely going to take care of some internal family matters - no need for George to get his dander up."

Devereaux leaned over the arm of his chair, reaching out to touch her wrist, even for Malcolm this was forward. Diane felt an instant sensation of warmth emanate through her from his touch, which she of course suppressed.

"Precisely my thought, darling. I told his majesty, 'Let the cousins ferret about the Euro zone. They always leave a broad wake, easy for us to sight from the shadows.' But then George took me into his inner ring of confidence. Scared the bullocks off me, his being hu-mane and all that. Said he was, rather is, concerned for your personal safety. Unlike the man, thoroughly."

Devereaux pulled back his arm and sat upright. He read the concern that lay on Diane's face like a rigid mask.

Mal continued, "His majesty may be *fith*, but he sips from a lot of different streams, most not available to ourselves. He is quite taken with you, in the professional context, of course."

"I am flattered," Diane said, in as sarcastic a way as she could affect.

"This is nothing more than to tell you to check your six, mind the gap, and all the other sophisms. Also, this," as Devereaux pushed a card across the table to her. Should there be any need, you call this number in Paris, and all the King's men come running, darling. Just drop the word 'corset' in the message, my touch there, and our side speeds the plough. Compliments of King George."

Diane looked at the fictitious, but very proper business card, "Rêves de Cuir, Rue de St. Denis, Paris" with a singular, discreetly embossed *fleur-de-lis*.

"Dreams of Leather? Really, Malcolm?" Diane knew this had to be his doing.

"Must be believable, darling..."

Diane stood, and as she did he did as well. She kissed his cheek, whispering into his ear "Thanks for playing the big brother. I'm touched."

She emphasized the last word with a warm exhale.

"Yes, thanks for that image," he said as he walked her to her blacktop cab. "Keep safe above all else. Cheers, or is it '*Auf Wiedersehen*'?"

She looked up from the seat of the cab with a look that said, "How the hell ..."?

Devereaux smiled, imagining her in the leather corset.

Preston Almesbury sat in his favorite chair in the drawing room with the wood log fire roaring. Occasional hisses of steam would remind Preston of the heavy London rain falling outside, as some found its way directly down the chimney, through a random combination of wind and of random chance.

He checked his mobile phone while his wife was conversing on the house phone with the chairperson of the heritage association regarding their upcoming fundraiser. The pretense and cliquish nature of the charitable community bored Preston to tears, and he used the few minutes to check his e-mail as international news editor at his small but influential independent newspaper, *The Westminster Conservatoire*.

Preston understood, while small newspapers were going under seemingly daily around the globe, it was their internet sites that could and would become very lucrative, but only if they had enough unique and relative material to draw searchers away from the more mainstream sites.

"Darling, might I remind you that silent auctions are quite *passé* these days," Preston heard his wife droning into the handset. "What we need are rather large, individual donations. What the Americans would call *'industrial sized'*. I am sure with the affluence of our members, this could be rather easily raised..."

Preston suspected she was just hitting stride and assured himself he had time to log into his work e-mail. He quickly glanced to assure everything in his inbox could wait.

That is when he saw the email entitled. "My name is Stanley Wisniewski: INTERPOL and the CIA are desperately looking for me."

"My Lord!" he thought. Opening the document immediately.

"My name is Stanley Wisniewski. I openly admit to shooting and killing Global Defense Analytics Executive Langston Powell in Warsaw Friday evening. I am retired CIA. I am sending you the attached files to verify my story. I only ask for you to independently verify my story and publish the factual portions herein."

The long elaborate e-mail went on to detail all the aspects of Stanley's being hired to research Powell's involvement in the death of another executive in Amsterdam. Attached were electronic copies he had made of the watermarked briefing materials supplied to Stanley by Global Defense Analytics.

Preston immediately forwarded the e-mail to his weekend editor, along with the following note: "Preston coming to office Sunday afternoon. Begin validation of materials herein straightaway. They appear genuine, but source could be suspect. He might be mad as a box of frogs. If authentic, then I am gobsmacked. Validate concurrently with preparing full layout for Monday print editions. Nevertheless, prepare immediate online news release *CIA Involved in Death of Global Defense Analytics Executive*?"

While the file had, of course, no contact information for Stanley, it did contain all his relevant information from his CIA career. It also went on to state that the CIA had been clandestinely purchasing the Daedalus Destroyer Drones from Global Defense Analytics for operational use in Afghanistan, Yemen, Iraq and Syria in the Global War on Terror – GWOT.

Stanley never directly stated why he took Powell's life, but provided enough information to allow *The Conservatoire's* staff to craft a release that did little more than identify the relationship of Stanley to the defense firm and its relationship to the CIA itself. He knew it was just enough factual information for the media to read their own undertones, and then to weave on their presses both print and electronic stories of interlaced facts and speculation. After all, speculation sold better than facts these days.

For Preston Almesbury, the details were to be readily checked in the coming hours and days. But tonight's release by *The Conservatoire* would only allow the news organization to report the receipt of the information itself and the questions that were raised. It lit the fuse of an investigative reporting cycle that once lit, would not be silenced until the entire story was known.

Preston could not believe his luck. The *Conservatoire's* own Edward Snowden? "Either that, or it's a massive fraud. If it is, and should we run with it, we will have dropped a spanner in the works. A very large, clanky one at that..."

Before Diane Sterling touched down in Berlin, the news release from the *Westminster Conservatoire* read: Rogue CIA Operative Claims Responsibility in Warsaw Assassination. {Subtitle} Defense Firm alleged to have employed killer in background vetting of victim {Second Subtitle} CIA feverishly searching for whereabouts of Stanley Wisniewski.

Later that afternoon Diane touched down in Berlin's Schönefeld Airport. It was the newest airport in the city, modern and sleek as opposed to the decaying but still functional Tegel Airport, which dated back to the Berlin Airlift. Diane was met at the airport by a bright eyed thirty something, named Emory, who had been stationed in Germany long enough to find his way about.

"Shall I take you directly to *The Blind*, ma'am?"

The hesitation in his voice was quite noticeable. Emory had been briefed on the importance of the woman he was escorting, and of the cutting nature of her temperament, especially when she tired of her exhausting transatlantic and cross-channel transits.

"Okay, Emory, let's get this corrected straightaway, (she noted to herself she was picking up the King's English from her extended London posting), I am not your mum and you are to address me as Diane. Got it? Good."

Emory stiffened in his posture behind the wheel, somewhat noticeably, in response.

"Yeah, sure, sorry M', … er, … Diane," he said, catching his mistake mid-stream.

"Emory, I saw from your file you've been over here for a couple years. How's your German?" she asked. She could see the slight smile of contentment crease his lips.

"Pretty good, if I do say so. Near fluent. But too much of a yank accent to be taken for a local. That will come with time."

Diane looked out the window, without turning to him, and said into the distance "Good, because I haven't got any..."

"Not a problem. We have you covered there," he said proudly. "Anyway, I've been over here for 18 months now and language skills haven't been a problem. I have no problem speaking to these folks at all. But that's really not the issue here, is it? Cracking the perfunctory ambivalence of these people, though, that's another matter."

"How so?" she asked.

"Everything is as efficient as hell, but there almost seems to be no joy in day-to-day affairs. No wonder these folks and the French have been dukin' it out for centuries, these people are total opposites. Even when the French are rude to you, they still have emotion tied to it. Here, everything is functional or it has no use. Order a meal, it comes quickly and will always be exactly what you ordered, but don't expect any small talk or smiles from your server."

"How did you end up getting posted to Berlin?" she asked, trying to hide the tired edge in her voice. "It still is a choice assignment. Usually reserved for the more experienced members of the company."

Speaking in the open, as she was, Diane had picked up the habit of referring to the agency as the company, or the firm.

"Oh, yes, the more senior members..." Emory said, as if correcting her. The younger operatives refused to believe seniority was equated with experience. While Diane found this equality to be generally true, even experience did not necessarily equate to good decision making or operational planning. The agency's history was full of the most experienced leaders planning horrendous ops that would blow up in the agency's face, so to speak.

"I was recruited with this in mind," Emory went on, as he merged in with the Berlin traffic. I majored in German Language and Literature at the University of Pennsylvania. Goethe, Hegel, Kant, Nietzsche and Hesse, I can recite them all from memory in the native tongue. At least portions thereof."

Diane was too tired to reveal that she herself was from Pennsylvania, as that was a lifetime ago, and she was sure Emory would have researched her bio before picking her up. She decided to test him instead.

"OK, give me a few lines of German from that impressive memory of yours that would pertain to our current circumstances, but in the English translation please..."

"OK. First thing that comes to mind is Nietzsche's, *'Man... cannot learn to forget, but hangs on the past: however far or fast he runs, that chain runs with him.'* Or perhaps Hesse's *'All men are prepared to accomplish the incredible if their ideals are threatened.'* How's that?"

"Impressive," Diane said, feeding the ego of the young man, who smiled, pleased, in response. "So how is the company putting your extensive knowledge of German culture to work over here?"

Emory rolled his eyes. "Busy work, actually. They have me deep diving the East German *Stasi* files. Interesting the first month or so, but all that totalitarian surveillance gets pretty boring after a few weeks. If you ever need to understand the workings of the *Stasi*, then I'm your man..."

Diane was half listening as Emory droned on, but she was now thinking of Stanley. Where was he? Had he crossed out of Poland yet? He would be cautious to do so, knowing that would be where the assets were placed immediately to contain him. Either flee like hell and get across, hoping you beat the agency from getting their teams in place, or you hunkered down for several days or weeks until you could have confidence in your crossing.

To brave a crossing on the second or third day would be hitting the border at its most fortified. Once a couple weeks had passed, Stanley would know the agents would be pulled back to broaden the search throughout Europe until a lead came in. Even then they would leave digital camera coverage behind with facial recognition software. Stanley would have to be careful, very careful. Diane knew he would be both patient and meticulously careful.

Diane was working on the assumption that he was boarded up in a safe house – and one not known to the agency – somewhere near the border. But which border?

Diane knew Stanley well enough to know Stanley hated the Russians, and no change of heart could possibly reach into the bleached crevices of his inner being where this animosity festered.

"Diane," Emory broke what had become an awkward silence, "We did get an answer to your inquiry from the researchers back home. They first said you had the spelling turned sideways..."

"What are you talking about?" Diane asked, coming back to Emory.

"You asked them to research who was *'Sarenka'* and could he/she have been in the states, specifically Baltimore, in 2008. Could they have been at any ceremonies at the National Katyń Memorial in East Baltimore?" he reminded her. "You apparently asked before you left the states."

Diane recalled the request that she had made less than twenty-four hours before. But with all that had transpired in that time, it seemed like weeks ago.

Emory continued, "They said you had the name wrong. Drop the 'a' and replace it with a 'y'. *'Syrenka'* is the sword and shield wielding mermaid that lore says protects Warsaw from invaders. A statue of her sits in the main square of the old town section of Warsaw."

This was exactly what Google had told her.

Emory went on, "Turns out our friends Stanley and Langston Powell were in that very square late Friday afternoon. Got picked up on surveillance video."

"I was sure it was *Sarenka* with an *'a',*" Diane said, checking her notebook, pulling it from the pocket of her Burberry trenchcoat. *Syrenka*, as his agent in *Solidarity*, made no sense at all, and besides Trellis said he went quiet and was not heard from again during the Russian purge at the time of Aldrich Ames and Robert Hanssen's betrayals in the mid 1990's.

"They pointed out," young Emory continued, "that Stanley's agent planted in *Solidarity* during the late eighties was also code named *'Syrenka'*."

"Yes, I was briefed at Langley on that much. No, my notes say very clearly '*Sarenka* ', with an 'a'. No way I mistook a script 'y' for an 'a'. No way."

"Turns out you made a very *deer* mistake," young Emory quipped, amused at himself for pointing out something not obvious to the agency's famous huntress.

"You want to let me in on the joke?" Diane was beginning to get perturbed.

"I will let Sophie tell you, as it turns out to be her joke," Emory teased.

"Who is Sophie?" asked Diane perplexed.

Emory glanced at her, taking his eyes from the road momentarily. "Our Polish cultural specialist. Added to the team to assist in Polish heritage and customs, but also provide language skills as needed."

He paused, and then continued.

"By the way, did you see your man Stanley contacted *The Westminster Conservatoire* to get his story out while you were in transit? Complete with internal Global Defense Analytics documents, including electronic transfer receipts of the cash. The amount of cash was massive. All the documents were transmitted electronically to the paper's editor by your man Stanley."

"More likely sent by his accomplice Jean Paul on Stanley's behalf. No doubt he routed the material through several burning-bridge servers to attempt to hide his tracks," Diane was recalling from the briefings at Langley.

"Exactly! How did you know?" Emory asked, amazed.

"Fits their MO," said Diane simply. "That is how the team tracked back where the original emails were sent from. But only from Jean Paul to Stanley. Those from Stanley to Jean Paul never had the burned servers behind them. Apparently, Stanley himself doesn't possess that technological insight."

"Well, the team is on it. They say they should have it traced back soon. We should know where Stanley, or at least Jean Paul was when they were sent."

Diane watched as the urban center of Berlin blurred by in the November gray white haze. The snow was picking up in its intensity. There was an incredible amount of building ongoing here. It grew more dense as they approached the city center. Cranes on top of unfinished high rise structures everywhere she looked. The town had changed dramatically since her last visit many years ago. Then the former section that had been East Berlin still showed pockets, if not large swaths of unused buildings, reminders of its communist era neglect.

Diane then thought again about the transmission to the *Conservatoire*. As good as the agency is, they will track it back to the original send location, and we 'll get a bearing on where Jean Paul was and a time stamp of when he was there. It could represent a stake in the interwoven trails of Jean Paul and Stanley.

Except Diane knew it could also be a planted message in an unsuspecting computer or server anywhere in the world that was triggered either by a message from Jean Paul, or was based on a countdown clock. It well could be the latter, an e-mail bomb that was set to go off by Jean Paul at a predestined time unless he sent an abort code.

In any case, Diane decided to let the IT Tech Professionals at the agency work through this. He doubted that Jean Paul had any tricks they would not have seen before.

Emory executed a turn, and continued. "This is damaging as hell to the Global Defense Analytics Execs, as well as to the agency itself. It's being picked up by all the major cable news firms. I heard Deputy Director Trellis was pissed."

"Trellis is always pissed," Diane said, knowing only too well.

"We are here. Welcome to *'The Blind'*," Emory said, pulling off the snowy Berlin Avenue into an inner courtyard as two electronic gate doors closed crisply behind them. The courtyard was secluded, but plain, and Diane followed Emory from the car into a very secure doorway into the classified operations center.

The Blind was an official annex of the US Embassy in Berlin, itself only a stone's throw from the Brandenburg Gate. Diane realized it was being used for the sanctity of its diplomatic immunity. It was around the corner, and to the casual observer would appear unattached to the embassy, but it was, in fact, an official American Embassy outpost. Originally devised as a garage for the Embassy fleet of cars, it had been converted into *The Blind* - an electronic ops center, complete with state of the art shielding to prevent outside electronic monitoring.

Meeting them inside was an old face Diane immediately recognized. As Trellis had told her, she was greeted by the smile of Dominic Reeves, an old hand in the Operations Directorate, often known by its more sinister moniker of "Covert Actions". Dom had grown up in this world of shadows, and was comfortable from Berlin to Buenos Aires, Munich to Macao, Warsaw to Washington.

"Great to see you, Diane," he said, offering a professional handshake in lieu of an awkward hug. "I took charge until you got here, but clearly it's your op now. We are all here for you to command and control. I trust Emory took good care of you."

"That he did, Dom," she said, with a quick smiling glance to Emory.

"We were hoping to see you yesterday, but understand that Trellis called you back to Langley for briefings. You've got a few miles on you at this point, so I thought we'd give you a little time to freshen up. We also have quarters for you unless you feel you need a hotel."

"No, I prefer to be here round the clock" Diane said, scanning the facility for someone who must be Sophie. "If we get to the point where I need outside quarters, it means we've been here way too long and the trail is ice cold."

She turned to face Dom, looking squarely in his eyes. "So, who is Sophie?"

Dom raised his arm, not unlike a *maître d'* in a restaurant. "*Zofia*, up!" he snapped, demonstrating the indifference with which he commanded this team.

From behind a series of electronic display screens in an otherwise dark corner, emerged a very beautiful blond of not more than thirty years old, and more likely in her late twenties. She stood in front of Diane, slender, lovely, in her gray turtleneck sweater. Sophie's face was as unadorned as her dress, her expression open and receptive, wearing only a hint of smile in the corners of her cheeks.

Sophie's golden locks appeared to Diane to be her only vanity. Well brushed, framing the serenity of her face, they cascaded down in straight lengths that spoke to her personality. She was shy and lovely, but she hid her own beauty in a shroud of modesty.

"Yes, I am Sophie," she said with a trace of accent that was anything but German. She anglicized it from its close, native pronunciation of Zofia.

Dom smiled, pulling Sophie forward through the narrow room now cramped with electronics and their displays. "Soph here is our resident Polish Princess. Brought her in to help with Polish Culture and firsthand knowledge of the country. But don't fret, Diane, she is fully vetted, and clean as a vestal virgin."

Sophie blushed hard. Diane shot Dom a disapproving glare. Catching it, Dom reminded himself this was not the usual gang of boys he was accustomed to being holed up with.

"You need some new analogies, Dom," Diane said, walking past him and taking both of Sophie's hands in her own, "So, Sophie, or do you prefer *Zofia* – no, Sophie is fine – OK, Sophie, so what is the joke about '*Sarenka*' and '*Syrenka*'?"

Sophie's face eased up with the question that she clearly knew the answer to. Clearly, she was not used to being the center of attention. She smiled meekly and said through what Diane now interpreted as a Polish accent, "You asked about '*Sarenka*', and the researchers assumed you were wrong, and gave you information on '*Syrenka*', the mermaid protector of Warsaw."

Diane noticed she pronounced Warsaw as '*Varsav*', pronouncing the W's as V's. "Go on, dear," Diane said in an attempt to ease her.

"Yes, exactly," Sophie said as young Emery cackled, again having a private joke.

Diane did not understand what had just occurred, and her disapproving look towards Emory stopped him in his tracks.

"He is laughing at you calling me '*dear*'," Sophie explained. "He thinks it is funny, because it sounds like '*deer*'. And so he laughs."

"I still don't understand," said Diane, struggling to make the overall context.

Sophie saw the confusion in Diane's eyes. She explained "A *sarenka* is a deer. A young deer. A fawn. It appears *Pan* Wisniewski used this polish word as an affection. *Pan* Wisniewski was affectionate to the one he called '*Sarenka*'."

Diane recalled the term "*Pan*" in Polish was like "*Herr*" in German or "Mister" in English. "*Pani*" was the feminine form.

"Now, why didn't the researchers pick up on that. They are so quick to connect the dots even when they haven't seen the overall picture. Thank you, Sophie, that is very insightful information."

Diane thought to herself, "It appears Stanley had an affectionate friend who paints and came to visit him in 2008? Or did his *Sarenka* paint the Monument from a picture and have it delivered to Stanley."

Either way, Diane had a gut feel that *Sarenka* was an important key in understanding what was driving Stanley.

"Sophie, dear, would you please contact Research and ask them to go through Stanley's contacts and find anyone who showed a talent for, or had a hobby of painting. Tell them this is top priority. It might be a shot in the dark, but worth pursuing. And thank you, I think you and I will be very good friends here in *The Blind* together."

Dominic Reeves escorted Diane to a conference room and brought her up to speed on every action their team had gone through since the news of Langston Powell's murder broke Friday night. Not a trace of Stanley. A couple of false sightings on the eastern Polish border and another further east in Lithuania. None proved out to be Stanley, just tall, graying old Slavs.

"Except for his height, Stanley is so typical of a seventy-year-old pole, or other Slav national, that these false sightings are going to be pouring in." Dom complained.

"That is precisely what Stanley will play against us. He will wait until we are tired of chasing false leads before he moves. He is betting we will tire and lower our guard." Diane spoke slowly, to make an effect upon her new team.

"So how exactly do you propose we go about finding Stanley?" Dom asked.

"We don't. It would be a waste of time. Stanley is too well versed in laying low. He is too smart to have anything remotely electronic on him that could be tracked. No way will he carry a cell phone. He likely discarded his clothes and changed into 'safe' clothes by now as well."

"My bet is he already is out of Poland," said Dom. "Maybe left Europe…"

"Could be," said Diane as she went through the briefing file update awaiting her arrival. "Leaving Europe would mean trains or aircraft, which would mean cameras in the stations, and ID checks that could be trapping points. Stanley is too much a pro to make a mad dash and leave a hot trail. He won't be using plastic - too traceable. No cell phones, not even throw-away burners. Likely had a go-bag before he took Powell out. Filled with enough cash to be on the run for several weeks and a number of passports and ID's from various countries. But, if we believe the timelines and he only had a few days to prepare for this attack, then chances are he is using ID's and Passports from his professional stash. Couldn't have had any made that fast that were any good."

"He blends in perfectly. He carries no plastic or electronics. So how the hell do we track him?" asked Dom with a look that said you just told me everything I already knew and nothing I didn't...

"Again, we don't. Since he has to have someone handling him, and I believe that person is the cryptic 'Jean Paul', we focus on finding Jean Paul."

"But we don't know who 'Jean Paul' is, do we? That appears to be a code name that Stanley came up with for his contact, whoever he is."

Dom was tired from two days with little to no rest setting up this *operation to find Stanley, only to have* "her highness, The Huntress" from another Directorate tell him they weren't even looking for Stanley himself.

"Dom, look, everything your team has done is dead right. We will catch Stanley if he slips up, I just know Stanley very well and he will likely not slip up. But Jean Paul is another story. I am betting he is an agent Stanley used to run who is now helping him out."

"That's one mighty huge set of assumptions you are throwing around," Dom said.

"Come on, Dom," Diane replied. "First, we need a search strategy. Once we have that, and we do, then the rest is all legwork. This is not going to be over very fast unless we are very lucky, or Stanley is very sloppy. And as I said, he is not sloppy."

"For all we know," Dom still wasn't buying in, "Your old buddy Stanley crawled off to some remote corner of Poland and finished himself off. We could be looking for a tall gray corpse at this point".

"I don't think so," Diane responded. "He is very strict Roman Catholic, wouldn't take his own life."

"He wasn't too Roman Catholic to murder someone. That would keep St. Peter from punching his card, won't it?" Dom's eyes screwed up, as if saying "This is making no sense at all."

"Dom, it is hard to explain, but Stanley is not thinking straight at this point."

"OK, *there's the expertise* they brought you in for," Dom said sarcastically.

"Let me finish, will you," Diane did not have a great deal of sleep and was starting to feel it. "Stanley was not after Langston Powell as a final objective. If he was he would not have put up that elaborate information release to *The Conservatoire* today. If he wanted to take out Langston and himself also, they would both have been laying in that square at the base of the Insurrection Monument. He has bigger fish to fry, but he is running out of time. I think he is somehow after the Daedalus Destroyer Drone program. He is justifying his actions as necessary to protect humanity overall. He expects to be taken out by us, which is exactly why we must take him alive. We take him for questioning so we can find out what is driving all of this."

"Saint Pete still ain't letting Stanley through them pearly gates. One thing is for sure, he scared the shit out of every Aerospace Exec in Europe, we're tracking them and they are all high-tailing it for either London or the East Coast of the US. Can't get back stateside fast enough." Dom had an evil grin across his meaty face.

"The key is knowing the relationship between Jean Paul, *Syrenka*, and *Sarenka*," Diane said, half to convince herself.

Dom continued his counter arguments.

"Three code names without so much as a face to put against any of them. I had the researchers check on your Sarenka lead, after Sophie came through for us. Nothing, anywhere in the files, or in the agency database."

Now for the significant storyline, Dom thought. "As far as Stanley's agent *Syrenka*, it turns out *he* went cold about the same time as the Aldrich Ames and Robert Hanssen investigations. Turns out a lot of our agents went missing during that time frame. Sold out by these bastards. Rolled up by the Soviets and Russians, and neatly disposed of. *Syrenka* could now be just a pile of bones in a Russian forest by now. And the code name Jean Paul is just a moniker that first popped out of the woodwork last week."

Diane was catching up on the news that the codename *Sarenka* was unknown to the agency database. Why would Stanley have two agents with similar code names? Not typical for field work, too easy to confuse. That is why code names were so random, so there were no relationships or meanings to misconstrue. Jean Paul was different. This was a cold agent that Stanley called only as needed. And he had apparently not needed him until recently, at least as far as the agency knew.

Diane looked at Dom as if she had just now had the insight that clarified the situation.

"That's why Stanley and Jean Paul must have worked together in the past. They knew their tradecraft from long before this opportunity popped up. Yes, it was crude codes and they did little to conceal it, but they knew how to reach each other, and how to speak to each other from the get go. Stanley did not care if the NSA was tracking all this, because he thought, no, he knew, that the Powell action was going to be completed before anybody put the pieces together."

Diane finished her argument with her gut feel. "I don't believe *Syrenka* was rolled up by the Soviets in the 90's. In fact, I believe that Stanley helped *Syrenka* go cold when the Soviets were getting close to him. Stanley salted *Syrenka* away with a new identity, likely outside of Eastern Europe. Then, when the opportunity to take action against Langston Powell came up, he contacted *Syrenka* through a prearranged code name – Jean Paul. My hunch is Jean Paul is *Syrenka*."

Dom was on the offensive now, "Well, even if he is, we still only have code names, and no one to trace. You said we had a search strategy, but I don't see what it is."

"You don't?" asked Diane simply.

"It may be clear to you, but it sure ain't to the rest of us..." Dom shot back.

Diane pressed forward. "Look, Dom, Jean Paul and Stanley are tied together – they have to be if Stanley expects to get very far. His survival over the long run is tied to intermittent contact with Jean Paul. Stanley is too smart to travel with him, for it will be much easier for us to track two men together than two individual travelers. If one assumes that Jean Paul must be out in front of Stanley, picking out safe routes, recommending shelters, replenishing his cash. In order to do this, they must be communicating somehow. Once we figure that out, we track Jean Paul, and he leads us to Stanley. I think Stanley saved his agent *Syrenka* from the Russians at the time when Robert Hanssen was betraying our spies overseas. And now *Syrenka*, aka Jean Paul, is repaying the debt."

"And since I was on the teams that brought down both Aldrich Ames and Robert Hanssen, I already have the agency researchers cross-checking known operatives that popped up on the Russians lists from these two, to anyone operating in Poland at the time."

Dom had wondered how long before *Miss Almighty* mentioned her two masterpieces – taking down Aldrich Ames and Robert

Hanssen. These were the two biggest sources the Soviets and Russians ever had in the CIA and FBI, respectively.

Diane had been on both teams, earned her bones, twice. Now, Dom, despite having over 37 years at the CIA, was taking direction and gut hunches from a woman who the agency had several years ago shipped off to babysit the Brits. Dom was sure he was not out of her league, and had hoped to bag Stanley before she got there, just to prove it. But now, she was here to claim the eventual triumph. There was a part of Dom that hoped that she failed.

"Oh, you got an *IMMEDIATE* cable from Trellis, I almost forgot," he said.

"Where is it?" She knew *cable* was dinosaur speak for electronic secure message.

"It says Trellis is sending his man Carlyle over to join our little team," he said, not giving her the pleasure of seeing it herself.

"Who the hell is Carlyle?" Diane asked.

"If you were in Covert Actions very long you'd know of him. Trellis' inside guy, Special Ops all the way. They say he can shoot the fleas off a rat at 100 yards." He watched her face as she blanked out. Dom added "Without hurtin' the rat. You're going to love this guy."

Diane was sure, as Dom was, that Trellis wanted this finished. Permanently. So why was it that Trellis appeared not to really want Stanley brought in for questioning?

In fact, Trellis didn't want Stanley answering anyone's questions. Anywhere.

Diane suddenly realized how tough this assignment would be.

Diane secluded herself in her makeshift quarters Dom had set up for her in *The Blind*. Her mind was racing, fatigued by her travels, stressed by Dom's insubordinate attitude. She decided to get some quick rest.

She stretched out on the cot in her corner of the darkened facility, shielded from the glare of the electronic screens by a heavy, dark curtain of wool cloth. Diane laid on her back, shutting her eyes, with directions for her to be awakened in twenty minutes. Last thing she could afford now was dropping into deep sleep.

She thought of Stanley. Were his surroundings any more comfortable at the present time? Where was he holed up? Did he sense that Trellis had sent her after him? Would he find this troubling? Would he respect her skills in tracking both Jean Paul and himself?

As she drifted off to sleep, she saw Stanley's face back in '85 in the Friday night darkness of a preselected bar in Georgetown. He was a half dozen stools away, locked in a mock camaraderie with the surprisingly handsome Bryce Weldon. His back had been to Diane when she first entered the bar, but Bryce had repositioned himself to the other side of Stanley so he could check her out. First in the reflection of the mirror, later in more direct looks down the bar. She played it cool, at first averting Bryce's prying glances. Only later allowing herself to return the sensual stare for a fraction of a second.

Finally, Stanley gave the rearranged signal, pushing back his hair with his left hand, palm outstretched. It was a very unusual movement for a man, but somehow Stanley made it look casual. None the less, it was an unmistakable signal.

Stanley drew close to Bryce, close enough to smell the Glenn Levitt on his breath. "I think our young friend over there has been eying you up, Bryce. How the hell do you do it? I don't understand," Stanley said, slapping him on his back.

Bryce just smiled, and raised his glass at Diane.

Diane decided to set the hook. She blushed and turned away, minding herself in the mirror behind the big oaken bar.

Bryce was slightly slurring, as Stanley and he had been here for the better of three hours, drinking constantly throughout. "Well, she sure as hell isn't waiting for a boyfriend. She's been down there for forty minutes sucking down Greyhounds. She's trolling my friend. And she's about to land the trophy catch. Watch and learn."

Bryce pushed past him, but as he began Stanley murmured he had too much and had to go.

"All the better, my friend. I have the tab. Take care," he said, never looking back. He pressed in on Diane as Stanley departed. Just as she and Stanley had prearranged.

Bryce stood before her now. He smiled the infectious smile of an old friend. His white shirt, even this late in the bar was immaculate, starched free of any remnants of his day's enterprise. The French cuffs set off by the gold links bearing his monogram BMW – Bryce Marcellus Weldon.

"My friend who just abandoned me up there swore you were smiling at me. I can only hope he was right…" The smile opened even broader than what Diane thought was possible.

"I smile a lot," she said, easing up her demeanor somewhat so as not to drive him away, but still distant enough to keep him interested in the prey.

"Well, you should," Bryce said, now in mock seriousness. "It is a very pretty smile."

Diane paused, and pretended coyly to enjoy the flattering comment.

"Now that your friend is gone, why don't you bring your bottle down to my end of the bar," she said, hooking her head in invitation.

He did, and they drank. And they talked and they drank. Unbeknownst to Bryce Weldon, the bartender was a wired FBI agent, who was mixing Diane's drink from a very special bottle of Vodka that contained nothing more than tonic water.

The joint FBI/CIA team had for weeks now been using wired agents behind preselected bars to get something on Bryce Weldon. Yet, despite his excessive drinking, Weldon never gave up so much as an industry trade secret. Every time Stanley would steer him away from his stories of sexual conquests among the many female employees of Marshall Analytics, to discussions regarding Dr. Ben Palmer, Weldon would pull back. As if to say, "nope, won't go there."

The team decided it was time to take a more aggressive approach. They decided to use Diane as bait to get Bryce to take her to his home, where she could look for evidence of classified materials from Marshall Analytics.

They had been drinking together for an hour and a half. Diane, protected by the impotent "vodka", noticed Bryce's speech had become heavily slurred. She leaned into him closely, affecting her own slur, pressing up against his chest for effect. She whispered into his ear in an earthy whisper, "Mr. Weldon, I have to go back to California tomorrow."

"No, you don't, you can stay with me," Bryce slurred.

She nibbled at his earlobe. "I don't think my husband in California would like that very much. Now, it is getting late. Why don't you take me home and show me that Georgetown brownstone you've been bragging about, unless you were just bragging..."

She giggled into his ear, as she removed his hand that slipped onto her breast.

"Not, now. Not here. Take me home and we'll both do some exploring," she teased. "And tomorrow you can drive me back to the hotel in your Porsche," she breathed heavily into ear, "Again, unless you were just bragging..."

"Young lady, I assure you, it ain't bragging if you got the goods." He reached for his wallet, exposing a wad of bills that would have impressed J. Paul Getty, slammed three hundred dollar bills on the counter. "And I got the goods..."

"Well let's go check them goods out…" Diane laughed as she put her arm behind Weldon's back to help him upright. She nodded ever imperceptibly to the bartender, and walked out onto the Friday night mayhem of the Georgetown scene, interlocked and supporting Bryce. They laughed as they stumbled the several blocks to his rented row house.

He unlocked the front door, pushing it wide before her.

"I expect to be properly invited in," she said.

"What you gonna do, have your California husband come after me?"

"Come on now, I want a proper invitation," she demanded.

"OK, then do please enter my humble abode, young lady." She knew the listening devise planted by the FBI outside his door would record the invitation. She was now officially an invited guest of his.

It was clear to Diane that Bryce had long forgotten her cover name of Catherine. As of at least an hour ago, he kept calling her "Young Lady", "Pretty Lady" and the like.

Once inside, he was all over her, but she was able to fend him off. "Not down here, I wanna see your place, show me around, and let's settle down with some drinks in the bedroom."

Bryce was on the verge of passing out, and clearly was fighting the elevated alcohol in his virile body to stay awake for his anticipated reward.

After grabbing a bottle of single malt scotch, Diane helped him up into the bedroom where she laid him down on the bed. She laid down next to him stroking his face as he hurriedly undressed her. She allowed him only so much discovery, just enough to entice him, when she got up to freshen up. He protested, but she insisted.

"Take a quick nap, baby doll, and I will wake you as soon as I am ready," she said suggestively.

She went into the bathroom, turning on the shower. She tracked her watch and counted off ten minutes, listening for movement from the bedroom. Then she heard the muffled snore coming from Bryce. He had given into the drowsing effects of the massive quantity of alcohol he had consumed that night, first with Stanley, and more recently with her.

She came out fully clothed and began her search. She located his briefcase that he had dropped off in the front room before walking down to the bar to meet Stanley. Surprisingly it was unlocked, and yielded a treasure trove of classified documents illicitly taken from Marshall Analytics. A quick walk through the house resulted in nothing save one locked door.

She listened to Bryce's breathing in the bedroom just down the hall as she worked the lock on the door with the training she had just received from the agency. It would have been seconds for a more seasoned agent, but Diane was able to get it open after a couple minutes of attempts and reattempts.

When she opened the door, what she saw made her skin tingle. The room had been converted into a photographic lab of sorts, with a table banked with high intensity lights for conducting the photographic duplication of the classified documents downstairs, as well as many others before them, she surmised. The table was shrouded with a heavy black felt, and the windows in the room were covered in blackout curtains.

Next to the table were a list of documents that was somewhat of a shopping list. It was handwritten, and Diane could only hope it was the handwriting of Dr. Palmer himself. Then she spotted the lock box, which took surprising little effort to pick for her, yielding a wealth of cash. A mix of twenties and fifties and hundreds. Diane estimated it must have contained thirty thousand dollars in cash. My God, how long have they been doing this she thought?

She retraced her steps downstairs, re-locking the photo lab door.

Once in the front room of the row house, she took her red handbag and placed it in the front window sill. She now had five minutes. The signal was set.

As they had agreed beforehand, no sense raiding a pristine town home, only giving Weldon the knowledge he was being watched. Better to send her in and confirm it was worth tipping their hand.

She quickly worked her way up the steps, removed her clothes except for her matching red bra and panties, and laid down next to Bryce Weldon. She rolled onto him, jarring him from his sleep. He smiled at her, slipping his right hand behind her waist as his left hand probed the soft skin behind her neck, pulling her face close to his. He kissed her passionately as he seemed to be coming into full consciousness.

Then they heard the crash of the front door being driven in below them. Footsteps and shouts of "FBI – Federal Agents, you are all under arrest."

Instantly, Bryce bounded over Diane to the hall, where he instinctively went to the locked door of the converted photo-lab. By the time Weldon reached it, the federal agents were on top of him, pistols drawn, directing him to lay flat on the floor as they handcuffed his wrists behind him.

Diane underwent the same ritual with the female federal agents, for Bryce's effect only, as all the raiding team agents knew she was an undercover member of the joint CIA/FBI task force. Both Diane and Weldon were wrapped in cape like coverings marked FBI. They were not given the option to dress, ostensibly to keep Bryce Weldon from destroying any evidence in the row home.

Diane did her best to act hysterical in front of Bryce. If he did not already suspect her role in this, it might help his interrogation. She knew he had a long night ahead of him, as the FBI convinced him to cooperate in turning over Dr. Palmer.

They would talk him out of his right for legal representation, stating that if he did so he would have the maximum sentence thrown at him. Diane actually felt sorry for him momentarily, before she realized the mountain of cash this creep had sold out his country for.

As they walked her down to the first floor and outside to the waiting escort cars, she was glad to see the first agent in had removed her handbag from the signal location on the front window sill.

Diane recalled from this scene in 1985, how the classified documents, the illegal reprographic center, and the thousands in illicit cash were to be used over that weekend to turn Bryce Weldon against his corruptor, Dr. Bennet Palmer.

Most damaging of all was the hand-written shopping list of classified documents. It partially matched the documents in the briefcase that were taken from Global Defense Analytics. Most importantly, it was later analyzed and found to be the handwriting of the very same Dr. Bennet Palmer.

Diane was suddenly wide awake back in the present – in Berlin. The call came from outside the curtains in *The Blind* to raise her. It was time to stop the haunting memories of Stanley from the past, and return to hunting him in the present.

Chapter Six
The River

STANLEY WALKED IN a slow strolling manner through Wroclawska Street, its newly built homes lining the rejuvenated riverside promenade of Zgorzelec, Poland. The cold November wind nipped at him through his overcoat, as if teasing him to play like an impatient dog at his master's side. His right hand still trembled, even now after three days since he had arrived here. The skin on his jaw was tight in the frigid air, as he had shaved off his trim beard to assist him in his modest attempt to hide in plain sight. He strolled the avenue hoping to reconnoiter the wide footbridge, *the Altstadtbrücke,* that crossed the Neisse River, beyond which lay the faithfully reconstructed old world town of Görlitz, Germany.

There was no border security here, and Stanley was free to walk across the footbridge, out of Poland, and into Germany, with no official query by German or even Polish authorities. But it was the spotter that Stanley feared, in his Görlitz photographer's nest just across the bridge. Stanley was now walking behind the buildings that shielded him from the river and thus the spotter's lens. The last building he was now approaching formed the base of the rebuilt medieval tower on the Polish side of the bridge. Stanley dared not walk beyond the buildings walls, exposing himself in the plaza from which the footbridge leapt on its majestic arc across the river. Stanley knew that even only a singular digital image captured by the spotter's lens could instantly be transmitted across Europe, and even to Langley itself. If it did not result in his immediate capture, then surely it would bring forth an army of trackers that would converge on Stanley, who despite all his deceptive skills, would fall. There was so much yet to be done, he could not chance even peering around the corner of the edifice that shielded him. Stanley pulled the woolen scarf tightly around his neck, cinching it up to his exposed face, to conceal from all the world not only his identity, but the guilt he was trying so desperately to deny.

For the first time in his life, Stanley indeed trembled like the stalk in the harvest wind that awaits the scythe.

Stanley now stood just behind the building adjacent to the bridge, raising his eyes to view the replica medieval tower. It rose some five or six stories above the river. In the medieval style it was square, with no windows save those on the top floor. Even these resembled portholes more than the windows of today. In the middle ages, they would have been deadly vantage points for the archers, protecting the town from a hostile river crossing. For today's precision weaponry, they would prove deadlier yet, to anyone trying to flee across into Germany. Stanley could only see one of the tower's four square faces, that which looked back into Poland. He knew that from the upper floor, each of the other three faces would provide a sniper excellent lines of sight into Görlitz, laying tantalizingly just beyond. Stanley knew so little of this building, neither of the tower nor the restaurant at its base, as it was not here during his time in Zgorzelec. He only knew its strategic importance, above the footbridge, especially opposite the spotter's position.

Stanley had assessed that while the windows from the upper level of the tower would afford a fantastic vantage point for one of the agency's snipers, his field of view would be limited to the three quarters of the footbridge approaching Görlitz. The windows were too restrictive to allow one to shoot down onto the Polish river bank. Stanley had never laid eyes on the riverfront facade of the tower, nor of the side that paralled the bridge's span. These were both blocked from his vantage point in the villa. Yet he assumed these were identical to the two faces he could see of the squarish tower. Each face had only four porthole-like windows on the top floor. From Stanley's reconnaissance, there were no balconies or other accessible openings that would allow the sniper a free sweep in a downward angle. His field of view would effectively only allow his picking up a pedestrian as he would reach the last three quarters of the footbridge. But from that height the reach of his bullet would extend well into the beautifully arcaded main avenue climbing the river bank of Görlitz.

Görlitz is a painstakingly rebuilt reflection of its former medieval majesty. After surviving both World War II and the Cold War era, it was restored, painted in the many muted but colorful hues whose charm alone would draw the tourists. Burgher houses and stone-arcaded shops lined the avenues, giving a display of vibrancy and wealth. It was the old world as it was meant to be remembered. It was a movie setting, and with the twin majestic spires of the Church of Saints Peter and Paul, rose in triumph above the Neisse river.

As Görlitz rose above the Neisse, it cast a darker, dingier shadow onto the opposing bank. Zgorzelec was not majestic, but painted in the dusty hues of the communist functionality. It was a remnant of communist Poland – harsh, unwelcoming, in its concrete solidity. It craved to become the Polish equivalent of the scenic Görlitz. Even though some architectural improvements had been made along the river promenade since the footbridge was rebuilt, Zgorzelec stood as a homely child does in the presence of her own elegant sister.

"Remember your mission," Stanley said to himself. He had come to confirm what he had observed from his villa window over the past several days. As the sun had only begun to set each day, Stanley had witnessed a man on the light blue and white bicycle from which a miniature Greek flag flapped just aft of the rider's seat. Stanley had marked him departing and returning twice so far, crossing the wide footbridge upon his bicycle, drawing the ire and disdain of the pedestrians he callously weaved through. Stanley had marked him as a food worker, maybe a dish washer, possibly a sous chef, at one of the many tourist hotels or Greek restaurants across the river in Görlitz. In his imagination, Stanley had named the man "Spiro".

Ever since Hollywood had "discovered" the fairy tale qualities of Görlitz, the tourist trade boomed. That meant jobs. That meant Spiro crossed the Neisse every day. Twice. He was becoming an expected traveler by the watchers. And this expectation would provide Stanley the opportunity to cross undetected.

Zgorzelec was a Polish town that had an extensive Greek minority, much of which were unemployed. They had come during the Greek civil war, when the many Greek communists were expelled or emigrated. Here in this western Polish town they found a tolerant, then communist, culture. Jobs were scarce here, but Stanley believed that Görlitz was Spiro's answer to the boredom of unemployment. The excitement of major motion pictures being filmed there, or the anticipation of those that were to come, could be pretty heady stuff for the late thirty something that Stanley had pegged Spiro to be.

Stanley looked at his watch. He had timed his walk down the hill from the villa to coincide with the time he had seen Spiro crossing over the bridge the past several days. As he had stood avoiding the edge of the building nearest the bridge, coming down the hill behind Stanley was Spiro himself. Right on schedule. Stanley heard the razor whip of his spokes before he actually saw him. Stanley began to turn to look back on the sidewalk path he had just travelled. Spiro, who had just negotiated the same path but in the middle of Wroclawska street, leaned into the turn as he negotiated the corner to which Stanley stood closest. Stanley smiled to himself as the Greek sped out onto the plaza, and then without Stanley looking around the corner, onto the footbridge itself. The footbridge was wide enough for a small car to readily negotiate, were it not for the barricade posts that fenced both entrances to the bridge. These did not deter Spiro, whose daily need for the transit outweighed the leisure of the *Altstadtbrücke's* pedestrians. Spiro surely had been crossing this span daily for years now. Stanley was even more sure of the fact that Spiro would be contemptuous of the tourists that provided the very job he sped to so callously.

The sun was now going down. With dusk settling in, Stanley shuffled into the building and down a narrow flight of stairs to a small restaurant. Its name *Piwnica Staromiejska* meant "Old Town Cellar". The restaurant was in the very base of the tower, and in warmer months its riverfront walk served as a delightful patio full of small cafe tables. Its western facade was now sealed in glass windows that gazed upon the beauty of the opposite river bank.

Stanley approached the windows cautiously, realizing these were beneath the *Altstadtbrücke* footbridge. The angle from below the bridge both shielded him from the spotter on the other bank, and afforded him a magnificent view of embankments of Görlitz. which appeared to Stanley, as an animal at dusk, cautiously kneeling along and sipping from the banks of the *Neisse*. It pleased him to notice that even along its sloping concrete ramps, there grew wild river grasses from the water's edge.

Feeling secure among the sanctuary of the bridge's vaulting

understructure, Stanley ordered a warm tea and a bowl of *Żurek*, a traditional sour soup made from fermented rye wheat. When the tea came, Stanley was careful to keep his cup from being too near the glass window, so as to keep its steam from clouding the pane, obstructing his vantage point.

The tea warmed him instantly. It was served to him by the young, dark haired woman running the shop. It was served in a beautiful saucer and cup from Bolesławiec, the world-famous pottery and earthenware producing town nearby. Stanley sipped at the tea heartily, as it was the first warm drink he had had since coming to Zgorzelec. The rest of the time he had lived off the cold provisions Jean Paul had stored up for him in the villa at the top of the hill.

Moments later, the familiar sour taste of the *Żurek* soup crept through him, producing in him the simplest of comforts of life - nutrition, warmth, and belonging. Stanley savored the flavors of the food, the styling of the surroundings, the native language that fell upon his ears like the drops of a cool spring shower. However, despite the illusion, he knew it was not the fresh growing season of spring, but the already barren late days of fall in which he found himself. Soon the winter would be upon him in its full fury, its biting wind chasing him to his ultimate destiny.

Stanley scanned the river as it flowed hypnotically beneath the bridge. But while the tea and *Żurek* warmed his body, it was the vibrant blue and pastel green pattern of the pottery, whose design was taken from the peacock's feathers, that made Stanley recall another fateful tea taken with his mother on a warm fall Saturday afternoon of 1985.

Stanley was 40 then, ten years after the loss of his father, some six months after being forced to leave his life's only love, Agnieszka, in Warsaw. On that Saturday, he met with his mother, only hours after having just the night before made the critical arrest of Bryce Weldon. Stanley hoped to soon be returned to his assignment in Poland. Soon enough he hoped to be reunited with Agnieszka, for each passing month extended a growing chasm he feared he would never be able to cross again.

Stanley, on this victorious Saturday, took a rare day trip away from his hotel accommodations in Washington DC to drive up to Baltimore and spend the afternoon with his aging mother in the Fells Point home they both had loved so dearly. His mother, his loving *matka*, had been through so much in her life, as his father had explained to Stanley on his deathbed. It was Stanley's pleasure to spend the day with his mother, and while she would never know the details of his efforts in Georgetown the night before, he was sure she would see the satisfied beam in his eyes. This would comfort her, he thought.

They sat in the warm sunshine in the small brick yard, amidst the garden his mother had created almost as soon as she and Stanley's father arrived in America. His mother, her face rounded by the years, her hair stressed white by strain of her memories, sat amongst the explosion of color in the pots of her garden. This was her place of solace, the calm center of her aging life. They had been talking of Poland, sipping their tea at the small cast iron outdoor table she so loved. They were using the very tea set that Stanley had brought back for her on his return, hand-picked by himself at the pottery stalls of Bolesławiec. The beauty of the green and blue hues of the peacock pattern rested between them on the jet-black cast iron table.

They had been speaking of Warsaw, with Stanley recounting the details of the rebuilding of its Old Town that even at this time was ongoing. His mother seemed to visualize her home country in every inflection of his words, all in the lovely Polish language that passed between them effortlessly and naturally.

"*Matka*, I realize sitting here now that you never told me of how you came to live here in Baltimore after the war." Her face seemed to instantly blush, and Stanley had no desire to have her recount the captivity she and his father endured at the hands of the SS officer Keller in the area of the 1944 Insurgency, near the Old Town in Warsaw.

Stanley knew from his father's deathbed ten years prior that his mother had been repeatedly raped by Keller until his father was able to kill the SS Officer with Keller's own Luger. Stanley had no intent in dragging his mother back to that devastating nightmare that surely was the horror of her life.

Stanley, in their discussions over the warm autumn scent, had realized that he never had understood how his parents had arrived in Baltimore. It seemed odd to him, 40 years old at this point, that this void in his knowledge about his mother and father had never struck his curiosity before. His mother looked tenderly upon his face and seemed to recognize an opening for a discussion she had desperately wanted to have with Stanley for some time.

"My son," she began softly, "I know your father tried to tell you so much before our Lord took him. It pained him so, to tell you so much of this, but it also was such a relief to him."

"No, my mother, I did not intend for you to go that far back. I know that you came here from London, and I was merely curious why Baltimore and not Chicago, New York, Cleveland or Philadelphia?" Stanley had offered the escape from this discussion his mother would not take.

"My son, as it is you who have opened this door, please allow me to speak without interruption. This is a discussion I have been trying to forge the will to have with you in the ten years since my husband was taken from me. So, please, allow me to do this as my will permits."

"Yes, *Matka*," Stanley said reverently. This was as stern a scolding as she had ever administered to him, but he knew his tender, loving mother had just rebuked him severely.

"When he passed away, your father tried not only to unburden himself in his telling you of our fate in Poland, but he tried to honor the truth that you deserve to know. I know that he was unable to tell you everything before his cancer choked out his life."

"No, *Matka*," Stanley interrupted cautiously. "He told me of Auschwitz, of the farm, of what went on in *Stare Miasto* in Warsaw. You do not need recall these things."

Stanley realized he was desperate in his trying to avoid this retelling, but did not realize it was for himself, not his mother, that he shielded his own heart.

"My Stashew," she looked over the mother of pearl frames of her glasses at him, "You have always obeyed me, why do you not now?"

"Yes, *Matka*," he said apologetically. He realized that this retelling was for her, as much as for him.

"Your father told you of *Stare Miasto*, and the manner in which Keller ravaged the young girl that I was. But did he fully explain the horrors he himself had been through at the hands of this beast?"

Stanley finally knew not to interrupt. She went on, "When I first saw your father in the dirt yard outside the farm, I could not bear to look at him. He was a skeleton, drawn from a horror, as if pulled from a nightmare into my very sight. I am ashamed that I turned my head away. I am ashamed that the world turned its head away. It was well known what the Nazi's were doing in those camps to the Jews, to the Poles, to the *Romas*. My own father taught me to hide whenever the Germans came to our farm, for fear that they would take me. I always feared that they would take me away. And it was not until that horrible day when Keller shot and killed my very father before me, only to take me in the way that he did, while my father's corpse lay not far from my feet. I felt my life had been pulled into every terror that I ever feared, but what I tell you next is the only thing that I am ashamed of from that day."

"After Keller was through with me that first time, I was ashamed, of course. Keller then locked me in the back seat, chained to the horror that then was your father. I screamed to Keller in Polish to not leave me to this ghost, as somehow, I feared that this gaunt, emaciated man would somehow harm me further than what this heartless, merciless Nazi had just done. My screams were just noise to Keller, who did not understand the Polish words aflame in them, but your father heard every word of my terror, and I can never fully know the pain that these cries ripped through what was left of him then."

"Yet it was that ride through war-torn Poland that afternoon that changed my life. My world had been completely and devastatingly shattered, my body ached from Keller's abuse, my heart broken from witnessing my father's murder, my soul was soiled black. My violation was complete. Now, I was chained to what I barely recognized as a man."

"Then, I came to know it was a man from his tender touch. He whispered in my ear in Polish, in my own language, not to fear. He said he would protect me. This soul, all but taken himself, calmed me with the touch of his bony hands and the comfort of the words of my own language. I never knew until years later that the reason your father was saved by God through all the years of abuse at Keller's hand was to so that he could comfort me. He was a tortured angel, my angel, whose message, over and over was *we must survive.*"

Her strength gave way to tears, but when Stanley began to rise to embrace his mother, she merely put out her arm for him to remain seated. She was not yet ready to concede her command over her memories.

"And so, survive we did. Keller continued to take me, until this became his very undoing. Your father took Keller's life. We escaped that courtyard with the keys from Keller's corpse. Soon we were rescued by the Polish Home Army. We found refuge in the *Stare Miasto*, the very old town that the Germans had surrounded and later would annihilate. But we were with our countrymen, they cared for us, nurtured us. As I learned English, I was always fascinated at how *Torture* and *Nurture* seemed to be opposite meanings of the same idea – to take care of something.

We were prepared to die there on our own terms, with our fellow Poles, until God interceded. Only days before the final onslaught, the insurgents, that is the Polish Home Army, succeeded in getting your father and I, among others, out through the sewers. Only days later, the Germans crushed the remaining insurgents, and after that Hitler himself ordered Warsaw itself to be leveled. So, when you tell me of its rebuilding, even in all these years that intercede, it brings a joy to my heart, my soul, that few alive can ever understand."

"We were smuggled north to the port city of Gdynia, not far from Gdańsk on the Baltic sea. We were hidden by the Polish Home Army with cargo as we made our way across the Baltic Sea to Sweden, and the weeks we spent in that country seemed to try to wash us clean from the terrors of war. But we could not escape these terrors simply by the calm of our new surroundings. Every look at your father reminded me of the pain they inflicted upon him for years, not merely on his flesh and bones which could be restored somewhat with time, but more so upon the recesses of his memory. This I was understanding all too well at that point."

Stanley looked at her aged frame, crippled by the years, bowed peacefully in this garden of her and his father's making. He had fashioned it from wasted bricks he recovered from throughout the neighborhood. She implanted the floral gardens, and here she would never recover from a youth laid waste by a monster. Yet the garden soothed her, especially in her later years.

"The Polish Government in exile in London got word to the British of our torment at the hands of the Nazi's. They desperately wanted us to come to Britain, in order that our tale could be dispositioned, so that it could be included in the case even then that the Allies were building against the Germans for the postwar proceedings that ultimately became the Nuremberg trials. They desperately wanted your father's account of the on goings at Auschwitz throughout the war. So, in early 1945 we were carried by plane from Sweden, over Norway and across the North Sea to England."

"London was the home of the Polish government in exile. They took care of us while your father testified the unbelievable truth of the abuses at Auschwitz, even of his taking Keller's own life. By now it was February 1945. Through the Polish Government in exile, we contacted your father's uncle who had emigrated to Baltimore before the war. He was quite well established, and with some assistance from the government, he offered us a place to live. I was desperate to get to America, for by this time, it was clear I was pregnant. I wanted my child born in the country that even then was driving the Nazi's back from the West."

Stanley now interrupted. "But, my *matka*, I was born in Johns Hopkins in early May 1945," he spoke aloud, doing the math in his head for the first time. "Does this mean I was conceived in Sweden?"

He was alarmed that his very beginning of existence in his mother's womb may have occurred outside his beloved Poland. He saw a ripple that distorted his mother's face and seemed to travel like a wave through her body. She closed her eyes in the sunlight, as if gathering the strength for what came next. She opened her eyes and looked warmly into her son's.

"No, my son, rest well in knowing you were conceived in Poland, of that there is no doubt." She began. "There is something that your father did not live to tell you, or perhaps the weight of it bore heavily into his soul, quickening his demise. It has been ten years, and I can no longer live another day without your knowing the truth."

Stanley still was oblivious to what his mother was telling him. For a man, even then, so adept at reading people, he was completely blinded by the maternal mask this woman before him wore. Perhaps she steadied her face and thoughts because of the damage it was about to afflict on Stanley. It was about to change Stanley's life as that last day at the farm had forever changed hers. But she could no longer keep this from her *Stashew*.

"My son, I am so sure you were conceived in Poland because your father, having seen the torment I was subjected to at Keller's hands, never attempted to touch me in that way for all the years we were together. What I am very ashamed to be telling you, my son, is that the man who died in this house ten years ago was not the man that fathered you." Stanley watched as her face crushed under a crimson blush of shame.

"I don't understand, of course he had to father me. Who else…?" Stanley paused, caught in the realization of the moment. In his mind's eye, for a fraction of a second, Stanley could see his mother being raped by the Nazi Keller. He remained seated, but his frame transitioned from a pleasant rest to a coiled tension, as if bracing for impact, "No, no, no. *Nie Prawda.* This cannot be true."

She spoke on over him, something that was very disrespectful to her humble nature, but was needed to console her son. Her voice was uncharacteristically rising above his.

"The man who died in this house did not father you, in the sense farm animals are sired. But the man who died in this house raised you from an hours old infant to the man you are today. He loved you and I know in my heart was sent by God to me to endure all that I have had to survive in this life. The man who died in this house was more a man, a parent, a father, a blessed husband than most people of this earth are ever graced to know. Do not dishonor him, *my Stashew*, by not knowing him as your father. Forget the brutish German who brought only the most searing pain to my life, to your father's life, and now to your life. Forgive me, my son, I could no longer live with this secret sowed deep in my heart for even a moment longer."

She began to cry gently. Her tears belied a tenderness, a sensitivity of remembrance of the pain of her many assaults at Keller's animal desires and whims; of the skeletal survivor of Auschwitz who held her, stroking her hair and face, whispering *this will all be over soon*; of the same man now in this foreign country, America, taking whatever odd jobs and charity he could for the survival of his family; and finally watching him die in agony from an illness few strong men could dream to defeat, let alone a man weakened so damagingly in his youth by three years in the captivity of a monstrous oppressor. And yet she had no remembrance of this man ever complaining of any of this, not so much as a word. She remembered him exiled in his own silence, but a silence he was forever forced to share with his own agonizing memories.

She remembered the days before he succumbed to his newest oppressor, his cancer, using all his strength to explain all that happened to his *Stashew*. Even at the moment of his death, he lingered in the shame that his Stanley, his *Stashew*, was not of his own flesh and blood.

He was not strong enough, for long enough, to explain to his *Stashew* that he was not his natural father. But, as being a father came naturally to him, and looking upon her only son, she could not disrespect the honor he had wrought from his indignity. That is why she decided, ten years after his passing, to complete the telling on this sunny warm day in the very garden her husband had created with his own hands.

Stanley's face was ashen white, his countenance enraged in disbelief. He struggled to stand, to escape the sunny comfort that now was somehow a trap to his senses. An anger within him was fueled by feelings of abandonment and deception, although these fought within his own being with the truths of love, belonging, and acceptance that his parents had always shown him.

The conflict that resulted deep within him tore at his reserved demeanor, and ultimately destroyed it, replacing it with anger. An anger that would no longer allow him to sit, to passively receive the long-hidden secret of his own being. It drove him to stand, as if this mere act alone was a rebellion to the assault on his very existence.

He stood, his blood now raged with adrenaline. However, in his abrupt rising to his feet, his thigh caught the edge of the table in the garden, toppling it, spilling the tea set onto the brick patio on which they sat. The pottery exploded into a thousand pieces of shattered Polish heritage.

"My son, my son, my son." His mother instinctively moved to him, embracing his suddenly shaking body. "You are my Polish boy. You are always my Polish boy. This is why your father insisted on the three promises, the first being foremost."

"...but you have just told me he is not my father," said Stanley, wounded, dazed.

"Keller was an animal, an animal that abused both your father's youth and my innocence. While he is the only man who ever defiled me, it was your father, your true father, who raised you in this very house, who laid these bricks upon which we stand, who laid the foundation for who you are as a man."

"Keller," Stanley murmured in disbelief.

"No, my *Stashew*," his mother tugged at his consciousness. "Remember your father in keeping the three promises. Please hold true to these."

Stanley was holding his mother close, looking over her shoulder into a non-existent space beyond the yard. For the first time, it dawned on him that his very life was conceived in a brick courtyard not unlike this one.

He spoke aloud.

"Always respect your Polish heritage..."

A weighty pause followed that tore at the heart of his mother. He heard her sobbing, but continued nonetheless.

"Always take care of your mother..." He squeezed her tight as he said this.

"My *Stashew*, my *Stashew*, my *Stashew*," she wept into his chest.

"Always protect the weak from the strong..." Stanley lost any resemblance of control of his emotions and his body shook vehemently as a wellspring of tears let loose in him. He held on tightly to his mother, as she was now the only part of his reality, his being, left as he knew it.

From the sun of that day in Fells Point, Stanley snapped back to the cold reality of the frostbit cafe in Zgorzelec, Poland. The *Żurek* soup was gone, and from the pattern of the empty bowl a hundred blue and green peacock eyes stared up at the old man before them.

For the last thirty years, since he was forty, he had to live with the knowledge that he himself was actually as much German as Polish. As he walked in front of the riverfront windows, Stanley glanced across the river into Germany.

It was then that Stanley remembered. The peacock feather that was the basis of the design of the pottery was also the sign of pride of the Teutonic Knights. These German warriors had long battled Poland for dominance of the Baltic lands. Ever since that day with his mother, Stanley felt the rage of these forces, Poland against Germany, within his own blood and bones. For the last thirty years, he had lived with the shame of knowing all that was most important to him for his first forty years in this world, was since tainted with an ineradicable truth.

It was then, as Stanley approached the door to the outside world, that he heard the call of the cook to his waiter.

“Now, it is time to take the food up to the American,” Stanley could hear him say clearly in Polish. “Remember to leave it outside his door, he does not like to be disturbed.”

“Does not like to be disturbed? Who has seen him?” asked the youthful waiter, who Stanley took to be a family relation to the cook.

“Yes, of course, I have seen him. I rented the room to him, did I not? He paints. He paints the river, but he wishes not to be disturbed. And he pays well. So just leave the food by the door and knock.” The cook feared the young man might spoil his good fortune.

“He is a ghost. No one sees him. Give me the tray. *Bigos* - he always eats *bigos*. That is hunter’s stew, not food for an artist. He is a hungry ghost who I will never see.” The youthful waiter began his agitated ascent up the stairs of the tower.

“You will see him sooner or later, as he has to eventually come down to use the WC,” the cook yelled up the stairs after him.

Stanley now had confidence that his sniper was on station, just as he had suspected all along.

“Tomorrow, tomorrow I will test my tired resolve. Tomorrow, I shall cross the river that ties together the two countries of my life. With my plan, I hope not to be taken by the sniper that I now know nests in the tower of this building that rises above me. I will have no one here to console me tonight.” He thought of the warm embrace of his Agnieszka that he would never again feel.

The room that was Trellis' *"Blind"* hung heavy with a darkened electronic humidity. Not to mention the stale sweat of the entire team working round the clock, still scratching for a lead, any lead. Some place to pick up the trail. Stanley, Jean Paul, *Sarenka, Syrenka.* 15 false sightings today, alone. Agents all over Poland, INTERPOL notifications throughout Europe.

Diane realized amidst the frustration, she could no longer focus her eyes on the arrays of video and computer monitors. Maybe that was what Trellis meant by calling it *"The Blind*". Her body ached, not of pain but of sedentary excess. She had been statically sitting, or worse sleeping, in conference rooms or executive jets for far too many hours.

She glanced at her watch. Six fifty PM, still might be some natural lighting outside she thought.

She reached for her scarf and Burberry trench coat. How cliché, she thought, spies in trench coats in Berlin. She laughed to herself. She was overtired and was now getting giddy.

"I am going for a walk for the next thirty minutes," she yelled out, as if to no one.

"I am calling for a security detail for you," echoed Dom from behind a bank of monitors.

"I don't want any damned security," she said, now scanning the darkness of the bunker like structure.

Dom retaliated. "Ma'am, we have had an Aerospace Executive gunned down last Friday night. Warsaw is not that far from here, you know."

"Great, if I walk into Stanley in the *Tiergarten* I will arrest him and everybody can get back to living their lives. Where's Sophie?"

"Here, Madame." Diane peered beyond a bank of monitors to make out a slim shadow rising, awkwardly unsure of itself.

"Grab your coat, I have some questions to ask you while we walk. Come quickly please."

"Yes, Madame," and Sophie followed.

They processed out of *The Blind*, Diane agreeing to taking a burner cell phone with one touch connection to security. Diane knew it was already assigned to a monitor screen, and they would be tracked along their walk on the digital map of the surrounding area. She wondered if Dom would have hacked it and thus be using it to listen to her conversation with Sophie, but guessed not.

Diane and Sophie stepped out into the brisk November night. The sun was already gone, the mixture of cold air and artificial lighting gave a halo like effect to their exhaled breath.

Diane thought they looked quite the pair - she in her designer overcoat and heels, Sophie in her blue Pea Jacket, jeans and fish heads. Diane grabbed her by the arm, as if to say, "let's stay warm together". They talked as they walked the short distance to the *Pariser Platz.*

"So Sophie, have you been to Berlin before this trip?" Diane asked.

"No, Madame." Sophie was stoic as always.

"No, really. I thought with it being so close to Poland..." Diane's face contorted, as if to suggest, "How could this be?"

"No Madame. I have been many places, but not to Germany. I am a Pole; I am lucky to have the whole country to explore. I live in Poznan, but I have been to Warsaw, Gdańsk, Gdynia, Kraków, Wroclaw, Katowice and even a trip into Kiev in the Ukraine."

Diane noticed Sopie's eyes evaded contact with her own. It was as if she was not worthy to be in her presence.

The cold was biting. Diane cinched her arm more tightly around Sophie's, telling her in physical terms "you and I have a connection, now."

"Sophie, how do you say 'please' in Polish?" Diane asked, arching her words to make them more friendly, more intimate.

"*Proszę*, Madame," Sophie answered, looking up at the Brandenburg Gate in all its sodium lighted glory.

"OK, Sophie," Diane said, grabbing the young Pole gently by the cheek to force her to look at her eyes, "every time you call me Madame from now on I will say *'prahshem'* in front of everyone, but it really is short for 'will you please stop calling me Madame?' OK?"

Diane had said this with a laugh, and for the first-time Sophie relaxed and laughed as well. In this night light, her skin was a wonderful porcelain white, highlighted by her long beautiful blonde hair.

"Tak," smiled the youthful Pole. "I mean yes, O.K."

Sophie pronounced the last two letters oddly, like the sound of two heavy stones separately thudding into the ground.

They now stood in the nearly empty *Pariser Platz*, looking upward at the magnificent Brandenburg Gate. The sodium lights cut it sharply out from the black night of the *Tiergarten* grounds that lay just beyond.

"You see the four horses and the chariot on top the gate, Sophie? Did you know that when Napoleon defeated the Germans, he took them back to Paris? Once Napoleon was defeated for good after Waterloo, they were returned here, but the Germans added the iron cross to the staff in the chariot goddess' hand, so they would always be German going forward."

Sophie stared hard at the Iron Cross. "Yes, and these people are those who once wished to destroy our Polish culture."

"Come, Sophie, let's walk to stay warm." Diane wheeled the two of them, and they walked along the promenade known as *Unter den Linden*. As they strode arm in arm along the thinning, mostly barren trees, Sophie broke the silence.

"Madame," began Sophie.

"*Proszę*!" Diane barked sharply.

"Miss Sterling," Sophie corrected herself.

"Diane. I insist - call me Diane. We are friends now."

Sophie seemed startled. "I could never have a friend like you. You are too beautiful, too elegant, too..."

"Too old. Say it, dear, 'you are too old to be my friend'."

"No, no, no. I was about to say you are too important to be my friend." Sophie was clearly embarrassed, perhaps not realizing Diane was playing with her.

"Well we are friends now, Sophie." Diane genuinely liked her new, unassuming companion.

Sophie hugged her new friend, but stopped almost immediately. She was ashamed that Diane might think her rude.

"What were you about to ask me, dear?" asked Diane in her most accommodating manner.

"Is he a bad man?" Sophie asked sheepishly.

"Who, dear?" replied Diane, truly not understanding to whom Sophie referred.

"Stanley Wisniewski, the man who committed the crime."

Diane recognized the fluid Polish pronunciation of "vish NEV ski," so much more endearing than the blockish "WIZ new ski".

"Well, Sophie, I have known Stanley for some thirty years. I have always known him to be a good, caring man. He was a close friend of mine."

"So why then do you hunt him, now?" Sophie's eyes looked mournful, concerned.

Diane stopped walking and took Sophie by the hands. They were halfway across the *Unter Den Linden* promenade.

"My friend needs my help, Sophie. I am doing this so he can get all the help he needs." Diane could see in Sophie's eyes that she understood. Diane had, of course, over-simplified, for she did not understand at this point what had driven Stanley's actions.

They cinched arms against the night, and walked on further. As they walked, Diane could not help but notice how capitalistic this former boulevard of East Berlin had become. Every high-end product was sold from these store fronts. How inconceivable this must have been in 1989 when the wall fell.

As if this city could not absorb enough of the materialism of the West, everywhere they looked were the skyward nests of construction cranes. They had just ended their day and were quiet now, resting for the onslaught of activity in the morning.

Diane returned her attention to her quiet Polish companion.

"Sophie, you have given me the only good information I have gotten since I have been here. *Sarenka* means 'deer' or more precisely 'fawn'. I know from this that Stanley had a very good friend, probably a lady, who came to America to paint a picture of a monument to Katyń, a painting that now hangs in Stanley's home. It was dated 2008, and I suspect it was painted at the monument itself."

"How was it signed?" Sophie asked

"*Your Sarenka*, 2008". Diane tilted her head forward to watch Sophie's face.

"The monument paid respect to the souls of Katyń?" asked Sophie.

"Yes, what are you thinking?" It was clear that Sophie was working something through in her mind.

"Very often, the Polish government contributes to these works through what in America is called the Polish National Alliance. What I am wondering is that *Sarenka* may have been in the Polish government and wanted to see for herself the monument she worked so hard to get money for."

Diane took Sophie's gloved hands in the cold, and looked into her eyes.

"Sophie, that is what I love about you. Your perspective is that of a Pole, you think like the man we are chasing. Where would you go if you had done this?"

Sophie had not even heard Diane's question. They had been amongst the Linden trees on an expanded promenade that separated the two flows of traffic. At the far end of the avenue, the tree lined promenade triangulated down to a single undivided avenue. Within this triangular plaza stood before them the equestrian statue of Frederick the Great. Amidst the cold evening, this silent sentinel faced east, near the Humboldt University, just before the avenue crossed the River Spree Canal onto what is now known as Museum Island.

"This is why I have never had any desire to come to Berlin," said a stoic Sophie as she looked upward at the Prussian leader, heroically poised atop his horse.

"I don't understand, Sophie," stated Diane.

"This so-called leader of the Enlightenment is well known for his contempt for the Polish people. He saw my country as full of savages to be stamped out. He considered our lands to be wasted on our people. In 1772, along with Catherine the Second of Russia and Marie Teresa of Austria they began dividing up my country. However, their greed outlived them, with only Catherine of Russia alive during the third and final partition of Poland in 1795 that completely wiped my country from the map of Europe."

"I am so sorry for that, Sophie. But that was a long time ago," said Diane in an attempt to pacify her emotional, young friend.

"In my country, it is as fresh a wound as what the Nazi's and Soviets did in 1939. They all attempt to drive the Polish and their culture from our homeland. Their greed still lies dormant in their country-men's hearts."

They began their walk back to *The Blind*. Diane asked Sophie again where she would go if she were in Stanley's position.

"Stanley is Catholic, yes?" asked Sophie.

"Are not all Poles?" Diane responded with her own question.

"Yes, nearly all. But he is American?" said the young Sophie.

"Yes, and very Catholic. Staunch Catholic," Diane emphasized.

"Then he will go somewhere very important to him to confess his soul." Sophie paused. "Unless of course, he is mentally ill and thinks he has done nothing wrong."

"Of course, Sophie, you are right. Whatever rationale he came up with for this, is now in conflict with his belief structure. He has to do something to relieve that conflict." It was something Diane should have seen. Her head was clearing, and she was learning to trust Sophie's insights.

"What would you do?" She asked Sophie.

"Me? Myself, I would not kill anyone. Of course," she smiled tightly at Diane, "but if I did, I would go to *Częstochowa*, and recant my sins to the Black Madonna. Either that, or go to *Wadowice*," the young girl said.

"Why ***Vadoveetz***?" asked Diane, awkwardly attempting to mimic Sophie's native pronunciation of the town. Diane could understand seeking the iconic image of *Our Lady of Częstochowa*, but the other city baffled her.

"Because that is the hometown of the Pope - Pope Saint Jonas Pawel II."

Upon hearing Sophie pronounce this, Diane's face was alight in revelation.

"Yes, of course, Pope John Paul II. Why didn't I see that?" Diane was amazed, her eyes only now opened by Sophie's reference. She spoke the names aloud into the bitter cold night air, "John Paul. Jean Paul. We humans can never be quite random enough. We cling to our vanities. Thank you, Sophie, I owe you so much. You are my friend for life now."

"For what?" Sophie's innocent shined from her face in a radiance that was undeniable.

Diane's energy levels were now spiking. "I still don't know who Jean Paul is, but I bet you are right and he is from Wadowice. Let's get back to *The Blind*, I have some inquiries to get the research boys started on. Besides, I am freezing my ass off out here?"

Sophie smiled a beacon's beam. "I teach you Polish - you are freezing your *dupa* off."

Diane smiled warmly at the young girl. "You bet your *dupa* I am..."

Despite its being very late on a rain soaked Sunday night, Preston Almesbury was now in the London offices of *The Conservatoire*, overseeing the postings of its breaking news to the fledgling website it had so recently established. His team was partitioned into three tranches, the first fact checking the material received via e-mail from the elusive Stanley Wisniewski. The second tranche prepared the paper's website postings, which became more detailed in the hours following as the treasure trove of material was vetted, the postings prepared, and finally approved by Almesbury himself. The third tranche had the most difficult assignment as it attempted to make contact with the fugitive.

All the return e-mailings attempted by the paper's team were regurgitated by the servers as undeliverable. It was clear this data feed was a one-way thoroughfare. But was it indeed a hoax? If so, Preston's decision to post the story earlier, despite his ever so dodgy disclaimers, could be the legal end of his *Conservatoire* enterprise. Only a few hours after the initial posting, the lawyers for Global Analytics were ringing up his office and mobile numbers with a vengeance.

Being such a massive story, Almesbury knew he had to take the chance. Initially, it appeared to be paying off richly, as the number of hits exploded exponentially, followed by his story being picked up by the premiere media outlets throughout the world, all crediting *The Conservatoire* with breaking the story.

Preston was simultaneously editing postings, returning text messages to his peers around the globe, when the call on his office number was rung up by his dusty, little used contact at MI6. Preston had planted a few stories as a favor to him over the years, but all before Almesbury had ventured solo at *The Conservatoire*. Preston quickly dropped everything else, cradling the receiver to his ear so as not to broadcast to the office using the speaker.

"Preston, I am afraid you have snared quite the beast, best you hang on for dear life," said the voice.

"Yes, quite. I am living that right now, as I am sure you suspected," he said laconically. "Is there anything from your side of the river that you can add to this dog's breakfast?"

"Preston, I only called to warn you to tread carefully here, as there are many parties who have planted mines in these waters. Just be sure all your facts are indeed that, facts, and not the conjecture of a raving, homicidal refuge from justice."

The line squawked in an unusual static that Almesbury assumed to be coming from the caller's end, possibly some form digital distortion intended to disguise the caller's natural voice.

"Preston?" called the slightly distorted voice after a few seconds.

"Are you receiving this quite clearly? Need I express in other terms the bloody squall you are now kicking up?"

Preston thought silently as to how he should express himself, before responding.

"One supposes when you and your mates across the Thames ring me up to express your angst, there must be a flaming tornado swirling around this Wisniewski chap."

"You have misread my message, dear Preston. You've got the wrong body of water centered in your concerns. It is not the men across the river in whose waters you are ploughing, it is the boys across the pond. And in case you are not aware, these are very little boys with very massive budgets. As such, they can wreak quite an exceptional havoc."

And with that the electronic static faded out, along with the voice in the night.

Diane and Sophie came in from the cold Berlin night. Two more sightings had been reported to *the Blind.* An old man in the wheel chair on the Charles Bridge in Prague seemed to raise everyone's hopes, and seemed promising. After all, Prague was only several hundred kilometers from Warsaw. Had Stanley gotten across the border quickly Friday evening, he could certainly have made Prague by early Saturday.

But as soon as they started describing this situation, Diane knew it was a false alarm. Stanley was too smart to run forward fast without a plan.

Stanley likely would lie low until he had a high probability of crossing the border, either totally undetected or in some manner to afford him a jump on the hounds at his heels. He certainly wouldn't draw attention to himself, hiding his height in a wheelchair, the first item on every watch list. He would certainly never draw even more attention by trying to access the medieval foot bridge, a major tourist site, in a handicap device that even modern thoroughfares had difficulty accommodating. He also wouldn't trap himself on the bridge across the river *Vltava*, where he would be bottled up by as few as two armed *Czech Policie*.

Sure enough, this turned out to be a pensioner coaxing coins from the tourists with his accordion. Might as well have a sign saying "if you are looking for a murderer on the run, follow the notes of my mazurka."

Embarrassingly, when the local law enforcement rather rudely separated him from his wheeled apparatus, he only measured up to five feet, ten inches.

Diane knew somewhere Stanley was lying low, allowing the hypersensitivity of the moment to overcome the patience of the pursuers.

The second lead to come in from during their walk turned out also to be from the Czech Republic, at its other end in the country town of Olomouc. An old gentleman walking his dogs near the old town section of Olomouc was detained by the local police. From the digital photo received, it was close to the description and photo sent out with the INTERPOL alert. Diane guessed that someone must have thought the two identical Pomeranians were just a nice touch in the disguise.

Diane knew this would happen. Everyone was looking too hard for Stanley. The airports and trains were sewn up tightly, but Stanley knew this and would stay away from both. Diane knew that Jean Paul was "handling" him, as Stanley had handled operatives in his day. In fact, Diane was now certain that Jean Paul was once Stanley's operative. She was convinced that he would be traveling ahead of Stanley, finding him locations where he, Stanley, could bed down, pay in cash, and not draw too much attention. Stanley would surely not carry anything traceable on him, no credit cards, no cell phones, and of course no computers.

Diane assumed at each of their rendezvous, Stanley would tell Jean Paul the next two meeting locations, likely each nine or ten days apart. They would have a protocol for meeting, complete with some safe sign. In the cold war days, these were a chalk mark of a specific type on an obscure but predetermined physical location.

Now the Internet made that all passé, as any posting to a Facebook account could be safe sign for Stanley to look up. Diane knew it could work something like this - if a photo of a person, any person was posted, it was safe. But if the posting was of a castle, a car or any inanimate object the meet was off. Whatever the code, Stanley and Jean Paul had likely worked this out years ago and refreshed the details more recently.

Sophie had assembled the researchers, and they now filed impassively into the only conference room in *The Blind*. It was a well-lit, glass enclosed oasis amongst the darkened sea of computer monitors. Diane addressed the weary eyes that had been scouring the illuminated screens over the past dozen hours.

"Gentlemen," and they were all, with she and Sophie being the only two women in *The Blind*, "Everyone out there is playing this game as Stanley expects we would. Cover as much as we can with our agents, along with INTERPOL alerts, and wait for the false claims to pour in as he hunkers down somewhere. Soon we are overly sensitized, become dulled by our non-success, and then Stanley will begin to move in plain sight, likely with minimal alteration of his physical appearance."

Diane looked out upon the tired faces lilstening as attentively as possible before her. They seemed to be waiting to understand their part in changing how this manhunt proceeded.

"Gentlemen, Stanley is running below the radar - no credit cards, no cell phone, no electronic emitters whatsoever. This I guarantee. We believe he has eyes out in front of him, in the person of an individual code named Jean Paul. If we catch Jean Paul, not only will he lead us to Stanley, but we will be out in front of Stanley as well."

She continued, "So here is our task for you. We have information that Jean Paul may possibly be from Wadowice, in southern Poland. We have a hunch that he may also be a former agent run by Stanley. I need a cross reference of every former known agent run by Stanley who had any association with Wadowice. The key here now is who is Jean Paul, and how can we track him? Start digging."

Then, as if caught in a receding tide, the boys were pulled back into the phosphorescent churning of the sea of darkness. Sophie had drifted out into *The Blind* proper, leaving Diane alone with her thoughts and memories of Stanley. Diane stood and walked over to turn the light switch off, plunging the illuminated lifeboat that had been the conference room into the darkened sea surrounding it.

Diane sat, putting her feet up on the adjoining chair, alone in the now dense darkness of the conference room. She remembered that phone call to her apartment on that gorgeous Sunday afternoon in 1985. It was not atypical for Stanley to call her on a weekend, as they had forged a tight professional relationship on Project Indigo. But this was different. Stanley's voice was weak and indecisive, wavering with a vibrato of fear and desperation.

These characteristics were very upsetting to the younger version of herself, as she had only known Stanley to be upbeat, or neutral in demeanor at worst. On the previous Friday, two days before, she and Stanley were elated on having rolled up not only Bryce Weldon, but his traitorously corrupt mentor, Dr. Bennet Palmer. Both were in custody, Palmer in a location she nor Stanley were entitled to know. But they were both aware that Bryce Weldon was being sweated at the CIA River House.

"I just came from the River House. I need you. How soon can you be here?"

The edge in Stanley's voice cut her to her core. She could taste the trembling, nauseating fear rising in him.

"Where is here, Stanley?" she asked in a perfunctory way.

"I need you," Stanley repeated almost pathetically, swallowing hard as the bile came forth with each word he uttered into the public pay phone. "I need you now!"

"Where are you?" Diane repeated, somewhat more sympathetically.

"Meet me at Holly's on Route Fifty at six. Only you. I need only you." Stanley's voice trembled; he was scared of something. She had never experienced this side of him before.

She knew Holly's well. The restaurant was on Maryland's Eastern Shore, not far from the River House. It was in Grasonville, and Holly's was well known to the area's duck hunters, crabbers and fishermen given that it was open 24 hours a day. The restaurant lived off its proximity to the main highway, sucking its life from this artery, every bit the leech to the travelers wishing to enjoy Maryland's cat-tailed marshes, creeks, rivers and open bays.

Diane well knew that the MI6 Headquarters on the River Thames at Vauxhall Cross in London was in many quarters referred to as the "River House". Since its opening in 1994, after the Secret Intelligence Services, or SIS, relocated from Century House near

Waterloo Station downriver, the MI6 Headquarters had become proudly visible to the city itself. It indeed had become emblematic of the clandestine services it housed.

The CIA's River House was altogether different. It was simply a safe house, not a headquarters of any sort. It was far off the well-traveled path. Adjacent to Grasonville, there extends a long neck of land separating the Wye River from the Eastern Chesapeake Bay. Known as Bennett's Point, it stabs out precariously for several miles, thinning to the eventual strip of peninsula that houses a community of upscale waterfront homes. Today, it is only a bayside collection of residences.

But not in 1985. At the very tip of this neighborhood, there used to lie a barely serviceable driveway piercing seven foot hedges with a simple white sign with black lettering, somewhat faded and peeling in spots, declaring "No Trespassing, United States Navy, Chesapeake Bay Tidal Research Facility." This ominous, though unassuming, sign kept out the very few curious eyes who ever wandered this far.

From the water, access was clearly marked as well, to keep the local watermen and recreational crabbers from getting too close. Of course, this facility was not a US Navy installation at all, but an agency safe house, usually used for interrogations, or convalescence of personnel as needed. It had been selected for its location, and the view over the blue confluence of bay and river was majestic.

When Diane found Stanley, he was not in the diner that was Holly's, but she soon found that he had rented one of the modest motel rooms set in its rear. Seeing his car, one of only two, parked in the motel parking lot, she inquired only to find that he had checked in under his real name.

Diane knocked on the unit door, soon opened by a very distraught Stanley, his red eyes the only sign of life in an otherwise ashen comatose face.

"My God, Stanley, are you OK? You look like you've seen Death itself". His red eyes immediately sheeted over, and he moved forward in a hug of her - less than an embrace, more of the clinging of a drowning man to anything that would carry him afloat.

She instinctively pulled backwards, but then forced herself to take his embrace.

She looked over his shoulder for any sign of empty liquor or pill bottles. Nothing. She really didn't think Stanley would resort to these crutches, but then again, she had never seen him this emotional before. The only disturbance in the room was the swirl of sheets on the bed, as if drawn into a fetal nest for this very tall man.

He held her a long time, not speaking, his head buried in her hair. Diane, not one brought up in a very emotionally embracing family, was uncomfortable with this unexpected intimacy by Stanley. While he was fully clothed, minus his shoes, he stood naked before her emotionally. She could deal with this in the only way she could think to - distance.

She slowly led Stanley over to the cheap pine bed, gently pushing him back onto its ruffled wake of sheets and blankets. She then slowly backed away until she found the thread worn wing chair by the window. A wooden lamp with a federalist eagle, its wings spread wide, was on the night table between them. Somehow, fittingly, the wings were wounded with several chips of missing wood defacing the pride of its feathers. Sitting below its equally damaged talons sat Stanley's revolver. She thought this must be the demon with which he was wrestling, but why?

"Stanley, you have to tell me what happened," she said firmly, from the safety of the wing chair.

"I shouldn't have come, not after yesterday. I should not have come." Stanley was tossing his head back and forth as he uttered these words. His face, red and drawn, leaked his wispy sinew visibly mixed with his tears.

"What happened yesterday, Stanley?" Again, firmness in her voice. Distance.

The forty-year-old man was slowly, unconsciously pulling himself back into the fetal position on the bed. Diane, fifteen years his junior, felt compromised just witnessing this. She would be required to report this event to the agency, as Stanley was unstable and nearly incoherent.

"I visited my mother in Baltimore." He paused to draw in a deep breath, as if it could retract all the inner feelings he had already revealed.

"Yes, I know. You were looking forward to it very much early Saturday morning when we left Langley."

Diane had thought, at the time, that it was sweet, a man in his forties, would be interested in seeing his mother on his day off.

A pause of indecision hung between them. Then Stanley decided he must unburden himself, if he were to resist the dark temptation that told him to quiet himself forever. He looked at the revolver before beginning to speak.

"My father died of cancer ten years ago." He was collecting himself a little now. "On his deathbed, he made me promise three things - to continue my pride in my Polish heritage, to look after my mother, and to protect the weak from the strong."

"The weak *who* from the strong *what*, Stanley?" Diane knew Stanley had always revered his father, but she did not understand this last "promise".

Stanley looked up, searching for her eyes. She could tell that whatever happened between him and his mother the day before, had been building like a pressure inside him since. He had no one to share this burden with, and certainly it must be something he could not share with the agency. She arched her eyes wide open, saying "It's OK, Stanley, you can share whatever it was with me."

"My father survived over three years in Auschwitz during World War II. The agency knows this, I disclosed it. Also, I disclosed that my father killed the SS guard, Keller, who had held him and my mother captive in Warsaw. I disclosed this also."

"So what happened with your mom?" Diane probed, fearing the worst.

"I can't say, I can't bring myself to say, but it was very disturbing news about my father."

"You can tell me, Stanley. I promise you I would not disclose it to the agency, if you don't want me to. I would do that for you."

"Then you could be fired, or even charged if you intentionally withheld. Better you not to know." He was stammering, excited.

"But, Stanley, you have to get it off your chest, it is eating you up inside. I can see it plainly. Is your mother OK?"

"Yes, she is fine. Just talking here, now, is good for me. Let's just say yesterday, what she shared with me, it was very disturbing to me. Made me question who I really am. Shook me to my roots. So, I should not have come to the River House today to see Bryce."

"But you did. What happened?" Diane felt as though she was reasoning with a small child.

"All the way driving down I couldn't shake the conversation yesterday with my mother. Driving down Bennett Point Road, I could not stop thinking of her - my mother. The sun was shining brightly, but I felt as if I was doomed. All because of yesterday."

Stanley began to tighten back into a ball again.

"I processed into the River House, as normal. They told me Bryce was sedated after an intensive interrogation Saturday night. They said he was up on the second floor. I went to see him. What I saw shook me."

"What did you see, Stanley?" Diane was now feeling the edgy unsteadiness of Stanley's emotional state, threatening to crumble altogether at any time.

"Bryce was strapped to his bed, arms and legs restrained. His skin was pale, his face blank. He appeared out of it, but when I stood over him, his eyes slowly sought mine out. His eyes pleaded with me - *how can you let them do this to me?*"

"What happened next, Stanley?"

"The orderly came in to check on his IV, so I decided to walk the shoreline to calm myself. I looked out over the river, knowing it was my work that put Bryce in there. But my thoughts still kept drifting back to the day before with my mother. I am a heartless bastard."

"Stanley, listen to me," said Diane. "Bryce and Palmer were selling technology to the Russians and got caught red handed. We, you and I, worked hard to stop that. They deserve what they got. They were the heartless bastards."

Stanley sat up and looked vacantly at Diane. "Bryce Weldon is dead."

"What?" Diane gasped as she stood, her hands covering her mouth. "What did you do, Stanley?"

"Not me. After I left the room for my walk, the orderly removed his arm constraints temporarily, before getting distracted and leaving the room to get some supplies. He swears he was not gone two minutes, but when he came back he found Bryce's body tied with his IV tubing around his neck and the headboard post. Bryce was able to undo his constraints and throw his body weight out of the bed. The tubing gave too much to allow his neck to snap, so he died a slow panic of asphyxiation. So much for the orderly's two minutes - more like ten or fifteen. It must have been a slow agonizing death."

The only words the shocked Diane could produce were, "Oh my God! No! No!"

Stanley buried his head in his hands. His fingers raked frantically through his hair as if they might dislodge the demons that tormented him.

Herself still shocked at the loss of Bryce, Diane took the opportunity to grab Stanley's revolver off the nightstand. She removed the clip, and pulled back the mechanism to assure the chamber was empty. It was. She noticed her own hands were now shaking. She could only imagine what Stanley was feeling.

Stanley talked through his hands, "I should not have left the room. This would not have happened. Bryce would still be alive. I could have protected the weak from the strong."

"Stanley, you're all over the place here, 'I should not have come', 'I should have stayed'. Bryce wasn't weak, Stanley, he was weak minded. Palmer, too. Selling their country for profit, they can both go to hell if you want one woman's opinion. I hate to see you like this, Stanley. You are my rock, and I will stay here with you until we work through this. Did you process out of River House before you came here, you're not AWOL, are you?"

"No, they told me to leave, said it was best if I did. Said they knew how to find me. They should, being they are the damn CIA, after all." Stanley delivered the last line deadpanned, but it struck Diane as amusing.

She laughed softly and awkwardly. Inwardly she was very concerned about Stanley's stability. She spent that night with him, nursing his confidence, but not allowing him too close, protecting her own emotions. It was almost as if she knew then, years ago, that this hunt was bound to come into being one day, and wished not to become too entangled with her future prey.

The next news broke on CNN late Monday night on the East Coast of the US, but was soon reverberated on every news channel as a lead story. After convening an emergency Board of Directors meeting to discuss the assassination of Langston Powell and the firm's involvement in hiring retired CIA officer Stanley Wisniewski, the firm fired current CEO Everett Roberts as well as cut all ties to former CEO Marc Constantine. It appeared the wounds produced by *The Conservatoire* were fatal.

One TV business analyst described the situation as the result of "Roberts and Constantine being incredibly stupid enough to hire Wisniewski to investigate Powell without the Board's approval, or the Board being astute enough to pretend they had not."

Either way, the firm had no CEO with Roberts departure, and no COO to promote, with Langston Powell's more permanent absence.

The board resolved this quickly by naming to CEO the other candidate who was in consideration when Powell was selected. And as such, in the span of a week, Virginia Ford, went from losing the most important selection of her career, to having the weight of this crisis thrust upon her as the immediately installed CEO of Global Defense Analytics.

Her first actions would be to clean up this mess, and then investigate deeply into her company's largest profit generator – The Daedalus Destroyer Drone program.

Chapter Seven
The Crossing

Crossing The Altstadtbrücke

STANLEY AWAITED ATOP the hill, monitoring the watcher across the river. The watcher had just left his post in the German riverfront window, and for a slight period of time was removed from Stanley's prying view. Stanley anticipated that this was exactly what he was so patiently waiting for, the relief break given to the sniper in the tower was about to commence. As soon as the watcher came out into the plaza at the German landing, donning the bulk of his ceramic body armor under his fisherman's sweater, Stanley knew it would be time to launch.

Stanley pulled the Greek's surplus army coat over his shoulders. It was awkwardly tight, binding in his armpits, cramping at his elbows. The helmet was only slightly too small for Stanley's head, the wrap-around riding glasses somehow miraculously fit well. But these would all suffice for the three-minute ride down the hill, across the bridge, past the armored watcher and through the town of Görlitz. Then, Stanley would ditch the bike, jacket and helmet, and move into what had once been East Germany.

The Greek was only too eager to sell the jacket, helmet, and riding glasses to Stanley, who had tracked him earlier this day to his dilapidated apartment in Zgorzelec. The Greek was less excited to depart with the bicycle, but when Stanley raised his offer from three to five thousand Euros, he realized this was a windfall opportunity he could not pass up.

As Stanley held out the Euro notes to *"Spiro"* - Stanley never did ascertain his real name - he reminded the Greek that he should keep this quiet, as the authorities might wish to confiscate his earnings should word leak out. *"Spiro"* looked cautiously at Stanley for a second, tilted his head as if to say, "I can do that", and grabbed greedily at the money.

Stanley then rode away from his *"Spiro"*, trying to regain the skills of his youth, balancing his aging weight on the bike's frame. Stanley had not ridden for years, but as he suspected, it came back rather naturally to him, and quickly so.

Through his binoculars, Stanley could now see the watcher walking out onto the plaza at the landing of the bridge across the river. Stanley assumed this meant that the sniper was stretching his legs, as it had been some six hours since the last time they went through this ritual. Stanley now pushed the powder blue Grecian bike out the front door of the villa, leaving behind the apartment that had been his survival nest for the past several days. He had spread the remaining cash in his clothes under the army jacket. The only other possession he had debated whether to take or leave behind - the 9mm Glock pistol - Stanley ultimately stashed in the pocket of the army jacket.

Stanley mounted the bike and turned left down the street on the hill overlooking the river. As he negotiated the second left, he began to descend the steep incline, picking up speed to which he soon realized he was unaccustomed. He braked the bicycle continuously, something "*Spiro*" would never have done, but Stanley knew he was out of the line of sight of the watcher. Soon he was at the bottom of the hill on Wroclawska street, now shielded by the riverside buildings. He was gliding along the street thanks to the momentum of descending the hill, and was soon enough in the shadow of the medieval tower itself.

Now Stanley knew all he had to do was negotiate the bridge, ride past the watcher who Stanley was sure would mark him as the Greek, and drift through Görlitz until he cleared the town. He hoped the sniper would not only be away from his shooting position, but also down from the tower itself.

Stanley leaned into the right turn that centered him in the plaza approaching the footbridge. It was just after sunset, though not fully dark yet. Stanley took in his first clean view of the bridge as he approached it on the bike. His momentum from the hill was ebbing, so he was now stepping into the pedals to pick up his speed across the bridge's length. The more speed he had, Stanley reasoned, the less reaction time it allowed for the sniper (if he was in position, after all), or the watcher, for that matter, to take him out. Of course, that was assuming neither the sniper's crosshairs nor the spot of his laser sight were not already burning into his back as he neared the center of the bridge.

Only a few pedestrians were on the footbridge as the night began to fall. At the end of the bridge in his fisherman's cable knit sweater was the youngish CIA operative, Andrew Kidd, known only to Stanley as "the watcher". Andrew walked briskly across the German fall of the bridge, waiting for the signal from his partner that he was back in place in the tower on the Polish bank. Andrew was cold, and the weight of his body armor somehow made the cold penetrate into his chest all the more quickly.

Andrew saw the bike come around the corner and make its way onto the bridge.

"The Greek's running a little late tonight," he thought initially to himself. But as the bicycle approached the first quarter length of the bridge, Andrew noticed something slightly amiss. The Greek did not have the same speed he normally did zipping across the bridge. Andrew could see him pumping the pedals, whereas every day before the Greek was effortlessly coasting at high speed across the bridge surface. Tonight, it appeared as if the Greek was giving a wide berth to the pedestrians, and not joyfully buzzing them as he had each night before. Their first night on the bridge, his partner and he had almost stopped the Greek, but did not, and soon became aware of his daily crossings. Tonight, there was something slightly unusual. The Greek was moving slower, more cautious, more considerate of those on the bridge with him. Now at the midpoint of the span, Andrew had a decision to make.

Stanley saw the watcher begin to walk towards him. His bike had just crossed the center of the span, but Stanley could see he had somehow drawn the attention of the watcher. Stanley crouched down to conceal his height on the frame of the bicycle.

Andrew walked out onto the footbridge, and saw the Greek ball up tightly on the bike. This is exactly the opposite of what he had seen from the Greek each night before. Every other night, as he coasted so quickly across the bridge, he would rise straight up in his saddle, arching his back slightly as if preparing to break an imaginary finish line tape across the German landing of the bridge. Andrew cautiously said so that his partner could hear over their radio connection, "Tango, Tango."

His partner, the sniper, was a CIA veteran of many years, unlike Andrew. He was now in the base of the tower, washing his face in the tight WC of the riverside restaurant. Hearing the call from Andrew, noting the tentative tone of his voice, the sniper's first reaction was "Shit! Andrew, could you not wait a few more minutes before getting yourself all wound up again?"

The sniper was a seasoned agency veteran of these types of operations. He had been a Marine Corps sniper, and found himself in missions around the world. His transition to the CIA was a natural one for him. In this second career, he had been around the world yet again. He was taking R&R in Bergenz, Austria when the call for him came, following the Friday night shooting in Warsaw. He had to report immediately to Görlitz, to cover this river crossing.

However, given the rapid onset of this event, and the multiple teams needed to cover multiple egress points out of Poland, the agency had to enlist more junior personnel who were already stationed in Europe. Andrew Kidd was every bit the junior partner - overly excitable, and under-experienced.

Andrew's "Tango, Tango" call immediately required the sniper to re-ascend the tower to the firing position he had been in for the last six hours. He was glad he at least had time to take the leak he so badly needed.

There had been several false calls by the neophyte Andrew since they arrived on station, and frankly the senior partner was getting tired of his jumpy teammate. Nonetheless, the sniper began to speed up the six flights of stairs to his shooting position.

Andrew Kidd now walked briskly out onto the bridge, closing the gap with the oncoming rider he was increasingly sure was posing as the Greek. He was peering iron rods into the rider's mostly covered face. The helmet and glasses obstructed the rider's overall identity, but as the bike neared him, Andrew could see the pale, gaunt cheeks plainly. These were not the olive skinned, tight youthful cheeks of the Greek. Andrew was sure something was now amiss. He would stop this imposter of the Greek, giving his partner time to return to position. He reached his right arm behind him and felt under the sweater to the small of his back to place his hand on the butt of his holstered revolver.

Stanley, not looking directly at the watcher, in his peripheral vision still could plainly see his mouth moving, which Stanley assessed was to signal his partner. Then, as Stanley closed even more, he could see the watcher's right hand loop behind his back. Stanley knew he was preparing to draw his weapon. If Stanley burst past him on the bike, he would be easy prey to one or two shots before he could turn his bike down along the river road. No, Stanley assumed he would not survive this scenario. Stanley began to pump his mount even harder.

Andrew saw the rider pedaling even more furiously. He raised his left arm as he moved directly in front of the cyclist, yelling the word "HALT!" Seeing the cyclist was not stopping, he began to draw his revolver. The gun snagged under the Kevlar vest that was protecting him, catching it just enough to slow the draw of weapon.

Stanley heard the watcher's command to stop. His heart was now beating furiously. His ruse as the Greek had failed him, and terribly so. How could he have been so incompetent? Why was he so arrogant to think he could leisurely jaunt across this footbridge? He was over confident and under prepared, and so he cursed himself.

Then Stanley saw the watcher's weapon come from behind his back. His immediate reaction was to pump the pedals harder, but they were already at the maximum they would propel him. He knew his only chance to escape was to intentionally collide with the watcher. And for this to work, Stanley thought, it needs to be a violent collision.

Andrew saw the cyclist accelerating directly at him. He feared his draw of his weapon was too late as the bike closed in on him. He began to pull the gun down into a shooting position, realizing he had never shot a person before in his life, which caused in him yet another hesitation. Realizing the bike would plow into him, he steeled his nerve to fire upon the rider.

That is exactly the moment when the missile that was the rider and bike crashed into him. The impact ripped at him like a razor mounted on a sledgehammer. The pain was initially sharp and cutting, and instantaneously afterwards seemingly pushed through his being from the inevitable momentum of the cyclist.

Stanley felt the moment freeze just before he ran into the watcher. He could hear a dead silence, not only an absence of sound, but as if every bit of ambient noise had been actively sucked out of the air by the gravity of the moment. Then, with a thunderous crash, he felt the impact ripple through him as Stanley drove directly into the crouching man, who was readying to shoot. The watcher's arm was still coming into position when the bike slammed into him, his revolver firing a round into the dusk, but missing the rider by inches as the collision occurred. The echo of the shot rang through the darkening river valley. It detonated like a bomb ripping through the tranquility that repeated itself each night along this border setting.

Stanley felt himself flying off the bike, over the handlebars and his shoulders slamming into the hardened bulk of the watcher, driving him backwards. He could clearly hear the gasps of the pedestrians, which turned sharply into unexpected screams as the watcher's gun fired into the night.

Stanley and Andrew collided violently, the momentum carrying both onto the concrete walkway of the bridge about a quarter span from its landing into Germany. Stanley had driven Andrew backwards, before himself rolling and scraping along the hard sidewalk. His head was protected by the rider's helmet. Andrew, after inadvertently firing his weapon during the collision, fell straight back onto the bridgeway, the mass of his armored ceramic vest whipsawing him, driving his head aggressively into the concrete surface. At this, Andrew released from his grasp the gun which clattered across the bridge.

The sniper ascending the tower was at the second-floor landing when he heard the shot. His annoyance at the young spotter's inexperience turned instantly into panic for his partner's safety. His fast pace was now accelerated as he bound three steps in a gait. He tore into this triple stride and shot up the remaining four flights of stairs as fast as he could to his rifle and his partner's aid. He yelled into his communicator for Andrew, but with no response. He continued to fly up the stairs, as quickly as his legs could master the steps.

Stanley became aware of himself lying along the quarter-span of the bridge. The shock of being tossed from the bike had clouded his senses, as if he were suspended in a thick and viscous fluid. He looked up, through the throbbing of his arm and back, expecting to see the watcher rising to his feet. But the watcher still lay on the sidewalk, moving, but almost in a random motion. Stanley began to raise himself slowly to one knee when he looked up at the tower.

What he saw initially stunned him, before its full terror descended upon his senses. Wrapped on the front facade of the tower, and around the side of the tower squaring the bridge, was a multi-colored appliqué painting of a highly-stylized face. Its explosion of color appeared to be out of place on the sullen medieval simplicity of the tower to which it was applied. Stanley had never seen these facades of the tower from his villa, and knew nothing of the artistic rendering it bore. To Stanley, it had the vibrant markings of his visualization of an African death mask. In his stupor, Stanley sensed it floating over him ominously. It stared down onto the bridge, and pierced into Stanley's clouded consciousness. Its message was absorbed immediately. Not in his brain, as in understanding, but in his nerves as an unexpected terror. The death mask looked hauntingly down on him, as if saying "This is the moment of your death. You will die on this bridge tonight."

Stanley looked about the bridge. The pedestrians were either fleeing or crouching for safety in whatever recess they could find. Regaining himself somewhat from the fear that had permeated him, he took his first steps after the collision with an uneven keel. He walked over to the watcher, who still writhed in pain on the sidewalk. His gun was gone, but Stanley could not locate it. It was then that Stanley looked back at the death mask floating over them both on the tower. On the tower facing the riverfront in one of the four windows, he thought he saw the motion of a darkened shadow. Stanley now feared not the floating ominous death mask, but the shadowed figure in the window he was sure would do its bidding.

The sniper had regained his position, and catching his breath looked down onto the bridge to see what appeared to be the Greek standing over his obviously injured young partner. The cycle itself lay mangled slightly in the foreground. He feared the man standing over his partner was preparing to finish him. Grabbing for his rifle, the sniper clearly saw the man dressed as the Greek looking up directly at his position.

Stanley instinctively dropped to the ground, scurrying behind the watcher. Reaching under the wounded man's armpits, he pulled the watcher up over his chest as one would don a blanket on a cold crisp outing. Stanley immediately noticed the sticky thick serum on his wrist and hand, but knew not if this blood was from himself or from the watcher's body, which now was shielding his own. Stanley crouched down behind his armored human shield, and could clearly see the source of the blood streaming from the back of the watcher's head. Stanley realized this wound was the result of the collision, and likely also resulted in the concussion of the awake, but traumatized, man.

Stanley looked up to the third window in the tower. Where he had seen the figure, he now thought he saw a glint of the lens of a rifle scope in the darkness, but was unsure. His own head was still pounding painfully, his blood raced through his veins like a locomotive. The haunting image of the death-like mask floated in his peripheral vision, taunting him. Stanley knew at this point, if he were to live, he needed to get off this damn bridge. He took small steps backward in his crouching position, careful to assure the watcher's flailing body protected him from the view of the sniper in the tower.

The sniper by now had his weapon trained on the mass of the two men slowly pulling back to the German side of the bridge. He knew the local police would be arriving any second, after the initial shot had rung out. He needed to act now, but the target was shielded by the injured Andrew. He assumed Andrew had been shot by the rider, thinking it was that shot that he and rest of the river town had heard. Andrew must have been onto him, he thought, catching him coming across the bridge disguised as the Greek. He trained his crosshairs on the receding tangle of the two men, but could not get a clean shot on the rider. He needed to flush the prey from behind his injured partner, and quickly. He decided the only way to do so was to rattle the rider into making the mistake of exposing himself. He moved the crosshairs directly onto the middle of his partner's bullet proof vest, knowing he wore his ceramic body armor when he came out onto the bridge. He would need it, for the Kevlar vest alone would likely not stop his rifle round.

The sniper's first shot rang out from the tower. Stanley felt it slam into the ceramic armor with the impact of blacksmith's hammer. The sniper's bullet impacted the ceramic panel within the vest, blunting its tip and absorbing its energy. In a millisecond, the ceramic was shattered. The flattened slug now had no chance of penetrating the Kevlar fibers of the vest itself. But the massive amount of energy transferred in the process of arresting the projectile now poured through the body of the wearer. Its impulse wave crashed through his torso. The watcher cried out in pain, as the shot's impact likely had broken his ribs just beneath the impact point. Stanley felt the round's impact ratchet through his human shield, and tightly held onto the back of the arm holes of his vest.

"Do not let them drive you into yet another mistake tonight," he said to himself, hoping to calm his nerves. The watcher, now his shield, writhed in tortured agony. Despite Stanley's clouded head, his pounding pulse, a certain clearness came back to his thinking. "Stanley, if you wish to stay alive, then calm yourself. He is trying to drive you from behind his partner. He means to kill you. Stay behind the watcher."

After freezing for a moment after the sniper's first shot, Stanley then began again to pull himself backward to the German landing of the bridge. The watcher still wailed aloud in pain, his screams ebbing into a howling sobbing. The sniper feared that Stanley would not budge from behind his injured partner. He decided to try again to flush his prey, selecting another portion of Andrew's vest, away from the now compromised location of the first round's impact.

The second round slammed into the opposite side of his partner's vest. Again, the ceramic in the vest absorbed the energy of the bullet. The ceramic insert shattering into small fragments as the energy of the round pulsed through it. It again blunted the projectile, preventing it from piercing the vest. The forceful wave of the impact caused the watcher to writhe anew in pain. His screams reignited, as a fresh panic roared uncontrolled in the man. The sniper watched as his partner began to shake in an uncontrolled, almost spastic, state of shock. Stanley fought to stay behind the agonizing watcher, but feared the sniper would time his next round to slip past the spastic watcher and into Stanley's unprotected self.

The sniper watched as his partner wailed continuously in pain on the bridge. The two men were now just at the landing on the German side. For the first time, he heard the wail of sirens from the Görlitz banks. He might have only one more shot. Through his scope, he could see the man posing as the Greek raising his partner to his feet against the side of the bridge. Andrew was still shielding him, although shaking uncontrollably. It was then that he saw his prey place his foot into the wall of the bridge, as if into a stirrup preparing to mount a horse. He placed his crosshairs carefully, anticipating what came next.

Stanley crouched low behind the watcher before thrusting himself up and over the bridge wall. Kicking off with his leg, he did not clear the broad wall of the span at the landing, but clumsily landed short and scraped across it. He lay prone across its girth when he heard the third shot, feeling a stinging in his leg and buttocks. He then rolled over the wall, dropping several feet down onto the sloped concrete embankment of the German shore. It was steep, and its momentum carried him down into the icy river below. Disoriented, but now shielded from the sniper by the structure of the bridge, Stanley grasped for the grassy plant growth at the river's edge to keep him from flowing downstream in its currents.

If the sniper was still in the tower, coming out from under the bridge would be suicide. His leg and butt were now burning, but in the darkness, Stanley could not tell how badly he was hit. The cold river water was already numbing it somewhat, but Stanley realized he needed to act quickly before its icy waters rendered him entirely into hypothermia.

Stanley removed the biking helmet from his head, and also the Greek's army jacket. He worked one arm at a time, clutching the growth to prevent his drifting into the sniper's lines of fire. That is if the sniper was still there. If he came down from the tower to the Polish river banks, then Stanley had only minutes to live.

Stanley wrapped the jacket around the helmet, such that the bundle floated on the river's smooth surface. He pushed it away gently downstream. It appeared to Stanley as the back of the jacket, sticking up just enough in the water to betray a man trying to swim beneath its surface. The sniper must also have thought it as such. As the floating clothing cleared the bridge, Stanley heard two shots ring out, the first tearing at the floating jacket, the second dislodging the helmet from beneath it completely.

"Good. He remains in the tower," Stanley thought. "My only chance is to swim back to the Polish bank. The embankment along the Polish shore will give me cover."

The river embankments near the bridge on the Polish shore were more vertical than the sloping German side. Stanley reasoned that if he could swim back to its side, they would possibly shield his escape downstream. The old man began swimming in the shadow of the footbridge, fighting the currents that would carry him exposed into the firing lines of the sniper. His breathing was labored as he fought to stay concealed beneath the bridge. The icy cold of the river made his muscles tight, threatening them to spasm. Stanley swam on as long as he could before his aging muscles rebelled. Eventually the current of the river overpowered him, carrying him downstream and directly below the tower itself. Stanley had abandoned his swim, catching his breath. He floated on his back, awaiting the bullet that would sink him in the Neisse's waters. These seconds along the River's surface stretched into a boundless band of anticipation of his own death.

In the tower, the rifleman had put two rounds into the jacket as it had emerged from under the bridge. He knew it was a ruse when he had seen the helmet float from under the jacket. He turned to leave the room and access the stairs to the roof when he heard the scurry of men climbing the stairs to his landing. He peered over the rail to see three men bounding up the stairs in uniforms. He knew he could not make the roof undetected, and returned to the porthole window, latching the door behind him. He had missed his chance to escape, and now was trapped in his nest.

He watched the river, and then saw it carry his target in its current directly below him. The sniper angled his rifle, and tried to resolve one last shot into the man carried on the Neisse's surface. He had to crane his neck just to look straight down from the limiting porthole window of the tower. But in no way, could he position his rifle to shoot nearly directly beneath him, for its barrel's length denied him the access needed. Outside the room, there was now an urgent pounding on the door. He could make out the word "Police" amongst the Poles shouting just beyond. He ignored them, and watched the limp body float a very short distance, frustrated he could not get off one last round. The sniper could only watch as his target floated to the lip of a small dam, crossing the river, creating a delightful waterfall for the tourists. It was then that he saw the target body slowly climb over it, and fall freely for several feet, along with the waters it failed to hold back. He still could not get a clean shot, as the Greek imposter slipped into the Neisse's pooled waters below. Stanley then floated unobstructed downstream and away from the joined towns of Görlitz and Zgorzelec.

The sniper turned to address the pounding at the door to his firing nest.

Emory was dispatched from *The Blind* by Dom to the airport to retrieve Carlyle, who was coming in on a commercial flight from the United Arab Emirates connecting through Munich. Diane was now concerned as to how she was to handle Trellis' special ops contribution to the team. Clearly, Carlyle would be getting direction from Trellis that likely did not align with Diane's decision to bring Stanley in alive in order to be questioned.

"Diane, can I interrupt you for a second?" It was Dom.

"As long as you are not going to give me the painstaking blow-by-blow of how we efficiently tailed what turns out to be another false lead," she snapped. "Sorry, Dom, after over 200 of these, my nerves are fraying."

"This may be something a little more positive." Dom smiled at her, looking up from the papers in his hand, as if to say "OK, we are all overtired and understandably edgy."

He continued, "The researchers came up with the data analytics you asked for. I had to get approval to have our kids hack the Polish Government archives from Trellis, so it took a few more hours than it should have."

"What did the brain trust come up with?" Diane asked, anticipating.

"We ran, per your request on Sophie's hunch, looking for known agents with ties to the town of Wadowice. No luck. But also on Sophie's hunch, we ran known Polish Government officials from Wadowice and came up with several hits. Then we re-ran it against the archived Communist Polish Government files, and zero hits from Wadowice. But, when we compared all communist officials to the list of post-communist free Polish government officials, regardless of where they were from, we generated a very short list. We were surprised to see one name pop up on both lists – Kazimierz Danuski."

"And why is this significant?" Diane asked.

"Because he was a Political Officer in the old Communist regime. Why would he get a choice position in the new, free Poland? Well, same question I asked. I had Sophie look at it. First thing, she recognized the name right out. Kazimierz' mother, Agnieszka Danuska, turns out to have been appointed Assistant Cultural Minister in the first government after the Communist regime. She was in the government under Lech Wałęsa, which later drove out the entire Communist regime."

"So why would Kazimierz, a former Communist official be carried over into the new Poland's government, along with his mother becoming an assistant to the Cultural Minister?" Diane was now thinking out loud. "Were they being rewarded for something?"

"Very good," Dom said, condescendingly. "Now a couple other facts. Kazimierz worked for the Communist Government in the Gdańsk shipyards. This was a choice job back then. It was set up for him by his father – the former Communist Economics minister."

"Where is the dad now?" Diane asked.

Dom smiled broadly. "He is in Russia. *Persona non-grata* in Poland. He was convicted of abusing the Polish economy in cahoots with the Soviets. One of the first bastards the free Poles threw out on their ear."

"So, you deport a minister and make his wife Assistant to the Cultural Minister. The son gets a new appointment in the free Polish Government, one of very few Communist Political Officers to make that jump. It must be that they were being rewarded by the new government for past services rendered. I think we are on to something, Dom."

"Here's the *coup de grâce* – Agnieszka, the mother – comes from Wadowice. Home of Pope Saint John Paul II!"

"So why didn't she show up in the search for Free Polish Government officials from Wadowice? I thought you said there were no hits?" Diane was truly confused, not effecting it in the least.

Dom's plump face broadened into a toothy grin. "Because that is not where she was born. They were resettled to Wadowice after the Germans drove her family from its farm in Görlitz. She is originally from what today is Zgorzelec, Poland, on the German Border."

"German border, you say?" Diane's mind was racing.

"Yeah, effectively the other half of Görlitz, Germany. We've had a couple watchers there from the get-go. There is a footbridge across the river we are watching very closely." Dom said, his pride flushing crimson in his plump, pale cheeks.

"Good," said Diane. "I would like to see this place as soon as possible."

"Not a problem, it is less than ninety minutes away by copter," Dom responded.

Diane said nothing as a wave of thoughts of Stanley and Agnieszka ran through her mind. She seemed to have left the present and gone deep inside herself. And she had.

Dom said quietly, not wanting to raise her hopes too high, "Agnieszka took a trip to the US in 2008. To visit the Polish National Alliance councils in the US Eastern seaboard."

"Did she stop in Baltimore?" asked Diane, snapping back to the present.

"Buffalo, New York City, Philadelphia, and DC." Dom was stringing her along. "Trip topped off in Baltimore to commemorate the National Katyń Memorial."

"Dom, I think we may have found our artist *Sarenka*, and Stanley's agent *Syrenka*." Diane was too excited to sit, now stretching upward in a manner that seemed to embody physical optimism.

Dom waited as the excitement and agitation built to a crescendo in Diane. Then, as if a lawyer closing his argument in court, he added, "Her father was a Polish Army officer massacred at Katyń."

"No doubt about it. She is Stanley's *Sarenka*. And I will bet my next paycheck that her son is *Syrenka*. Stanley's spy inside of *Solidarity*. This is all making sense now. Stanley used Agnieszka, his *Sarenka*, to get the US funds and information to *Solidarity* through her son."

"Why wouldn't Stanley have dealt directly with the son?" asked Dom.

"Protection," Diane jerked in response. "Not Stanley's, but the son, Kazimierz, his agent *Syrenka*. He would have been watched like a hawk as being suspected of sympathizing with *Solidarity*. But no one would have thought twice if he saw his mother on a recurring basis, not even the communist bastards are that heartless. Stanley gets the dollars, equipment and information requests to Agnieszka – very difficult, but not impossible – and she passes them onto her son. If young Kazimierz gets caught with an excessive amount of Polish zlotys currency, he just says that he is carrying this sum at the request of his father, the economic minister. I want to talk to both of them as soon as possible."

Diane was now exuberant.

"That's where it gets tough." Dom was about to bring her back down to earth. "Kazimierz disappeared in the mid-nineties, same as *Syrenka*, during the height of the Robert Hanssen manhunt. Thought was that the Soviets picked him up, as we have now confirmed that the code name *Syrenka* was passed to the Russians. We just never had any confirmation, so it was assumed he was arrested and executed."

"Or that he was relocated and resettled as Jean Paul..." Diane mused.

She thought before continuing, "That's a code name, of course, but he could be resettled anywhere in Europe. Let's get a search going for men of his description who don't have a history before '95. Chances are thin they would not have built a backstory, but it is worth the researcher's time."

Dom's eyes were now wide with success. "I'll get them on that. If we can find Kazimierz', now Jean Paul's, resettled identity, he'll lead us right to Stanley. Just like you said, Diane"

As Dom began to walk away, Diane wanted to complete the narrative - "Now, why can't I talk to Agnieszka?"

"Well, I almost forgot," Dom said, as he turned to her and held open the file, pushing it up to where Diane could read it plainly. Even in the dim lighting of *The Blind*, the news jumped off the pages.

"Oh, My God. No wonder Stanley snapped." Diane's face went pale. Within her, she felt the pain that must have, like years ago in the Holly's Motel, stabbed deep into the very being of Stanley Wisniewski.

Emory interrupted them at this point.

"Ma'am, we have a very solid lead. We think Stanley crossed the Polish border into Germany today. Our team caught him crossing dressed as a Greek restaurant worker. Stanley apparently bribed him for his clothes and his bike."

"Did they take him down?" asked Dom.

"Negative," blurted the young man. "They bungled it badly, from the reports we are hearing. Our shooter is in the custody of the Polish Police. The spotter is wounded, and in the hospital in Görlitz."

"Aw, shit!" blurted Dom. Diane was surprised that she actually felt a sense of relief.

"Where did you say?" asked Diane incredibly. "Where did Stanley cross?"

"Görlitz, Germany. Over the footbridge from Zgorzelec, Poland."

Diane turned to Dom. "Now that's a town you don't usually hear of twice in one day. Dom get us that chopper, quick."

Dom reached for a phone, holding it before his round face, barking commands into it.

"Where is Stanley?" asked Diane.

"Escaped down the river. They are searching it as we speak, but the German and Polish authorities are slowing them up. They both appeared to be pissed. They don't like a third country shooting up their shared border, even if it is the US of A," said young Emory.

"Chopper will pick us up in twenty minutes. Tops. But Carlyle is in the air from Munich, and he won't be here for another hour or so."

"Well, Mr. Special Ops will just have to catch up to us, won't he? Let's see how good he is." Diane had no intention of waiting.

Stanley did not know how long he had floated in the river's waters. He was in and out of consciousness as it carried him away from the bridge. Its currents deposited him along the river's bank, stopped by a tangle of exposed roots of a clump of trees. He awakened, and pulled himself out of the river's frigid waters only to feel the sting of the cold night air. He lay on the bank in its grass, and slowly realized that as the river carried him north, it had deposited him on the German side. He knew he could not stay here, even concealing himself in the brush. Soon enough the searchers would be along with their infrared devices. If he did not freeze to death first, his body temperature would scream like a beacon to these instruments. After several minutes, he stumbled to his feet to get some warmth, by moving through the patch of forest that lined the river.

Immediately his leg began burning. He remembered the third shot and assumed it had caught the back of his thigh. He knew that if this was the case, he surely would not be able to move about on it. But he was, although with a sharp, but not debilitating, pain.

He continued to hobble until he came upon a dark, country road that ran alongside the river. He decided to follow the road north, away from Görlitz, for as long as he could.

Several minutes later, Stanley could see an approaching set of headlights following the road south towards him. The car slowed as it approached, clearly having spotted the aged man walking along the northbound lane. The car coasted to a stop on the nearly pitch black road. Its headlamps shone accusingly on Stanley, who shielded his eyes and face. Stanley expected this was a recon team for the agency racing along the river looking for him.

"Excuse me, good sir," shouted the young man driving the Mercedes sedan in German. "Can I be of assistance to you?"

Stanley could hear the music he was listening to within his car. He thought it was Mahler, "Good. Then, he likely has not heard any news out of Görlitz," Stanley thought.

"No. Leave me alone," snapped Stanley.

"But you will be killed walking along this darkened road," said the man, who sounded to be perhaps forty years old. "I almost did not see you myself until it was too late."

His German accent was native, and likely not that of an agency pick-up team. But Stanley knew, after his errors on the bridge, that his instincts could be wrong. His instincts said the man would certainly not be listening to music if he were from the agency. Also, he would certainly not be alone. Stanley decided to take a chance. For he knew the man was correct. If he kept walking along this road, he would surely end up dead.

"Then I could not be more fortunate that you came along," responded Stanley in a hoarse trembling German voice. He thought of a location that would take him away from Görlitz. "I am trying to get to Leipzig. I am old and I have become lost. That is all."

"But where is your coat, my friend? You must be freezing." The Mercedes was now parked, its hazard lights flashing. The driver exited the car, and came towards Stanley with a heavy wool blanket he had taken from the back seat. As he began to wrap this around Stanley's shoulders, he noticed the lightly stubbled and heavily razor scarred scalp of the old man. He could also see the man was wet, saturated from head to toe.

"Sir, we have to get you out of those clothes immediately. It is amazing you are still able to walk on your own. What happened to you?"

The man began compassionately shedding Stanley's clothing there in the middle of the road along the car. Upon removing his pants, the driver noticed a white shard sticking out of Stanley's bleeding thigh.

"What is this?" he asked, carefully removing it from the old man's leg. He returned to the car, bringing back a second, smaller cloth that he applied as a bandage. "What has happened to you, my friend?"

Stanley removed the rest of his clothes. "I am freezing," he said to the driver, beginning to tremble without having to effect it. Stanley was anxious to get moving, before other vehicles came along.

"*Ya, ya.* This I can see," the driver said, as he wrapped the blanket around the now naked old man and eased him into the passenger's seat. Having thrown the wet clothing into the trunk, he climbed back in behind the wheel of the sedan.

"You are quite lucky that I found you before you froze to death," said the driver. He was indeed in his late thirties or early forties, and seemed to be quite prosperous from the look of his clothes and his car. His appearance was neat and proud, his hair was elegantly coiffed. "What happened to you? How did you end up in the river?"

Stanley looked at him as the man returned the car to motion.

"I was foolish. I was hitch hiking to get to Leipzig. I was picked up by some youths. I think they were immigrant young men. They said they would take me there, then once we got out of town they robbed and beat me and threw me in the river. I am ashamed for being so weak." Stanley bowed his head in shame. The scabbed razor marks atop his head were thus presented to the affluent man again, who thought immediately of his own good fortunes in life.

"I need to get you to a doctor," said the driver.

Stanley felt the throb in his wounded leg. He now knew the third shot had missed him completely. His companion had pulled a shard of ceramic from his bleeding leg.

"No, no more doctors," rejected Stanley. "I am dying, let an old man die with dignity."

"Yes, dignity. Crawling out of a river and wandering lost along the roadside. Some dignity." The man shook his head, as if he was used to arguing with the aged.

"Thank you for your kindness. But no more doctors. Let me out here, or take me to Leipzig." Stanley could feel his situation tugging on the sympathies of the young German.

"You say you are dying? What from?" his voice was now bold, almost demanding. As if the information were the cost of the fare.

"I am dying of cancer. I do not have much longer to live. My sister in Leipzig has a kindness in her heart for me. She told me if I could make it to her, she would take care of me. I could not afford the train, so I thought I would hitch hike to get to her. I never thought I would be attacked by these immigrants."

He was playing on every sensitivity he could detect in the man. He was a good man, with a kind heart. What was he thinking? Would he offer to drive Stanley to the Görlitz *Hauptbahnhof* train station? How do you put a naked, beaten old man onto a train? Even if his clothes somehow miraculously dried, would he be a target for other belligerent youth? Stanley could sense the man's reasoning, when the driver affected a U-turn and headed north on the road, away from Görlitz.

"Well, my friend, you are indeed fortunate. I was heading south along the river to make my way to Prague. I cannot take you to Leipzig tonight, but will take you as far as Borna. Do you know it? A small coal mining town about 30 minutes outside Leipzig. I was raised there, behind the iron curtain as a young boy. You can stay with my father at his home there. It is small, modest, but warm. How is that blanket, is it warming you?"

"Yes, yes, very much so. Again, thank you for your many kindnesses," said Stanley appreciatively. "You do not live there with your father?"

"No. I live outside Berlin. I left years ago to study at the university. I stayed and learned programing. I have done well over the years, but my father does not approve of how I live. He has closed his heart to me. He is about your age, a pensioner. He is very frugal, but will rent you a room for a few days. I will give you the Euros you need, as he will not take money from me. I will drop you and then take the Autobahn to Prague tonight. It will make me very late tonight, but I will be able to sleep in the morning. I am not expected until tomorrow afternoon."

Stanley wondered how much of the money in his clothes was still there. Clearly the young man had not detected the stashed Euros.

What of the Glock 9mm? Did it become dislodged on the bridge or in the river?

"How often do you see your father?" Stanley wanted not to pry into their relationship, but needed to understand what he was being delivered into.

"Perhaps once or twice a year. We share a meal and perhaps a beer before he begins attacking me. *'Why can't you go to church services? Why must you have so many vices? Why are you so addicted to your wealth?'* " he said, mimicking a raspy old voice.

"You will see, he will complain to you about me. I am not religious, and by his standards, too materialistic. So, we fight and I leave."

"Yes, well, I believe I understand. The fathers always fear their sons will suffer the fates they themselves deserve," said Stanley, not recalling where he might have read this line.

The driver looked at him quizzically. "For being an old, drenched, and naked man, you are quite philosophical. What is your name my friend?"

Stanley had anticipated the question, and offered only "Mariusz" in response.

"Polska, no?" asked the driver. Stanley's German accent was not good enough to fool the young man.

"Yes. Polish. From Wroclaw," said Stanley, remembering the street name along the river in Zgorzelec.The street was named after the Polish city to the east.

"Ah, Breslau," said the driver, choosing the city's German name. He looked at the old man and smiled. "My name is Deiter."

Stanley said the name aloud, "Deiter", as if he was weighing the sound of it.

"Well, Mariusz. I should thank you for giving me an opportunity to see my father again. Ah, here is the A4 to take us to Borna," he said, pulling onto the ramp of the Autobahn. Deiter then reached for the dash to turn off the music that had been playing since he stopped.

"No, Deiter, please allow it to play. It soothes me," said Stanley, as he pulled the blanket tightly around him. He made a hood around his head from it, hoping to shield himself from the highway cameras. He reclined his seat back as far as he could for the same reason.

"It soothes me to know there will be no radio news broadcasts," thought Stanley, before he unexpectedly drifted off into a deep sleep.

Ninety minutes later the Special Ops agent Carlyle sat in the dark confines of the Berlin *Blind*, waiting on the COMM specialist to connect the encrypted secure link with Trellis in Langley. The darkened edifice had the feel of a prison, secure but confining.

It was a feeling Carlyle felt naturally aligned to. He was lean, and no nonsense. Always ready to act, to move, to uncoil the training that had been drilled into him since his creation as the killing weapon that he had become in life. He had learned long ago to suppress all his original thoughts – and surprisingly to any who would take the time to discover, he had many – and execute the assignments given to him. Trellis had been clear on his initial communication of this assignment, very clear. Take out the target, preferably before he could converse in any way with Diane. Let Diane lead you to the target, and then take Stanley out. Period.

Carlyle did not ask why – not his place to. Orders came from Trellis and that was sufficient to satisfy Carlyle. Especially since Trellis was the man who had swept into the theater in Iraq eight years ago and hand selected Carlyle for this post-military career with the CIA.

Carlyle knew there would be few safe locations to communicate directly with Trellis, and he knew he would be able to catch up with Diane and the rest of the team in just a few hours. If Stanley was as good as they said, he would stay ahead of Diane for some time. But from what Carlyle had just heard of the bungled crossing, Stanley might not be that good of a field agent after all.

Carlyle was now in the COMM station inside *The Blind*, effectively a bunker within a bunker.

"Deputy Director Trellis. This is COMM specialist Phillips. Initiating secure contact from location Bravo. I have Carlyle physically in station and requesting a dialogue with you."

"Thanks, Phillips," was the only response coming over the secure line.

Carlyle was now staring at the young man's face, the headset wrapped around a disappointed countenance that registered insult at the lack of banter. No "How are you, Dennis?" No "Dennis, great to hear from you." After all, early in his career, Phillips was actually assigned to Trellis. Phillips had mentored under Trellis, that is before Trellis' career took off into the stratosphere.

Phillips started again. "Before I turn the headset over to Carlyle, Deputy Director Trellis..."

"Get out," said Carlyle, rising to stand over Phillips, his lean but muscular frame extending a hand for the headset. The hand stood, palm outstretched, and without a flinch, said to Phillips, "give me the headset and get out."

Carlyle implied, but did not say "... or this hand will punish you."

"Excuse me, you can't talk to..."

Phillips now heard the static of the voice in the headset. "Give him the *f**king* headset, Dennis, I don't have all day."

Phillips ripped off the headset and stood angrily, but found himself slowly slapping the headphones into the thirty something's palm. No need to make new enemies, Dennis thought.

"I'll be outside if you..."

"Just get out, now," Carlyle said, slipping the headphones over his extremely close cropped post-military razor cut hair. His face was muscular, highlighting the intensity with which he appeared to address everything.

Phillips left the COMM center, securing the door behind him. Trellis knew and appreciated Carlyle would be no nonsense. And so, it was.

"*The Huntress* has a bearing on the prey. They embarked just before I arrived."

"Where?" asked Trellis.

"Görlitz, Germany," said Carlyle crisply.

"How old is the sighting?" Trellis seemed agitated.

"Two hours or so."

"Shit. There goes trying to contain him in Poland. Why the *f**k* are you still in Berlin?" Trellis' agitation was now elevated.

"I need confirmation on the second target." Said Carlyle outright. It was less of a statement than a demand.

Trellis was uneasy with this reference. He knew this line was secure, crypto-encoded at the highest level and would not be recorded in *The Blind's* COMM center. He knew it was secure from virtually anyone in the world, except the NSA. He did not trust his brothers in Fort Meade from intercepting and breaking the encryption.

Better be on very sure footing here.

"What about the secondary target?" Trellis asked.

"If secondary target intercepts primary target before I do, define instruction." Carlyle barked the statement at Trellis, not asking at all.

Trellis wanted no errors. He decided to be direct with Carlyle, damn the NSA. This had to be done right.

"Take out the secondary target, only if necessary, after taking out the primary target. Carlyle, listen to me closely. Do nothing to risk taking out the primary target. Only after successfully taking out primary target, proceed to take out secondary target, but only if secondary target has interfaced with primary target."

Carlyle understood only too clearly. Stanley's got a secret that Trellis doesn't want to see the light of day. If *The Huntress* talks to Stanley, assume the secret has been passed and take her down. The trick would be to let *The Huntress* lead Carlyle to Stanley, but for Carlyle to close in on Stanley before Diane did. This would make things cleanest for everyone.

"Roger. Over and out." Click. Carlyle terminated the connection.

It was now time to move.

Later that day, Trellis received a grade-A grilling in the Intelligence Oversight Committee in closed chambers in the Capitol Building.

"*F**king* bureaucratic politicians" he thought. Of all things, they were barbecuing him on his directing the team to break into Stanley's Fells Point home without proper court approval, and even then, they expected proper coordination with the FBI. God knows they were touchy with his team operating within the US against the rights of American citizens – even those who had committed cold blooded murder of an American abroad. The Maryland Congresswomen Malinksi went so far as to threaten to have him dismissed from his office over this.

Trellis knew they wouldn't. They never had the balls to actually do something. Not when they could just talk about doing something. They always feared the voter backlash. If they even vaguely appeared to protect Stanley, the Aerospace Executive killer, their precious approval numbers might go south.

The grilling was well worth it. Trellis had his team in place now. Part of getting Diane up to Stanley's home was to slow her down enough until Carlyle could be in place. Even with pulling her back to the states, she got a jump on Carlyle. Now, Trellis was certain Carlyle would close that gap quickly.

The only problem was that damn painting alerting *The Huntress* to *Sarenka* – Agnieszka Danuska. He was hoping Diane wouldn't make the connections as quickly as she had, but she in fact had. Why didn't his team find the inscription on that damn picture and report it? Now it was too late, but Carlyle would fix everything, if needed.

Chapter Eight

Post Mortem of Incompetence

LATE THE NEXT morning, Diane with Dominic Reeves stood in the center of *the Altstadtbrücke*, the footbridge where the botched shooting occurred. Carlyle had caught up with them in the night, and he joined them on the bridge.

The Neisse river flowed beneath the three of them, its chilled waters on their long arduous path to join into the Oder River and beyond into the Baltic Sea. Despite the frigid temperature, on the German side a restaurant with an outdoor beer garden adjoining the river was already full of European tourists drinking from tankards. They were heavily dressed for the wintery chill, but joyful to frolic in the day's short hours of sunlight. The early hour of the day did little to dissuade them.

Diane pulled her Burberry trench coat tight around her, wishing now she had a heavier lining in it. She tried not to show the chill she was feeling to Carlyle or Dom. Reeves looked tense, and that is how she wanted him to be. She looked up into the towering structure that rose above the bridge on the Polish side, standing like a sentinel to all who crossed in its shadow. She noticed Carlyle was doing the same.

"Your sniper was stationed up in that tower window facing the river," she said to Dom, "and his partner over here was operating from alongside the German landing of the bridge?" The question was more of a fact being recited aloud.

"Yes, Diane," responded Dom. Ashamed. Looking away from the woman he knew was now running this manhunt.

"And they both watched this crossing the last several days with no relief, other than occasional naps, never at the same time, of course, to regain some energy?" she added.

"Yes, Diane," Dom replied, again in a defeated tone.

Diane thought they had to be exhausted - two men trying to cover this crossing 24/7. But with Poland bordering Germany, The Czech Republic, Slovakia, Lithuania, The Ukraine, Belarus and the Russian enclave of Kaliningrad, there was a tremendous amount of border to cover. Therefore, a second relief team could not be afforded.

"Why station him in the tower?" she asked Dom. Diane answered her own question aloud, "Only rational reason is to snipe from that location."

"Yes, Diane," admitted Dom. "The agent in the tower was a sniper, in case we needed him."

"And his partner watches from the footbridge's German side, also along the river banks. The watcher alerts the sniper if he sees the target coming from behind the sniper's position, that is from beyond the tower. This gives the sniper time to prepare his shot even before he sees the target on the bridge. The sniper would have a tremendous field of view with his scope from that high up the tower. What were his orders?"

"Shoot to immobilize, not kill, just immobilize," Dom snapped back. He was anticipating the question. "I would know, I gave them the directions myself, didn't I?"

Diane looked at Carlyle, who like Diane wasn't buying Dom's well-rehearsed answer. It was Carlyle's eyes that said so. His mouth said nothing. This was his area of expertise. But he said nothing.

"Well your boys didn't immobilize, Dom, did they?" accused Diane. "And now we have the sniper in Polish Police custody, the spotter in a German hospital with three cracked ribs, a split skull and a pretty severe concussion. Sounds like they were the only two that were immobilized. Oh yeah, thanks to them, we also have an international incident to resolve as well."

The ice in her comments was highlighted by the frost her breath created upon meeting the cold river air. Diane looked at the picturesque scenery around her. Why did Stanley pick this quaint town to make his crossing? She suspected she knew exactly, because he knew its terrain. Why had he crossed in broad sight and not downstream wading or swimming across the river, as he ended up being forced to do eventually? He must have thought there was less of a chance of being killed outright in the crowded town center. She could see he had laid this out from the beginning, likely even before Stanley's killing of Langston Powell.

"Stanley watched those two for the last several days. He couldn't see the agent up in the tower, but he knew he was there. The younger agent must have stuck out like a sore thumb over here on the German side – day and night watching this footbridge for days straight. Stanley knew they were getting tired, and he knew they had no one to relieve them, especially since you there was only one shooter and they couldn't swap positions. He let them get used to that Greek coming across on his bicycle every day to work, he lets them get used to the rhythm of it. Then he attempts to cross as the Greek on the blue bike. But young Andrew catches on, doesn't he? But our Stanley has watched them, measured their tempo, and waited until Andrew's partner was out of position. This is exactly what I meant when I said how good Stanley was."

"Yeah, so good it nearly cost him his life..." responded Dom snappishly.

Diane stared hard at him. "OK, Dom. I grant you, maybe Stanley is slipping up a little. He didn't make it past your team unrecognized. But today we stand on this bridge, and he is still on the run, now outside of Poland. If you assume we have the airlines and trains shut down cold, he could still be anywhere in continental Europe. Great!"

Diane had thrown her hands up in the air, frustrated, punctuating the last point. Dom looked around at the surroundings to evade her stare. He looked off into the old town of Görlitz, across its maze of century old homes beneath the twin spires of the Gothic Church.

"Look at me," Diane now snapped back at Dom. "How did this get so botched up, Dom?"

But it was Carlyle who answered. He said plainly, "Because they weren't fully committed."

"Hey, I am not going to take that from you, you don't know sh..." Dom reacted explosively to Carlyle.

"Shut up!" commanded Carlyle loudly, and Dom indeed did just that.

"You *are* going to take this. I was not here, but I will tell you exactly what happened. First, your team got into a regular relief cycle, and

Stanley was watching them, probably from somewhere up there," said Carlyle pointing to the homes atop the hill in Zgorzelec. "Second, your sniper took up a restricted firing position inside the tower. He was limited by the window being round, long and narrow. Limited his field of view, especially on firing down on the quarter of the bridge nearest his position. He should have been on the roof, but wasn't. Either he didn't want to be seen by the houses up the hill, or he didn't want to be freezing his balls off. By the time he thought to escape to the rooftop, he was trapped in his position by the locals. Smart move would have been to build a camouflaged shelter on the roof that he could fire from without being spotted from above. Finally, when the shooting started, your sniper was out of position. Stanley has time to attack his partner, Mr. Kidd, and use him as a human shield to get off the bridge and into the river. Your sniper takes three shots and still allows Stanley to make the water. Incompetence. Sheer incompetence."

The pause that followed allowed Dom's rage to build within him. When he did speak, the words seethed out slowly and tensely. "OK, Mr. Special Ops, our sniper fired two rounds into his partner's armor to rattle Stanley. But Stanley didn't rattle, did he? The third shot, as Stanley went over the wall, spalled the ceramic high on Andrew's vest. A lot of it went into Andrew's neck, luckily not his face or eyes. Some of it hits Stanley in the legs. We know because we found his blood trail downriver along the road, not enough to think the round hit him. Then it stops, so somebody must have picked him up. Now, what would you have done so differently?"

Diane saw a steely look come over Carlyle's face. He turned to stare intently into Dom's baggy eyes. "Mr. Reeves, I assure you Stanley would not have gotten off that bridge alive if I had been in that tower."

The comment was more a reprimand than a statement. Dom, however, pressed him further. "You still haven't said what you would have done differently."

Carlyle looked at Diane for an instant, then retrained his look deep into Dom's eyes. "I would not have been out of station, so Andrew Kidd would not have been run down as he was. Secondly, as I said, I would have been on the roof of the tower, so Stanley could have been taken out later as he floated downriver. But as I also said, he would never have made the river. Because even if he was using Mr. Kidd as a human shield, Stanley would have died on that bridge from my fire."

Dom was not backing down. "How so, hot shot? How would you have gotten Stanley out from behind Kidd?"

Carlyle stepped closer to Dom. In a tense whisper, Diane heard him clearly say to Dom, "I would have done what your guy was unwilling to do. I would have put a round into Mr. Kidd's skull. It's my experience that even the most experienced people freak out when the gray matter starts flying. Even if Stanley didn't panic, he would now have Mr. Kidd's dead weight to try to keep in front of himself. Stanley would not have gotten off that bridge alive, Mr. Reeves. Because immediately after opening up Mr. Kidd's skull, I would have done the same to our friend Stanley!"

Carlyle turned away from Dom, and marching past Diane headed off the bridge to the Görlitz bank of the river.

Diane looked at Dom, who had a look of shock tightening his otherwise flabby face. He slowly recovered, saying to Diane for effect, "Do you believe that shit? He would kill his own partner to get to the target? The guy needs to be committed."

Diane said to her rattled colleague, "Yes, Dom, I do believe Carlyle would have done exactly that. As far as his being committed, as Carlyle himself had said in not so many words, he would have been fully committed, and have done whatever it took to bring down Stanley. I have every reason to believe him."

She then turned from Dom and also walked back to the Görlitz side of the river.

"That is exactly why Trellis wants him so close to me," thought Diane. "He wants me to lead him to Stanley, and then Carlyle will take it from there…"

Preston Almesbury had been warned by the voice in the night. Beware the Americans. Yet now, before him sat a very prominent American businessman, William Hobson, who had long been rumored to be unofficially affiliated with the CIA.

"Preston, do you mind if I call you Preston? OK, Preston, my friends in the States are somewhat concerned with this entire Stanley Wisniewski drama, as it is unfolding. Of course, we recognize you boys are just doing your jobs- free press being the foundation of both our Western democracies and all that. But, there does come a point where illegal breaches of security must be considered. And in that regard, our team is asking, in the best interest of all concerned, if you could reveal to us your source in all this matter."

Almesbury knew that this was not the message his longtime professional acquaintance was sent to deliver. This was merely the opening discourse, designed to feel out the would-be media baron.

"Mr. Hobson? You prefer William? Well enough, William, I have not known you very well, just having seen you about London's society functions over the years. However, certainly long enough to be completely earnest with you. When I could not track the original messages, I brought in experts in telecommunications. The first thing they made me rather mindful of was that all my computers, servers and my personal mobile phone had been hacked. Not by those that had sent the *'Vish-nev-ski'* material, but by a rather finessed team a few hours after our first internet posting. The experts I hired said this hack had gone out of its way to be noticeable. They thought it was as if to send me a message. One has to believe that '*your boys*', as you so deftly describe them, at this point have all the details that I do."

The two men stared at each other across the elegant Louis Quinze desk adorning Almesbury's office. Preston broke the silence. "I think it is high time you come forth with the intended message you were sent to deliver. Time for you to be earnest in return."

"OK. Here's the whole nine yards, Preston. You are to stay off this story. You've had your run, your paper got its fifteen minutes of fame. Now in the best interests of all involved, ignore any more material that may come to you on this topic in any manner: e-mail, snail mail, spiritual apparitions - all forms, mind you. You are not to post anything else regarding our elusive Stanley Wisniewski and his whereabouts."

Preston allowed his American brethren to finish his discourse. Then after waiting a respectable few seconds in mock consideration, he responded.

"How very Wellingtonian of you. *'Publish and perish'*, is it? Isn't that precisely what the Iron Duke retorted to the seedy publisher who threatened to include his name in the memoir of a London socialite courtesan? Yes, I am quite sure it is. How interesting a clandestine organization such as '*your boys*' would have me turn the blind eye to the most legitimate story to come along this decade - our Stanley's wanderlust, and his back-story, as your cinema would call it, is exactly what the masses are craving to read."

The American was astonished that his warnings had been so flagrantly brushed aside.

"To use another phrase from our county, allow me to show you the door," continued Almesbury, rising from behind his magnificent desk.

"Preston, I would encourage you to think closely about your next move. It may result in undesired consequences," said Hobson.

Moments later, the American having left the office, Preston pressed the number in his mobile phone associated with the mysterious voice in the night.

"Did you get all that clearly?" asked Almesbury, referring to the bug that had only days before been planted by MI6 in his office.

"Very much so. They can be such a predictable lot, can't they, these cousins of ours?" said the now unadulterated voice of Malcolm Devereaux. "I liked your Wellington and Nelson references – turning the blind eye, and all that. Too bad it surely was lost on our Mr. Hobson. Perhaps our cousins will realize that if we once brought down the mighty Napoleon, we can surely cause them much concern as well. So, good of you, Preston, to allow us to prepare you for this."

"Yes, of course," responded Almesbury. "However, I am quite

stupefied about one thing. You directed me to call you on this number, but isn't it likely the Americans are listening to us at this very moment."

Devereaux laughed into the phone. "That's why you are calling me, my friend. We want very much for them to know we are watching their every misstep, as it were."

Almesbury suddenly felt himself uncomfortably caught amidst a family squabble. That is, a very dangerous squabble of a very dysfunctional family.

Diane, having arrived in Görlitz late in the evening the night before, had immediately split her team into two parts – the first was in pursuit of Stanley, and the second to scour Zgorzelec to discover the site where Stanley had holed-up the preceding days.

She knew Stanley would be somewhere deeper in Germany by now, if not even further into Europe. They had scanned the woods along the river with night optics and FLIR's (Forward Looking Infra-Red devices). They found nothing. The search at first light yielded only a small blood trail that ended mysteriously along the center of the German river road. He apparently had someone arranged to pick him up after his crossing. Was it Jean Paul, perhaps? Whoever it might have been, finding them in an unidentified vehicle along the German roads, even if they were traveling upon the camera-laden Autobahn network, would likely be a futile effort. Nonetheless, she had her team of researchers back in Berlin analyzing the Autobahn's cameras by automated facial recognition software, but didn't expect

Stanley would allow enough of his features to be captured by the cameras to trigger a hit.

Although she knew Stanley would avoid the trains, Diane had teams dispatched to continuously ride circuitous routes on all the local trains servicing Görlitz and the surrounding towns. They had started this morning, hoping to make a random sighting. Diane was sure Stanley would continue to travel by car, the most anonymous means of transportation. She thought most certainly not with Jean Paul though, as Stanley could be quickly trapped had his cohort been compromised.

Her hopes were more focused on the other half of her team that was combing through the Polish side of the Neisse River. Where had Stanley been hiding? Assuming it was not a hotel or inn, as they would have certainly been notified to look for this tall aging American, then the question would be "who owned the property? Who provided the critical shelter?"

Diane already knew the source of Stanley's funds. She had the forensic accounting team track the payments made by Global Defense Analytics to Stanley for his vetting of Langston Powell. It was easy work for the money tracers, but took a few days only because of the route through Europe the money had electronically traveled.

The money in question, some three hundred and fifty thousand dollars, was deposited into Stanley's personal account. The same account he nearly emptied on the Monday before Powell's death while in London. The bulk was transferred to a Swiss account, where it was instantaneously split and redeposited into several smaller accounts, all behind the confines of the Swiss banking system. While the Swiss bankers no longer had the ironclad refusal to participate with international investigators as they once had, Diane sensed

Stanley knew that routing the money through Switzerland could slow the investigation over the course of many days, if not weeks. But in this case, enough pressure was brought by the Americans to assure timely cooperation. The money trail became instantly known to the forensic accountants.

In addition to the briefcase full of thirty thousand Euros cash carried out of the Canary Wharf bank by Stanley on that Monday, the electronically routed Swiss funds were withdrawn over the next several days in banking offices in Paris on Tuesday, Berlin on Wednesday, and Warsaw on Thursday. The equivalent of over three hundred thousand dollars were legally withdrawn before the crime of shooting Langston Powell had been committed in Warsaw on Friday night.

All funds were withdrawn by the same individual, in whose name each of these accounts had been opened many years before, but had never seen any activity until the week before Langston Powell was murdered. This man was dark haired, mustachioed and overweight, wearing the thick corrective lens glasses that obscured much of his face. Even the lenses themselves were darkly tinted. But it indeed was the same man emptying each account.

And each account bore the same institutional name – The Franco-Polish Confederacy. The authorized withdrawing signature, that of the dark haired, plump, sight-impaired Wojciech Grzymała.

Only a few hours later, after a detailed search of Zgorzelec, the villa was exposed. Later research would find it was purchased in the early 1990's - in the months shortly after Poland was freed from the Communist grip that had strangled it. It was purchased by none other than the same Franco-Polish Confederacy, whose president was one Wojciech Grzymała.

They now sat around the warmth of the massive ceramic stove in their small suite of their Görlitz hotel. It overlooked the fountain on the east end of *the ubermarkt* square. Outside their third-floor accommodations, as night was beginning to descend, pigeons nestled in the stone ledges framing the stained-glass windows of the church, which was across a narrow alley-width path from their hotel.

This was their makeshift operations center, now that they had distanced themselves from *The Blind* in Berlin. The papers for the villa ownership had been sent in the last hour, as well as the records Diane had requested for the multiple bank account withdrawals.

She yelled across the room at an agent on station with her, "We need to have the team in *The Blind* run this Wojciech Grzymała and see what we can find about him."

Sophie was sitting upright quietly in an armchair. "I will tell you what you will find," she offered modestly.

"Yes, Sophie, please go on," Diane said encouragingly. She had learned to listen whenever Sophie had something to say, for she did not say much, but her few words were always heavy with insight.

"You will find that Wojciech Grzymała is a joke. He does not exist. I know because Wojciech Grzymała was a close friend and financier of Frederic Chopin while he was living in Paris. And that is why this fictional organization is called the Franco-Polish Confederacy. They are laughing at their cleverness."

Diane realized that this so-called Wojciech Gryzmała must have been none other than the mysterious Jean Paul racing across Europe, emptying accounts, and preparing for Stanley's murder of Langston Powell. All at Stanley's behest, the two men having met in London that Monday before the Friday murder. Stanley surely detailed a plan to Jean Paul which would keep his friend moving fast. Since there was no crime at that point, so no one would have been watching them.

"Their vanity will be their undoing," said Diane, not appreciating their joke, as Sophie had described . "Get the researchers looking for anyone who fits Jean Paul's general description on trains or planes between London on Monday, Paris on Tuesday, and Warsaw on Thursday."

Chapter Nine
Germany

STANLEY AWOKE IN a large, nearly empty room, containing only the bed in which he lay, a wooden chair nearby, and a decorative wooden stand atop which was an old, but beautifully hand decorated ceramic wash basin and matching water jar. The decorations were decidedly Germanic to Stanley's eye. His body ached, most notably his thigh where he had been wounded. An angled winter's morning light cut through the room, despite the fact that winter was still a few weeks off.

Stanley raised himself carefully from the bed. His leg had been tended to, he noticed, as it was cleanly bandaged. Otherwise he was completely naked, and the cool air in the room reminded him of this. He had been sleeping under an old but heavy goose down quilt, which he now realized had been keeping him remarkably warm. He grabbed the old robe which had been laid on the wooden chair and wrapped it around his aging frame. He then moved to one of the two windows, which overlooked a small square, lined with other creme and mustard colored adjoined homes, some with Saxon exterior markings. At the end of the square, attached to the end of a row of houses, he noticed a six or seven story tall tower.

Initially, he cringed, remembering the tower over the footbridge where he very nearly lost his life. The height was similar, and this tower was also square in design. However, the similarities ended there. This was no medieval tower, or recreation thereof. This tower was bright and alive with light, unlike the dreary Zgorzelec tower. Whereas the Polish tower had only three porthole type penetrations atop its barren facade, this tower had three large rectangular windows across each of the floors of its face, except the lowest two which formed an impressive, open archway.

It had four tiers of windows decorating the upper floors. The highest tier of which appeared to be only half the height of the previous three courses, as demanded by their yielding to the sloping terra cotta colored tile roofline, which was adorned with yet a final single small dormer window. The entire tower was stucco, in a hue of creme that bordered almost on a subdued pale blend of butter and orange. Its corners were highlighted with white stone blocks, its arch and structure outlined in matching broad white stonework, giving the structure an overall imperial dignity.

"It is the *Reichstor*. All my guests who rent this room, as modest as it is, comment upon its charm," said a soft, wispy voice in German from behind him. "Do not mind me, I am just an old man who has long lived in a silent house alone, so your footsteps, as light as they were, seemed like thunder to me."

Stanley turned slowly to face the man. He was older than Stanley's seventy years, and stood haunched in the bedroom's doorway. Behind him, Stanley could see the top of the staircase leading down to the ground level.

"Yes, it is very impressive." said Stanley slowly in German. The two men were measuring each other in their minds. "It was a gateway to the town at one point?"

"*Ya, ya*" said the German. "It was functional in its day, but now is merely a decoration. Like so many of us that crawl in its shadow."

Stanley smiled at the man, as he himself had felt the same lack of purpose in his years as a retiree.

"I owe you and Deiter much thanks for taking me in, and caring to my wounds," said Stanley, grasping his thigh through the robe.

"Yes, of course, you are wondering if Deiter is here now," the elder man said, apparently reading Stanley's mind. He paused. "*Nein, nein*, my son has left me once again. He tires of my spying on him, so he stays for a few hours and then leaves me. He left the night he dropped you with me to continue on to Prague, two nights ago."

Stanley searched his German vocabulary. Did he actually mean spying, or perhaps he meant his gazing upon him? Stanley noted from what the old man had said that Stanley had been asleep for over 24 hours straight. This would explain the stiffness in his back that he thought could only have been from his exploits in the river.

"Come now, your clothes are dry. I had them by the fire. Also, the money that you were carrying, over seven thousand Euros. Not bad for an old man dying of cancer."

There was a twinkle in the old man's eyes, a sparking ember from the flames of a fire that had long ago burned itself out.

"Forgive me, I do not understand," said Stanley. His host seemed to be antagonizing him. "I am going to live with my sister. This money was my life's savings. I will give it to my sister, who has agreed to take care of me until I die."

"My friend," started the old man, "you will find I have no time for the stories that you so fancifully told my overly sensitive son. My son is a good man, in his own way, but even for as successful as he is, he is full of folly and compassion. He left this house long ago because I am not. He was full of hope and ambition."

Stanley stared at the old man, wondering where this was leading.

"You see, my friend, I pulled more slivers of ceramic out of your thigh while you slept so soundly. If those immigrant youths tossed you in the river, as you told my son, they must have beaten you first with beer steins, eh?" The man laughed elfishly at his own joke.

Stanley could only look at the man, careful not to say anything that would incriminate himself. The man was demonstrating his powers of perception, blatantly showing off for his houseguest.

"These immigrants also missed your stash of euro's, which was hard as they were bulging from your soaked clothes." The man paused. He was enjoying this game of cat and mouse. "But where are my manners? You must be starving after so long in bed. I will leave you to wash. Come downstairs to eat and we will talk over a meal."

The man departed, closing the door behind him. Stanley washed, and still in his robe, he went downstairs to join the man at the humble wooden table and chairs within his kitchen.

The man heard him coming down the steps, and called out aloud to him. "As you know I am Deiter's father. My name is Tobias, but please feel free to address me as Herr Reinhardt."

Stanley could smell Herr Reinhardt boiling sausage. His hunger was like a flame that danced erratically in the hollow of his stomach.

"You have lived here in Borna all your life, Herr Reinhardt?" asked Stanley carefully, so as to have the appearance of making small talk.

"*Ya, ya, ya*. You are wondering how old is this Tobias? Gauging from his son, he must be in his sixties. That is correct, although I know I look much older. You my friend, are Polish, or so says my son. Tomorrow I will drive you to your sister's home in Leipzig, *ya*?"

"Yes, that will be fine," Stanley answered, still working through his thoughts as Tobias fished a boiled sausage out of his pot and placed it carefully onto Stanley's plate.

"You are thinking, who is this man to whom I have been abandoned?" said Tobias aloud. "He pries and surmises, and is quite analytical - this is what you are thinking, *nein*?"

"Yes, Herr Reinhardt, that is exactly what I was thinking. Precisely, but you seem to have displayed a knack for discerning that in the few minutes we have been talking," said Stanley.

"Allow me to continue. You casually ask how long I have lived here. Indeed, all my life, which you now know is more than sixty years. You have deduced I had been here when this was the German Democratic Republic - you would say in America the East Germany, *nein*?" He smiled at Stanley.

Stanley was now eating his meal. He cut and ate the sausage with the skin intact, along with the boiled potatoes Tobias served as well. "Why do you think I am American?"

"You are betrayed by your German. It is quite good, but you use words and pronunciations that are the corrupted German of the Americans. As I say, it is very, very good, but not as good as your Polish, I am sure."

Tobias was clearly enjoying the company of Stanley, but Stanley sensed it was more than just loneliness. Stanley's senses warned him that this man was a former intelligence professional himself, and was enjoying having a colleague in his care. Even if that colleague was previously unknown to him.

Stanley continued to eat greedily. The coffee now being poured by Tobias was bitter and black, but no cream was offered. Stanley assumed it was a luxury this pensioner had denied himself for some time.

"It was very easy to discern who you really are, my friend. Or, should I say, *Herr* Wisniewski?"

Stanley stopped, frozen. His fork with sausage now inches from his mouth, before he realized his reaction was only validating the old man's accusation. Had Tobias wanted to turn Stanley in to the authorities, Stanley would have awoken in chains. Stanley listened and continued eating.

"Do not look so startled. Do not worry, my friend. You are safe here. The townspeople do not call on me. I am an *Ausgestossene* - an outcast. They barely look at me when I walk the square. This is a small town of only twenty-two thousand people, but nearly all know and despise me. I do not have the money to move away, so I live here a very lonely and very poor life. Now it is your turn to tell me who I am."

Stanley finished his plate, and was still enjoying the coffee. It was clear Herr Reinhardt was showing off his power of inductive reasoning. Now, he wanted to test Stanley.

Stanley swallowed his mouthful and began. "You were raised in East Germany - not *the* East Germany, we say only East Germany - and now you are retired. You have your home, and while it is modest, you are prideful of its appearance. This shows, especially to the unexpected lodger. You live simply, and are a stern man, who neither approves of your son's lifestyle, nor will accept the money he offers that comes from his success. He loves you but also fears you. Your townspeople only fear you, or did once, but that fear has now grown to be an open disdain. So why do they detest this observant, bitter old man? Because as you mentioned upstairs, you spied on them. For years, you spied on your neighbors and friends. You turned them over to the *Stasi* - the East German secret police. The *Stasi* paid you, no? A little here, a little there, and along with your wages as a coal worker, you got by. Did they arrange for your son to get into University as part of this deal? I assume not, as the wall had come down before that. No, he earned his degree on his own, which makes you even more angry with him. But what angered you most, was when the wall came down and the *Stasi* were driven out. After Germany reunified, the *Stasi* files were made available to everyone who they had once spied upon. Your townspeople started to access their files, only to find out that you, their nice but curious neighbor, had spied on them. Soon you were shunned every time you left your door. Your own son came to despise you for what you did. Am I close?"

Stanley was reining himself in now, as he had gotten too prideful of his own perceptive abilities. He knew that East Germany had been one of the most spied upon populaces of all history. Anyone having any contacts or commodities that were even remotely deemed to be Western were turned in to the *Stasi*. The whole East German government leveraged fear in lieu of liberty. Unlike in Poland, where the Poles resisted the communist state, in East Germany nearly everyone yielded to its abuse. It was estimated one of every six citizens had a *Stasi* file. Neighbor spied upon neighbor. Husbands had even spied upon wives. Once the *Stasi* files were opened to the German people in the 1990's, rifts were torn throughout the population as they became aware of those who had betrayed them to the state secret police.

"Very good, my friend. I am amused by your insights. I liked the coal miner profession observation. Good guess, as this is an area that was built on coal for many years. But *nein*, like you, I was a professional. I was not an informer, but I was the *Stasi* agent to whom so many here informed. It was to me they told their every suspicion. To me they told what comments their coworkers had made in confidence over a schnapps or two. To me they told whose husbands they suspected were cheating on their wives. I was a powerful man, once. I was a man of special skills. Now, there is no need for these skills. Now, I am only a hated lonely old man waiting to die."

Stanley noted his reference to dying, as if mocking Stanley's own tale of waiting to yield to cancer.

"If you give me my clothes, I will dress now and leave you now. I hope you will accept my thanks and will take payment for my lodging and care." Stanley felt the need to continue towards his rendezvous in Vienna with Jean Paul. He felt staying any longer in this home was not safe.

"Relax. Do not fear me. I am a silly old man who is enjoying the little company I get. Besides, I have no benefit in turning you in. These people that you run from, they will only cause trouble for me.

With my background, they will think I am part of your network, as if this all had been planned. I do not need this. For this same reason, I will not take your money. You are free to go, if you like, just promise me when you are taken, you will not speak of your time in this house or this town."

"I appreciate all you have done for me. I will respect your wishes," promised Stanley.

"I will drive you to Leipzig myself. I will drop you at the *Hauptbahnhof* where you can catch a fast train to Frankfurt, Dusseldorf, or wherever. It will be my pleasure. It will be nice to see the world outside Borna again," said Herr Reinhardt, underscoring how rare this trip was for him.

"Of course, I will pay you what I would pay any other driver," said Stanley, finishing his sausage breakfast.

"I could not possibly allow you," protested his host, who in reality longed to hear these words from Stanley. His protests collapsed altogether when Stanley insisted.

Tobias looked at his guest curiously. What drove him to the murder in Warsaw? Stanley saw the curiosity in his eyes, but also realized the old man was professionally smart enough to resist asking. It was a case of what he knew could indeed hurt him. At this point, if Tobias was to be questioned by the authorities, he could deny knowing who Stanley was.

"You do not blend in, my friend. I have some German clothes for you. I think they will fit you, though you are quite tall. Also, a coat and a large hat for you, to keep you warm. *Ya*?"

Later they rode into Leipzig in Tobias' remarkably maintained 1989 Trabant 601 Universal station wagon. The puttering of the two-cylinder, two-stroke 600cc engine made Stanley marvel as to how this vehicle had remained usable over the last twenty-some years. Trabants were the automotive laughingstock of the East Block itself, yet were popular within East Germany. Nearly four million had been produced over thirty-plus years in this small country. But none after 1991, when the capitalism of the German reunification killed off the inefficient brand. German carmakers were known for their efficiency. Like so much else of his past life, Tobias held on to this last vestige of his past importance.

"You know, Herr Reinhardt, a collector in the west would pay handsomely for this vehicle," Stanley said to his landlord turned driver.

"And what would I drive then?" dismissed the cynical Tobias.

Stanley decided not to waste the energy to make him understand the incredible value of this vehicle, which must have been one of the few remaining of its kind.

Herr Reinhardt dropped his passenger at the Leipzig central train station, where Stanley paid him well for his effort. He gave the pensioner one thousand of his remaining Euros.

"These funds are clean, no sequential numbers, untraceable. But you can always exchange them again yourself, if you desire." Stanley did not bother to tell him how, as he was sure Tobias already knew from his past life.

"*Ya*, I will be careful. You should be careful also, my friend. They will be watching for you, whoever they may be." With a laugh, he said, "Tell your sister to take good care of you."

"I prefer you pay attention to your driving," Stanley said calmly and slowly. "I recently lost a very close friend to a motoring accident. I will hold your phone until we get to Munich, and pay you another one hundred euro's for doing so." He could see he had the driver's attention now. Stanley methodically removed the battery and the sim card from the device.

"For one hundred Euros, I can wait to talk to my wife," said the Arab.

He knew from the agency they could track a phone from its GPS bearings. He also knew the agency had software which once pushed onto a phone, could mimic it being off, but it's microphone and GPS locator remained functional. Their prey turned off their cell phones, unaware that the agency continued to track and listen in on them. Stanley's removing the battery from the phone rendered it to a lifeless piece of cold metal and plastic.

Arriving in Munich, Stanley had the young man drive him to the downtown east train station. He paid the driver in cash, and after returning the Arab's phone, decided to eat before repeating the process to find a driver to take him to Vienna. Before he ate, however, he purchased from a street vendor a *Landhaushut* - a traditional German country hat in a muted alpine green, its tassel flailing from the headband at its aft.

He also procured a new jacket, not as warm as Tobias' battered coat, but certainly a random purchase to change his appearance. Especially if the agency were able to track him somehow to Herr Reinhardt or the Arab driver. Finally, he procured a scarf in the colors and insignia of the FC Bayern München – Munich's soccer team.

An hour later, the driver was a young, blonde German, and the car a Mercedes sedan. Stanley sat quietly in the back seat again, having already paid the driver for the luxury of holding onto his cell phone. It rested in Stanley's right hand, its battery and sim card in his left.

The countryside was very flat as the Mercedes motored out of Munich. Leaving the city in the late afternoon, the farmlands rolled out before them in a great plateau. The German villages were discretely visible as strategic intersections, where competing hues of wheat, barley, and ochre colored fields came together.

The edges of the fields were militarily rigid, never meandering, always having highly delineated borders, extremely precise. It was a strangely soothing, peaceful and prosperous surrounding. It effected in Stanley a feeling of calm and melancholy. Yet, in this Bavarian farmland lay the very seeds of aggression that ultimately led to the conquest of his beloved Poland. Here the Nazis under Hitler planned their conquests of Austria, Czechoslovakia and beyond.

Stanley could not help but think that it was Munich, itself, where the last great war could have been averted. But rather than confront Hitler in 1938 with strength and resolution here, the Allies squandered peace, mistaking appeasement as its equal. But the appeased only became the emboldened, and the subsequent war ripped apart the world. Ripped away at his Poland, ripped away at his family and friends, ripped apart the family of his beloved Agnieszka.

Chapter Ten

Rendez-vous in Vienna

ON THE MORNING of the sixth of December, Stanley rested, on one of the ornamental benches that decorated the luxuriously detailed grounds outside the Belvedere Palace in Vienna. The morning had left a touch of frost that lay like mirrored glaze atop the expansive manicured lawns. The cold morning air stung of the pending, bitter winter.

Stanley had walked the short distance from the third-rate Turkish hostel where he had stayed over-night not far from Vienna's *Ungargasse Strasse*. He had risen early, donned the wide brim wool *Landhaushut* hat he had procured in Munich. It felt loose atop his shaven, now stubby head, but still captured its heat in this cold, gray December morning. Along with his Bayern München scarf and sunglasses, he felt inconspicuous enough. He was careful that the scarf was pulled across his mouth and chin to deny any cameras and their facial recognition software the chance to pull his image from the sparse morning crowd.

Earlier that morning, he had walked through the narrow streets of this Viennese neighborhood, past the prominent white mosque, complete with two free-standing minarets, which in the brightening morning sun seemed to punctuate the solemnity of this young but advancing day. Stanley took in his surroundings, constantly assessing figures that might be following him, or loitering passively ahead.

He saw virtually no one, and felt the empty, anonymous contentment of being unnoticed. He knew this could be a deception, if the agency had a bearing on him. They could be tracking him from pre-positioned spotters or cameras well out of sight. His senses remained sharp as he walked the brisk early morning streets.

Weaving through the maze of narrow streets, he passed a Uniate style building, it's massive onion dome surrounded by four others in a manner reminding him of the Mosque's minarets. He crossed an elevated walkway over a couple of train tracks, and coming down the stairs of the walk, found his way through the courtyard of a large Western hotel – what had once been the stately Imperial Riding School.

It was still early, and the sweepers hosed and scrubbed at the hotel's grounds. Stanley tilted his head down as he passed, knowing the hotel's video coverage would be extensive. Stanley pushed past the posh hotel gates onto the *Ungargasse Strasse*, in search of the *kaffeehaus* he had found the night before. Soon he was upon it, only a few blocks down the boulevard, across the avenue, and back through an alley.

Stanley stepped in past the front of the store. Its ravaged facade spoke of a poor proprietor who could not afford the luxury of fresh paint nor proper signage. Stanley minded his hat as he negotiated the door, with its soap scrawled text upon the glass panel reading "free internet".

Inside Stanley calibrated to the warmth, purchased a coffee and

Viennese croissant, and was pleased to notice all three internet computers unoccupied. The young proprietor, likely Albanian or Serbian from his looks, was pre-occupied in preparing for his hopeful morning rush. Stanley keyed in the web address that Jean Paul had supplied him- the address that Stanley had committed to memory in the villa at Zgorzelec, before burning the only written evidence, crumbling the ashes, and washing the fine residue down the sink with water as hot as he could convince the tap to produce.

Stanley sipped the coffee, which he found to be acidic from the over roasting of the beans. The website came to life on his monitor. It was in French and discussed the merits of the *Musée d'Orsay* and its cache of Impressionist art.

The code they had worked out was simple and readily recalled from memory. Stanley and Jean Paul had agreed to two physical locations in advance for each city where they were to meet, and these were known only to the two of them. The website was elegant in its simplicity. It showed one impressionistic photo cropped by an effusive volume of detailed text describing the work. The number of words in the first sentence of the text told them of the time of the meeting. Stanley counted ten words. The meet was to be at ten AM.

The nature of the artwork depicted which of the two locations would be the meet site for today. If the artwork contained one or more people in it, the location was the pre-agreed primary meeting location. Easily remembered – "people meant primary". If it was a landscape or still life with no human forms, then the meeting location was the back-up location - "Scenery means secondary".

The image centered in this website this morning was one of Monet's water lilies series. Backup location - Vienna's Belvedere Palace at Ten AM. The other site – the Primary site, had been agreed to as outside the *Wurstelprater* amusement park in the *Wiener Prater* in Vienna's second district.

Stanley was pleased not to see the one picture that was reserved for the abort signal - Van Gogh's famous self-portrait with the bandaged ear. If this image was displayed then the meet was aborted, and no further contact was to be attempted. It amused Stanley that this famous masterpiece was not even resident at the *Musée d'Orsay*. It resided in the Courtauld Gallery in London.

It was now later that morning, at quarter to ten, and Stanley rested on the bench within the manicured lawns that formed the promenade leading up to the Belvedere Palace proper. The hat, scarf and shaded glasses were his only protection from being recognized by man or machine. Stanley was confident in the simplicity of this tradecraft.

Only he and Jean Paul knew the primary and alternate locations. Only they knew the website address declaring which site. And only they knew the meaning of the images displayed.

Jean Paul walked up to Stanley at precisely ten o'clock. Stanley knew that now was the point at which the real danger hung over them both. Whenever they were both together, it meant they were then at risk of being exposed to anyone who followed either of them. For this reason, they were to keep these meetings as brief as possible, despite their obviously being elated at seeing each other again.

There was always the risk of one of them having been compromised by the authorities to entrap the other. For this they had also long ago worked out a safe-word, and safe-word response.

Jean Paul walked up to Stanley, and in Polish said to him as he patted his own chest in the cold Viennese morning air. "*Dzień dobry*, my friend. How has life been treating you?"

Stanley looked up at him and answered with only the safe-word, "Handsomely".

Jean Paul grinned broadly with the response, "Handsomely? *Dobrze*!"

Any other response from either of the two would have warned the other that they were being watched or listened to. Also, any other question or opening phrase was Jean Paul's opportunity to declare "not safe".

Jean Paul had carried a small khaki knapsack, which he put down next to Stanley's leg. He had expected Stanley to have had the rucksack he had left with him in Zgorzelec. The two knew to grab the opposite bags on their exit in only a few minutes. This day, however, Jean Paul would leave empty handed.

Jean Paul began in Polish, "My friend, you have no bag this morning?"

Stanley had practiced the response to himself the night before in the Turkish hostel. "I am well. There was trouble, but it is well behind me now."

Jean Paul was surprised that Stanley would have lost the bag and its contents. The bag was prepared so that its contents were untraceable, but it bothered Jean Paul that the man his mother once told him to always trust, appeared to be slipping.

"Where is the handgun?" Jen Paul asked the old man. He was confident from their tradecraft that the meeting was safe and they were not being monitored.

"Somewhere in the Neisse river, I believe," said Stanley stoically.

"In the river? You threw it in the river?" Jean Paul was again surprised.

"No, but I believe it became dislodged from my pocket while I was in the water." Stanley looked impassively at the palace.

"You don't know for sure? What were you doing in the river?" Jean Paul became more animated with each revelation.

"I was stopped in my attempt to cross the bridge. I had to escape into the river. That is enough about that. I am here, the bag and the pistol are not."

Stanley did not appreciate the bevy of questions being lobbed by Jean Paul. He then passed a folded note to Jean Paul, naming the city, date, as well as the primary and secondary locations for their next meeting. Jean Paul took it, noting this physical act was intended to end the verbal discourse. Jean Paul unfolded the note, but carefully shielded it against his body, bowing his head over it to assure it was obstructed from all viewing angles. He studied it, committed it to memory, refolded the note and returned it to Stanley.

Jean Paul looked hard into Stanley's eyes, which were all he could really see of his partner's face, as Stanley had pulled his sunglasses low enough on his nose to look over. His eyes looked like those of a tired old man. They were fatigued, reflecting the weariness of this seventy-year-old man in playing the games of his youth.

"Why do you continue this, my friend? Pick a spot and rest, stay out of sight." Jean Paul thought he was comforting his friend.

"I do not kid myself," began the old man. "My days are numbered. But for the first time since I have retired, I have a task I must complete. It is what drives me."

Stanley continued to look upon the grandiose upper Belvedere Palace before which he sat. The grounds were separated into the upper and lower. The upper grounds possessing the elegant white marble palace, along with the tremendous reflecting pool. The lower Belvedere, after descending the outdoor steps of the immaculate garden, yielded the orangery and other components of the palace.

"But your task is complete. You finished it in Warsaw. I have now sent your message to the British press. You are done. Now rest and stay put somewhere." Jean Paul spoke, gauging his mentor's weariness.

"No, my friend, I have only begun my task. Your mother, my dear love, always wanted a simple thing I could never give her. We both loved the master's music. It is where we first met. She always yearned to lay a bouquet of white lilies on the master's grave. This, I now must do for her. Out of respect to her, I must live long enough to place her flowers upon those stones. There, and only there, will my task be finished." Stanley's tired eyes were now ringed in a moistened pool that collected near each temple. Jean Paul noticed this and became concerned that this hiding and running was becoming too much for him.

Jean Paul understood the master to be Frederic Chopin. As a young boy, he remembered his mother playing his nocturnes on the phonograph. Always Chopin. Rarely a waltz. The young boy that Jean Paul was then loved the upbeat waltzes. His mother, however, always played the somber nocturnes, which, while beautiful, were mournful. Much as Chopin himself was mournful for his beloved Poland, while he was self-exiled in Paris. Much as Jean Paul's mother was mournful for a truly free Poland that the Soviets had stolen from her. Finally, she mourned her own father, who the Soviet's took from her at *Katyń*.

"Yes, yes, my *matka*," Jean Paul said fondly. "We both loved her while she was with us. Come with me, I can take you today to the master's grave. By tomorrow you are done. But this is sheer foolishness. My mother is gone. It is not your fault, my friend. We both loved her. She is gone, she led a good life. She died in a terrible accident. It is no one's fault."

Jean Paul looked softly at Stanley, sensing his increasing pain of remembrance.

"What I am here to tell you is that it is someone's fault," said Stanley harshly. "Warsaw was only the beginning. The other one profited from his dealings with that man taken in Warsaw. One has been stopped, the other must be brought to justice."

Stanley's eyes were now dry and hardened, reflecting the tone of his voice.

Jean Paul knew the references were to the slain Langston Powell, and "the other one" was the very Jack Trellis who now hunted them both. To Stanley, Jean Paul repeated, "What do you mean, someone is responsible?"

Stanley paused to regain himself. "Long ago he pulled me back from Warsaw. Away from your mother. Do you remember?"

"Yes, of course, my friend. I had never met you in person before that. My mother said to always trust you, and then she sent you to see me in Gdańsk. You saved me that night. If I had not listened to you that night, I would have perished, I am sure of that."

Jean Paul reflected on all that Stanley had done for him, getting him out of Poland and relocated to Paris back in 1996.

Stanley did not desire either praise nor thanks. He continued, "Soon after that, I was recalled back to America. He then tried to discredit me. I had found out that he was enriching himself on the misery of others, so he forced me into retirement. Do you know how?"

Jean Paul knew that Trellis had driven Stanley out of the CIA. This Stanley clearly needed to get this off his chest. "How, my friend?"

"He told me that he had discovered my *Sarenka*. He knew her name. He knew she was your mother. But they thought you were dead. Executed by the Soviets in '96. They did not know that your *matka* and I had started a new life for you in Paris. He then threatened me that if I did not retire immediately, or ever spoke a word to anyone of what I had found of his treachery, that he would kill my *Sarenka*! I would never see her again. In that moment, he took her from me."

Saying all this for the first time to anyone, Stanley bowed his head in shame. While he had not lied to Jean Paul, he was not completely truthful, either. Trellis had learned *Sarenka's* identity years earlier, but this was another tale for another time.

"My God," said Jean Paul. He was shaken with this new knowledge; crushed by the denial of a long-held truth. "Are you saying that the accident in which she died was his doing?"

Stanley ignored the question directly. "She came to see me in 2008 in America. I had worked with her to fund the building of a Katyń Memorial in Baltimore. The Polish Government supported this. Our friend found out that I had been communicating with her, and that she had visited me in Baltimore. Less than two years later she died in that supposed horrible accident. I hold him responsible. I know it was his doing."

Stanley now raised his head again, his eyes relit with a passion of the tasks that remained ahead of him.

"My God," repeated Jean Paul, in shock.

Stanley looked away from Jean Paul to hide his tired eyes. He pushed his sunglasses high onto his nose. In looking at the grand white palace that lay majestically across the lawn and fountained ponds, he said aloud to Jean Paul, "This really is a beautiful palace. Perhaps more beautiful than those in the other European capitals, but still it is certainly less lovely than the Belvedere Palace of home."

Jean Paul knew Stanley spoke of the other Belvedere Palace in Łazienki Park in Warsaw. And he knew now that Stanley was tiring of this game of hiding from his inevitable fate. Stanley was homesick, not for his physical home, but for the home that was Poland. The home that had once been his and his Agnieszka's together.

The alarm on Jean Paul's watch sounded, noting they were not to stay together for any longer.

"*Do widzenia,*" said Jean Paul, rising abruptly to his feet.

"*Do widzenia,*" said Stanley, sitting still in his lonely reflections.

Stanley carried the knapsack as he walked away from the Vienna meeting.

His thoughts reminisced back to 1993. Poland was now free. Lech Wałęsa had been democratically elected as its first free President. The yoke of communism was now cast behind them.

Stanley had returned to Communist Poland in 1987, renewing the output from his agent *Syrenka*. Over the next six years, he continued his relationship with *Pani* Agnieszka Danuska. By 1993, this was done in a much more open manner. Her husband was gone, exiled to Moscow, along with so many other of those Poles who had laid low this great culture at the direction of the Soviets. And in a fitting move of reward for her services, Agnieszka was awarded an under-secretary position in the Cultural Ministry of the new free Polish government. Her son, Kazimierz, Stanley's agent *Syrenka*, also was rewarded, continuing to serve the state as a customs official in his adopted home of Gdańsk.

Stanley was now able to invite Agnieszka openly to lunch with him in Bolesławiec, the town renowned for its remarkable pottery. On its town square, there stood a restaurant he favored. Traveling separately, she met him there. No longer shackled with travel limitations, or Communist minders as the Economic Minister's wife, it was refreshingly easy for her. She also no longer had a husband to which she had to explain her movements, either. The Soviets had him in Russia.

She had taken the train, and Stanley his car. He met her at the station, driving her the short distance through this small but beautiful town.

After they had finished their meal, Stanley asked her to take a ride in his car through the countryside. The sun shone brightly on them. Stanley drove the battered country roads. He doubled back at times, to assure there had been no one following him. This was no longer needed for the Communists. Now it was his fellow Americans to which he wished not to reveal his secrets.

As they neared the river Neisse, they parked his car and he walked with her. Stanley boldly took Agnieszka's hand and pulled her up the walk to a modest, but beautiful villa, sitting upon a hill, its rear facade overlooking the river.

"You know this place?" she asked, smiling up at Stanley.

"It is why I asked you to come with me to Zgorzelec." They walked up a short length of brick paving to the heavy oaken door. Stanley reached into his jacket to produce a single key, which he handed to her. She inserted it into the lock. Together they pushed open the heavy door, and stepped across the threshold.

Her eyes were amazed, her face raptured. Its features were transfigured to those of a very young child.

"It is beautiful," she said, so softly that the words nearly clung to her lips.

"I am glad you think so," exclaimed Stanley proudly. "It is yours."

"*Nie, Prawda*!" she exclaimed, almost in a schoolgirl squeal.

"My dear *Sarenka*, it is most certainly true. This lodging is modest, and certainly much too modest for a woman of your accommodations," Stanley said, smiling at her. Around them were wooden chairs and furniture, all hand made locally, all bearing traditional Polish carvings. From the kitchen, she could see across the Neisse into Görlitz.

"I am amazed. It is like the home I remember as a very young girl.

We had a small family farm. This side of the river was all Germany then, long stolen from Poland. But even that was not enough for the Nazi's. The Germans forced us from our farm, and we were forced to resettle with my father's family in Wadowice. But all this is yours, my Stashew?"

He looked at her with a snappish move of his neck. "No, my *Sarenka*, this is not mine. As I have said, this now is all yours."

He pressed the key he had removed from the lock into her palm with both of his hands. Her eyes moistened. "Why do you tease me, so?"

He moved his hands to her cheeks, wiping away her forming tears. "I do not tease you, my lovely. This is my government's gift to you. For all you have done. For all we have done together."

His fingers wiped away her tears, only to soon have a profusion of tears stream that he could not possibly hold back.

"*Czy to prawda*?" she asked of him.

"Yes, my dearest fawn, it is true," Stanley replied. "But we must keep it a secret, your government must not know, your friends must not know. Only your son may know."

"It is too much! *Chwała Bogu*!" she said, praising God for this unexpected blessing.

Her tears flowed now with no constraints. She threw her hands around his neck, pulling him down to her. Her lips found his. And now, this time, there was no hesitation. Her mouth searched his, her tongue traced its corners, seeking its every crevice. The joyous tears of the young girl had transformed into the woman's cries of gratitude. Agnieszka was deeply struck by all Stanley had done for her. He had risked his very life. Her tears moistened the dry skin of his face.

"My Stanley, *jak cię kocham!*" She breathed huskily onto his tear-moistened face

"I love you too, my *Sarenka,*" he responded, his emotions rising in him like an animal heat.

His hands moved down from her tear moistened cheeks, outlining her enchanting feminine form. They came to rest along her hips, until, she reached down to gently lift them upward onto her clothed breasts. She knew this was new to Stanley, the delicate softness of a women, which made her cherish the moment all the more.

Stanley's breathing quickened. He was now forty-eight years old, his adult life now exposed as a clandestine ruse. This man of secrets was about to discover the most anxious and delicate of mysteries.

Agnieszka, some eight years his senior, was still as beautiful as any woman he had ever seen. Her face was younger than her years. His hands now roamed awkwardly across the expanses of her form. He pulled back from her lips, to kiss the gentle dimple of the tip of her nose. He had always loved this wonderful crevice, for it was the identifying feature the night he sat next to her in the symphony, to assure it was she that he addressed.

He remembered holding her grace and loveliness in his sight that first night so many years ago. Tonight, he held her grace and her womanhood in his trembling hands.

She took him by those fumbling hands, back to the modest bedroom she had not yet seen. There she embraced Stanley as she had long desired to, pressing herself into him, as if attempting to merge their bodies and their souls into one being. And soon, this is exactly what came to pass – one being, one breath, one pulse.

Wave after wave of emotion enveloped them. Expressions raced across Stanley's face that she had never seen. Then she realized, deep within herself, within her consciousness, that she also was feeling emotions she had never experienced.

Of course, she had made love to her husband, this she had surely experienced. But it was a forced undertaking, with a man she neither loved nor respected. A native Pole who willingly enslaved his mother land in the chains of the Soviets for his personal gain.

Tonight, for the first time, Agnieszka made love to a man she respected, and now was sure that she loved. It was truly *love* that she now made with this man.

With this man, from across an ocean, from the land of excess that was America. To her came this unexpected, yet wonderful old soul. Like Agnieszka, his wounded spirit had so much already taken from it. In his own way, he was like her: humble, caring and passionate. They were the same. They yearned, for so long, for the culture of Poland itself to be freely reinstated. And now, they had succeeded. This day, despite the fears of the many tomorrows to come, they took solace in each other's tenderness.

When they were resting afterwards, naked, exposed but without shame, Agnieszka noticed the lilies on the table by her bedside. The flowers' bouquet mixed with the sweat of their lovemaking, creating a distinct scent that they both would associate with this day forever.

She rolled over onto him, her tender bosom resting comfortably upon his naked chest.

"One day you will take me to Paris, and we will lay white lilies upon no other than Chopin's grave. I hear it is always draped in flowers, fresh every day from his visiting admirers the world over. One can only feel pity for the rest of Paris' dead."

Stanley, exhausted, consumed, looked into her eyes above him. "This is a promise I make to you. Your lilies will be laid upon the master's grave."

Jean Paul left the meeting with Stanley in Vienna, returning to his old green Audi. "Always trust this man. Do only as he says. Never question him."

It was his mother's voice ringing in his ears.

It was the early 1990's. The communist government of Poland had been replaced with Lech Wałęsa's *Solidarity Party's* free government. His mother, no longer worried about hiding her son from the Soviets, was about to introduce Jean Paul, or Kazimierz Danuski, as he was then known, to the CIA agent for the first time.

"You can always trust *Pan* Wisniewski. Always trust Stanley."

Since the late seventies, Kazimierz only knew his mother was communicating with the CIA. He never knew who, or how. Nor did he want to know. It was safer not to. *Solidarity* trusted Kazimierz, who trusted his mother, who in turn trusted Stanley.

Now she asked her son to trust Stanley as well. And trust Stanley he did. When Stanley asked him to buy the villa in Zgorzelec, he did it.

Jean Paul, then Kazimierz, bought the property with money taken from Stanley's operational funds. Stanley had told him it was to be a secret gift from his government to his mother. Jean Paul provided the fictitious name, and its equally fictitious organization, for the documents.

Then, five few years later, in 1996, Jean Paul received the call from his mother that would forever change his life. She was crying uncontrollably. She was hysterical. Kazimierz Danuski tried to calm his mother, but she would not be consoled. She told him to immediately meet Stanley in Gdańsk. It was incredibly urgent. He was to meet Stanley at the medieval port crane, known in Polish as the *Żuraw*. He was to go directly there and nowhere else. His mother made him promise to do exactly this.

The *Żuraw* was a massive structure along the Motława river in Gdańsk. It stood impassively along the waterfront like a gothic sentinel. Originally built in 1367, destroyed by fire in 1442, and rebuilt a few years later, this cycle continued many times over the years. It was finally destroyed in World War II, like so much else of Poland. Then, after the war, this medieval sea crane was reconstructed once more. A massive dark wooden crane supported on two large, round buildings made of brick. It had been remarked as looking like a shrouded spectre's head haunched out over the sea, its massive brick shoulders shrugging at time itself.

Stanley had meticulously always used Agnieszka as the intermediary to protect his agent. A cut out, to protect *Syrenka* from being observed with Stanley. It was also a comfort for Agnieszka to protect her son in this way.

Since 1991, when Stanley first met Kazimierz Danuski directly, they decided they would continue to use Agnieszka as a go-between. It was safer. Although the Communists in Poland had disappeared, the vengence of the Russians never would.

That night in 1996, on that frantic phone call, she told her son to go to the *Żuraw* and meet Stanley alone, without her. She cautioned her son to look for Stanley's safe signal - sweeping his hair from his forehead with the back of his left hand, its palm outstretched to the world. That would be the signal that Stanley had not been followed and it was safe for them to talk.

Jean Paul went to the massive crane, found Stanley, and noted his unorthodox signal. They embraced and conversed under the massive brick and wooden structure of the *Żuraw*, looking out on the river. Stanley explained to Kazimierz, that he, his agent *Syrenka*, was in grave danger.

Stanley had just learned that the Russians had very recently been given not only his operational code name, *Syrenka*, but his identity as Kazimierz Danuski. The Russians would surely be coming to eliminate him. While Stanley could not predict when, it could be literally at any minute, in any location.

Stanley told him he had to drop everything and flee. Every hour he stayed in Poland, his life was in severe danger. The agency would provide him with a new identity. Stanley handed the young man a backpack containing multiple currencies - Polish Zlotys, German Deutschmarks, and French Francs. (This was the mid 1990's, and the Euro currency was not introduced yet). There also was a one-way train ticket to Paris. Finally, the backpack contained false passports issued in French and Swiss documents.

"Trust this man with your life," Jean Paul heard his mother saying. And so, he did this day in 1996.

The young Kazimierz did not return to his apartment, and went directly to the train station where he boarded the train to Paris. When he arrived in Paris, he stayed in a location supplied by Stanley for thirty days. During the third week, Stanley met him there, and provided him with his new French identity, a permanent apartment and a swiss bank account holding a half million US Dollars. It was then that they set up emergency contact procedures. During that visit in Paris, many conversions occurred. This is when the young Pole Kazimierz Danuski had transformed into the young Frenchman Étienne Chaton. The agent *Syrenka* was now dead, replaced by the man with the emergency code-name "Jean Paul".

"How will this information be protected? How will you assure the Russians never find me here?" he asked Stanley that week in Paris.

Stanley looked at him, and weighed his response carefully. "Because, my friend, only I know this information. The Russians will not find you. The Americans will not find you. I made this promise to your mother. Only I know how to find you, and you may never hear from me again. Unless the emergency sequence is activated, exactly as we have arranged here this week, trust no one who comes in my name, or in the name of the agency."

That was nearly twenty years ago. Jean Paul had indeed trusted no one but Stanley. But the Stanley he trusted had become old. Vienna was the first-time Jean Paul began to question the skills of this aged, retired spy. It dawned on him, that, true to his deceased mother's advice, he once again was trusting Stanley with his life.

On the tenth of December, Preston Almesbury's *Conservatoire* ran a featured story on its webpage of the difficulty the American CIA was having tracking the fugitive Stanley Wisniewski. There had been no additional receipt of e-mailed material from Stanley via Jean Paul, but Almesbury's team of journalists were beginning to tie together the relationship of Stanley to the CIA, the CIA to its procuring and using the Daedalus Destroyer Drone system in several theatres of the GWOT – the Global War on Terror. The article then highlighted how Ted Barber, the Daedalus' chief designer, and Langston Powell, the system's program manager, had both died mysteriously over the past month.

It then went on to question whether this entire operation was indeed a sweep-up by the CIA. Had the agency decided that too many knew too much of the efficacy of this weapon system. Did the agency need to tidy up the scene, if nothing else than to protect its own image?

The story went on to question if the trove of information provided by the fugitive Wisniewski suggested that the CIA and Global Defense Analytics were working closely together in some capacity. Global Defense Analytics had just purged its own Executive Leadership. When would the CIA hold their own leaders accountable?

The story was picked up by the international news organizations, and once again brought significant prestige to *The Conservatoire*. In fact, the story was a plant supplied to *The Conservatoire* by Malcolm Devereaux from MI6. It had been conceived by his superior, George Chartwell, to turn up the heat on one Jack Trellis.

Shortly afterwards, in a story largely ignored by the mainstream press, Italy became the first European power to allow American drone systems to operate in their country's airspace. While explicitly explained as allowing launching from Sicilian NATO airbases only for strikes against Libyan targets and other threats throughout the Mediterranean, MI6's George Chartwell feared it opened a new gold seam in the many illicit accounts of his personal nemesis, Jack Trellis.

A few days later, Devereaux found himself in Chartwell's office in MI6 headquarters, overlooking the river Thames. The call for him was urgent, and he assumed it was tied to the Wisniewski case, which all but consumed his superior these days.

"Malcolm, you began your career in GCHQ, did you not?" asked Chartwell, knowing the answer all along.

The Government Communications Headquarters, or GCHQ, were today located just outside Cheltenham, on the very edge of England's famed Cotswolds. GCHQ was today housed in a behemoth metal and glass ring of a structure. "The doughnut", as it was often called within the trade, had neither the elegance nor the noto- riety of its predecessor at Bletchley Park, where a team of scientists, including Alan Turing, broke the German Enigma code in World War II.

At least none of the notoriety until in 2013 Edward Snowden, a contractor working for the NSA, revealed among his exhaustive data dump to the London's Guardian newspaper that GCHQ was conducting a program, codenamed Tempora, that was collecting massive amounts of on-line and telecommunication traffic within the UK.

Devereaux had worked as a crypto-analyst at GCHQ at the onset of his career. It was, in fact, at a nearby resort in the Malvern Hills that he first met his wife-to-be, Petula. Once she had taken him to her father's nearby sprawling estate, *Millhaven*, Malcolm became ever more enamored with his Pet. She clearly was from a family drenched in the old money of the aristocracy. Her father, himself having done some clandestine work for MI6 and GCHQ over the years, was taken with young Malcolm.

Devereaux ultimately proved to have a greater affinity for the nicer things than he did for his lovely Pet. They soon became man and wife. After their first year together, Devereaux seemed to have little more than a platonic relationship with her. Pet really did not seem to be bothered by it, doting on her new husband whenever they were with her parents or friends, but showing little affection when they were alone. It was only in their third year that Malcolm hired an investigator to confirm his suspicions. His wife was having a very extensive lesbian affair with one of her closest friends.

Confronted with the photographs that his investigator had produced, Pet seemed rather blasé.

"Good God, darling, don't tell me you spent your modest income to investigate this..." Pet said, holding the very illicit depictions of her and her Connie in various intimate embraces. "Quite honestly, Malcolm, I thought you had known for some time now. Just precisely how thick are you, dear? I would have simply told you, had you merely been chivalrous enough to ask me outright."

As their discussions that night unthreaded, and the emotions were driven out of the misrepresentation upon which their relationship was based, Devereaux found himself with a pragmatic proposal from his Pet.

"Come now, Malcolm. Of course, we don't have a traditional marriage. I never actually expected you to be the monogamous husband. After all, we are not a pair of bloody swans. I rather took you all along for something of a bounder. Well, if you one-day fancy owning a piece of *Millhaven*, then remember this: I don't need a faithful husband; I just need a husband. At least for as long as dear Daddy is with us."

She could see the rational side of Devereaux was now overtaking the spent emotional side of him. Pet went on.

"You know Father is quite fond of you. He is currently pulling some strings for you in London. A nice promotion and executive position at MI6. When this comes to pass," Pet shot Malcolm a look which said that it certainly would come to pass, "then we can set you up with a lovely little flat in London where you can entertain all the birds that your heart, or other attributes of your anatomy, may desire."

At that point, Malcolm Devereaux decided there were worse lies in life to live than posing as window dressing as the contented mate to a closeted Cotswolds heiress.

"Malcolm, are you hearing me?" asked George Chartwell, "I asked if you began your career at GCHQ?"

"Yes, sir, I did begin my service there, actually." Devereaux said, bringing himself back to George the FITH's question.

"Well, your mates in Cheltenham have just provided an intercept out of Munich from Diane's traveling party. Something having to do with a someone identified as 'Carlyle', no name other than 'Carlyle'. I had the analysts run it, and the only valid connection that came back was a para-military type employed by my good friend, Jack Trellis." Chartwell looked into Malcolm's eyes for a response to his sarcasm. There was none.

King George continued, "As it were, this Carlyle, he's a bloody assassin. Handpicked by Trellis out of Iraq. Born and raised in ..."

Chartwell held the page in front of him as if it were lit aflame, "can this possibly be an actual place? Bucksnort, Tennessee?"

"One cannot accuse the Americans as failing to be descriptive," Devereaux said. Then adding, not wishing to appear obtuse, "Yes, yes, I see your concern, sir. What with it already being so long since Wisniewski assassinated that Aerospace executive. The fact that they are in Munich suggests that Wisniewski was not contained within Poland. Wherever he is, they either have him on the run or are just waiting for their great white whale to come to the surface."

"Malcolm," Chartwell resumed, "this situation has become quite volatile. I don't wish to see our lovely Diane waylaid in all this, but with a mercenary like Carlyle tagging along, just waiting for her to flush out the quarry, my apprehension is elevated. This is precisely the *modus operandi* of Trellis and his team. Heaven forbid that Diane should sense what is to come and attempt to capture this 'Stanley' whilst protecting him from Trellis. I know exactly where that will lead."

"Yes, sir," said Devereaux. "I would not prefer such an outcome for Diane. I have grown rather close to her over her time with us."

"Excellent. Then we are agreed," said Chartwell.

"If I may, agreed to what, sir?"

"Come now, Malcolm. Trail her in the field, not too close, but let her know we stand ready to assist her in any manner she finds necessary. Don't startle her with it, but let her know if she wants to protect Stanley from Trellis, she can arrange through you for us to take him into custody. I wouldn't mind hearing his tales of Trellis' indignities over the years."

Devereaux now understood his superior's intentions - secure Stanley from Diane to antagonize Jack Trellis. Chartwell would use Devereaux's relationship with Diane to do just that.

"Yes, I am sure Director Trellis, as well as the rest of the American cousins, would find that to be a burr in their knickers," said Malcolm, smiling.

"That's *Deputy* Director Trellis," Chartwell frostily corrected him.

Chapter Eleven
Mistakes in Milan

"DIANE, WE HAVE a bearing on Stanley. Confirmed, rock solid."

It was Dom. They had moved their headquarters south from Berlin to Munich, attempting to get themselves positioned in Stanley's expected vector of travel.

Carlyle was in the room they had used as a makeshift operations center within the US Consulate there. Sophie was also there.

"Where is he?" asked Carlyle, beating Diane to the question.

"Milan," barked out an excited Dom, his sagging cheeks now crimson and aflame.

"How long ago?" asked Diane.

"Less than an hour, but I have my team moving there already," Dom said proudly. For once he was ahead of *The Huntress*.

They all rose at this point and started grabbing the few things they needed to take with them. They had a fueled jet at the ready to carry them in whatever direction they needed.

"I already have a flight plan in work for Malpensa," said Dom, huffing with excitement. He referred to the airport just outside Milan.

Diane snapped, "OK, this trip is for Dom, Sophie and myself only."

"Bullshit," yelled Carlyle, "you don't have to like it, but I am going unless Trellis himself tells me to stand down."

Diane knew Trellis would not, so she agreed to take Carlyle along.

Soon they all were moving in an extended black sedan carrying them briskly to the executive jet now ready and awaiting the four of them. Their town car moved with purpose through the bustling streets of Munich.

"Where was he spotted in Milan?" asked Diane of Dom, thinking the whole time of how she might protect Stanley from Carlyle's deadly aim.

"Of all places, he was caught by the security cameras at the fresco of *The Last Supper*. He made the mistake you thought he'd never make." With this Dom smiled broadly at Diane, as if to say, "you gave this guy too much credit from the get-go."

"What was his mistake?" asked Diane, understanding in full his underlying intent.

"He went in to see Leonardo's masterpiece all bundled up against the cold. Hat, sunglasses, scarf wrapped over his face." Dom was enjoying his moment. He went through the two airlocks the Italians had installed to protect the climate inside and meter the flow of visitors. I was surprised he would do that; given he was trapped like a rat if we were tracking him there. But as soon as he came out of that second airlock and turned to face *The Last Supper*, he appears on the video to stand still for about thirty seconds before beginning to shake, and then ***bam***!" Dom slapped his hands loudly.

"What, Dom, damn you, out with it." Diane was restless to know.

Sophie spoke next, softly. "He dropped to his knees and cried."

Everyone looked at this quiet child, who only spoke when she had something significant to say.

"How the hell did you know that?" asked Dom, astonished.

"He is saying his penance," added Sophie, "confessing his sins, cleansing his soul."

"Just as you had predicted he would," Diane said to Sophie.

"Now just wait a minute, here," Dom blurted, feeling slighted. "I am the one who tapped into their video feeds and fed them to our facial recognition signal processing analysis system."

No one said a thing, they just all knew that this fresco was on Sophie's list of possible locations Stanley might seek out after his exit from Poland. She had also included the Crypt of John Paul II at the Cathedral of St. Peter in the Vatican, the Shroud of Turin (which was not currently on display), the Holy Grotto of the Blessed Mother at Lourdes and several others.

Dom broke the silence. "Well the bastard made a royal *faux pas* when he removed his hat, scarf and glasses. That's when our recognition software picked up the features of his face and gave us a match. The bastard had shaved his beard and his head, even his eyebrows. That along with the fact that he must have dropped about fifteen pounds or so, makes it look like he just crawled out of Dachau."

Diane cringed at Dom's reference to the concentration camp that was only ten miles or so from them as they drove rapidly through Munich. "Is he doing this in some ritualistic or even subconscious homage to his father, the concentration camp survivor?" she thought.

"It is no mistake," stated the young poignant Sophie. "He is preparing himself".

"For what, to be captured?" the voice was Dom's. Carlyle just listened, never saying a word.

"To be sacrificed," answered Sophie, now looking intently at Carlyle, never breaking his angry stare. "Stanley knows he is to be sacrificed, and while he can evade his hunters with distance and disguise, he knows his sacrifice is due. As such, he cleanses himself beforehand, so when the moment comes he can stand tall before those who would slay him down."

There was a chill that pervaded the cabin of the town car. It was cold and dense and unrelenting, suppressing all other dialogue. Soon the car came to a screeching halt as it had entered the airport and pulled directly onto the tarmac next to the agency's jet.

Diane and the team converged on Milan's *Santa Maria delle Grazie*, or Our Lady of the Graces convent and church. The church itself is a beautiful Renaissance house of worship, still used today in that capacity. Across the piazza, the convent refectory, or dining hall, had been converted into a full-blown tourist destination because of the painting on its wall from the late 1490's - Leonardo Da Vinci's beautifully iconic *The Last Supper.*

The team fanned out with assignments, hopeful to spot Stanley nearby in the piazza or in the church vestibule or among its darkened pews. Diane knew this was unlikely as it had now been nearly three hours since he had visited the painting. After establishing her team's assignments, Diane viewed the security video in an office in back of the ticketing office. Not only was video available from the fifteen minutes Stanley, like every other tourist, was allotted to view the masterpiece, but video was also available to view from the hall where the tourists waited on simple benches to access the painting, as well as the two clear plexiglass enclosed air locks where the fifteen or so visitors would spend fifteen minutes each waiting to access the refectory and its images.

That meant 45 minutes Stanley knew he would be contained in a camera rich environment. This was an incredible risk for Stanley to take, and he surely knew he could be trapped without hope of escape in either of the airlocks or the refectory itself. Diane could only conclude one thing from his decision to come here. It meant more to Stanley to come before this iconic image, copies of which he would have been exposed to as a child, adolescent and throughout his adult years in Poland and the US, than to evade being captured.

Then Diane recalled, in his home in Baltimore on Shakespeare street, above the oak legged table with the painted old-country metal dining surface, there hung on the wall a bronze, bas-relief image of Leonardo's *The Last Supper.*

Diane fast forwarded through the tapes. In the waiting hall, most tourists sat on the benches provided, but Stanley was not to be found except for a glimpse of him entering the hall before disappearing off camera. He had spotted the camera and found the blind spot where he waited, further evidence that he was aware of the risk that he was taking.

Stanley could not evade the cameras in the airlocks as there was no blind spot in which to hide. He stood with his back to the camera, looking onto the courtyard, which was natural enough. When he turned briefly to face the camera, he looked German enough in his *Landhaushut* hat. Stanley's eyes were covered with dark lensed sunglasses. His face was nearly fully covered with a scarf, ironically bearing the Munich Bayern football team logo.

As Munich was the city from which Diane had just departed, she wondered how close their paths may have come to crossing, assuming Stanley had even been in Munich at all.

His entrance into the refectory was where he lost his awareness, or his desire to conceal himself. He stood silently before the great image on the wall. It was not a true fresco, as any art historian would tell you, for it was not painted in wet plaster, but over an existing dry wall. Just like the image, the Stanley they were now so close to apprehending, appeared to Diane to be just an overlay painted on the man she knew and once respected so highly.

In the tape, Stanley removed his hat and glasses, but not his scarf at this point. He began to sway slightly, and then visibly shook until a few seconds later, when he dropped to his knees. With a motion one could only describe as exposing himself, he ripped the FC Bayern München scarf from his face. At this point, the crowd which had been giving him as much space as possible, peeled away visibly from him as they were now seeing his scarred and gray-stubbled skull.

Stanley was visibly weeping in the video, on his knees, hat in hand, prostrating himself before this image of the Lord Jesus and his Apostles. Leonardo had caught the moment just after Jesus had told the twelve that one of them would betray Him. Why was this image so moving to this cold, hardened professional spy?

Stanley knelt and wept openly for several minutes. While most visitors had more reserved reactions to this iconic artwork, Stanley's reaction was neither unprecedented nor even rare according to the security chief. People were generally moved on seeing this great work for the first time. Often, their response welled up inside them, uncontrollably, and totally unexpected.

In the video, Stanley then raised himself, replaced his scarf and hat. He then migrated to the other wall in the refectory, opposite the *The Last Supper*. On that wall, was another tremendous work of art, *The Crucifixion* by Montorfano. Stanley stood under the picture looking back onto *The Last Supper* from across the refectory. Diane could not help but notice that he stood at the base of the cross bearing not Christ, but the sinner that according to the New Testament, would be saved because of his faith in Christ.

After viewing the security tapes, Diane was permitted to enter the refectory from the exit to join a group of visitors to see the image of Leonardo's masterpiece for herself. The colors were more vibrant than she expected, the details sharper. Beyond that, she had no feelings of emotion other than those of any artwork to which she had been exposed throughout her life. She did not share the emotive reaction that Stanley displayed.

The security lead explained that there was great controversy over the most recent restorations of the artwork, but in his view this was true to the original artist's expression.

"Alas, who will ever know for sure, only the master!" his hands pinching the air in front of him, pulling it down like heavy curtain.

Diane looked away from the image and up to the vaulted ceiling. Three semicircular arches ran its length, causing three lunettes where they intersected the top of each fresco. On *The Crucifixion*, these lunettes were filled with Christ and the two sinners on their crosses. On *The Last Supper*, these were filled with coats of arms. Diane continued to span the ceiling, remembering that an allied bomb had scored a direct hit on it in 1943, and if not for sandbags and other reinforcing precautions taken, both images would likely have been lost to man's lust for war. Was this divine intervention or just dumb luck?

Diane exited through the door she entered. The fifteen minute sessions were over, and the timing of the exit door, as well as the doors controlling the two airlock chambers, were coordinated to control the steady flow of visitors.

Soon she was receiving reports back from her teams. No evidence of Stanley Wisniewski, but the team was now requesting city video surveillance to hopefully catch him walking through the area. Spotters had been posted to the train platform a few blocks away, but they had no luck with intercepting him.

Stanley was too smart to linger in the immediate area.

Diane walked up to the young Pole, Sophie. "Sophie, what is the tie between *The Last Supper* and Poland, other than the fact that it is well known to be a Catholic icon?"

Sophie looked at her directly and said slowly to her, "You saw the painting itself, *The Last Supper*?"

"Yes, yes I got to see it in-person," responded Diane

"Did you notice the coats of arms near the ceiling?" asked Sophie.

"Yes, yes I did," Diane responded, wondering where this was going.

"That coat of arms belonged to the Duke of Milan, Ludovico Sforza, who commissioned the masterpiece. The Sforza family became very close with the Polish nobility, with even one of the Kings of Poland taking a Sforza princess to be his wife. It is this long association which explains why one of Leonardo's other masterpiece's, *The Lady with an Ermine*, is today on display in the Wawel Royal Castle in Kraków. It was sold by the Sforza family to a Polish Nobleman, and that is why this masterpiece today is in Poland."

Diane was amazed, but this was becoming a regular state of wonder and discovery in her discussions with Sophie.

"There is a Renaissance castle only a few blocks from here that belonged to the Sforza family. Perhaps your people should inspect it to see if Stanley had been there?"

"Yes, yes, I will get someone over there straight away," Diane's use of the British term made her think of her deliciously mad Malcolm Devereaux. It had seemed like an eternity since their tea together at the St. Ermin's hotel.

"Well, that squares that circle, doesn't it - I am the Lady with a Saint Ermine," thought Diane, intentionally corrupting the Leonardo masterpiece with the London hotel name. Something inside her couldn't wait to tell this anecdote to Mad Mal himself. Now that Carlyle was in the mix, it was comforting knowing she had an emergency contact in Devereaux's "Rêves de Cuir" telephone line.

Stanley had indeed met with Jean Paul in this day in Milan. After making his pilgrimage to the Santa Maria delle Grazie to see Leonardo's *The Last Supper*, he then met Jean Paul. Stanley had earlier visited the impressionist website and recognized the safe signal calling out the alternate site, the Sforza Castle, at eleven AM. Stanley remained disciplined, always checking the website the morning of the meet to assure there were no last-minute changes between alternate or primary locations, or worse, should the abort signal be given.

Again the meeting was over in fifteen minutes. They agreed on Albi, the French town about an hour east of Toulouse, as being the next location, on December 21st.

After their agreement had been reached, Jean Paul asked Stanley the question that had been burning within him since Vienna.

"You say he knew of *Sarenka*, then why did you have me take you to the villa?" His tone was demanding. Stanley understood the "he" to be Jack Trellis.

"Because I was sure it was safe. I practiced utmost care when I took your mother there. We were there only a half dozen times or so together. She swore she would never go there without me. She said it meant nothing to her without me. That night in 1996, when I was permanently withdrawn from Poland, she swore she would never visit there until I returned."

Stanley looked at Jean Paul, as they both stood within the massive courtyard of the Sforza Castle.

"How did you know they had not followed you both there on one of the handful of times you and my mother were there together?"

Stanley could not understand if Jean Paul's apparent anxiety was with Stanley's relationship with his mother, or merely concern over the couple's ability to keep it a secret. In either case, he was sensing a level of agitation from Jean Paul he had not in the past.

"Well, my friend, now we know for sure they had not because they did not come to the villa to collect me, did they?" Stanley reasoned aloud. "As I told you, I had been extremely safe over the years in taking your mother there."

Jean Paul looked intently at Stanley, "But you weren't sure! I could have been picked up there when I provisioned it for you. They could have tracked me since then."

Stanley was unaccustomed of being quizzed at this level by Jean Paul. It suggested a lack of faith in his abilities. Or perhaps a concern of the decay of age setting in the old man.

"Jean Paul, if that were the case, we would be in their clutches by now. Stay calm, my friend. The villa was completely safe for us. They did not know of it. It was always my secret hideaway from them all." Stanley looked at his watch. The beep of his timer's alarm was only a few minutes from sounding.

"I will see you at the next location. You have the date and the sites." Stanley said this, knowing Jean Paul was still troubled. Stanley sensed the younger man was fearing being caught. Possibly for the first time Jean Paul's confidence in the old spy had been shaken.

Jean Paul looked at Stanley, still concerned his partner was faltering under the pressure of this manhunt.

"Yes, yes. *Do widzenia*, my friend." he said, somewhat hesitantly, to the old man.

Stanley decided to give his partner an option. Jean Paul could still flee and restart his life once again. Stanley reached out to touch Jean Paul on the shoulder.

"Calm yourself, my companion. If you cannot search your soul and convince yourself by our next meeting that you have faith in me, then do not show. We will be over, and you will never hear from me again. I will understand completely, of course. I will always remember all you have done for me, and will always be grateful." Stanley looked hard at the younger man. "But if your soul says you still have faith in me, then I will see you at the next location. *Do widzenia*, my friend."

Jean Paul looked tenderly at Stanley, realizing this might be the last time he would see him. "Thank you, my friend. I owe you so much, but I am afraid I may not have much more to give. *Do widzenia*."

They departed, each with the bag with which they had not arrived. Similarly, each now carried concerns about the other that had never before been felt. Each was unsure if Jean Paul would indeed show at the French town of Albi on December 21st, the first day of winter.

Two days later, Diane's team was now gathered in the bunker-like Sheraton Malpensa hotel, adjoined to the airport just outside Milan.

Diane began by addressing the small crowd in her oversized room.

"We got a very lucky break that afternoon," she began. "After Sophie made the connection to the Sforza Castle, even though our surveillance team got there too late to intercept Stanley and Jean Paul, we got a real breakthrough."

Dom began his normal caustic response. "Sounds really lucky. If they got there too late, Diane, then how do you even know they were there?"

Diane smiled broadly at young Emory having his moment. "Tell him the best part," she said, in a tone that both celebrated Emory and eviscerated Dom at the same time.

"We also scanned the street cameras and picked him up getting into his 1997 Forest Green Audi. Would never have picked this up had Soph here not tied us to the Sforza Castle, and that tied that to our boy here to Stanley."

Dom unknowingly walked into the next trap. "Well, youngster, the bad news is that old a car has no GPS built into it and we will have no way to track it."

Diane jumped in again, "Precisely why we believe that is why Jean Paul - and that is who we are tracking here, our beloved Jean Paul - that is precisely why he bought it for cash from a private party in Amsterdam. Did so two days before the Langston Powell shooting. Drove it through Germany and into Poland just in time to make the meet. But Emory still has more to share."

Emory jumped in before Diane finished her lead in. "We got the bastard's plates. Dutch plates. Didn't show in the pic, or any of the pics from the street that afternoon. We interviewed everyone we could find that afternoon, and we found the shopkeeper in front of whose shop Jean Paul parked. This shopkeeper had quite a lot to say. He detested anyone who wasn't his client taking his parking spot. *Everyabody knowsa thata isa mya shop'sa parking spota*," said Emory in his most offensive Northern Italian accent.

Diane pressed it from there. "For whatever reason, that shopkeeper had a long festering hatred of the Dutch. He was quick to tell us this while he pointed out this car had Dutch plates. He was not so polite as to have written down the tag, but once we started interrogating the Italian surveillance cameras for 1997 Forest Green Audi's with Dutch plates, we only found…"

Dom cut her off, "Pray tell, only one in all of Italy..."

Diane Smiled even more broadly, "Funny thing Dom, we actually picked up three. Who would have thought that was such a popular combination? But the other two were way in the south, in Nola and Reggio. Turns out one was a '99, and the other was more gray than green, but who would have figured even three that close. Later, from the cameras on the Autostrada, we found our subject car and got the plates."

"Which means you can track him from the highway camera network and he'll lead us right to Stanley," said Dom, almost as if it was bad news.

"Well, before we do that, we need to figure out how he is communicating with Stanley. Otherwise we spook him, and he gives Stanley the ABORT signal. Then we have nothing but an ex-spy who knows how to clam up."

The next voice was one seldom heard. It was Carlyle. "Track him. I'll intercept him, and I will get what I need out of him."

The room became strangely silent, which Diane broke after a few seconds. "You mean what ***we*** need, right Carlyle? No, we do this my way, we let Jean Paul think he is still not being traced until we figure out their little code. And one last thing, Dom, the street teams found Stanley's scarf in a nearby trash receptacle, and we found a young vagrant wearing a freshly acquired *Landhaushut* hat. In other words, Stanley is morphing again."

Two hours later Diane was alone. She walked out of the hotel and into the adjoining airport. She walked about in a manner of someone lost in an airport until she came upon an American couple, middle aged, waiting on their luggage to be spit out of the temperamental Italian carousel.

"Excuse me," she interrupted the couple. "Could I beg a big favor of you. I can't find my boyfriend who is picking me up, and my cell phone is dead. Could I bother you to borrow yours for just a second? I'll call him from right here in front of you."

The husband was fat and suspicious. Diane noticed he reached immediately for the wallet conspicuously in his front right pocket, fearing she was a picket-pocket's distraction. "I dunno..."

"Oh, of course you can, hon. Where in the states is that accent of yours from? It is so cute." From the twang in her voice, Diane marked the wife's accent as Texan, maybe Austin or San Antonio.

She handed Diane her phone. "I just called home, it is working just fine. So, where exactly in the states are you from?"

Diane took the phone from her and thanked her profusely. "Philly, by the way. My accent and I are both from around Philadelphia." It was easier to say than Bucks County.

Diane called the number from "*Rêves de Cuir*" that she had committed to memory over the last several weeks.

An operator answered on the second ring. "*Rêves de Cuir.* It is my pleasure to assist you." In French. Dead perfect French.

In English, Diane mentioned that her boyfriend was in their store buying a corset, and she needed to speak to him immediately. The voice switched to English, and said without trace of a French accent, to hold and she would connect.

"Hello, darling, I thought you would never call." It was Devereaux.

Diane smiled at the American couple. The husband arched his eyes and said "ooh-la-la" at the corset reference, and the wife slapped him on the shoulder. But now they were both listening intently.

Diane was happy to use their phone, as she had reason to think everything around her was potentially bugged by Trellis. She didn't want Trellis, and by extension Carlyle, finding out what she was up to.

"Honey, I was expecting you to meet me," she said, smiling at her audience.

"As fate would have it, darling, I am just down the road from you in Florence. If you can make it down here before too long, I should be glad to take you across my knee..."

"Yes, Dear," Diane said slowly. "Where should I meet you?"

"Come to the Hotel Tournabuoni Beacci. Precisely above the Tiffany's store there. You shouldn't have any trouble finding that, not with your tastes. Well, until tonight, my darling."

"OK, Honey. I have to give this nice couple back their phone. I will meet you there, but it will be late tonight."

"I suspected it will be after hours, but I will be waiting for you. Drop my name with the night doorman. It has some cache. They all know me well. After all, I'm a great tipper," said Malcolm. "You are alright aren't you, all in one piece, I mean?"

"Just the way you remember me, darling," Diane said.

"You cannot begin to fathom the ways I remember you," Devereaux said slyly as he rang off.

"*à toutes les heures,*" she said in his favorite French.

"Yes. *Tootles*, darling." He rang off.

Diane returned the phone to the Texans. She thanked them, and said she was sorry, but had to go. This was to get away from the wife who was prattling on about some time they had been to Philadelphia.

The husband was leering at her, still imaging her in nothing but a corset. "Damn Devereaux," thought Diane. "He had to be the wise guy with his inside joke code word. And how did he know she was in Milan? What the hell was he doing in Florence? He was trailing her at a safe distance, no doubt. What the hell were the Brits so afraid of?"

Diane walked away from the Texans and found the escalator between the airport and the Sheraton that went down to the train platform. This was going to make for a very late night.

Diane went to him that night. She did not arrive in Florence until shortly after midnight, and walked the few blocks past the darkened *Basilica di Santa Maria Novella* and its empty piazza. She walked the shuttered upscale shops of the *Via Tornabuoni*.

No Tiffany's, no Cartier, no Hermes at this hour, only the inelegant metallic sheen of their protective enclosures dully reflecting the moonlight onto the ancient stones of the darkened facade.

She found the etched glass doors that read *Hotel Tournabuoni Beacci*. The accommodation was actually the upper floors of the renaissance palace whose ground floors had hundreds of years before been converted to shopping for the richest patrons of Florence. Diane pressed the ringer, introduced herself as needing to meet Mr. Devereaux, and was rung up immediately. As she stood at the top of the palatial marble staircase, she looked past the night porter and saw Malcolm coming toward her.

"*Buona sera*, my darling," he said pressing past the porter, wrapping his arms seductively around Diane. He was in a very stylish Azure blue silk robe bearing a Florentine motif over his crisp clean cotton pajamas. Diane blushed to herself realizing this was a new first in their relationship, her having never before seen him in sleeping clothes.

"Georgio, this is my Diane, the one I told you to expect," he said, turning to the porter. As he did, the silkened arm slid effortlessly low around her hips, his palm coming to rest on the upper round of her buttocks. Diane pressed into his embrace, fearing if she did not, it would weaken any cover story Devereaux may have been using for her late arrival. At least that is what she told herself, denying to herself the sheer sensuality of being desired by this attractive man.

Malcolm said to the porter, "Georgio, is the champagne on ice in the bar as I requested? *Si, Eccellente... Grazie.*"

And with an effortless move, Malcolm palmed a twenty Euro note to Georgio, who then led them down a hall, up a few steps and around to a small but stylish bar. Its two leather wing chairs were facing through the glass windows onto the darkened rooftop garden.

Soon they were left alone, after Georgio had served a silver tray of cheeses and fruit to be enjoyed along with the opened bottle of Piper Heidsieck champagne, sitting in the silver ice stand which was positioned perfectly between the two chairs.

"Sorry, darling, they were all out of Dom on short notice," said Devereaux.

"That's OK. I've had about all the Dom I can handle lately," said Diane. Malcolm did not understand Diane's play on words.

Malcolm poured champagne into Diane's flute while he watched her peel her Burberry trench coat from her mature but shapely form.

"Darling, it is truly a shame you could not have made it here with me earlier in the year. The garden is beautiful in the June moonlight, and a delightful way to spend an evening together. Especially in the morning when the sounds of the Arno river rise like a delicate scent of rose, only to be exceeded by the joyous peals of the bells of the Duomo later as the day progresses." Devereaux smiled, his darkened, dashing features becoming animated, as he raised his glass to her, toasting her with term "*Salut*".

Diane raised her glass, "*Salut*" she said smiling back to him.

"Well, Mal, I am almost disappointed to not be invited back to your bed chambers for this discussion. Perhaps the hotel proprietors would not appreciate that..." she said jokingly.

"Oh, they'd be fine with it," he said, smiling warmly, letting her swim momentarily in the waters of a rejection. "However, I don't think young Camille would appreciate it much. Sharing me on the first night, and all that."

"My God, Mal, I am terribly sorry. I didn't realize you were traveling with someone." Diane felt the blush rise in her cheeks. She was stammering softly.

"Oh, come now, Diane, of course I am not traveling with anyone," he said, tilting his face to peer deeper into hers. "I just met Camille at dinner this evening. Beautiful young girl from Perpignan. I sensed her girlfriend was somewhat glad to get rid of her for the night. Even the best traveling companions wear on each other somewhat after a few weeks."

"Well, I will hurry through this to allow you to get back to her." Diane's words were now as rushed as her thoughts about Malcolm and Camille.

"Don't bother to rush, love. Young Camille is in a very satisfied repose as we speak. I'll have trouble waking her for breakfast. Let us enjoy our evening together in Florence, peering out onto the moonlit rooftops beyond the garden. What could be more romantic?"

They drank the champagne, only to have Georgio reappear to with an already chilled second bottle. Diane suspected Mal was attempting to loosen her tongue, but she was massively enjoying the impromptu company, after weeks of the tension of the chase.

"Mal, dear, there is something I need from you and your brethren on the Thames," she began her request cautiously.

"Anything, darling. King George specifically said the fortunes of the realm are at your beck and call."

"Yes. Chartwell. Yes. Well anything that would agitate Trellis would be certainly be welcome by George Chartwell," said Diane out loud, meaning not to. "OK, my dearest mad Malcolm. Here is a Dutch license plate number we are currently interrogating."

She slipped a small slip of paper into Devereaux's palm. He grasped her hand as she did so.

"What I need from your team is to trace where this car has been since it left Amsterdam." She left her hand in his, enjoying the warmth of his touch.

"But, darling, your boys at Fort Meade can do that faster than anyone. Why come to us?" He looked into her weary, alcohol dilated eyes. "Unless, of course, there is something you don't want that nasty Deputy Director Trellis to know?"

"I was just getting to that," she said, her words only slightly beginning to slur, yielding to the combination of the late hour and the early vintage. "We think our prey is communicating with his handler through an unknown website. What I was hoping your team could do is figure out where the car had been over the last few weeks from the network of road cameras, and then search for common website hits accessed from those physical locations."

"Darling, that could be hundreds, if not thousands of websites." Mal already knew where she was going, saying aloud as he realized "... but not if we limit it to those having a very small number of hits per day, say fifty or less. You really are a clever little bag of bones, aren't you Diane?"

His eyes showed a glint of professional respect. She picked up on his look. "And I thought you just wanted me for the carnal desires of the flesh. Now that you are complimenting my bag of bones, tell me, what's the beef between Trellis and Chartwell, anyway? No telling where this could be heading. It would be good to know."

"First, darling, why do you desire to hide this from Trellis? This is the kind of thing that makes powerful men very angry," Devereaux said, nonchalantly inspecting the rise of bubbles within his flute.

"He is shadowing me with a special ops snake. Kid from Tennessee." Diane unconsciously raised her finger to the rim of her lips. Had she said too much?

"Bucksnort, Tennessee. That would be your Carlyle." Said Devereaux. "We know him well. You had best be very careful not to come between him and his dinner, if you know what I mean." Malcolm's face was registering real concern.

"So, you *are* trailing me," Diane said, taking both his hands into hers. "That is so sweet. Now, where did Chartwell hone his legendary dislike for Trellis?"

"Well, I believe it all goes back to the eighties. Both Trellis and Carlyle were playing in the Eastern European sandbox, digging holes under the sandcastle that was then the USSR. The Poles haven't trusted the Brits since Chamberlain did little-to-squat to defend them in '39. Therefore, Trellis and his boys, including your Mr. Wisniewski, got the preferred treatment from the Polish underground community, and together they subsequently brought down the 'evil empire'. That simple, I'm assured, as most clever stories always are."

"OK, Malcolm. This has to go further than professional envy. What's the real scoop?" Diane pressed.

"King George doesn't share his private interests with me in detail, but what little kindling I have gathered all points to money. The American cousins love to brag about all the cash they pumped into Poland, and specifically supporting *Solidarity*. George says it wasn't so, that the real support was only a fraction of what was claimed. The difference is missing, but no one thinks it is, so no one's looking for it. Trellis is a hero, and gets promoted to ticklish heights at Langley. There you have it, darling."

"It really is professional envy, after all?" Diane asked aloud.

"That was my take all along. But I did a little further digging. It turns out that the powers that were on the *Solidarity* side all agree they never saw the money the CIA claims to have sent. Now your Mr. Wisniewski would have had a ringside seat, so that is why George Chartwell is so interested in this perspective. He believes Trellis has long ago absconded with tens of millions of dollars. The closer you get to Trellis' prey, the more dangerous this game becomes for you. Please remember that as you go forward. We are here to help you anyway we can."

"Well, get me that damn website. And make sure Trellis and Carlyle don't get a whiff of it. I intend to bring Trellis' prey in, kicking and screaming. Screw Jack if he has other plans," she said defiantly.

"You know, Diane, as well as I do, if you bring him in, he won't be kicking and screaming for long. You could always bring him to us, just for safe keeping, as it were," quipped Mad Mal.

"Yes, wouldn't your King George love that?" Diane shot him a look that said she knew this was impossible. "Turning one of our own over to a foreign state. I can't do that, Mal. I think your country has the same term for it as we do – treason. If I recall your English Kings had played that card a few times. Can you just get me that website?"

"I should be able to get you something in a few days' time, assuming your idea of their communicating through a website is accurate."

"That works for me," said Diane, realizing she needed to sleep. She pushed back into the plush wing chair. "I owe you one. I am getting very tired now, so I hope you'll forgive me if we end our conversation here."

"Of course, my darling. Rest." Malcolm Devereaux watched her as she faded into a very deep sleep. He gathered the Florentine blanket that Georgio had very considerately placed next to Mal's chair and covered Diane. He kissed her cheek softly, returned to his chair and stayed awake, watching her, protecting her from the evils of the Tuscan night. Her words rang in his ears, "I owe you one."

"I intend to collect that debt, someday," he thought to himself.

"Our secondary target, Jean Paul, is on the move." The voice, wobbling with uncertainty, was Dominic Reeves. It was as if Dom was waiting to be contradicted, even in this factual information he knew to be rock solid. "He appears to be headed back to Paris."

"Dom, he is not our secondary target. He is our target. He will lead us to Stanley." Diane was still suffering the fatigue of half a night in a wing chair, and half the morning sleeping on the train. She had only enough time to get to the Sheraton Malpensa, shower, and make the session with the team.

"What do we know about Jean Paul that is new?" Diane asked.

Emery's voice rose high and confident. "Jackpot. Treasure trove!"

"Go on," Diane commanded.

"Well, we know by matching up records and facial analysis that Syrenka indeed lives and breathes. We know this individual started life as Kazimierz Danuski, son of the lovely *Pani* Agnieszka Danuska. We have file footage of him from the Polish Government archives, which I personally hacked. Kazimierz was very active in the Gdańsk shipyards, working for the communists, but must also have been working with *Solidarity*. Why? Because after the Polish state was once again free of the Russian/Soviet influence, the Danuski family split. Bronislaw, the father and Economic Minister under the communists, was run out of Poland and popped up in Moscow. We suspect not for long, as he was never spotted again."

"That makes sense. Poles always made second rate communists and third rate Russians, according to our friends in Moscow," stated Dom blandly. "The Russians surely executed him for screwing up the economy in Poland, costing them a satellite state. God knows they would never lay blame where it should be – that their Communism economics experiment failed. Easier to kill a former Minister of Economics, instead."

Emory pressed on. "So, what happens to Mother and Son? In President Lech Wałęsa's first free Polish government in the early 1990's, they both get some very nice government positions. Agnieszka becomes an undersecretary of the Cultural Ministry, and Kazimierz becomes a customs officer in the very shipyards of Gdańsk where *Solidarity* was nurtured. That is until 1996. Everyone was relaxing after Aldrich Ames, that treasonous bastard, was captured by a team including our own Diane Sterling," said Emory, nodding at Diane and winking condescendingly at Dominic Reeves. "Just as everyone felt safe again, we know that the code name, *Syrenka*, showed up on a Russian hit list, but now for the first time, along with its agent's real identity - Kazimierz Danuski. Thanks again to a team including Diane, we later found out that other treasonous bastard, Robert Hanssen, was double dealing detailed information to the Russians."

Emory once again winks at Dom, as if to say, "Look at how much *The Huntress* has done in her career – what have you done, my friend?"

"Go on, Emory, we knew most of this, I am waiting for the treasure to be unearthed," Diane said flatly.

"Just framing the picture, ma'am," Emory said, remembering too late she hated the "ma'am".

Diane gave a hard look, one that Emory had no issue understanding. Emory proceeded, "Since then, both *Syrenka*, and Kazimierz have disappeared. The agency had concluded that the Russians had rounded him up. Likely executed him, paying him back for his spying during the *Solidarity* days. Case closed."

"*Syrenka*," pronounced Sophie, saying the word in her native Polish, correcting his American pronunciation.

Not one of the Americans in the room could tell the difference between the two pronunciations, but Diane knew the change in inflection was important to Sophie. She shot a look to Emory.

"Yes. Of course, Sophie," said Emory, not troubling to repeat his mispronunciation.

"Next thing we know, almost twenty years later, this fellow named Jean Paul pops up and helps Stanley in a very major way, assassinate an asshole executive of Global Defense Analytics."

"Still waiting," said Diane, now becoming impatient.

"OK, those are the muscle groups, here comes the connective tissue."

Emory had been waiting to use that phrase for some time, since his Pre-Med courses at Penn State. This was before he found his courage to defy his father, and switched his major to what he tuly loved, German Language and Literature.

"Jean Paul is Kazimierz Danuski. He is also Wojciech Grzymała. No, not Chopin's financier," Emory was speaking at Sophie now, "but the President of the real estate procuring and money laundering Franco-Polish Confederacy."

"How do we know all this? Are we sure this is the same person?" asked Carlyle coldly.

Emory paused and glanced awkwardly at Diane. She nodded, "Go on, tell Carlyle what he asks."

Emory looked at Carlyle. "The boys at Langley ran some pretty advanced processing algorithms on all the imagery, from the Polish Government files I hacked of Kazimierz, to the bank files of Wojciech withdrawing the funds, and of Jean Paul from the social media posts from Milan. They are as sure as they ever get, and that is damn sure, that these are the same person. It is definitive."

"Very impressive," congratulated Diane. "Now we just need to learn what name he lives under today, and where."

"You should have let me finish," said Emory, now very sure of himself. "We were able to backtrack to new names that came up in London, Paris and Amsterdam in the time after Kazimierz went missing. Got a strong hit in Paris, six months after Kazimierz' last sighting. We have a lot of activity on a middle-aged man establishing a new identity. Lost identity card application, followed by passport application, soon followed by a small business application. We pulled his photo from the passport, and bingo – same dude. Now living at large in Paris' Montparnasse district, calling himself Étienne Chaton. Since the late 1990's, he has put some weight on, darkened his hair, but the analysts confirm he is Kazimierz Danuski, Wojciech Grzymała, and Jean Paul all the same." Emory looked up to Carlyle taking notes, and Diane noticing this also, wearing a very painful look.

"Any records of a young child deceased by that name?" asked Dom.

"No, by that time the French, as the rest of the world, were using computerized cross referencing of birth and death certificates. Sorry Dom, but that trick died with the nineteen seventies. More likely he created a story as a French national who migrated from Algeria, Guyana or one of the other former French colonies. That, along with a well-placed bribe, would have done the trick. We traced the records overnight and found no trace of Étienne Chaton before 1996. He is definitely our man. According to this morning's camera sightings, he is making a bee-line back to Paris. Using the French highways, it's only a nine hour run to Paris. He appears to be making no attempt to avoid the detection cameras. He must feel pretty damn anonymous at this point. He'll be back in Paris by tonight."

"Any chance Stanley is with him?" asked Carlyle, his interest growing as the quarry was now in sight.

"We don't think so, as the cameras are only picking up one driver in the car," Emory answered.

"Stanley won't be with him. Too risky," Diane said flatly.

"How has he been making his living, for all these years?" asked Carlyle, again without any trace of emotion.

"He has been living off tourists along the Seine. Buying mass produced canvas paintings and selling them through several *faux artistes* as their own, along the banks of the river. Apparently, he has been making a fairly lucrative living from this trade, even after he pays off his fake street painters. The tourists love them, especially the Americans. He seems to have focused on copies of the impressionists, as well as Parisian street scenes." Emory was proud of himself, positively beaming.

"How on earth do we know all that, so quickly?" asked Diane.

"It was all on his home computer, I hacked it. The embassy translators helped me with the French." Emory was waiting for Diane's reprimand, which did not come. "This guy is very careful, though. Nothing in Polish, nothing tying him back to his previous life. Also, nothing tying him back to Stanley. Certainly, nothing showing a recent massive influx of cash."

"We are tracking his car, we know where he lives, we know how he makes his money, when he is not taking blood money from Stanley. We need to take him down now, and force him to take us to Stanley." Carlyle's voice was not flat now, it was loaded with forcefulness.

"No, absolutely not. Not until we know how they are communicating for their meet locations." Diane was meeting his level of forcefulness. "He sends one abort message and the tie to Stanley is cut forever, and our trail goes cold."

"Well, pardon my ignorance, '*Your Huntress*'," said Carlyle, cynically. "But did it ever occur to you that Stanley, the master spy we all seem to respect so much, is dragging our asses all over Western Europe to stall until he and Jean Paul can arrange a more permanent solution to their problem. Perhaps a way to relocate Stanley to Chile or Australia. Plainly said, we are giving them too much respect. Let's close in on Jean Paul and force his hand."

Diane responded as forcefully as anyone in the room had ever seen her. Almost yelling, she said, "Absolutely not. No, we move operations to Paris and focus on how they communicate. We have heard from you, Carlyle. Force of hand and permanent solutions. Trellis can redirect me, but so long as I am leading this team, we do this my way."

Carlyle, seemingly ignoring her, turned to Sophie. "What's Stanley going to Paris for, Sophie? You seem to be the one with all the answers."

Sophie cautiously looked at Diane. She tried to hide the fact that she indeed did know the answer to this, but instead she turned, looked at Carlyle, and said simply in her heavily accented English, a lie. "This, this is something I do not know."

Jean Paul had thought about the man who he had assisted in evading the CIA and INTERPOL for several weeks. His beloved Stanley, the man who had saved him from Russians once his identity had been betrayed to them, was slipping. Stanley was now putting them both at significant risk.

Jean Paul drove along the French countryside. He was to meet Stanley in the French town of Albi in a couple days. After the discussion in Milan, Jean Paul decided he would not make that meeting. He felt it was too dangerous. Stanley was slipping, and his errors would turn Jean Paul over to those who now pursued them both. He decided to return to Paris, collect his essentials, and restart his life for a third time. It would be somewhere new. He certainly had the funds he needed to do so from aiding Stanley throughout this undertaking.

He remembered his darling mother, now gone forever from him. He had always consoled himself that she was lost in a terrible accident. In Vienna, Stanley had suggested that this perhaps was not an accident all, but the wrath of Jack Trellis having been inflicted upon Stanley. Had Agnieszka merely been the instrument of Trellis' torture upon Stanley? Was her death a punishment for the spy who would not follow Trellis' demands?

Jean Paul would skip Albi. Unknown to him, that also meant the

American CIA team now trailing him throughout France, would as well. Jean Paul's loss of faith in Stanley would insure the old spy remained on the loose a little longer.

Chapter Twelve

The Preparations of Christmas Week

STANLEY WAS DETERMINED to arrive in Paris in the week leading up to Christmas. He traveled by an indirect route, always using random drivers and changing them at each leg of his travel. First, he journeyed from Italy to Bern, Switzerland. His driver was an Italian he had watched for two days in Turin from the apartment he had rented overlooking the train station. He knew the Italian drove a private car, most likely his own, trying to earn a meager living picking up tourists coming into town, stealing them from the legitimate taxis. He then offered them "special tours of Torino" to run up the fare. He would not be able to resist the payday that Stanley would offer him.

Stanley, masked by a new scarf, but no hat, exposing his stubbled head, told the driver that he was sick, and needed to get to Bern as quickly as possible for treatment. When the Italian suggested the train, Stanley turned and looked to the terminal.

"*Si, Signor*, perhaps, if you do not want the two thousand Euros I am offering."

"The train will not offer you the comfort and company that I will. I will gladly take you to Bern," and so he did. Stanley took advantage of his driver to rest, lying flat in the back of the Fiat, claiming to be exhausted from his sickness.

They stopped only once during the four hour drive, in the small village of Bourg Saint Pierre in the Alps. Stanley and his driver ate at an inn just off the roadside along the Route Grand-Saint-Bernard. Stanley had risen to take a few sightings out of the rear window of the Fiat earlier, when they were negotiating the snow laden mountain switchback roads. The snake-like road, meandering back and forth upon itself as it rose up the mountain, afforded him a clear view of the traffic behind them. Taking a window seat at the inn, Stanley noted the few cars he saw in the village, comparing them to what had trailed behind them on the switchbacks. Stanley soon convinced himself they had not been followed.

A few hours later Stanley was dropped on the outskirts of Bern, where he soon found a modest room for his overnight. The next morning, he bought a new hat, needing it against the biting cold of the Swiss mountains. He then took a taxi to the nearby train station, where he quickly found a new driver, this time a Czech living in Bern, who would drive him to Avignon, France. He continued this pattern, moving in a very inefficient manner, tacking across Italy, Switzerland and southern France. He never used the same driver for more than one leg, as he knew for anyone trailing him, it would be monotonous work, at each destination to discover the next link. Those chasing him would have to be incredibly thorough to find the next driver. Stanley knew that thoroughness would mean time, and that time worked to his own favor.

The next morning, in Avignon, he shopped in town and replaced his overcoat, and shirt and scarf, adding a wide brimmed hat in the regional Provencal style. He discarded his old clothing, and again found a private car willing to drive him to the town of Albi, some forty kilometers outside Toulouse. Here he found lodging for the night. That evening, on the small town square, he dined on local specialty of warm, thick Cassoulet, a stew of white beans, along with shredded duck confit.

He looked through the plate glass window of the restaurant, gazing upon the Cathedral across the empty square as he ate. He knew that this was to be a solitary meal. He had checked the website that morning in Avignon, only to see the abort image - the self portrait of Van Gough with the bandaged ear. He was not angry with Jean Paul for losing faith in him, but was concerned for his safety. If Jean Paul rushed back to his Parisian life, even if only to collect enough things to reinvent himself, he could be falling into their hands. They could have discovered the life his friend had carved out for himself in the capital. It was no longer safe, Stanley feared, for the first time. He felt a tremendous guilt for having involved his friend into all this.

Stanley looked up at the cathedral as he drew only small spoonfuls from his cassoulet. He barely touched the confit. Instead, he thought of his *Sarenka*. Had he betrayed her, by dragging her son into all this? Stanley had struck hard at Trellis, by taking his partner Langston Powell's life. He did so to have revenge over Trellis, who Stanley was sure had endangered Agnieszka's life. The only problem was in the process of revenging her death, Stanley had now endangered the only thing Agnieszka cherished more than life itself – her son.

He inspected the quiet town square around him. This town of Albi was the origination of what came to be known as the Albigensian Crusade. In the twelfth and thirteenth centuries, throughout this Languedoc region of southern France, the Cathars, or "pure ones" rebelled. They were against the materialism and decadence of the dominant Medieval Roman Catholic church. They believed there was an ongoing war between themselves, the pure, and the evil that had permeated their time. Albi was the town where these Cathars were most heavily concentrated.

In 1208, Pope Innocent III declared the Cathars heretics, and called for a crusade against them. This crusade went on for the next twenty years, with extensive fighting in the walled cities of Toulouse and Carcassonne. The Inquisition was shortly thereafter introduced to the French region of *Languedoc*, and murder and torture ripped apart the families of this otherwise tranquil land.

Stanley could not resist seeing himself in the role of the Cathars, being hunted unrelentingly by the established institutions. The powerful were threatened, and when this occurred, there was bound to be dire consequences.

The evil of his own time had already afflicted the lives of his father, mother, and his *Sarenka*. He thought especially of his Agnieszka. He remembered the last conversation they had in his modest Fells Point townhouse in 2008, when Agnieszka came to stay one last night with him.

"This is so wonderful, your being here with me," he remembered saying to her over a modest meal in his kitchen. His face was beaming, as the burden of loneliness was, for at least one night, eased from him. "Come stay with me in America and we can grow old together."

"You jest, my *Stasiu*," she responded, using his affectionate name in Polish, "but I may come and stay with you one day. This waterfront is very lovely. It reminds me of Gdańsk. No, it does not quite have the charm of our homeland, but it is lovely in its own way."

"Then come," said Stanley, still radiant. "Nothing could make me happier. Even if you only stay for a few weeks or months, come stay with me."

"I have to stay in Warsaw a little bit longer," she now pulled back, "for I have been invited to the seventieth anniversary ceremonies commemorating the Katyń Massacre. It will be a tremendously solemn event. However, in order to honor my father, I must be there."

It had been an emotional few days for her. The day before she was the guest of honor at Baltimore's National Katyń Monument ceremony. Now she spoke of another ceremony, which would soon mark the seventy years since her father was so brutally killed by the Russians. With this, her eyes, which were so radiant only moments before, began to tear. He knew this event was still nearly two years away, but just thinking of it wounded the delicate spirit of his cherished Agnieszka. Stanley moved to her and held her close as he sought to console her.

"Yes, for your father. His life was ripped from yours there. And you were so young, only a toddling child. After so many years, the scars of our youth are still the most tender of all."

Agnieszka cried on Stanley's shoulder as a child does in a father's embrace. Through her gentle sobs, she whispered in his ear, "You are so good to me. You are so pure."

These words rang through his mind, over and over, until they were etched in his soul. They were remembered, not as the compliment she intended, but as the ominous mantra of the ghost she had become.

It was Saturday April 10th, 2010. Stanley had taken a long walk around the Fells Point waterfront, and upon returning to his

Shakespeare Street row home, turned on the television. Soon, the program he was watching was interrupted by the news that a Tu-154 aircraft, carrying the official Polish delegation to Smolensk, had crashed in heavy ground fog. It was carrying the official entourage to the commemoration ceremonies marking the seventy years since the massacre in the nearby Katyń forests.

All 96 persons aboard were dead. This included the President of Poland, Lech Kaczyński and his wife, Maria Kaczyńska, and nearly the entire Polish government leadership. Also perishing onboard was the ninety-year-old former President of the Polish Government in Exile during the Communist years, Ryszard Kaczorowski. Even the beloved hero of the *Solidarity* strike of 1980, *Pani Anna Walentynowicz*, perished on board. In his mind's eye, Stanley always imagined that next to her on that ill-fated flight, sat his beloved, Agnieszka Danuska.

In a final twist of fate, Stanley soon came to learn from his contacts in the agency, that the plane did not merely fly into the ground and crash. It had come in low, but in the heavy fog, the plane was off course, and struck the trees of the nearby forest. Damaged, the plane rolled over, and plowed into the ground upside down. It smashed into a patch of forest not far from the runway of the Smolensk airport. Like her father before her, Agnieszka died violently in the forests surrounding Smolensk.

Stanley remembered breaking down emotionally that day. He tortured himself reliving the last seconds of her life over and over. The sheer terror that must have enveloped them all as the plane rolled over. His only solace was the speed in which it must have occurred. He could only hope that those last few seconds of her life were not stretched into an infinite horror by the relative nature of time. For him, he would never escape these last few seconds of her life.

He remembered Diane calling him on the phone later that day, as she had heard the news. Diane, at that point, did not know of Agnieszka, nor, of course, Stanley's relationship with her. Nonetheless, she could not help thinking of him, and how this tragedy would affect him.

Stanley recovered slowly from that fateful tragic Saturday. He soon travelled to Warsaw, which was in a heightened state of crisis. With the government having been essentially lost, the country suspected this crash was the work of the Russians, and as such, feared an invasion.

Stanley travelled east to Smolensk, where he laid bouquets of white lilies not only at the crash site, where Agnieszka's soul departed her body, but also at the Katyń site, where her father's love had been denied to her at such a young age.

It was at the crash site that Stanley heard the echo of Trellis' words that haunted him. "We know about your beloved *Sarenka*, and you are never to contact her again. If you do, she will be taken from you. You will never know when it will occur, but at some point, she will be taken from you."

Stanley was convinced that Trellis had found out about Agnieszka's visit to the United States two years before, and had somehow arranged this crash to fulfill his threat. It was here, in the broken tree line of the airport, that Stanley vowed that Trellis would one day pay.

Carlyle opted out of the jet to Paris. He was trailing now several miles behind the team of five cars following Jean Paul across France. The team of cars were professional trailers, each taking turns dropping the target only to have another pick up the surveillance in apparently random patterns. In this they were successful, not drawing Jean Paul's attention.

Jean Paul, for his part, was making it easy on them. He was on the highways, and was progressing toward Paris in a very direct fashion. He made no attempt to access the country roads where these cars were more readily spotted. He made no attempt to double back on his route of travel. Jean Paul was intent on getting to Paris, and was taking the most direct route available. Any vehicles he would see repeatedly upon the highways, he would naturally assume were also headed to the capital upon the same route.

Carlyle was listening in on the radio communications between the tailing team of cars, but the special operations agent was a good seven miles behind them on the highway. As they passed the southern walled town of Carcassonne, Carlyle exited the highway, and drove away from the fortress town sitting proudly upon the hill, and into the countryside. He drove through the country until he came upon exactly for what he was searching.

Carlyle pulled the car alongside a rocky outcropping by the side of the road. The large white stones were naturally occurring, and generally scattered across the countryside. Exiting his vehicle in his country overcoat, Carlyle slipped on a pair of rough leather gloves. He pulled at the individual stones, weighing them in his hands, inspecting them, and then casting them aside. After about twenty minutes, he found exactly the stone for which he had been searching. He strained to lift it, carrying it crablike over to the trunk of his car. The weight would not allow him to carry it much further. It was nearly two feet across, smooth, with gently rounded edges. Carlyle released it, dropping it into the trunk. The car sank a bit under its weight. Carlyle smoothed his gloved hand over the stone's cold upper surface.

"Yes, this will do nicely," he thought to himself. A sadistic grin creased his lips.

Carlyle then re-entered his car, drove back to the highway, and re-entered in the direction of Paris. He was now a good twenty-five miles behind the chase, but he knew he would gradually make this up. By the time they entered Paris, Jean Paul would still have his invisible shadows, and Carlyle would be lurking tightly behind them all.

The next day, Diane and Sophie, along with the rest of the team, were working out of the American Embassy in Paris. They now had Jean Paul under constant surveillance in a flat in the Latin Quarter. Unfortunately, this meant Carlyle, who had joined them in Paris, was getting information at the same rate that Diane was. This she feared could prove deadly for Stanley. She had on three occasions requested Trellis to recall Carlyle, and on all three occasions was rebuked. She had to figure out a way that she could isolate Stanley, and get to him before Carlyle became aware.

Diane wanted to hear Stanley's rationale for his murder of Powell, and for leaking the finite details to the press. It was clearly a striking out against the Daedalus Destroyer Drone program, but why?

This afternoon, Sophie had asked Diane if they could go for a walk alone. They had just processed out of the Embassy and walked along the Avenue Gabriel that soon adjoined the Place de la Concorde.

"Sophie, you have never been to Paris, you said?" asked Diane.

"No, Madame, this is my first time here. There is so much history here," she said, clearly taking in the ambiance of the capital, unencumbered by the unseasonably cold weather they were having this December afternoon.

"Is there anything you would like to see? We could walk up the Champs-Élysées to the Arc de Triomphe, or along the Seine to Notre Dame? Whatever you like."

"I would like to buy some flowers," responded Sophie. Coming to the northern edge of the Place de la Concorde, Sophie led Diane to the left, proceeding along the Rue Royale.

"You've never been here, so where are you taking me, mademoiselle?" Diane asked Sophie tenderly.

"I am taking you to buy flowers. Anyone trailing us will see we are simply buying flowers in Paris. What could be more natural?" Sophie was moving at a determined pace, which was in stark contrast to the casual and innocent task she claimed to be endeavoring with Diane.

They soon came upon the grounds of the Church of the Magdalen, known to Parisians as "*La Madeleine*", where indeed upon its dormant grassy surroundings, were several stalls of merchants, which despite the bitter weather, sold their magnificent and colorful array of greenhouse grown floral wares.

As they picked through the blooms, Diane said quietly to young friend, "Sophie, why did you bring me here? Certainly, not to buy flowers."

"Please look up, Madame," requested Sophie, her own head down, inspecting the blooms. "This is why Stanley is leading us here."

Diane looked up onto the Church of the Magdalen. It stood

imposingly before her, bisecting the Rue Royal into two great boulevards forming one of the busiest intersections of Paris. "*La Madeleine*" loomed over them impressively.

"Sophie, I must admit that I know very little of *La Madeleine*," Diane said, still gazing upon the massive structure that looked to her like a replica of the Parthenon in Athens.

"Allow me, Diane." Sophie's head was still down in the flowers.

"Well, at least, I have finally got you to stop calling me *Madame*," Diane laughed.

"Only because you have requested me to treat you as one of my friends. Therefore, I will now call you Diane, as you have asked. And you will call me by my Polish affectionate name, *Zosia*."

As if to accentuate the request, Sophie raised a bloom into the air to inspect it in the afternoon sun.

Diane felt a warmth spread throughout her. She realized the significance of Sophie allowing her this intimacy, this privilege of their deepening friendship.

"*Zussia*?" repeated Diane phonetically.

"Yes, *Zosia*. Sounds like Russia with a 'z' instead of an 'r'. This is the easiest way for you to say '*Zosia*'." Sophie smiled warmly.

"OK, *Zosia*, why does this church interest Stanley?" asked Diane.

"This Church was originally not a church at all. It was intended to be a memorial tribute to Napoleon's *Grande Armée*. After he fell from power, when the monarchy was restored under King Louis the

Eighteenth, it was repurposed into the Catholic Church it is today, honoring Mary Magdalen. I believe that Stanley will come here when he gets to Paris. I just did not wish for Carlyle to know. I am aware you do not wish for him to know."

"Yes, you are certainly correct on that point," said Diane, now deadly serious. "I still don't understand - to know what exactly, *Zosia*?"

"I did not want him to realize that this is the Catholic Church in which the funeral of Frederic Chopin was held. After which, his body was taken to lie in rest within the walls of Père Lachaise Cemetery in eastern Paris. These are the two locations we need to watch, without Carlyle understanding why."

Diane smiled at her *Zosia*. She was so perceptive. Diane, looked back down into the wealth of greenhouse delights her hands sorted through.

"You really are something, *Zosia*. Yes, I agree, these two locations must be watched. However, let's keep this task to those I trust – yourself, Emory, and me. The rest of the team need not know about these two sites."

The two women stood in the presence of the massive church, looking more like an ancient temple with its fifty-two columns wrapping around its exterior.

As *Zosia* had detailed, it was begun as a tribute to men, specifically Napoleon's Grande Armée. But this was before its crushing defeat in the winter snows of Russia. *The Grande Armée's* size and prestige was diminished with every mile of its winter retreat from Moscow in late 1812. *The Grande Armée* was fighting not only the fatal cold of the Russian winter, but also the dehumanizing hunger, as well as the debilitating typhus that ran rampant through its ranks. The original invasion army of some 690,000 strong would yield only 93,000 men who would survive its retreat.

However, at this Church of the Magdalen, the real irony was not of men, but of women. When Frederic Chopin died in Paris in 1849 at the age of thirty-nine, his will was specific as to the music that would be played at his funeral – Mozart's Requiem. This required female voices, but women were forbidden at that time from singing in the Church of the Magdalen. The compromise that was ultimately reached, but taking two weeks and delaying Chopin's funeral by that interval, was to have the women sing from behind a large black velvet curtain. Here, they could be heard, but not seen.

Chopin's funeral crowds were massive at *La Madeleine*, with thousands of attendees drawn from across all of Europe, to pay their respect to this great virtuoso. Thousands came yet had no tickets to attend, and as such, could not enter the church itself.

The next day Stanley was able to arrange for a driver to take him to Paris. He did this through the owner of the inn at Albi. There were many unemployed drivers in the area, most being unemployed Algerian immigrant men, who Stanley feared might well be under surveillance of the French Government. Instead, Stanley convinced the inn owner's son to drive him, for which he was richly compensated.

The drive was uneventful, except for the end in the outskirts of Paris, when a Gendarme behind their car lit his flashing lights. Stanley thought of the irony of coming this close, relaxing only when the Police passed by them in pursuit of his intended pursuit, another offender of the laws of the French Republic.

After paying the innkeeper's son, Stanley had now only several thousand Euro's left. These would burn quickly in the capital, but Stanley had calculated he now had enough left for what he needed. Jean Paul still had posted the abort image on the website, the painting of Van Gogh's bandaged ear, meaning he would not be showing up with fresh funds. Jean Paul knew Stanley planned to place Agnieszka's lilies on Chopin's gravesite, and he could readily guess the timing. Stanley, however, did not count on seeing him in the cemetery.

Stanley was tiring of this hiding as a way of living, for it was not living at all. It was avoiding life, and it was exhausting him.

After being dropped by his driver in the 10th arrondissement, he walked first to the northern train station, the *Gare du Nord*. Only blocks from it, along a minor side street was a small family owned hotel where he checked in under an unused fictitious Latvian identity, with a matching passport supplied by Jean Paul in the last bag transfer in Milan. It was not good enough to get him out of the country, but certainly official looking enough for his use at hotels within the city.

That night he walked the street that was the Rue Saint-Denis as the grocers were closing, and the night life was beginning to come alive. Throughout the avenue, in the gates of the alleyways and doors of the edifices of this working district, were the women of the Parisian night. Several greeted him as he passed, but Stanley merely smiled as he continued walking. He wondered if they had ever had seventy-year-old clients before, and decided surely, they had. These were likely the lonely clients who would have most needed the brief interlude of their companionship.

Stanley now realized that this was exactly what he, himself, had missed the most during the past several weeks - the ability to take a mind clearing walk without fear of being taken captive. Stanley walked several blocks along the Rue de Saint Denis, before circling back through adjacent streets. It was not that he was safe in Paris, just the contrary. He knew he was still wanted by INTERPOL, and specifically the agency. But Paris had always been his goal. He had outwitted the agency, and whatever came next, came next. Stanley had won. In his own mind, Stanley had survived longer than he had dared to hope.

Along the Seine, at nearly the same moment that evening, Diane walked alongside Malcolm Devereaux. He had called her on her cell directly, inviting her to dinner at a quiet eatery just down the left bank from the famous Shakespeare & Company bookstore. This was the very bookstore where Earnest Hemingway, in the Bohemian Paris of the 1920's, borrowed reading material from the proprietor.

The name Shakespeare forced a memory from Diane. She recalled Stanley's home, in the Fells Point section of Baltimore, was on Shakespeare Street. She knew he would never return there, but hoped that would be because of a lengthy incarceration. If only she could keep Carlyle from Stanley, she knew this could be.

Malcolm and Diane had dined on an exquisite meal of escargot, baked oysters, and lobster, unlike any meal Diane had ever had in Paris. She had joked to Malcolm that she was sure he thought this meal was nothing more than a disguised aphrodisiac. Malcolm responded that having already spent the night together in Florence, it was not needed. Diane playfully defended her virtue, or at least her virtue relative to his desires.

"Well, darling, you may never know what privileges I took with you in that wing chair, will you? Mum's the word to Georgio, so long as he finds a few Euros in his palm...."

Diane noticed the flicker of the candlelight in his eyes, and was thankful to have this hour or so of relief with him.

It was after dinner as they walked along the left bank. The chill off the Seine was so penetrating that Diane wrapped her arm inside his, catching him somewhat off-guard.

"We finished our little research project for you, darling. Not so tough a chore as one might think. Turns out your friends are playing a very simple game, same as back in the days before the Wall came down."

Diane could not help but feel safe with him. She knew she was likely being watched by agency spotters, but she was known to be friendly with Devereaux. He called her to dinner on her open line, nothing suspicious there. They crossed over the Pont Neuf and stood upon the *Île de la Cité*, the island in the middle of the Seine river upon which Notre Dame cathedral stood. They soon stood before the monument to the French King Henry IV.

"*Et donc, la nouvelle devient l'ancien,*" Devereaux said to Diane. "You do speak French, darling?"

"Very poorly, yes," she replied in English. Translating, she said aloud, "And so, the new becomes the old!"

"*Tres bien, ma Cherie,*" Devereaux rewarded her.

Diane mentioned in response that she knew the Pont Neuf, or New Bridge, was misnamed as it now was the oldest in Paris. The cold was biting hard at both of them now.

"Paris is full of dichotomies, Diane. Take this monument, for instance. It was destroyed during the French Revolution. But the Sans Culottes, or the Jacobins, or whoever else despised the monarchy at the time, were never able to destroy the mold. So later it was, thankfully, faithfully re-cast from the original mold and placed here."

"I can think of a lot warmer places to get a *'leçon d'histoire française'*." She was now gripping hard at his arm.

"Let's take a stroll in the park, darling," he said leading her down the darkened stairs to the vacant park that below them, rested just above the river's crest. Along this lower tier of the *Île de la Cité*, the island's banks separated and then reunited the Seine river.

"Are we safe?" asked Diane, for once worried more about street thugs than alphabet agencies.

"Don't worry, darling, we have a chaperone, so do keep your hands to yourself." Devereaux flashed her his knowing, sly smile.

She understood this to mean the Brits were providing cover. Then she saw a series of two short and three long flashes from a very powerful light along the opposing bank of the river. "Looks like we are cleared to talk," Devereaux said, as he watched her.

They had reached the park, and the sound of the Seine rushing past the stone embankments of the quay was loudly audible. Not another soul was present. Only the cold, the dark, and the unseen eyes of the

Brit watchers. Devereaux took her free hand and placed in her palm a small piece of paper.

"This is your website, darling. Looks like it has been maintained and updated by your number two quarry, awaiting your Stanley to access it each time before the meet. It is tied to the *Musée d'Orsay*, at least thematically, and only shows one image at any given time. In between their meets, it appears to be a safe image exhibited – the image of the Musée itself, with open and closing times. But usually the evening or two before they meet, there is a change of the image and text. The image is usually a single impressionistic painting from the *Musée d'Orsay*. It appears the variable could be by the artist painting the image – Monet, Manet, Degas, etc.- or by the painting content somehow – does it show people, landscapes, etc. Likely the latter, as it is simpler, and less likely to be misconstrued."

"We had thought something along those lines, just did not have the website." Diane was pressing his hands tightly in a sign of gratitude.

"Darling," Devereaux pressed on. "We also noticed that all the site's images are pre-stored, so all your man has to do is switch the images. But for some strange reason, he feels compelled to edit the first line of text before posting it."

"How is that significant?" asked Diane.

"We think he is declaring the meet time to your target. Could be something complicated, but more than likely they are keeping this very simple. Number of words in the sentence for the hour of day. We know it matches up for Milan."

"You are not supposed to know about that," she said to him smiling broadly.

"You are leaving a broad enough wake for a blind sailor to trail. Be very careful," he said, taking her into his arms, his hands pressing the small of her back. "This beautiful park used to be the site where French Kings tortured their subjects. Don't be fooled into thinking your royalty is any less malevolent."

With this, he smiled again wryly, reaching his arms around her.

"I would never forgive myself should anything happen to you, Diane," Malcolm breathed, more than said, to her.

And with this, he kissed her hard pulling her in to him and upward. Initially, she resisted him only slightly, perhaps to register the height from which her submission would fall. Then, throwing her arms over his neck, she pressed into him, eagerly probing his mouth. She fought with herself for control of her emotions. Then her fingers that had hungrily framed his face, turned his head away, until her lips, full from his gentile biting, slid from his mouth. She whispered into his ear, barely above the sounds of the surging Seine, "I am taking him this week, after which I am coming to take you."

Devereaux pulled back gently, searching her eyes. "Well, darling, there is this rather nasty man from Tennessee who may have a little problem with that. We are very concerned about your safety. I want all this in one piece," he said running his hands up her waist and cupping her breasts through her overcoat, before returning them to her waist.

He continued, "Just tell me where the location for the meet is, and my traveling circus and I will provide you three ring coverage."

Diane pulled back from him. Her face hardened from the melted edges of her ecstasy, to the sharpened spikes of a pit of betrayal.

"So, now I get it! You don't give a damn about me, do you? You're just letting George Chartwell use you to get to me. Then he can gain access to Stanley and find out what else Stanley has on Trellis. My God, what an idiot I have been all along!"

Enraged, she pulled away from Devereaux and headed back to the stairs ascending to the Pont Neuf. Devereaux caught her from behind, grabbing her hand.

"Diane, this isn't about Chartwell and Trellis. George just knows that bastard Trellis inside and out, and we both fear for what comes of you." He seized her arm hard to get her attention. "If we figured out that website so quickly, I guarantee you Trellis has. The only missing piece is where Stanley and your number two meet. If Carlyle gets that location, this is going to get as ugly as it possibly can."

"I have caught bigger catches without being bitten," she half snarled at Malcolm.

"Diane, this is not about catching traitors by going through their trash and their financial records. There is no telling that your dear friend Stanley - yes, we know about your connection to him also – that he won't be the spitting serpent they think he is. God knows he's been crawling on his belly for over a month now."

"Stanley wouldn't hurt a ..." Diane stopped herself, thinking of Langston Powell.

"I am not flying away," said Devereaux, picking up on her unfinished thought. "Call the number if you need me. I will be close. Just tell me where to meet you, and I am here for you."

Diane pulled away from his grip and raced up the stairs. Atop the Pont Neuf she walked briskly away, across the river, heading north, before turning left and heading back towards the American Embassy. Her anger had turned to embarrassment, and she felt the sting of tears forming in her eyes.

"I will be damned if I will let that British bastard's spotters photograph me crying." She continued to walk with a vengeful gait.

Diane returned to her hotel room. She was furious, having felt betrayed by the one man she thought might really have had a romantic interest in her. She was silly to think so, she reminded herself, as Devereaux was nothing more than a professional charmer. He used these skills like any other - to get what he wanted. She was only angry that he wanted Stanley, not herself.

She opened her laptop computer. She began searching the *Musée d'Orsay,* the impressionistic art museum that had once been a train station along the left bank of the Seine river. She was going through its many webpages as cover for the site she was about to access. She was acutely aware that her web searches were being monitored. After about a half hour of going through an endless parade of impressionist information, she accessed the website that Malcom Devereaux had just palmed her an hour or so earlier.

Up popped a very simplistic webpage full of text and one image. The text described the history and art of the *Musée d'Orsay.* However, as soon as the image in the center of the page loaded, Diane immediately responded aloud with the word she rarely used. "Shit!"

She recognized the painting of Van Gogh with the bandaged ear. She knew it had nothing to do with the *Musée d'Orsay*, because she had recently seen the original painting in London. It was part of the permanent collection of the Courtauld Gallery. She had been there with a friend, after which they lunched in nearby Covent Garden. She remembered the artwork specifically, with Van Gough wearing his country overcoat and his fur trimmed hat resting above the bandage covering his self-mutilated ear.

Realizing that this work had nothing to do with the *Musée d'Orsay*, she immediately knew it must be the abort signal.

They were trailing Jean Paul to get to Stanley, only to have the link between the two broken for good. She may never find Stanley, she feared. He could not be in Paris at all. Her mood plummeted further into depression.

She then remembered Sophie, her *Zosia*. She would double down on having the church and the cemetery watched. If Stanley was here, she would bet he would show at either location based on *Zosia's* hunch.

Deep inside the US embassy in Paris, Carlyle spoke to Trellis directly through an encrypted, secure line.

"The timing suggests another meet soon between Stanley and Jean Paul, or as we now know him, Étienne Chaton." Carlyle sat in the darkened room. He had asked Dom to wait outside the door to the secure section of the embassy reserved exactly for this purpose.

"I don't want us losing track on that *f**ker...*" they had been talking for several minutes, and Trellis had already whipped himself into a frenzy.

"Don't worry, Jean Paul did not return to his, or should I say Chaton's, usual apartment. He's holed up in another sleazy hotel in the Latin Quarter. He thinks he's safe. He doesn't know we are onto the car he bought in Amsterdam, and that we are tracking him wherever he goes."

"That's not the *f**ke*r I was thinking of," said Trellis.

"Jean Paul will lead us to Stanley. It's Diane that I am worried about. She's keeping something from me, about how they communicate via website. She's been talking to the Brits; I think they are helping her," said Carlyle.

Trellis was quiet for a second, as if deciding whether to say what followed. "That is her weakness. She is too proud to accept help. We're watching the Brits, especially Devereaux. She appears to be talking to him, but nonetheless she appears to be keeping him at bay."

"Good. They won't get in my way," said Carlyle.

Trellis went on, "Besides, I have already had our Fort Meade friends run the website they are communicating through. NSA says it is an art related site, and that they are communicating through visual signals in the art that is posted. By tracking that back to Jean Paul's movements, it appears that he is very diligent about posting the day before the meet. But they think he has now posted an abort signal."

Carlyle cringed on hearing exactly what Diane had feared all along.

"We need to force Jean Paul to think there is a meeting. Then I can follow Jean Paul to the location. I can force Mr. Chaton to tell me how to track Stanley. After which, I will take care of business." Carlyle was glad to be coming to the end of this tedious trail, so he could wrap this up, and move on with life.

Trellis blasted, "It won't be quite that easy. We still don't know the meet site. Diane will also likely be trailing Jean Paul, with possibly the *f**king* Brits in tow as well. We can't turn this *f**king* thing into a convention of witnesses."

"I agree. This needs to be a small party. Just me and Stanley with a clean-up crew waiting to be called in. I don't want Diane or the Brits in the vicinity."

"This is what we are going to do," said Trellis, explaining in detail the plan to assure no crowds. "I've got the cyber team standing by. You just need to prepare yourself for all *f**king* contingencies."

Siting on the desk in front of Carlyle was an opened case, allowing him to gaze upon the sniping rifle. It was complete with laser sight and night scope, as it had been issued to him from the agency's embassy stores.

"I am ready for all contingencies," said Carlyle.

Chapter Thirteen

Christmas Eve

Père Lachaise Cemetery, Paris (Kiev.Victor/Shutterstock.com)

THE NIGHT SKY of Paris was painted gray with an opacity that absorbed and re-radiated the city's celebratory luminosity. The day's air had been bitterly sharp and cold, crisp in its condemnation of those who dared out against it. The city's church bells tolled to awaken the otherwise indifferent Parisian masses to the joyous majesty of this night of nights.

The tolling of the bells coincided with the falling of an accumulating snow, very unusual for this early in a Parisian winter. It fell heavily, engulfing the city of lights in a pristine blanket of silence, pierced defiantly by the bells of Christmas Eve.

Jean Paul peered out the window of his rented hotel room, taking it all in. He was preparing to leave Paris. He had over the last few days collected the things he needed from his apartment two blocks away. Tomorrow he would drive south, and journey across the Pyrenees mountains into Spain. From there he would decide his next steps, while lying low for several months. He could journey into North Africa or even on to South America, after any searching for him died down. He had nothing but time to decide. He also had all the time and money needed to recreate himself once again.

Jean Paul looked out his window. In the distance was the illuminated Eiffel Tower, and emblazoned in its lights across the Seine was the *Trocadéro*. Over these and the rooftops along the Seine, snow fell in a thickened, cleansing veil, preparing the otherwise unworthy city of decadence for the ceremony of the occasion of Christmas Eve.

As Jean Paul had prepared throughout the day, his thoughts continued to return to Stanley. He sensed his friend was in the city also, but had no way of being completely sure. After Jean Paul posted the abort signal, it was not unlikely that Stanley could have cancelled his earlier plans. But, Jean Paul remembered Stanley insistently speaking of laying lilies for his mother upon Chopin's grave. He knew that if Stanley was to do this, he would do so upon the symbolic stroke of midnight, as Christmas Eve became Christmas day. *That would be pure Stanley*, Jean Paul thought. The Stanley that he had come to know. Père Lachaise Cemetery would be closed, buttoned up tight, but Jean Paul also knew that would not stop Stanley.

"*Zosia*, when will Stanley go to the Church or Chopin's grave?" Diane asked Sophie in private.

"Given the time of year, it is likely he will do this on Christmas eve," said the young Polish woman.

"You sound very certain, why?" Diane was always intrigued by Sophie's thought processes.

Sophie looked at her as if she was surprised Diane did not know. "In Poland, the celebration of Christmas begins on Christmas Eve. This is tradition. There is the celebration of the first star, the family then sits down to a great meal, always fish, never meat. At this meal, there is always an extra place set for the unexpected guest. This also is tradition. If someone comes to your home whom you do not expect, like a poor soul or a traveler, you are expected to seat them and have them join your family. Later the whole family celebrates together the *Pasterka*, or Christmas Midnight Mass. Given these traditions, Stanley will celebrate Christmas Eve by being close to his people. He may even visit a Polish family in Paris, of which there are many, as the unexpected guest. More likely, he will attend mass at the Church of the Magdalen or visit Chopin's tomb at midnight."

Diane was amazed at how simple it all was. She now knew that Stanley was surely in Paris just days before Christmas, for exactly this reason.

"OK, *Zosia*, you and Emory will cover the gravesite. I will cover the church. We will see if your instincts are true."

Jean Paul looked at his watch. Ninety minutes to midnight. He needed to be moving, getting out of Paris. He would forgo celebrating Christmas. He needed to head south. He pulled on his woolen French frock coat, wrapped a warm scarf around his neck, and donned a woolen cap of his own. What he did next from habit, he would have been better served, as having not done, for it may have changed his destiny.

Jean Paul checked the website one last time. Force of habit, more than anything else, he always checked it just before leaving for the meet. Tonight, he would not meet Stanley, but perhaps due to the guilt of abandoning his friend, he checked it anyway. What he saw terrorized him.

Instead of Van Gogh's bandaged ear, the abort signal, the website now displayed the muted undertones of a Gaugin still life of an apple and bottle of wine. No people meant the alternate meet site!

Who had switched this? When, since last night? Hours ago, or minutes? Jean Paul sensed a heaviness on his chest, and an immediate feeling of being watched, possibly trapped.

Jean Paul knew Stanley planned to be at the gravesite, likely this evening, but the alternative location was *La Madeleine*. Was Stanley aware of the change in the website image? Could it had been Stanley, himself ? No, Jean Paul knew Stanley did not have access to change this site, ony to view it. Who, then, did this? And why?

Jean Paul thought through the situation, attempting to calm the tremors he could now feel rising involuntarily within him. His first instinct was to repost the emergency abort of Van Gogh and his bandaged-ear self-portrait. But whoever had hacked his impressionistic website had now blocked him from doing so. It was as if they had commandeered this site to divert Stanley to the alternate site, *La Madeleine*, the Church of the Magdalen – the site of the funeral of Frederic Chopin.

Was it possible Stanley would arrive there, instead of the primary site, expecting the signal was a change of heart by Jean Paul? It depended on when this site had been hacked. Had it been hours ago, Stanley could certainly have seen the change. But had it been minutes ago, then Stanley was surely already en route to his original plan.

If Stanley was now heading toward the Church of the Magdalen, then this certainly was nothing more than a trap. Jean Paul wondered how he could warn his friend. Then it came to him, and he had just enough time. If only Stanley would recognize him, before the watchers recognized Stanley.

Jean Paul decided he would go first to the Church of the Magdalen, and look for Stanley, to warn him. If he did not see him, he would proceed to Père Lachaise Cemetery, and meet Stanley at Chopin's grave. There was just enough time, but before he left the room, Jean Paul bandaged his right ear. This was a clear reference to the Van Gogh abort image. Jean Paul hoped if Stanley only saw him at a distance, he would know to abort immediately.

Dominic Reeves had his spotters ready and they easily trailed Jean Paul into the Metro stations after he left his rented apartment. By radio link, they noted he was carrying a knapsack, which was expected, and that his right ear was bandaged, which was not. Dominic passed this information on to Carlyle, who was driving circles through central Paris, awaiting Jean Paul to tip his hand and show his destination.

In his car's trunk was the case containing the sniper's rifle and laser sight. They sat atop the massive stone Carlyle had hand-selected outside the walls of Carcassonne.

"Subject is on the move. Appears to have right ear wrapped in heavy bandaging. Into the tube he goes. We have a team surveilling subject. Advise if we should intercept."

The voice was tiny, but clear in Malcolm Devereaux's ear. He smiled across the table at the stunning, dark haired young lady. She was gorgeous, her wine-red lips becomingly full, warmly framing a radiant smile. Her eyes were alive and wondrous, taking in her surroundings.

"More champagne, darling?" asked Malcolm, not waiting for the nod of her head to begin filling her glass.

Devereaux did not respond to the voice in his ear, knowing that the MI-6 team was trained to not engage the subject unless they positively and unmistakably heard from Devereaux himself. To the team tonight, he bore the code name "Chamonix".

He leaned across the small white tablecloth that separated him from the twenty-seven-year-old Parisian beauty who was enjoying the show on-stage immensely.

Devereaux caught her attention, smiled at her in his rakish manner, and said, "My dear Nicole, I cannot believe you have lived in Montmartre your entire life, and have never before seen the show at the Moulin Rouge."

She smiled, turning her head at him. "But Monsieur, I could never afford all this," she said, raising her arms high over her head to define "all this", but at the same time highlighting her exquisite breasts to Malcolm's blatant gaze. Her eyes were alight with excitement, her mind awash in expectation and champagne.

"*Mais, non*, Nicole, you could always afford it" he thought to himself, "Just tonight you'll be paying with the proper currency."

Jean Paul exited the Metro on the south side of the Place de la Concorde. The omens of the night continued, as this is where the nobility lost their heads to the guillotine during the French Revolution. He moved northward, checking his watch, he realized it was already eleven thirty PM. He walked faster. No time to properly circle the Obelisk of the Luxor Temple to assess if he was being followed. He was too late. Only thirty minutes until the meet. He had to find Stanley. He had to warn him of the trap.

"Subject has exited Metro at Place de la Concorde station. He has crossed the square and now heading north along the *Rue Saint Florentin* toward the Church of the Magdalen." Dominic Reeves relayed the message to Carlyle, who was circling in collapsing circles as the position was updated nearby. He began looking for a temporary place to leave the car. He found an open passage of sidewalk along a side street, and ditched the car there.

"He's staying off the *Rue Royale*, one block over on the more secluded *Rue Florentin*. If we can grab him there, we are a mere couple of blocks from the American Embassy." Dom suspected Carlyle had other plans for Jean Paul.

Carlyle had jumped the curb in the side street, put on his flashers, and exited the car. He slipped and nearly fell on the snow now accumulating on the cold concrete of the city.

Carlyle knew forcibly detaining a French citizen into a foreign American embassy, even one who was an undeniable criminal, as was Jean Paul, would create an international incident. "Besides, what I need from this man cannot be extracted in the embassy," thought Carlyle.

On another encrypted frequency, a separate discussion regarding the tracking of Jean Paul was ongoing by Her Majesty's finest. They discussed the fact that Devereaux, tonight codenamed "Chamonix", had not responded earlier. Thus, there was no approval to act beyond merely monitoring Jean Paul.

The head of operations, having no response from Devereaux, said into the microphone for his team, "Lads, we have no interaction from Chamonix. Therefore, no intercession. Right. Understood and acknowledged. Our objective has climbed out of the Tube at the *'Place de la Concorde'*. Coming up the *Rue Florentin*. Appears to have grown a yank tail. Walking straightaway toward *La Madeleine*. Might be attempting to shed us, or the cousins, in her large and growing crowd for midnight mass."

Malcolm listened while hungrily smiling at the very lovely Nicole. She was, in turn, enjoying the exquisite and lovely dancers on the stage. Mostly female. All topless. Her eyes sparkled with excitement. Her body swayed in her chair with the choreography of the dancers.

Malcolm thought to himself, "Of all the nights for our boy to be foraging about, why in the hell did it have to be tonight?"

"Diane, something unusual is going on," said young Emory from his car parked outside the Père Lachaise cemetery. He glanced at his smart-phone again. "Sophie is inside the cemetery, watching the gravesite. What's weird, is someone changed the image on the web-site. Maybe it is Jean Paul, trying to re-vector Stanley for a meet. Looks like he changed the abort image, to a piece by Paul Gaugin - fruit on a table top."

"Or perhaps it's Devereaux and the Brits interfering in our op," thought Diane, as she scanned the crowds entering the Church of the Magdalen. "OK, Emory, stay put. So far no signs of Stanley or John Paul here."

Diane had no idea that Carlyle and Dom were flushing out Jean Paul by the change in the image on the website. Just then, Diane heard

Emory say aloud, "Well, I'll be! Little Miss Sofie comes through again."

Diane continued to examine the crowds approaching the church. "How so?" she asked Emory over the connection.

"Sophie just spotted Stanley in the cemetery. You better get over here," said Emory, trying to contain his excitement. "We are at the *Rue Gambetta* entrance which is at the top side of the hill. We bribed the caretaker who unlocked it for us."

"On my way. Tell her to watch him from a distance, don't get close at all, and don't spook him." Diane was moving now, walking briskly away from *La Madeleine*.

"And, Diane," Emory said, his excitement which was fully evident in the pitch of his voice, "just as Miss Sophie predicted, Stanley is headed to Chopin's gravesite."

Jean Paul walked the several blocks along the *Rue Saint Florentin*, which changed its name to the *Rue Chevalier de Saint George*, before he made a left turn onto the angled *Rue Duphot* that very immediately dumped into the square surrounding the Church of the Magdalen in central Paris.

Now standing on the corner just opposite the eastern half of the church, Jean Paul could see the structure in her full majesty, bathed in the floodlights as her patrons gathered under her pediment for midnight mass.

Jean Paul searched the crowds frantically for anyone who could possibly be Stanley Wisniewski. Instead his attention was drawn up to the sculpture adorning the pediment itself, which depicted the Last Judgment. The long shadows cast by the floodlights made this the most ominous of the night's signs.

It was then that Jean Paul felt a pressure in the small of his back, below the knapsack he carried. He heard a whisper in English into his bandaged right ear.

"Étienne Chaton, Jean Paul, Wojciech Grzymała, and Kazimierz Danuski. My, how I have been looking for you all."

Jean Paul's heart sank. He knew what he had feared most, that this was indeed a trap. Now, and only now, he realized it was not set for Stanley, but for himself. And that he had been played.

"You will now come with me, and we will talk pleasantly enough. When we are through, you can go home to your apartment and your amassed fortunes. Just don't make me have to use my quiet little friend here." Carlyle pressed the silencer of the pistol hard into the back of Jean Paul. "One outcry and I'll take you out. Here and now. No chance to spend that little treasure you've been squirreling away."

Again, he felt the pressure in the small of his back.

They walked a short distance. Jean Paul was frozen in his own fear, deathly afraid of the stranger whose words he had heard, but whose face he still had not seen. Even more, he feared the cold metallic presence radiating from along his lower spine, awaiting only the command from this stranger's trigger finger.

At that same time, a static-laced voice called out the situation over the encrypted British radio frequencies that sliced through the Parisian night.

"Our lad is getting into a Renault with a rather nasty looking gentleman with sharp features and a military cut crop of blond hair. Likely 30 or 35 years old. Subject may be coerced, difficult to ascertain. Do we intercede? Now or never, they'll be lost to us in a moment."

Again, no response from Devereaux, who was given direct orders from Chartwell. Trail the objective's. Get Diane to turn Stanley over to us. But whatever comes to pass, do not interfere with the American's operations.

"No response from *Chamonix*. We are desisting." The operational voice was crisp and authoritative, but subtly accusing Devereaux of being non-committal.

Devereaux listened intently to the one-sided conversation in his ear. Before him the famed, young, lithe dancers of the Moulin Rouge were vigorously assaulting his senses. His young female companion was wide eyed in her excitement, enjoying the gala spectacle.

Devereaux turned his head away from her, feigning a cough. Activating his microphone, he spoke a single word that was transmitted to the entire British operation - "Desist".

The metallic voice in his ear replied instantly. "Roger, Chamonix. Desist. All parties desist. Over and out."

The Renault soon pulled off into the cold gray Parisian night, leaving the frustrated British team in the thickening veil of the midnight's snow.

Carlyle drove with one hand on the wheel, the other on the grip of the revolver, now openly visible in his lap. Its silencer-capped muzzle pointed lazily toward Jean Paul, who was now free to observe the features of his captor's lifeless face. His brain was racing. Knowing the grave danger he was in, his mind seemed to avoid the peril by a wash of random thoughts. The streets of Paris raced by his window, east past the *Hotel de Ville* into the less heavily tourist sections of the city.

Carlyle headed out of the congested center of Paris, soon passing the *Place de la Bastille*, marking the site where the infamous prison once stood. Now it also was just another congested intersection. Carlyle continued away from the heart of the city.

"Étienne Chaton, where is your friend Stanley Wisniewski?" he asked coldly.

Jean Paul stalled, looking at the silencer on the pistol pointed at his stomach. He had to stall for time, he thought, knowing Stanley was only now likely arriving at the cemetery.

"Answer me, or my friend here will speak to you," threatened Carlyle, as he waved the barrel and silencer with his wrist in a menacing manner.

"I was to meet him at the Church of the Magdalen, before you illegally apprehended me. I demand to speak to the Paris Police immediately." Jean Paul was mustering every ounce of indignation he could, when all his body could produce was fear and the bile he tasted in the back of his mouth.

"Yes, I could see the very sizable donation you were about to make to the collection basket in your knapsack. Don't worry, if he shows at the church I have friends waiting for him. He won't. I am surprised you fell for our ruse. Now I suggest you quickly tell me where I can find Stanley, or you will not like what follows." Carlyle was business-like, and it added to Jean Paul's terror.

"I told you. He was to meet me at *La Madeleine*. He likely saw my abort signal of my bandaged ear, and never got close to your team. He has slipped through your fingers, I suppose."

Jean Paul was trying to calm himself. He looked at the dashboard clock – just past midnight. He expected Stanley would be at the grave site by now.

Jean Paul thought of Stanley, and his undying love of Chopin. He had tried to tell Stanley how dangerous it was to go to the gravesite, but the old spy seemed driven to do so. It was as if this function, this homage, of laying his mother's lilies on the master's cold tomb, was his ultimate goal of evading his pursuers. For this noble, but foolhardy action, Jean Paul had fallen into the hands of what he realized now was the CIA.

Jean Paul realized, it being just past midnight, all he needed to do was delay the man beside him. Stanley would surely hold to his protocol and leave after only fifteen or twenty minutes. Jean Paul would delay the agency, and Stanley would slip back into the night.

Grounds of Père Lachaise Cemetery (Pascale Gueret/Shutterstock.com)

Midnight crept curiously in the form of a cold, heavy snow falling across the cemetery grounds. Père Lachaise is cut into a hillside in the twentieth arrondissement of Paris, an area that only the truly motivated tourists wander out to see. This cemetery had become a tourist attraction of its own, with the graves of many famous artists lying within its massive walls. Oscar Wilde, Camille Pissarro, Honoré de Balzac, Georges Bizet, Eugene Delacroix, Marcel Proust, Edith Piaf, and the French icon Molière are interred here. Even the American rock star, Jim Morrison, so beloved in this city where he died, rests in one of the most visited graves here, often strewn with freshly emptied whiskey bottles in homage to his vices.

Père Lachaise's thousands of granite monuments, arrayed above ground as a city scape of markers, tombs, crypts and mausoleums, are remembrances of the multitude of lives and talents long departed. The stones are tightly packed like the remnants of personalities clawing, resisting the inevitability of death. These cold granite slabs are but mirrors where living men come to reflect on the souls they are surely soon to lose.

The dark, snowy night shrouded the grave of interest that lay three quarters up the great hill. The gravesite ascends into the climbing hill, surrounded by a thicket of other tombs in this densely-packed cemetery. It is comprised of a square granite monument bearing the bas-relief profile of the interned artist. Atop this monument is the marble statue "*La Musique en pleurs*" by Chopin's friend, the sculptor Auguste Clésinger. It depicts the mythical muse of music, *Euterpe*, bent in great remorse, crying over her broken lyre. This represented the grief of Paris, if not the world, at the loss of this exquisite composer, who died at an unbelievably young age of thirty-nine years. It was an insurmountable loss in 1849.

Outside of the decorative wrought iron fence, on either side of the tomb, stone steps climb the graveyard hill. These would often be full of clusters of his admirers, always in numbers to show their respect. This tomb of Frederic Chopin is most recognizable by the near continuous bouquets of fresh cut flowers, still placed there by those who love his music more than 165 years following his death.

As the clock struck midnight, the snow continued to fall upon the white marble of the gravesite, before which stood the tall, silent and weary silhouette of Stanley Wisniewski. Tonight, beneath the many leafless trees that stood guardians of the dead, Stanley had come to honor the master, Chopin, and fulfill his promise to his forever-lost love, Agnieszka.

Stanley had truly not expected to make it to this, his ultimate destination. Indeed, except for the clumsiness of the agency upon the footbridge of Görlitz, he would not have. Even now as he felt the grip of inevitability tighten around him, he knew not to where he could run next. Despite all, he had made it here, to this sacred place for all who are Polish. He had now lived to place the fragrant breath of Agnieszka's lilies on the damp stones that marked the remains of the man who forever captured the beauty and simplicity of the Polish soul. Stanley could ask fate for nothing more.

Stanley respectfully, carefully, stepped over the decorative iron fencing. He used his height to gently place the fragrant white lilies just below the marble feet of the grieving muse. The lilies were high above the collection of other flowers lying at the tomb's base that had not yet been cleared away by the cemetery staff.

The cemetery had now been closed for six hours, and as such, Stanley had only the chilled night and falling snow with which to share the expanse of its grounds. He had entered before closing, long enough to find a hiding spot behind a row of crypts near the cemetery wall. Somehow it was appropriate that tonight, of all nights, he should do what he had spent so much of his life doing - hiding, waiting, anticipating.

Stanley had waited until the stroke of midnight, but not beyond, to lay Agnieszka's white lilies upon the snow that accumulated on the wind etched marble of the monument itself. The delicate white powder subdued the torment of the years. The marble, upon which lay the snow, upon which lay the lilies formed a progression – each a fresher, more delicate hue of white.

Tears formed upon the tired cheeks of this old and weary spy. No matter how delicate, how perfect all these abstractions would become, none could replace the most delicate perfection of his remembrances of Agnieszka, his fawn, his *Sarenka*.

"Merry Christmas, my love." He said aloud in Polish. "I am here as I once promised you. But know that I long to be with you soon again."

Chopin's Tomb (Kiev.Victor/Shuterstock.com)

Stanley reached into the pocket of his overcoat. With great care, he placed the bulky form of a portable CD player against the monument of the Chopin grave. Earlier that day, he had bought it as a replacement for the player he had lost with the knapsack on the *Altstadtbrücke* footbridge. He leaned the device carefully against the sculpture that adorned the memorial.

Next, Stanley took the small speaker he had also bought earlier in the day, so that he and his *Sarenka* might listen to the music of Frederic Chopin in the presence of the master.

From his pocket, Stanley inserted a new, never-played disc of Chopin's Concerto No.1 in F minor by the Warsaw Symphony. This very music had played the night Stanley so audaciously took the vacant, worn velvet chair next to the lovely Agnieszka in the concert hall. She was to be the woman who would weave her velvet touch onto his heart, one that had never before been caressed in such a delicate embrace.

The effort of his days of running now over, Stanley's hand trembled openly, forcibly beyond his control, as he pressed the play button on the device. The reverent, circumspect silence was now slowly infused by the strings of the Warsaw Symphony. Magnificently it played the beginning of Chopin's first piano concerto. The symphonic movement pleasantly built to a zenith that then smoothly cascaded down the hillside. The notes searched across the pale white night of the vacant cemetery, as if to settle at the base of the hill, seemingly searching for the shores of an invisible sea. The strings would recede to allow the initial plunking keystrokes of the piano, not unlike the first flailing strokes of a swimmer undertaking a last great journey. Stanley could taste the salty brine of the open sea, only to realize it was the salience of his own mortal tears.

It was then he sensed the unhurried footfalls behind him. He knew this was to be the end of his great journey. Without turning, he said into the vacuous night, "I knew they would send you, and I am glad for it to be so."

Stanley reached to stop the music.

"Let it play, Stanley. It is too beautiful to stop," Diane said warmly into his back. "Why don't you turn slowly and face me, it has been so long since I have laid my eyes on you."

Stanley turned slowly, keeping his hands in plain sight. He turned to face her trench coated form, shrouded in the thickening snow that continued to fall. She stood with her back to the open night, the hillside slanting away behind her, so that only the falling snow and the thicket of frosted branches from the cemetery trees formed her backdrop. The revolver in her right hand was not a surprise to Stanley.

"How did you know to find me here?" he asked.

Diane looked at Stanley's hands. No weapons. He was calm, unthreatened. His face wore a mix of fatigue and recollection. Diane listened to the poignant beauty of the concerto as it played aloud, and somewhere in her perception of the old man she sensed the subtle satisfaction of triumph.

"I have a young Polish friend, Stanley. Her name is *Zosia*. Once we knew you were headed to Paris, she told me it was inevitable that you would come here. I had the grounds covered. You were spotted. *Zosia* knew you would return to your Polish heritage."

With this last comment, she smiled at the old man who had meant so much to her for so long. Diane noted that the triumphant demeanor seemed to grow upon him, and for the first-time she felt that she, herself, may have been played. Had Stanley hoped that she would show?

"Yes, of course, I am betrayed once again by the reflections of my past," he said aloud.

The calm of the music played into the vacuous still of the night. The falling snow seemed to absorb every note, as if stolen by a thief, only a brief second after it was played.

"I was able to have the groundskeepers admit me to the cemetery, Stanley, as it was after hours. The wall around this place is well over twelve feet high in places, so we suspect it was likely you hid among the tombs at closing tonight."

The music played a tender sequence, the piano seemed to trill in mournful yet angelic notes before rendering a solemn, beautiful passage. It was as if the master spoke through the recordings into the night around them both.

Stanley listened to the music, its effect upon him was visibly noticeable to Diane.

"I have made a living hiding amongst the dead," he said solemnly, and with this began again to cry softly.

Diane immediately thought of the night in the Holly's motel room, the only other time she had seen him shed tears.

"They sent me to find you and bring you in, Stanley," Diane began. The revolver pointed into his stomach, aimed for maximum cross section requiring minimal lateral movement. Stanley knew she was deadly, but he knew his life was in danger not from *The Huntress,* but from those who trailed her in the night. He knew she would be the hound before the weapon's barrel, even if she, herself, did not yet realize this to be the truth.

"They will never let you bring me in, Diane," Stanley said to her. He peered into her eyes, much younger and energetic than his own, yet he found contrasting shadows of sadness. Stanley perceived an unexpected tinge of indecision.

What was Stanley reading in them? He expected her satisfaction of the conquest. While it was there, it was offset by a sympathy for the conquered. She knew what awaited Stanley, and could not bring herself to deliver him.

"Trellis will never let you bring me in," Stanley clarified. "I know too many of the shades of darkness that stain him."

The Chopin concerto continued to play mournfully into the night. The snow began to let up, as if it could not compete with the purity of the music.

"Nevertheless, Stanley," Diane said flatly, "you must answer for what you did."

She spoke with the moral authority of those who have never tasted the bitter seeds of injustice, nor the sweet promise of its revenge. Stanley respected her tremendously, but knew her for what she was - an indifferent capitalist whose only love other than money was the thrill of the chase - taking down men in their "men's world". He mourned for the emptiness that had become her soul.

Diane was also processing the situation. She knew Stanley was dangerous, but she did not fear him. Not here, not now. She had also sensed that he was exhausted by the running, but somehow was not fearful of what lie ahead. She watched his hands for any motions that belied a weapon, or even a signal to a second person who might be hidden within the cemetery. But the only motion, was that which surprised her most, was the understated, yet continuous, tremor in both of his hands.

A quick glance to Stanley's razored face - his characteristic, trim beard long gone - convinced her of what she had suspected. Stanley was drawn, gaunt, and spent. The tears rolling down his cheeks made her avert her eyes back to his hands. Her full consciousness was now on not screwing this up. She had to bring Stanley to justice. A living justice. Not merely the sentence of permanent silence that she knew was Trellis' sole reason for imparting Carlyle into her team.

As Stanley and Diane talked, a few miles away in a massive park complex known as the *Bois de Vincennes*, Jean Paul was marched at gunpoint by Carlyle, into the darkness of the open space adjoining one of the four man-made lakes. Carlyle had forced Jean Paul to carry the weighty stone from the trunk of his Renault. Jean Paul sensed this was a trial that his captor had effected on other prey before him. Jean Paul imagined this location had been pre-selected for its solitude. The weight of the stone wore him down, as he carried it deeper into the emptiness of the darkened park at midnight. The white snow covered the grass lightly. He wondered if this might be the last sight of beauty his eyes would ever see. The thought sent a horrifying chill through Jean Paul.

Carlyle suddenly commanded, "Stop!" which Jean Paul did instantly. The voice continued to come from behind him as Jean Paul struggled with the heft and mass of the stone.

"Étienne Chaton, Wojciech Grzymała, Kazimierz Danuski, and most appropriately Jean Paul: you are given one last chance to tell me where I can find Stanley Wisniewski. I am running out of precious time, so I will give you one pain free chance to free yourself. After that, I will offer you only '*motivation*'."

Carlyle's eyes were cold and flat, lifeless. Jean Paul readily sensed that he was enjoying this.

"Please skip the Church of the Magdalen nonsense, as it was us who changed the website you used to contact Stanley. One last time, where was is Stanley?"

"I do not know," mouthed Jean Paul, his voice quivering with fear.

No sooner were these words out of Jean Paul's mouth that he heard a muffled discharge from the gun, and felt the immediate shattering explosion of pain in his foot. Jean Paul dropped the massive rock he had been forced to carry. He, as well as the stone, fell to the ground. Jean Paul rolled away from the stone, its burden which he had been forced to bear. He knew not what was to come next, only that it would be unbearable.

Jean Paul's heart raced, his chest pounded, and all hope of surviving this ordeal now left him. He felt the gloved hand of Carlyle cover his mouth, muffling his loud screams of pain.

In the isolation of this snow-laden park field, on the merging minutes of Christmas morning, there was little chance of anyone being present, let alone responding to his screams. He felt the gloved hand release from his mouth, and in an instant Carlyle was gone. The pain in his foot was intense, as if someone was probing his wound with a ragged shard of glass. A fire in it burned white hot licks of flames, whose tips stretched into taut wires of nerves, pulsing with incredible pain. Where had this madman gone?

Carlyle had been lost to the night, reaching for something that was hidden from Jean Paul's sight. As Carlyle came back into his view, Jean Paul could see the large flat stone that this strong, young man was struggling to hold over him, just as he had struggled with it moments before.

"You are likely thinking you are willing to die to protect Stanley. Very noble. It is what you all think, before you realize the agonizing pain of a slow death."

Carlyle's voice was unemotional. Businesslike, but frighteningly enjoying the anticipation of what was to come.

"Where is Stanley?" he asked again of Jean Paul.

"I don't know, I don't know, I don't know!" squealed Jean Paul, the pain in his foot seemingly consuming every element of his consciousness.

With this, Carlyle stood with one foot heavily on Jean Paul's right hand, preventing him from raising it in defense. Carlyle then, with great exertion, raised the great flattened stone above his head.

"Where..." he grunted "...Is ...Stanley?" The three words came out as short clipped breaths, as he held the stone aloft.

"You have to believe me," cried Jean Paul, whose consciousness now recognized the imminent terror of the moment that was far more dangerous than the agony he was experiencing in his wounded foot.

Carlyle, with all his might, thrust the stone into Jean Paul's chest as he lay on the ground. His right hand pinned under his torturer's foot, Carlyle raised his left arm in defense. It was the first to feel the massive smashing contact of the stone, seconds before the crushing contact with Jean Paul's chest. The surge of pain ripped through him like an unstoppable wave, his limbs ached in echo of the trauma he had just experienced.

Jean Paul had no air in his lungs, and the panic of his breath evading him raised his terror. The pain that had moments before licked at him in flickers of severe pain was now massive. There was not a singular nerve in his being that did not cry out unbearably to him.

Carlyle stared down upon the excruciated face of Jean Paul. A wicked smile creased the corners of the torturer's mouth. He could hear the breath rattle as it escaped from Jean Paul's lungs, making it impossible for him to scream. The pain seared throughout Jean Paul, yet he could not draw a breath to respond.

"You are going to die, my friend. Tell me where to find Stanley and I will make it fast for you. Or I can draw this out for what will be hours for you."

"I do not know," he wheezed, barely audible upon his exhale.

"Where is Stanley?" Carlyle demanded as he struggled to raise the now bloodied stone.

"I do not..." began to escape from the mangled broken remnant of a man lying at his feet.

The stone came down a second time, this time smashing his right pelvis.

The scream that came from within Jean Paul was one that Carlyle had heard many times before, but mostly in the battlefields of the Middle East. It rolled out of the wounded man, a combination of low pitched sobbing and rolling guttural moaning.

Jean Paul's pain was amplified instantly, surpassing even what he had endured only moments before. It was inescapable and intolerable, like the clawed hands of a demon wrestling the life from his body. Through his squinting tearing eyes, he could vaguely make out the stone, elevating in the hands of this madman, unknown to him only an hour before.

"No, no, stop!" Jean Paul spat out the words, along with blood and thickened fluids directly from his lungs. The agony cut through him like a heavy dull throb trying to mask the spiking edges of terror rising yet again within him.

Time, he thought. *It must have been enough time for Stanley to have left the cemetery. I am not giving him up, for he is surely gone.*

It was less of a thought than an electric arc that sparked through the aching, throbbing horror of Jean Paul's brain. It was but one such spark among millions of others. Pain, terror, the last seconds of his mother's horrific ending, all flew about randomly in what he knew were now his terrifying last moments.

"Tell me," said the American, now threatening the stone again, "and I will kill you quickly, mercifully". Carlyle struggled to raise the stone higher.

Jean Paul looked at the stone that now seemed to float over him. He could not take another strike. In his ear, he could feel the breath of his mother's sweet warm voice.

"Tell him, my son. Tell him and come to me. I will soothe you, my magnificent boy…"

Jean Paul struggled to speak. His words fought the fluids choking in his lungs and throat. Carlyle heard them weakly, coming out in pulses almost too painful to deliver.

"Cemetery… Père Lachaise...He is waiting ... Chopin ... Midnight... Grave".

Again, Carlyle heard a rattle of breath escape Jean Paul.

He lifted the stone and thrust it down. It landed with a quiet thud in the snow covered grass next to Jean Paul's head, missing him completely. Despite the mercy shown him by Carlyle's last act, Jean Paul's eyes remained filled with the terror of realizing his every second to live was to come accompanied by agonizingly unbearable pain.

"Make … it …stop, … stop, …I …have …given …you …him! Please… God… Stop!" whimpered Jean Paul like the wounded and dying animal he had become.

Carlyle lifted his silenced revolver to Jean Paul's head, as the latter repeatedly cried softly one word in his native Polish tongue.

"*Proszę … Proszę … Proszę*." He begged.

Carlyle pulled the trigger and the cries for mercy stopped.

Carlyle looked at his watch. 12:39. He needed to rush if he was to have any chance of finding Wisniewski. He called in his location to Dom to send the crew who would come to collect the remains of Jean Paul.

Then he pointed the silenced pistol into the mangled chest of the corpse at his feet. He pulled the trigger a second time. The gun fired. No response. Nothing. Good.

Carlyle looked at the mangled human form at his feet. He thought to himself, one of the few unharmed parts of the body before him was the bandaged ear, the pitiful attempt of Jean Paul to warn his accomplice, Stanley.

"They always talk when the serious pain begins," Carlyle thought. Now, he had to rush to Père Lachaise Cemetery if there would be any chance of silencing Stanley tonight. He thought himself lucky it was not far. Yet, he feared his prey might have already escaped.

As the concerto played the delicate, yet frenetic, notes of Chopin into the cold night air, it was then that the question first formed in her being. Diane looked at his shaven head, his gaunt frame, his beleaguered appearance. She dared not ask it, but the more she suppressed the intellectual aspect of the query, the more she felt it pressing into the core of her very being, into her very existence. It now demanded to be asked, in so much as breaths are required to be drawn.

"Stanley, how could killing Powell have possibly been tied back to your father? How could this be so? I know you, Stanley, and you would not have taken this action if it were not tied back to your father in some manner. "

Diane was horrified at the sympathy in her voice betraying the control she needed to maintain. It morphed, without her intention, into a compassionate tone that was evident to them both.

Stanley searched Diane's eyes, pausing before answering. He weighed the proper level of response. He drew his words with caution, as one draws back the strings of the bow that will launch the sharpened arrow.

"My father only warned me of the dredges of the human heart. It is a nutrient to the evil that lies dormant in all men. Langston Powell was but one whose greed festered into corruption. Jack Trellis was also corrupted from this source."

"What source, Stanley? Is this all about your leaks and manifestos to *The Conservatoire*?" she asked incredulously. "Don't you see that they will paint you with your own brush. Stanley Wisniewski was a deluded, disgruntled embezzler of operational funds, who in a desperate act of revenge strikes out at the CIA by striking down the executive of the supplier of its most sinister drone program."

Stanley raised his moistened eyes to hers. His voice was firm, unaffected by the residual tremble still affecting his once stoic hands.

"Is that what you believe, Diane? That is exactly the story that they wish to tell. For you to believe. That is why Jack Trellis will never allow me to be brought in. He can't allow me to show the world the source of his illicit fortunes."

"Now it is over, Stanley. You will be locked away, and your *source* will still be unknown." Diane knew she needed to stop this conversation, but it's lure to her would not be denied. She needed to get Stanley out of the cemetery and into custody, but she hesitated as she decided whose protection to place her former mentor under.

"Nothing is over, Diane," he said. "The truth will continue to be told without me. Another will finish what I have started."

Stanley looked at her carefully. Her face told the story. She was listening to the ravings of a madman. He knew that she did not understand what he was telling her. So, he decided to elaborate his point.

"Diane, listen to that beautiful music, that resonates here, upon Chopin's grave tonight." He stood quietly before her, fearing that she, for the first time in her life, believed him to be completely crazed.

"Diane, I spent my life fearing that the talent of Chopin would die with the great masters of my day. After all, who cares, really? Rubinstein, Horowitz and others pass, but the spark that refused to die over 150 years ago at this very grave refreshes itself in most unexpected ways. The music you hear tonight is a nineteen-year-old Canadian virtuoso playing with the Warsaw Symphony."

Stanley could see she still did not understand.

"I took Langston Powell to light the spark," he continued. "You are here to take me, but before you can claim your trophy, Trellis will take me permanently. I will be as silenced as these graves that lie before us. But as these notes of the masters are played tonight by those who come next, I am confident others will come to pick up my torch and search for the *source* of the greed that continues to betray our profession. I only pray that person will be able to stamp it out."

"Stanley, there is no one else. Surely not Jean Paul. We have been tracking him since immediately after Milan. What makes you so sure Trellis and Powell were connected, anyway?" Diane asked.

Stanley watched her carefully. He was now well beyond the period of safe engagement. Every minute they stood talking in the graveyard was only working in Trellis' favor.

Despite this, Stanley continued, "Powell told me just before I sacrificed him that he was aware I was ex-CIA, and that I was accused of embezzling five million dollars. Only Trellis could have told him this. I was accused by Trellis of stealing that exact amount. I admit tonight to you, I did misappropriate funds from Poland, but only eight hundred thousand dollars or so. This money was used to relocate my agent *Syrenka* and purchase the Zgorzelec villa for *Sarenka*, our safe haven. Where did the other over four-million-plus dollars go? At just this time, Powell needed monies to fix his Daedalus Destroyer Drones? Then, after it was corrected, Trellis and the CIA would buy the drone in great numbers for the War on Terror."

"So, Stanley, this is the business we are in," Diane said, not seeing the conspiracy. He spoke so coldly of sacrificing Powell, it sent a shiver through the normally staid *Huntress*.

"Diane, what I know, but cannot prove, is that Trellis enriches himself with each drone the CIA bought from Powell. The profits to both men were great - great enough that their greed could only see one future. Expand the Global War on Terror, perpetuate it, until no man, women or child was safe, as our freedoms were being extinguished in the name of the safety and security."

Diane could just then recall Devereaux telling her of the corruption that George Chartwell had accused Trellis of perpetrating.

Stanley finished his discourse. "This is the tangled knot of greed tying together these two corrupt men. This is why Powell had to be taken. This is why Trellis does not want my story told."

Carlyle pulled his car into the driveway in front of the immense locked main gates of Père Lachaise Cemetery. He glanced at the luminous digital display of his wristwatch. It was forty-two minutes past midnight. Stuffing the silenced handgun into the waistband of his slacks, he exited the car to assess the incredibly high walls of the main entrance of the cemetery. Scaling these walls was certainly possible, but even if he did so with all his gear, it would be time consuming and he would be at the bottom of the hill into which the graveyard was built. The adjacent apartment building offered a quicker alternative with its rooftop providing a decidedly better shooting angle. From the trunk of the car, he grabbed the case containing his Barrett 98B sniping rifle. In this case also was the low-light optical scope, and his alternative modification for night operations, a laser sight.

This was essentially the same gun as the Barrett Light Fifty caliber he had used for sniping in-theatre in Afghanistan and Iraq. But the .50 caliber was too much round for what he had to do tonight. He had brought from the Embassy annex the 98B that he had shipped in under the auspices of the diplomatic courier. Its .300 Winchester Magnum rounds were more than enough firepower for this prey.

Carlyle left the car, readily accessed the interior of the building, and quickly ascended to the rooftop. In total darkness, he assembled the tungsten grey components of the Barrett 98B. Stock, bolt, and 26 inch barrel segments all snapped together thanks to its precision guides. In just over a minute, he was fully operational. He used the night scope to locate Stanley, if he was even still at the tomb. It was, by that point, nearing a full hour after midnight.

Carlyle was now aware of the general location of the grave, as Dom had researched and relayed the information to him as he drove over to Père Lachaise. He used the optical scope to begin the narrowed search, starting at the right-hand crest of the hill and scanning across the densely packed rows of the eleventh sector of the grounds. The snow had stopped now, and the reflected city light from the overcast sky, as well as the white blanket of the graveyard grounds, provided near optimal conditions for his scope.

Soon he was locked onto the living. Carlyle found Stanley in his sight, but Stanley was obstructed from his line-of-fire by a second figure.

"What the hell was Diane doing there with Stanley?" he thought.

They were 166 yards out, according to the scope. Due to the relative lack of elevation of the rooftop to the ascending hill, Carlyle's shot would be almost level. Diane had her back to Carlyle, partially shielding Stanley. His bullet's trajectory was going to have to be dangerously close to the right side of Diane's head.

There was another problem. The canopy of trees climbing the hill, even barren as they now were, obstructed his shot. If his round caught a limb, it might deflect the bullet and ultimately render his shot useless.

Carlyle decided to employ the laser sight. So long as the laser beam could find the target, he would have a clear line-of-sight through the thicket of barren tree limbs. If a branch obstructed his beam, and thus his shot, he would know. So long as the red dot was seen by Carlyle on the target, then his round would find its way through this unexpected tangle of obstacles. Stanley would never see the laser upon himself, but there was certainly a risk Diane would see it and react before he pulled the trigger. Carlyle decided this was a manageable risk, as he felt if he waited until the last second to turn on his laser sight, he could then quickly fire before she could warn Stanley.

Carlyle moved his position until he had a visually clear line-of-sight through the branches. He optically sighted-in on Stanley's forehead, but given their positions, the shot was going to be just over Diane's right shoulder. He had to be sure his shot was true. A wasted shot would make them aware of his presence, and give them both time to seek cover.

Carlyle would turn the laser on just before triggering his shot to confirm his round would not be deflected, and to minimize its telltale red spot from being detected. It was clear to him that Diane and Stanley had talked for some time, and by Trellis' rules of engagement, both would have to be silenced tonight. In any case, Stanley had to go first. No sense in risking taking out *The Huntress*, only to have his primary target escape.

Carlyle flipped on the laser sight. As long as its red laser dot appeared onto the target, he would be sure the line-of-fire would not be obstructed by the thick web of barren tree limbs.

Stanley and Diane had been talking for an extended period time. Stanley had unburdened himself to her. Strangely, Diane felt safe here in the solitude of this land of the dead. She knew as soon as she took him into custody, her chance to talk uninterrupted with him would vanish into the labyrinth of the agency's procedures. Or worse, she feared her access to Stanley might be taken from her altogether.

"The music. The lilies. The stroke of midnight," Diane stated to the old man before her. "This is a ritual, Stanley? For Agnieszka?"

With her mention of Danuska's name, Diane could see Stanley's jaw begin to quiver. The flow of tears pooled again in his eyes like the return of an ebb tide. A veil of grief overcame the tired mask that was his face.

"I never got to say goodbye to her, Diane," he said, attempting to control his emotions. "This is not a ritual as you say, but my requiem for her soul."

"Stanley, we know all about your *Sarenka*, Agnieszka," she said. She was truly sorry for him. "I was in your home in Baltimore. I saw her painting of the Katyń monument. She came to you, didn't she, in 2008."

Stanley hung his head before her. "Yes, she came to me then. She had arranged for the cultural ministry to donate to the Katyń National Memorial that was built in Baltimore in 2000. She did this to honor her father. At her urging, Poland provided the last of the funds needed. Eight years after it was triumphantly raised, she came to America to see the incarnation of her efforts."

Diane could see the emptiness in Stanley's eyes as he recalled this. She thought he would be joyful in recollecting this memory.

"That night she came alone to my home. It was my last night of unburdened pleasure in my life. We talked, we laughed, we remembered. That night she gave herself to me, for one last time."

Diane knew the bitterness of this last statement. Stanley continued.

"She planned to retire two years later from the government. She told me it was important to her to make one last trip to visit her father's resting place in the mass grave at Katyń. In 2010, she traveled with an expanded delegation of the Polish government for a remembrance ceremony of her father and all the other thousands of Polish souls taken by Stalin's butchery in the forest, seventy years before."

He hesitated, collecting himself. The next sentence came from his lips heavily choked with tears of most bitter regret. "Our night together in Baltimore was the last we would ever spend together."

Diane recalled what she had read in the file about Agnieszka's death. The plane carrying her and most of Poland's government had crashed in the woods outside Smolensk under, what many consider to this day to be, mysterious circumstances.

Agnieszka's earliest memories would be of the Katyń massacre stealing her father's life. Stanley had often thought that, in her moments of terror aboard that aircraft, the last of her thoughts must have been that Katyń would also claim her own life.

Stanley raised his head and looked directly at Diane, no longer ashamed of the tears that cascaded down his cheeks.

"She was a truly magnificent woman. A woman forged of sacrifice. She continued to sacrifice until her last seconds so that her nation's sons and daughters could again be free. Today, because of her, they are exactly that."

Stanley's face was hollow, gaunt, and vacant. He bitterly cherished the memories of Agnieszka that he had for so long adored. He had lived since her passing in a barren emptiness, knowing he could never again enjoy her presence.

"For what she sacrificed, throughout her life, she was the only woman I ever loved," he added.

Diane felt the weight of his heavy sorrow. Despite this, she still understood the need to bring Stanley to justice.

The somber music of Chopin continued to lace the snow-laden grounds of the cemetery. It was a mournful, solemn passage that played. In the heaviness of the chords, Stanley suddenly sensed the inherent danger that they both were in.

Stanley had been reading Diane's face when he first noticed the red laser's dot. It was diffused in the fringes of her shoulder length hair, and thus visible to Stanley, who thought it dangerously close to her right ear. This elicited immediate action from him, with not a second of hesitation.

Stanley lurched forward to drag Diane down to the ground. As he did, he yelled a singular word, "Shooter!"

Diane had lowered her emotional guard, but she had maintained her situational awareness. She was surprised by but nonetheless prepared for Stanley's charge. She was totally oblivious to the sniper's laser fringing in her hair, just beyond her ear. Diane heard Stanley yell out what sounded like the command "Shoot her!" as he lunged forward. She lowered her aim away from his mid-torso and shot a singular round into his right thigh, consciously aiming to miss the femoral artery. The shot was intended to immobilize the threat Stanley suddenly appeared to pose, and not eliminate it.

Carlyle had solved the problem of the sea of barren tree limbs. He steadied his finger on the trigger, preparing now to gently squeeze it with as smooth a motion as he could, to in no way divert his carefully aimed shot. As he steadied the laser sight onto Stanley's head, he could see Diane shift her weight. He had been forced to aim the shot just over her shoulder, and her slight movement caused the electronic glow of the laser to become visible in the fringes of her hair. He was certain Stanley would notice and react.

Suddenly in his view, Stanley went from a static position to dynamic, thrusting forward at Diane, but with the expected lethargy of a seventy-year old man. He saw Diane lower her pistol in preparation to squeeze off a defensive shot. Stanley had already lowered his shoulders and head into a tackling thrust. Carlyle's ballistic solution had been compromised by Stanley spotting the laser's reflection, and now he had one instantaneous chance to react, to rapidly squeeze off a shot at the diving Stanley. He lowered his rifle instinctively to compensate for the Stanley's motion and jerkily squeezed the trigger.

Diane had squeezed the trigger to hear not only her own shot, but also what she thought was a loud echo simultaneously from deep behind her. As Stanley went down from her well-placed shot into his leg, he hit the ground just before her, and rolled into her legs just as the sniper's round slammed into her right shoulder. It passed through her upper torso, before it slammed violently just behind, and barely clear of Stanley's head.

The round slammed into the base of Chopin's tomb, before ricocheting off and dying in an explosive puff of soft cemetery dirt nearby. The shot's echo rang loudly through the snowy white graveyard, as well as the surrounding neighborhood.

Stanley and Diane both lay wounded on the ground. Stanley had dragged himself over to her as she lay in the soil. His face grimaced in pain. The sniper's shot had missed him totally, but Diane's shot to his leg had not. He was convinced that his wound was not fatal. Diane had clearly taken a shot from the sniper to the upper torso. Her wound was bleeding profusely and required immediate medical attention.

Carlyle's round had blown through Diane's right shoulder. Several inches in from where her upper arm joined its socket. The thrust of the round's impact had pitched her violently forward onto the walkway that had seconds earlier separated her from Stanley. She was lying in a state of shock; her consciousness was both elevated and blurred at once. Her heart beat rapidly in her chest.

It was then that she realized Stanley was on top of her, shielding her body with his. Her initial reaction was to try to force her way up through Stanley's embrace.

"Diane, stay down," Stanley whispered, as they both lie in the snowy, grassy walk just in front of the composer's grave. That was when she saw it, a phosphorescent red insect, slowly flying just over them, probing the marble facade of Chopin's tomb. The laser searched for its prey, and given their position, it's red glow in the Parisian night was fearfully fatal.

Stanley dug his arms into the ground beneath her until they joined in the middle of her back. Stanley was assessing their exposure in the path where they lie. He found them perilously out in the open, realizing it would only take the shooter a few seconds to reposition to take advantage of their lack of cover.

"Carlyle," stated Diane, moaning the name more than speaking it.

"Who is Carlyle?" whispered Stanley. He had been retired long before Carlyle had been recruited by Trellis, so he did not know the name, let alone the menace of the man.

"Trellis' Special Ops goon," said Diane. "I made sure he did not know we were here tonight …"

Her voice trailed off, and Stanley feared she was ready to pass out.

Without warning her, Stanley grasped around her tightly, which must have been excruciating given the gunshot through her upper torso. He then used his un-wounded leg to push off the walk, while he torqued his shoulders enough to roll them both as an awkward singular, but unbalanced, entity. Diane screamed in pain in a staccato shrill that overpowered the eerily morose concerto of Chopin, still playing from Stanley's new but antiquated disc player.

They rolled away from the Chopin monument, off the walk and down a three- foot bank of hill to come to rest behind another crypt tiered just below the Chopin grave. Diane was in unbearable pain, but Stanley hoped it would keep her from lapsing into shock, as she had appeared to be doing moments before. They now had the critical cover, and time, Stanley needed to reassess their situation.

Diane lay on the ground, behind the unknown grave's granite memorial, her shoulder was an incendiary of pain. She knew the shot had passed through her without slamming into bone. But the blood flowing from her shoulder was massive, and she realized at that point it was likely the bleeding, itself, that would be fatal.

"Diane, listen to me," Stanley said, ignoring the throbbing and intense pain in his own thigh from Diane's shot. "I know that was not from you. We have been talking for nearly an hour out here, and Trellis would surely never have allowed that. They must have compromised Jean Paul – it is the only answer to how they found this location."

Stanley at that point knew Jean Paul was dead. He would never have given up Stanley, at least not until the pain would have become completely unbearable. Stanley blamed himself for lingering here for so long in conversation with Diane.

"I am sorry my friend, so very, very sorry!" Stanley thought to himself.

Stanley lifted his weight off Diane, and in his pulling back Diane saw the massive amounts of blood upon his overcoat, near his chest.

"My God, Stanley," she gasped, "you are dying!"

Stanley looked at his chest, touching it beneath his coat to confirm what he already knew. While his leg continued to bleed, this much blood could only have come from Diane's wound. Stanley made sure not to raise his head clear of the marker they lay hidden behind.

"It is not mine, my dear," he said calmly to her. "If we don't get you out of here, you will surely die. Either by their mark, or the fatal mark of time."

Diane's entire frame now began to shake violently, beneath her the blood began to pool in the snow. "Carlyle is here to kill you," she sobbed.

"Yes, of course he is," Stanley said as a matter of fact. "We have been speaking too long. They will not let you live, Diane. Not fearing what I have told you."

The adrenaline flowing through Diane had her replaying the second before over in her mind. The shot hitting the tomb just behind Stanley's head would have killed him had she not shot him in the thigh during his lunge. Or had her body not gotten in the way of Carlyle's line-of-fire.

Stanley noticed her revolver was gone, escaped to the darkness around them, lost to the force of the round passing through Diane's upper frame. He knew that she was unaware of the sniper from her reaction, but also from her obstructing positioning of herself between Stanley and the sniper's firing position. Had this been set up in advance, the sniper would have been afforded a clean shot.

Stanley pressed forward and kissed her on the cheek as they lay in the cover of the unknown grave marker. "I do not blame you, Diane. You were doing what we trained you to do. You had found me. But now, Trellis is here for my silence. You will now need to leave me here. With that sniper, we will not *both* leave with our lives tonight."

She looked into the old man's eyes to see a mixture of pain, mourning, and, most of all, resolve. It was then that she knew the state of his mind.

"Stanley, I could turn you over to the Brits. They have offered to protect you. Come with me," she pleaded.

Stanley crouched behind the crypt. She was delirious, and did not understand how tenuous her own life had now become.

He whispered to her. "It is now too late for that. Even if it were possible, it would start a war that would claim many lives besides our own. My time has come, Diane. The only way I will leave these grounds tonight is in your memory. So long as you remember me, I will continue to live in this world."

"Oh my God! No! Good God, Stanley, No!" she cried aloud frantically.

"We have but seconds, Diane. I will distract him. You must flee. Run quickly between the markers as soon as you hear his shot. Run to the crest of the hill, beyond it you will be safe. It is not far. Mind your cover behind the tombs, let the respite of the dead protect you tonight." He was once again instructing her in a clear, unconcerned voice, as he had once done so many years ago.

"No Stanley! No! I cannot allow you to do this." She wept openly. "You cannot waste your life for me, no!"

He looked at her tenderly, knowing his next words would be among his last.

"A life that is lived with purpose is never wasted. I fear only for those who have wasted their talents and their passions, for these are God's gifts."

Diane could not believe what Stanley was about to do for her. She could not stop him. She could only obey his commands, just as she had long ago as a young recruit. She painfully pulled herself into a crouching position behind the monument protecting them.

"Remember, once you hear the gun, do not stop moving. Stay behind the crypts as much as possible. Do not look back." Stanley's voice was strong, thick with authority.

He kissed her face just below her ear tenderly, whispering into it, "Thank you for saving me that night at Holly's from taking my own life. You saved my soul. Thank you for saving *Syrenka*'s life by telling me his identity had been passed to the Russians. You saved the secrets of my heart. Now it is time to save yourself. Prepare yourself."

He said this as he reached for the top of the marker they hid safely behind, to pull himself up.

Diane was crying uncontrollably, definitely knowing she had not the strength to save him. She did not know, however, if she had enough strength to save herself. She would allow herself to live for no other reason than to hunt those who hunted Stanley tonight – Carlyle and Trellis.

She pulled herself into as much of a sprinter's crouch as her pain would allow. She almost fell in doing so as her blood-soaked hand slid across the frigid stone beneath it. The night air was cold enough for her to see the mist of her breath. She knew from it that she was alive, and would fight to stay so.

"Thank God I have done my duty!" Stanley said aloud as he grimaced, struggling to stand upright.

Stanley pulled himself up onto a standing position. His own weight bearing down on his wounded leg was a deep dagger of pain. He fought this, raising himself as tall and as proud as he could. Diane was sobbing, knowing what was coming next, but at Stanley's request, she waited.

Through his sight, Carlyle could only make out the silhouette from this distance. He hesitated for a second because of the obscuring canopy of dead branches - Was it him or her? Was this an attempt for Stanley to escape?

Carlyle trained his laser sight on the silhouette's forehead. He knew whichever person stood before him, the other would attempt to escape as soon as he fired his next round. But whose forehead was his laser sight trained upon? Even with his night scope at this distance he could not tell.

Stanley glanced down at Diane. She appeared ready. Then he raised his eyes into the night, peering into the darkness. Why was the sniper hesitating?

With a deliberately slow move, Stanley raised his left hand, palm outstretched in his telltale fashion, to brush back the hair he had since shaved from his forehead, which he cocked to the right. Diane screamed aloud as he made the identifying gesture.

Carlyle recognized the gesture – Stanley's tell.

Diane looked up from her position at his feet as he wiped his hand across his forehead. Then she heard the rifle's horrible echo through the night. In the instant of its reverberation, Diane clearly saw, just as Stanley's left palm passed centered on his forehead, both hand and scalp explode into a violent cone of grayish-pink fleshy debris.

The view of Stanley's head blowing back burned into her consciousness. His body fell, twisting awkwardly to the ground. Having seen what her mind could not comprehend, Diane felt something within her snap. Her every emotion crumpled into the vacuum within her. She suppressed the terror and channeled her energy. She sprang forward with all her effort, knowing any delay would afford Carlyle the time needed to re-aim and drop her as well.

Diane pushed herself off as hard as she could and ran for the next crypt, only in doing so to hear Carlyle's next shot ring out. She heard the bristling snap of the round go by her as she ran. She realized it had just missed her as she lunged between the two grave markers. She had made it safely behind a row of large family crypts, in fact a literal cemetery's street worth of them. She heard another round crash into the crypt she was now behind. Diane knew she just had to keep from over-reacting, and allowing Carlyle to flush her out into the clear. She felt she was somewhat safe now. Unless there were other shooters...

Her energy was draining from her. The sprint to the crypts had caused a heaviness to settle into her body. She felt cold. Her awareness was fading from her, everything was becoming fuzzy. She looked back onto Stanley's lifeless body, laying mangled, yet prostrate below the tomb of Frederic Chopin. She realized then, that like his heroic master, death had saved Stanley from the agony of life. He was now free. He was free to rejoin his *Sarenka.*

As Diane caught her living breath behind the crypts of the Parisian dead, she heard a most beautiful music. It was not that of Chopin, but the checkerboard sirens of the French Gendarmerie, coming closer from the distance.

Had the shots that rang in the night been called in by one of the residents of the neighborhood? She knew this would be Carlyle's cue to exit the killing grounds. Diane numbly bolted between markers until she found herself safely behind the crest of the hill and soon at the gate where Sophie and Emory awaited her. They were both panicked, having heard the shots ringing out, not knowing if they would see her again. Then they saw the blood drenching her beloved Burberry trench coat.

They both examined her eyes, and saw the shock, uncertainty and doubt that had settled there. The very opposite of what they had ever known to expect. Diane caught Emory's eye's, and said a single word. "Drive."

In the car a few moments later, they left the streets surrounding Père Lachaise Cemetery behind them just moments before the French Police arrived, sirens and flashing lights fully engaged. Diane was having great difficulty in the back seat, next to Sophie, trying to manage her cell phone. It was not her muscles that fought her, but instead her concentration. Her mind was clouded by the sight of Stanley's corpse laying frozen in the dirt. A fog of intense pain had descended upon her.

The throbbing in her shoulder now seemed to draw it's radiating energy away from her consciousness with each wave. It clouded her mind like thick heavy ribbons pulling through a shadowing solution of thickening confusion, in what only minutes before had been pristine clarity.

Sophie took the phone from her hand. "What number, Madame?"

Diane looked at her with confused eyes. Sophie thought she was ready to collapse, if not die outright. Diane drew her every bit of focus to come up with three French words - "*Rêves de Cuir.*" They came out of her mouth in a slur, but Sophie somehow understood. She found the number in Diane's phone and hit call, holding the mobile device to Diane's face.

"*Rêves de Cuir*? How may I help you?" answered a light French woman's accent.

Diane could hear the voice that seemed a million miles away, through an increasing shroud of agony. She felt herself slipping from the pall of sensation into a congealing crimson darkness.

Diane began to voice her own words before the blackness collapsed in around her. Her residual energy seemed to have totally drained from her. Diane now teetered at the edge of consciousness.

Sophie grabbed the phone and screamed in French, "*M'aidez. M'aidez.* She is dying. You must help us."

The trained voice on the phone did not lose its professional bearing.

"My apologies, Madame. We are a clothing establishment of sorts. What product can I help you with?"

The voice waited tensely for the code-word.

Sophie continued to protest, continuing to plead with the unnervingly pleasant voice as the streets of Paris bled by.

Diane thought, fighting her desire to allow herself to completely release herself from the night, "If I die, this was all for naught."

She forged every last bit of will to mouth the single word, "Corset." It nearly crumbled on her lips, but Sophie understood it.

Sophie repeated the word "corset" into the phone, nearly screaming it. Immediately the phone voice became more mechanical. "Yes, of course, I will help you. Hold please."

A few seconds later it came back. "Take her immediately to the funicular at the base of *Sacre Coeur*."

"Funicular, *Sacre Coeur!*" yelled Sophie, uncharacteristically.

"Got it. Not Far!" yelled Emory.

Diane slumped, near lifeless, into the corner of the backseat.

Emory parked the car as close to the funicular as possible. The streets of Montmartre were dark and threatening this late after midnight. Emory left the driver's seat, and not knowing what to do, stood leaning on the front wheel well. His arms were folded. His revolver was nestled underneath his left armpit. He was unnerved at the thought of watching the most vibrant breath of life he had ever met at the agency expire in the back seat.

In a surreal scene, a tall dark man in evening clothes approached the vehicle. Emory heard his crisp British accent say with the most proper pronunciation. "We can do without any theatrics, my young friend. Put away your weapon. Where is the lady with the ripped corset?"

The last word eased Emory's angst. "Back seat," he mumbled.

Upon opening the door, Malcolm Devereaux was stunned to see the volume of blood smeared everywhere. He reached beyond Sophie, who hovered protectively over her, for Diane's wrist. Diane was pale, her pulse nearly imperceptible. Devereaux rattled off commands into an unseen radio in French.

Hearing his voice, Diane opened her eyes, but they focused on nothing. She said in the direction of the ceiling, "Another night of yours I have ruined."

Sophie was amazed she could even talk. She seemed to draw strength from him.

"Well, darling, it doesn't appear you had a wholly enjoyable outing yourself," said Malcolm.

With his saying this, a black van pulled up behind the car. Its rear doors opened, with several emergency medical technicians rapidly emerging. Emory was moving toward them threateningly when Devereaux stuck his head out of the car and barked, "Stand down, lad. I called for them. They are here to patch up our distressed damsel."

Emory stayed frozen between the two vehicles, his pistol in clean sight. Events were happening far too fast for him to comprehend. He was confused, disgusted at what he had witnessed, what had been done to his Diane.

Devereaux thought "If the idiot young man wants to get himself shot, we can patch him up also."

Just then, he saw Emory drop his pistol to the ground before walking off into the night.

Devereaux was still leaning over Diane. She fumbled reaching up to touch his face.

"Easy, darling, conserve your strength." The words came through the waves of pain to her, almost in separate pieces. She had to struggle to reconstruct them in her altered consciousness.

"Mal, I need you." Her words were labored, and fluttered on the edge of her weakened breath. "I really need you."

Her last words were choked out by a gurgled gasp, that escaped her involuntarily. She recovered after a second to plead, "I need my Malcolm."

Devereaux kissed her cheek tenderly. "I am here, darling. Here to look after you, and nurse you back to health, but you will owe me dearly…"

Devereaux smiled, but was very concerned that they might be too late. The fear rose in him, as if to say, "Your bravado is only a mask for the others. You, Malcolm, know how deadly this wound really is."

Suddenly, Diane Sterling collapsed in the back seat of the nondescript car, in the darkness that shrouded the base of the ascending steps that led to the immaculately lit Parisian Shrine to the Sacred Heart.

The team from the black van removed her unresponsive body from the car, carrying her into the van's interior. Its doors closed. Malcolm grabbed Sophie by the hand and led her into the cab of the van, which then pulled off into the darkness of the night.

Sophie, now separated from Diane by the wall cleaving the van's cab from its rear interior, could hear the medical technicians frantically working to save the life of her new friend. *Zosia* feared her Diane would slip into a final darkness. To calm her fears, she remembered what she had been taught years ago as a young girl in Poland:

"The darkness of man is but a valley that will be lit by the ascending sun, its secrets forever for all to know."

The End of
Chasing The Winter's Wind

To Be Continued in ...
War of the Nocturne's Widow

"These cold granite slabs are but mirrors where living men come to reflect on the souls they are surely soon to lose."